EMMA PRIDE

After graduating from Cheltenham
Ladies' College, Diana Raymond
entered the Civil Service, eventually
becoming Personal Assistant to
General Ismay. Her first successful
novel, *The Door Stood Open*, was
written at the age of nineteen,
followed by *The Lonely Guest*, and
Doves in Flight under her maiden
name of Diana Young. In 1940 she
married Ernest Raymond, the
novelist. She has written twenty
novels to date, her most recent being
The House of the Dolphin. Many have
been translated into different
languages.

Diana Raymond

EMMA PRIDE

A·PIATKUS·PAPERBACK

Copyright © 1981 by Diana Raymond

First published in Great Britain in 1981
First published in this edition in
Great Britain in 1987 by
Judy Piatkus (Publishers) Ltd of
5 Windmill Street, London W1

British Library Cataloguing in Publication Data

Raymond, Diana
Emma Pride.
I. Title
823'.914[F]   PR6068.A947

ISBN 0-86188-902-9

Printed and bound in Great Britain by
Biddles Ltd, Guildford and King's Lynn

Gratefully remembering
URSULA D'ARCH SMITH

and to her son
TIMOTHY
with love

Part One

Chapter One

The sound killed the air, killed sense, killed thought. In a city street the sound was familiar, but because it concerned me, Emma and Carey, it was new. I remember that it burgeoned in strength, in its impact on the nerves; and then from the window I could see the white body of the ambulance, with the turning aquarial blue light above. I saw the two of them, a man and a woman, uniformed, step down to the pavement, with red blanket and folding chair. The red of the blanket carried an air of danger, just as the noise had done.

It looked like a rescue, but I couldn't be sure. I waited; time was nothing to do with hours and minutes: it was time between life and death.

If I try to tell the truth about Emma and her daughter Carey, I shall of course be contradicted: all I can tell is *my* truth; that's all anybody can tell. One is limited by everything one is: I am limited because I am a man (Rick Ashley: at the time of writing thirty-seven years old); and because of the way Emma—and Carey—so violently affected and changed my life.

I thought about it for a long time. I talked to others, some of whom said, "But you can't know it all: you can't know everything about Emma"; and I said no one could know everything about anyone except God. Much of what I write I learned from Carey, and from others of our strange and multiparented company. True I was not

3

present—could not have been present—for some of the triumphs, anxieties and disasters: to begin with, I was too young, and later other forces constrained me. But whether I was there or not, I was greatly concerned, and whatever happened, however much contrary winds drove us apart, I never lost sight of Carey; nor of Emma.

There is a particular difficulty in writing of someone like Emma, whose name was (still is, I suppose) known to great numbers of people, to audiences in London and New York; to the wider audiences who knew her from the films she made. I say 'films' rather than 'movies' because although even from childhood I lived a transatlantic life, I was born in England, and talked mostly of pavements and the Underground rather than sidewalks and the subway. Sometimes the occasional Americanism would slip in, and then if I was in England I would be accused (as a boy) of showing off.

To know well a woman whose name could make headlines is to have double-vision. Or perhaps double-hearing. There is the sound made by the name of 'Emma Pride', a sound which spoken anywhere brings immediate recognition—that half-eager, half-mournful condolence which, because of its eagerness, never quite rings true. And then there is my own private knowledge, and Carey's too: the pictures of a woman with violent swings of mood, from ecstasy to the dark and creeping despair. There is the mother who at some point in her nature wished to be a mother, but wished (perhaps it was not her fault) more strongly to triumph in the field where her talents lay, so that she was never quite content. (You may say Who is?, but Emma not being content had a difference, a cutting edge.) There is the woman who had to be in love, and be loved, not only by men, but by everyone, audiences, producers, directors, stage-hands and cameramen. She didn't always go the best way about it; Emma could spit like a cat when she wasn't charming the birds off the trees.

4

I try to think back to the first most memorable moment, and it seems to be that time many years ago not long after the war, when she came running towards us across the sand. There were to be other sands, the supine bodies, oiled and famous and dieted to the necessary shape: some (the sands and the bodies) on this side of the Atlantic, some on the other. But it was on this beach that my memory lights, the quiet beach of Squibnocket on the island of Martha's Vineyard, off the coast of Cape Cod and within sight of Nantucket Sound.

I loved the island, with its Indian names (like Squibnocket, Chilmark and Menemsha; Manaquay and Wintucket) and I never questioned—as children do not question—how it was that we all came to be there at my stepmother's lovely house on its hill. I didn't question why my father was so seldom present, nor why Carey (then four) and her half-brother, Jonathan, nearly seven and my contemporary, were given the freedom of this paradisal place of bearded sand-dunes, rough Atlantic seas, legends of old whaling country, and the green bushy quiet of Up-Island. This quiet carried the scents of the sweet pepper bush and swamp honeysuckle; the Indian heritage of Gay Head, and the ripening of wild grapes. These places were ours for the summer, until Carey, Jonathan and I returned to England to school.

We—Carey, Jonathan and myself—were inspecting the carcase of a horseshoe crab, large black and disgusting, fossilised by the sun. My stepmother, Marguerite Ashley, lay in a low-slung chair, wide straw hat on her head, dark glasses making a mystery of her face, long slim bare legs stretched out into the sun. She was knitting, which did not surprise me then but surprises me now, for she was an elegant handsome creature who moved with that long-legged grace of many American women, and had a dry turn of phrase which for some reason didn't match with knitting. She had also the American warmth, the generosity of spirit which I am sure we traded on. I knew so little then, of course. I knew that she was Emma's 'American cousin'. I was at first puzzled by this, for Emma was English; but it seemed that Emma's Uncle Dan had married an American and produced Marguerite. Uncle Dan lived far off on the West Coast in California and made few incursions into Marguerite's life, some ancient quarrel enduring into a new generation.

I knew also that she was my father's second wife—my own mother had died soon after my birth—but those were words then. Words too that Carey and Jonathan, both Emma's children, had different fathers, neither of whom made any appearance, ever. Well, one of them was dead and couldn't; but the other?... The adult world is mystery to a child, he moves through it like a sleep-walker. We were all there for the summer—except my father, Lance Ashley, who was in New York: he was a 'theatrical agent', though I didn't know precisely what that was. Marguerite was an artist: she had done much work on theatre design which even then fascinated me; I could draw a little, and wished to follow her. All this was ours, and we made no question—least of all Carey—and had no intimation that it would ever end, nor how that end would come.

It was Jonathan with his light hair and delicate features, brown from the sun, who saw Emma first and said, "Here's Ma!" (Perhaps it was fitting that Jonathan should speak first, since he was, in one sense, to speak last.)

I sat back on my heels and watched as Emma leaped and sprinted over the sand, with all her triumphs and cruelties still to come.

The changes to come were great, and some were savage, but I can still, though I was so young, see that picture in my mind's eye. Emma was not tall like Marguerite: in time I would grow taller than she. ("Who's Rick Ashley?" "That tall young man over there.") But she was slim and perfectly made; she wore a bikini, which was then a new fashion, and a skin of smooth polished tan. She was waving and calling, "Hi!", stumbling as the scalloped sand made her path uneven. "Hi, all of you: Maggie and Carey and Jon. And Rick." She was laughing and her face in laughter had always that quality of extreme excitement; the breaking ecstasy of a child who a moment ago has been in tears, and may be again.

She flung herself on the sand, kicking off her sandals. She was still laughing, breathless, and I can see her face with the enormous shadowed green-grey eyes, the light brown hair, blown now in the sea wind; the look of someone too slight-boned, too delicate-faced to contain the excitements and violence which dwelt within her.

But on that day she was young, in her late twenties, but looking younger because of her slight body and the ecstatic smile. She was golden, so filled with delight that it spilled over us and brought us to silence.

Even Marguerite stopped knitting and said, "You look like you just won a hundred grand. What cooks?"

Emma clasped her knees with her arms and buried her head on them. My glance fled for a moment to Carey who had stopped playing with the sand. She stood in a small pair of pants and nothing else, one finger in her mouth, looking towards her mother who had given her no especial attention.

Emma lifted her head. "Lance just rang." I too looked up, as Lance was my father, however infrequent his appearances; and of course Marguerite's husband. Marguerite said with a twitch at her dark glasses, "It must have been terrible news."

Emma laughed again. "Terrible. Yes, terrible. He sent you his love."

"Big of him," Marguerite said: I remembered that she accepted such casual crumbs from my father with a salted calm. "Come on, give."

Emma said, "I've *got* it. The lead in *The Newcomer*. Guy Forster's new play. With Jeremy Hirst directing.

Rehearsals start in London next week. When I auditioned I thought I hadn't a hope. I wanted it too much, and I knew I could play it, but I couldn't *convince* them. I went home and cried. It was like the end of the world. But *now* . . . I don't know what's happened; maybe someone let them down . . . doesn't matter: I've got it—the best part I've had in years. A pre-run try-out: Edinburgh, Manchester, Liverpool, Cardiff and Brighton. Then the West End." It was as she spoke these words, as if they were not railway stations (as they sounded to me) but places of paradise, that Carey took her finger out of her mouth.

She said, "Where's Mama going?"

Marguerite resumed knitting. "Like all points of the compass."

Carey looked bewildered; Emma threw herself towards her on the sand. She scooped sand as if it were gold dust, something greatly desired. "Mama's going on tour, darling."

"What's 'tour'?"

"Oh darling, you know what 'tour' is—"

"Bit young, isn't she?" asked Marguerite with another twitch at her glasses.

Carey looked at her mother as she lay sprawled on the sand. "Going away?"

Emma was still playing with the sand. "Yes; just for a little while."

"How long's 'little while'?"

"Not long," Emma said, giving her daughter the full power of her smile; but Carey stood silent, her mouth turning down. I knew what was coming then. Without sound, Carey's face turned red, her mouth square. Then she began to scream, and tears ran down the scarlet cheeks. Her screams echoed across the sand, and seemed too loud for anyone so small. Marguerite said, "Now, c'mon, honey; nothing's as bad as that"; and Emma made a move to comfort her. But Carey's screams continued, ripping the air about us, until Emma lost all her gaiety and her wide smile, and putting her hands over her ears, shouted, "Oh, for God's sake, *shut up!*"

For a moment Carey stood, face scarlet, shocked into silence. Then she turned and stumbled towards me, put her arms round my neck and began to scream again, holding me tightly. Her face was hot and red and it was like being clasped by a warm wet sponge. She smelled a bit and I think she'd wet her pants. At first—since small boys aren't much given to compassion—I tried to push her away, but she clung more closely, and so from embarrassment I patted her head where the fair hair was damp too, and put one arm round what there was of her waist.

Gradually the screams subsided.

"*That's* better," Emma said; "Mama's around, somewhere; she'll always come back."

Carey stood, solemn now and still breathing heavily with the aftermath of sobs. "When?"

"Soon, darling; soon. And you'll have Jonathan with you—"

"Don't like Jonathan; he pinches me."

We all laughed, but Carey still looked solemn. Jonathan said with a dismissive smile, "I don't, for goodness' sake." (Even then Jonathan had an adult turn of phrase.)

"When's Mama going?"

Emma gave a quick glance of supplication to Marguerite, who said, "From what I know of the theatre, the day before yesterday."

We all watched Carey, especially Emma, but Carey didn't cry again. With the casual movement of one years older, and which I can see now was both incongruous and touching, she turned away from us and stumbled some distance off, crouching where the waves washed the sand. Here she seemed entirely preoccupied, as if her attention had left her mother and where and how far she was going.

Emma called to her but Carey didn't reply. Emma with the grace of any trained actress got to her feet and went

9

barefoot over the sand. She put one hand on Carey's shoulder, but Carey made a small but emphatic movement away.

I saw Emma's mouth tighten, and she turned abruptly. For a moment she didn't look beautiful any more. Marguerite said, "Best leave her be."

Emma, childlike herself now, kicked at the sand and was silent. She said at last, "It's no good: she's got to get used to it. I don't want her to be miserable, for goodness' sake, but I can't sit at home and do nothing but look after her. How *can* I?" She flung a look at all of us in appeal. "*You* don't mind when I go on tour, do you, Jonathan?"

Jonathan's delicate and controlled features showed nothing but caution. (But it occurs to me now that more than caution was there.) "No, Mama."

Emma frowned, as if this didn't please her either. Marguerite said, "When d'you leave?"

"Tomorrow to New York. Lance has arranged it all. Then London—"

Carey had said something. Emma said, "What?"

"Take Carey with you."

"Darling—I can't."

Carey said nothing, bending once more to dig at the sand.

Later we drove back to the house. Sitting on the rear seat of Marguerite's car, I could see a brief section of my face in the driving mirror: dark hair still damp plastered on my forehead, a broad face, unformed, scowling a little. I cannot think why, for a child doesn't brood long on the distress of another child. In any case, Carey now sang tunelessly, playing with a broken comb.

Once home, I wandered barefoot about the house. Marguerite went, as she usually did, to the kitchen. The house was built of Douglas fir—the smell comes back to me now, in woods and forests. The wide window of the living-room drew me as it always did with its magic view

10

of sloping green land, and water on three sides: the water of Menemsha Pond, of Vineyard Sound and the far ocean, the Atlantic which seemed great and even alarming with its massive and desert-like sea.

As I watched the small white sailing boats skim over Menemsha Pond, I heard Marguerite and Emma as they talked together in the kitchen. I was alone and listening; this seems to me now to have formed the pattern of my childhood: perhaps it's the pattern of all single childhoods. More especially when the mother has been replaced by a stepmother. Even when Jonathan joined me and began work on a jigsaw puzzle of Brooklyn Bridge, I still stood, a solitary listener.

What remains to me now of that conversation? The kitchen led from the living-room through an open door so their voices came clear to me. Emma's voice, with its English intonation had depth; it was both clear and husky like someone who is recovering from a heavy cold. She and Marguerite, as I remember, talked easily together; perhaps because their blood relationship was not so close as to inspire antagonism.

Emma was protesting, "I have to go, don't I?"

"Sure."

"Why does everything get spoiled? The best thing that ever happened to me, and then Carey—"

"You'll forget about Carey when you're an hour out from New York."

"No, I won't . . ." A pause, while I heard the sound of chopping on a board . . . "Well, yes, maybe I will; there'll be so much to look forward to. But when I'm back in London, in the middle of the night I'll think of her—"

"There's always the middle of the night."

"*Why*? Why can't I just sleep through till morning; there are people who can."

"Temperament," said Marguerite. "The luck of the draw."

"Well, why couldn't I have that sort of temperament?"

"Maybe you wouldn't be so good an actress if you had."

Another pause, and the sound of mixing in a bowl.

Then Emma: "You don't often say things like that."

"I don't go in much for flattery, as you must know. Not ill-will; it makes me shy."

"All right—I'm a good actress. And I'm going to be *very* good."

"The best thing since Sarah Siddons."

"It's not a joke—I've worked for it. No one knows how hard actresses work—"

"They can't've been listening."

"But it's *true*." I could hear the rhythmic sound of Marguerite's chopping, and Emma's bare feet as they went to and fro on the wooden floor. "I've rehearsed in trains and on park seats—in my head, I mean. I've been miserable in digs and eaten disgusting meat that looked like grey flannel, and I've played Beatrix in a high wind with toothache. (I mean *I* had toothache, not the wind.)"

"Sounds hell."

"I've listened to directors being sarcastic or lascivious or even full of praise which is marvellous but frightening as well. When you're told: 'Darling, you did that beautifully; that pause before you pick up the table lamp and hurl it through the window' you go into a spin and wonder what exactly you did, and how the hell you can do it again."

"Uh-huh," said Marguerite, as one who's heard this before: "quite a life."

"I've auditioned before a cloud of cigar smoke and expressions that give you as much as an empty slot machine, and I've played in films where the lighting made my face look like a tadpole (it *did*)"—as Marguerite laughed. "All right—I know this isn't only *me*; we all go through it while we wait for the bit of luck—but now it's come, I've earned it, haven't I?"

"Sure."

Perhaps the brief word carried some reservation: Emma said, "I suppose you could say if I want to succeed so much I shouldn't have married—"

"I don't go in much for telling people what they should or shouldn't do. They do it anyway."

Now I look back, that seems to sum it up: Emma's life so far was a pretty good example of someone who 'did it anyway', and it's doubtful if advice of whatever kind would have made any difference. In the first place that brief headlong war-time marriage to a young actor, Desmond Pride: a marriage which had produced a son, Jonathan, before Desmond had been swept like so many others into the war of '39, and killed within a few weeks in Norway: did she ever think much of him now; did Jonathan remind her of him? I couldn't know.

Emma had not remained a widow for long—had she done so, I imagine, everyone would have been greatly surprised.

I can remember Emma's second husband, Geoff Gardner; he was an English lawyer and Carey's father. A serious young man whose defective eyesight had kept him out of the war, he had met Emma because he was dealing with Desmond's estate—not that there was much estate to deal with. He had fallen so heavily for Emma, it appeared, that he wondered what had hit him. A year after Desmond's death, Emma and Geoff had been married. It had been a fashionable wedding at St George's Hanover Square, for Geoff's family set store by fashion. War-time muted extravagance, but Emma had already made enough name—or was, at any rate, attractive enough for a rather smudged photograph, labelled 'young actress marries again', to appear in one of the curtailed newspapers.

I saw Geoff Gardner—now in his fifties—not long ago when I'd been invited to lunch with a friend at his club. He hadn't changed much: hair going a bit thin, but the closed handsome lawyer's face, the glasses, the good but

13

humourless mouth remained. I went over and spoke to him. I don't know whether it was the right thing to do. It had seemed to me that after so many years, after another marriage—successful this time—and other children, Emma could be no more than a far gleam of memory: a brief wild midsummer dance under lighted trees before the lights went out. But at the mention of her name he took his glasses off, and his face showed an expression of sombre shadow, as if he'd been given the date of his death. Putting his glasses back on, he said, "Well, of course I remember Emma"; and no more. Uncomfortable, aware of having trodden clumsily, I moved away. I didn't speak of Carey, for that would have been too difficult.

How long had the marriage lasted? Not more than a few years: Emma, someone said, was 'a lady much fallen in love with'. If Geoff Gardner could accept that he'd married a woman who was, instead of playing hostess to his friends, off to places like Cardiff and Manchester, he could not, it appeared, accept one whose fidelity was uncertain.

He divorced Emma, leaving the child, then a year old, in Emma's care. Whatever doubts and stings of conscience attended him on this, his second wife, Daphne, did her best to smother them. Emma and Carey belonged to a past which they'd put behind them.

But if Geoff Gardner and his family were out of sight, Emma, and Carey, too, were most surely present. As was Jonathan, the son of the perhaps forgotten young man, Desmond Pride. I glanced at him, in the sea-dazzled room, where he frowned over the jigsaw of Brooklyn Bridge, which was very difficult because of the mass of wires and bits of metal structure which could go anywhere. Did he feel, as I did, an outsider? Impossible to know; Jonathan always kept his secrets.

But he, like myself, was listening, and when I heard Emma say, "Was Desmond lucky to die young?" I saw

14

him look up at this mention of his father. "They all say it's sad," Emma went on, "but look at all the things you miss—"

"Like this extraordinary mess I'm cooking up now."

"I'm serious."

"I know, honey. That's your trouble. You can't see being old, anyway. It's too far off."

"But some day ... it'll come." The voice was almost inaudible. "I'm afraid of that. Oh ... Maggie ... to be *old*—not beautiful any more, not wanted, ugly and stringy and lame—"

"Oh, c'mon, who says you'll be lame? Just stringy, maybe."

Emma laughed. "You can cheer me up. You always could."

"Thank you kindly."

"You're good to me, Maggie ... Except that you married Lance."

An odd silence then. My attention deepened. What difference could it make to Emma that Marguerite had married my father?"

"Subjects not discussed," Marguerite said briefly. "One of the rules."

"I don't like rules."

"Maybe not, but we have some now."

Out of humour, Emma came swiftly into the living-room; took us in with one glance and said, "Meal's nearly ready ... where's Carey?"

"Somewhere about," said Jonathan, eyes on his puzzle.

When Emma'd left the room, he said, "It's always Carey. Sometimes you'd think there wasn't a me at all."

I had no idea how to answer him. I felt something the same myself.

The next day Emma, leaving Jonathan, Carey and myself in Marguerite's care at the Vineyard, left for New York, and after that, London.

C

If I'm to explain Emma, ...hing of her life before that scene on Mai... ...I shan't go too far back: as far as I'm concerne... ...ways skip family trees, however they're presented: sooner or later I get the father mixed up with the grandfather and discover I'm one generation behind (or in front) and have to start all over.

Amongst the many albums which now lie on my shelves there's a photograph of Emma as a girl of about thirteen, looking oddly old-fashioned, with drooping frills, a bunch of patently artificial flowers in her arms; unsmiling, haunting of face even then, with the large eyes and the closed mouth; and a defiance slumbering there as if she might, held longer, throw down the tawdry flowers, yell and stride off. This perhaps says it all.

Of Emma's father, I knew little: he was wounded and what they then called 'shell-shocked' in the First World War, and though he lived on for a while in and out of mental homes, he died not long after Emma was born. Emma's mother was something of a puzzle: she had bursts of ambition, would take large and sudden decisions; then retreat into moments of aberration when she lost vital possessions, left rail tickets behind and forgot the names of people she knew well. The ambition lighted on her child, and from the beginning Emma was dressed, paraded, made to recite, to dance. You might have thought that all this would send the child into reverse, of shyness and drab clothes, but it did not. Though Emma and her mother could strike sparks from each other, there was a likeness there: a love of dressing up and bowing to an audience.

Emma's childhood coincided with that age of the cinema when—in Hollywood—large money flowed from films whose stars were not more than ten years old. No one in those days was making films in England, not so you'd notice. After some abortive visits to theatrical agents in London where she got no further than the reception desk, Susan Denzil borrowed the money and took her daughter Emma one summer to Los Angeles. This plunge into adventure had perhaps a trace of the wildness which attended Emma: it wasn't after all a very sensible thing to do.

I don't know from whom she borrowed the fare. Emma used to talk of gentlemen who came and stayed to dinner—perhaps longer. (Susan Denzil in her early years had a rather untidy prettiness, with a trace of Emma in the large grey eyes.) The child Emma used to lie in bed listening to the two voices, her mother's and the masculine companion. From one of these companions, presumably, the money came: for what favours, Emma could only later guess. She was not at the time much interested in money, and why it was or was not available.

But she remembered the journey to the West Coast, which was long, hot and for a child uncomfortable; she was sick with the movement of the coach, tearful and weary when they at last arrived at the shabby hotel in the less fashionable part of Los Angeles. The casting offices were overflowing and without welcome. "It was like," Emma once said, "being offered on a slab in a fish market. I didn't know all of what was happening, but I knew that whatever was needed I either hadn't got it, or nobody was going to see it if I had. I sang 'They'll never believe me' in a rather frayed treble to a fat man with a bald head who wasn't paying attention; after that I

17

suppose the money ran out—anyway, we went home."

I don't know exactly what effect this experience had on Emma. She spoke of it in later years with dry amusement, without self-pity. Through all her disasters and despairs, Emma never blamed anyone but herself. She could be maddening, demanding, hysterical; but she held that what happened to her, happened. This was the hand you'd been dealt: you had to do your best with it. Maybe you failed (as I suppose you could say, in spite of much success, she ultimately did) but however much she telephoned her friends in the small hours, or wept, or shut herself in her apartment when the dark moods came on, she never blamed her childhood. In fact I think the abortive experiment of Los Angeles put more steel into Emma than it took out. She'd been ignored, humiliated, turned down: when she told her friends at school that she'd been to Hollywood, no one believed her. After losing her temper once, she shut up: the mouth which could look so appealing set firm; she didn't speak to them of the adventure again.

Now, so many years later, when I think about Emma, I don't see how any person can be viewed in a vacuum. Try as you may, somewhere in your genes or subconscious or blood and sinews, or in all of these, the deadly gifts lie, like bacteria which flourish in warmth; and what are you to do with them? Every person has so much fear, so much duplicity, so much sex, so much guilt, so much compassion, so much awareness—or non-awareness—of God. How do you deal with it all, and where does it come from? I see Emma with some traits of her mother's; and I see Carey with something of her mother, and something of her grandmother too. How far back does it go? To the distant ancestors who casually bred and passed their strengths and inadequacies down to their unknowing descendants?

Certainly, from that failed endeavour, Emma caught the stage bug. It was the stage that pulled her: she wanted an audience of living people to love and applaud her, not a critical camera crew and a director in a canvas chair. She would queue for seats in the pit at the West End theatres, wait at the stage door for autographs, and as she grew older, learn the classic speeches by heart and say them—with gestures—in her bedroom.

Leaving school at sixteen, Emma went for a time to a small private house where an ex-actress of late years taught 'dance, drama and elocution'. Perceptive always, Emma knew when she'd learned all that this elderly and out-dated lady could teach her. She was off to every audition for young actresses: singer ... dancer ... walk-on. Emma had talent (already she knew that); would travel. She would play pretty peasant girls in pantomimes, or understudy young women of greater fame who kept in maddening health. She would prompt, act as A.S.M.; she'd do anything to get near a stage and the shabby strong-lighted dressing-rooms which lay behind it. Pantomimes closed, plays ended; she knew times of despondency, frustration; auditions which got nowhere, but Emma pursued her way.

And as Emma's ambition increased, so did her mother's for her. Rumblings from Europe all but passed Susan by; she had lived through a war; talk of another could be nothing but the distant sound of drums, signifying nothing but man's need to live on the lip of danger. Emma was eighteen at the time of Munich: Susan saw the crisis as a threat only to Emma's prospects. Understudying the part of Jessica in a production of *The Merchant* in Liverpool, Emma had for the first time struck oil: the chosen actress went down with mumps caught from a nephew, and Emma was, as it were, trying on the costume while the casualty came out in mumps and no doubt fury.

Among the many photographs I have one of Emma playing Jessica. She looks very young and very pretty and rather wooden, but that may be just the photography and

19

the make-up. Perhaps her expression (unsmiling and faintly anxious) mirrors the difficulties she encountered. The director was a man of uncertain temper; he had as Portia an actress of some stature and he found Emma not sufficiently subservient or over-awed or at any rate, not sufficiently *something*, and when rehearsals went awry he would blame it on Emma. (She was after all only the understudy.) He was one of those directors who cannot let well alone, and like to plan every movement, each inflexion of voice. In all her acting life, Emma never responded to this: she acted with brain as well as heart, but she was an 'instinctive' actress—so often instinctively right—that to have each move plotted put her nerves on edge. What was more, Emma didn't get on too well with the leading lady: to begin with, Emma believed herself the better actress (she may have been right).

One occasion was perhaps significant. The dress-designer, who was the scene designer as well, had in a moment of aberration produced for Jessica a dress which was like the star's not only in shape but colour (a misty blue-grey). The star with casual certainty said that Emma's dress would have to be changed or dyed, or at any rate made to look different.

An air of crisis took hold: murmur of costs, the stage-manager scurrying from dressing-room to dressing-room, arguments between the designer and anyone who happened to pass by. The star stayed inflexible: no one else was going to wear grey-blue the same time she did. Outside this small conflict the world rocked, but the challenge remained and the atmosphere grew more disturbed, not helped by a steady fall of grey north-England rain and the news placards which together threatened to keep all but the minimum of audiences at home.

"Look, darling," the director said, catching Emma by the arm outside the basement dressing-room which she shared with two other young women—"sorry and all that, but we'll have to change your get-up. Don't know if it'll dye—if not we'll have to find something in *eau-de-nil*, or maybe..." He became silent (not usual with him) at something in Emma's face. Her mouth set firm. She said, "This dress suits me."

"Darling, I know, but you're the juvenile and—"

"Juvenile be damned."

"Possibly," said the director; "but the fact remains that understudies of eighteen don't tangle with people like Audrey, and if you haven't learned that it's high time you did. Darling," he added perhaps as a palliative.

Emma said, "I look better in grey. It suits me better than it suits Audrey; you know it does."

"Oh God," said the director, "that has absolutely nothing to do with it. Audrey wants your dress changed. Curtain. Full stop. Got that?"

No, Emma hadn't got it. Or if she had, she wasn't going to say so. "I look good in the dress—"

"If you looked like Helen of Troy, darling, it wouldn't make any difference. In fact, it'd make it worse."

Emma swung round. Anger gave her wings—not always rational wings—to fly to the nearest point of danger. She knocked on the star's dressing-room door, heard a lazy "Come," and went in.

Audrey Byers was a woman of thirty or so, dark, with a face in which the eyes (dark too) and the full mouth and the short, blunted nose seemed to form a pattern of sensuous power. She smoked continuously and with indolence. Just now she was dressed in a robe of black towelling, cigarette in hand, face clear of make-up, shining and pale in the strong lights. She was reading a letter of several pages. Whether it pleased her or not, one couldn't tell.

Emma expected fireworks.

Audrey Byers said, "Sit down."

Emma thought of refusing, but the calm face with its heavy-lidded eyes prevented her. She sat on the edge of a small hard chair.

Audrey went on, "Listen. You're—how old?—eighteen. And you're very pretty and you've got—lots of people will tell you—a beautiful voice. Just don't become too conscious of it or you'll spoil it."

Emma sat, silent, the colour riding up on her cheeks, perhaps from unexpected praise.

Audrey put ash into a saucer. "But you've a lot of things to learn and sense is one of them—no, don't explode; exploding marks the face. Or it does later. This fuss is a waste of everyone's time and energy, most of all yours. You're trying to play a trump hand without any trumps. In ten years' time you may be able to get away with it. But you can't now. Is that clear?"

Prepared for rebellion, Emma paused, aware of authority. She nodded without speaking.

Audrey gave a glance to the lighted mirror, where she briefly examined her face with a lift of dark brows, then said, "You have what I have—magic and the determination of whatever animal it is that eats through boards with its front teeth to get where it wants."

Emma sat, tranced, the dress forgotten.

"I'm not saying, mind you," Audrey went on, "that either of these attributes guarantees anything at all—"

"You've got there!"

The dark eyes turned slowly. "I had luck—first and all important. I worked hard. I kept my head." The glance which stayed on Emma was summarising, judicial. "When I was twenty I married a sane man and stayed married to him. You need to watch that—"

"Watch what?"

"The men and the booze."

"I don't drink. And—"

"Oh, I'm not interested in your love-life. Other people's love affairs, I'm afraid, unless they're *very* unusual, bore me to the bone. All I'm giving is general advice. You'll have much love, and you'll like it (who doesn't?). What's more you'll want to get married—and

22

have children: you'll want everything. People like you always do."

"Why shouldn't I?"

"I don't know. Except that it doesn't work out that way—"

"It did for you."

"I told you—I had luck. And I missed out on part of it. I haven't had children—they say I can't."

"Do you want to?"

"Oh, I daresay I did once. Years ago. Now ... I don't think of it often."

The dark eyes clouded; smoke from the cigarette swung quietly upward. Emma caught the scent of mystery, of a closed subject. That nerve of perception which stayed always with her, watching the old woman in the bus, the typist on a park bench, the woman customer making a row in a shop, came alive. Now she observed a woman no longer young, full of success; but with regret buried deep.

Audrey Byers made a movement as if she dismissed the past. "All I'm saying is—use your head. In spite of this silliness, you have got sense. Question is, whether you've enough."

"I have!"

"Perhaps. You've nearly everything else. But—"

Emma wasn't concerned with 'buts'. "If I've got everything else—"

"There's luck," Audrey said thoughtfully.

"I *am* lucky! Look how Christine got mumps!"

"Then no more fuss about the dress, there's a good girl?"

"Very well..."

It's possible no more was said. The performances of *The Merchant* came and went, like so many performances, full of sound and fury, followed by the whispering quiet of an empty stage as the scenery was struck, and the actors moved on. I doubt if anyone now remembers that

23

pre-war *Merchant*, or if they do certainly not what colour dress Emma wore (a bright rather unbecoming yellow). Nothing remains of that small scuffle, except perhaps the words of advice which Audrey offered Emma in her dressing-room. It's a question how long Emma gave them any heed.

Chapter Three

So Emma left the Vineyard and flew from New York to London, leaving me, with Carey and Jonathan, in Marguerite's care. If, as Marguerite foretold, Emma thought of Carey much beyond the first hour of the flight, it isn't recorded.

She landed at Heathrow in the early hours of a grey morning. The fresh cool air made the Vineyard and the blind-hot streets of New York seem far off. Rain was drying on the tarmac, and as she walked, anonymous, with the company of travellers she met the first twist of unease which accompanied every new endeavour, even now, years after that talk with Audrey Byers (now overweight, with suitable plays hard to find).

Customs, passport, the punctuation which marked change from one side of the Atlantic to the other. No reason why these mundane processes should be accompanied—as they were—by dread.

She had made her mark; no one could deny that. For a limited run of *The Master Builder* on the fringe of the West End the reviews had been such that Emma had for a while seen herself walking with gods; she had bidden all the cast to a champagne party which she couldn't afford. But the play came to its end as the party had: Emma returned to her flat in a subdued part of Chelsea, met the usual pile of bills and congratulations and a leaden quiet.

Emma never became used to quiet. She met it now and knew the first surge of panic. She had the best chance of her career; but a fine chance was two-edged: if she succeeded, golden prospects could lie before her—but if she failed? . . .

Such things could happen. Nerves, over-ambition, antagonism between herself and the director or another member of the cast—any of these could undo her assurance, give her that most daunting sense of being off-balance, of losing command. Nothing worse than that; nothing worse than failure. . . .

Though it was still morning, she took a strong whisky because the spirit dulled anxiety, did something to quiet the voice in her head which was repeating, "You can't do it, you've lost it; you can't command the audience any more. It's happened to lots of people and now it's happened to you."

She refilled her glass, turned over a letter, found a cutting from the theatre page of a newspaper which, under a more or less unrecognisable photograph of herself, said, "Emma Pride, who has been making a name for herself in repertory and out-of-town classic roles, has her big chance now in the lead of Guy Forster's *The Newcomer*. The leading role of Daisy will be a departure for Emma; it's up-to-date, witty, a play—we're told—halfway between comedy and pathos. Guy Forster is one of the new playwrights to emerge since the war, and his style is astringent, belonging to a post-war age. Are we going to see a new Coward, and perhaps a new Gertie Lawrence? The play goes on tour and is planned to open in the West End in six weeks' time. . ."

She read and re-read the notice and observed the photograph which made her, she thought, look forty and on the point of tears.

In the end she threw it away and booked a call to New York. To my father.

(I did not, at the time, of course, know that she was telephoning my father, since he was in New York, Emma in London and myself on the Vineyard. In any case, had we

26

all been much nearer, I wouldn't have known anyway, for the adult world pursued its own course and paid small attention to the three of us who were children then.)

About half-past ten that morning in the Chelsea flat, the call came through. A voice rough with sleep said over the long distance cable, "Who the hell's that?"

"Lance—I'm sorry—I'm really sorry. It's me. Emma."

"For Chrissake—d'you know what time it is?"

"Half-past ten—"

"Here it's half-past five. In the morning."

"All right."

"It's not all right."

"I know what your time is. I just had to talk to you—"

"Why me?"

"Because I'm scared."

"Oh God, oh Lord. What about? And why d'you have to tell *me*?"

"You're the only person who can help. Other people don't *know*."

"Hell, I'm half asleep. Don't know what?"

Emma held the receiver in a hand that was already sweating. She took a gulp of whisky. "How I feel. How I get scared. There's a press cutting about me playing in *The Newcomer*."

"So I should hope."

"It reads like a question mark. As if they were all waiting to see what I can do." She took another gulp of whisky.

"You're drinking—"

"Water."

"I don't believe you."

"I tell you, I'm frightened. Out of my wits. Oh, do wake up and concentrate. It's serious, how I feel—"

"You shouldn't be drinking whisky at half-past ten in the morning."

"Oh, shut up about what I drink. I'm scared blue, stiff,

all the things you're scared like—"

"This call must be costing a bomb."

"It'd cost less if you'd stop interrupting and try to help me."

"Oh God; *help* you. It's half-past five and I had a late night."

"But I need help, and you're the only person who can give it."

"God knows why."

"I don't know why either, but it's true. It always has been true."

"I'm surprised. Dead sleepy and hungover like hell, but surprised."

"Surprised? Have you forgotten everything? No, you can't have."

"Oh . . ." the voice said. "No, I've not forgotten. Though I do my best."

"That's unkind."

"No; only reasonable."

"Lance—please help me." Emma lit a cigarette, coughed as it followed too quickly on a drink.

"Now you're asphyxiating yourself."

"Lance—*please*." In the quiet room Emma felt a true rise of panic. "You got me into this—"

"You wanted it."

"They're saying I ought to be a kind of second Gertie Lawrence."

"Darling, you're not a second anyone: you're yourself, Emma Pride: you're a wow—magical and if not exactly beautiful, you have something in your face that can break anyone's heart."

This brought Emma to silence, as praise always did. She lifted the glass with a shaking hand, then said unsteadily, "It didn't break yours."

A sleepy chuckle. "It takes a lot to break my heart. You should know that by now."

"I feel alone. I can't play this part, it isn't mine. And if

28

I fail—the critics'll be after me."

"Critics . . . pay no attention."

"What's the *good* of saying that? I have to pay attention: you know I do."

A sigh across the long distance. "Yes, I know. But it's part of the job. Either you quit, or you take whatever they sling at you. T'ain't no other way."

"I wish you were here."

"Dear duck, you know very well I can't be. I have work to do over here, and after that I have a wife waiting for me, with the patience of six saints, on the Vineyard."

Emma was silent again, then said, her voice husky and shaken, "Can *she* break your heart?"

Another chuckle. "I've no intention of discussing Marguerite with you in the small hours—or at any time, come to that."

"Now you've made me miserable again."

"Not intended. What's Marguerite to do with it? We're not talking about my wife, we're talking about you playing the part of Daisy in *The Newcomer*. And there isn't a doubt in hell that you can. You'll smash them, because—as well as much else—you're unique. There isn't anyone else quite like you. Maybe that's why you find life difficult—"

"Like hell I do."

"Yes, darling, I know it: we all know it. Life is something you've never really got under control. But the theatre is another story."

"Why's it taken me so long?"

"Oh, everything takes for ever, you know that. Including this call. You're on the up and up, baby, and you've nothing to lose—except your bank account if you talk any more."

"Will you think of me? Pray for me?"

"I'm not much of a one for praying. Let's say I'll send a lot of fine vibrations across the sea. . . . Cheer up, darling: the world's before you. Now can I get back to

29

sleep?"

Emma put down the telephone and immediately banished three thousand miles of the Atlantic, and Lance woken from sleep. The quiet of her room returned, with her luggage still unpacked. Now that the call was over, she began to think about the cost of it. Always the same, she reflected: she spent first and sweated afterwards. Now her anxiety was the cost of the call to New York: how much would it be? Ring the operator and ask? . . . No; better to stay in ignorance, wait till the bill came in; by the time it did she might be able to pay it; good things might have come her way.

In her bedroom she sat before the looking glass. Face weary with travel, smudges beneath her eyes, hair astray. An actress? A star actress? She leaned closer. In spite of the fatigue and the sweat of travel, she could perceive, with the detachment of the professional, a look of near beauty, of appeal. What had Lance said? ". . . a face that can break anyone's heart." It might be true. All the things he'd said might be true. But the silence of the room prevailed, and there seemed, in spite of her good fortune, a voice which whispered that none of this would come to good; that the road grew darker.

"I don't like this," she said. "Why did I ring Lance? It's never any good ringing people: they're on with their own lives, eating or working or making love; or asleep, like Lance . . . *Was* he asleep? Was there someone in his bed? Might have been; you can't know. You can't know truly about anyone. That's what makes it frightening: you can talk and talk as I've just done to Lance, but none of the right things get said, the things inside you, what you *really* feel; and the other person doesn't understand, so you end up with silence, a worse silence than if you hadn't spoken."

She moved from the glass. Best to unpack, make some sort of outward order, if she had none within. Her clothes spoke of the Vineyard, of the sun and sand dunes, and

30

Marguerite in dark glasses and her wide-brimmed hat. . . .

A wife with the patience of six saints . . .

I wonder, Emma asked herself, why I don't hate Marguerite? Because I so easily could. Long ago (or it seems long ago) Lance was mine.

Yours? a voice seemed to question.

All right; maybe Lance hasn't ever been anybody's; but it seemed like he was mine.

He never married you. And he's Marguerite's now . . . A cousin-by-marriage, you might say.

But I still rely on him. No one since—and there have been others since, I can't deny—has had his strength, his command.

So what are you doing accepting (as they say) Marguerite's hospitality? Her help with *your* children?

I don't know. It's just easiest.

Are you trying to get him back?

No. No.

Are you sure?

Damn; I don't want to think about it. I admire Marguerite: she's my cousin, and a far better person than I am—

Could be. But none of that, as you well know, cancels the determination of love.

I don't love Lance any more.

Don't you?

To hell with this: I don't want any more questions. We were lovers once. It's over and done. I just need him to *be* there; to reassure me.

Says you.

Oh, hell—

The sound of the doorbell startled her, and cut the inner dialogue short. Who on earth? . . . she wasn't yet ready for the world—

When she saw her mother she took a fall of guilt and apprehension.

31

Susan Denzil was equipped to inspire both of these. The woman who had taken the young Emma from coast to coast in the States now looked as if she would find difficulty in making her way from Ealing to Earl's Court. Her hair, long and pinned up, escaped in tendrils of brown and grey; her shoes were shabby, her skin sallow and her eyes (Emma's eyes) sad. Emma looked on all this with dread for there was a saying (wasn't there?) that all women became like their mothers.

"I went to the airport to meet you," Susan said. She held out a small bunch of marigolds which seemed to have wilted from the sweat of her hand. "Didn't you think I'd be there?"

Perplexed, Emma found a vase for the flowers (and why is there *never* one which fits?) and said aloud, "I didn't think anything. I was tired and knocked sideways with travel and distance, the way you are when you come back from the States."

"You gave me the number of your flight. I went all the way to the airport and I've been there nearly two hours."

"Oh . . . hell. I'm sorry. I didn't *know*."

"I suppose it doesn't matter." Susan Denzil wandered to a chair and sat down. "Nothing matters really, does it, except this marvellous thing that's happened to you."

Emma looked at her mother with doubt. "What marvellous thing?"

"Why, darling, this wonderful *chance*." Susan Denzil was foraging in a large lop-sided handbag. "I had something here," she murmured . . . "I got it for you: I thought it'd be useful." Emma watched with deeper foreboding: her mother could be taken with sudden enthusiasms for gadgets of one kind or another, driven by the shining terms of some advertisement; these nearly always turned out to be less than they claimed to be, or even failed altogether.

Her mother produced a package of small bottles from her bag. "It's for your face, darling, when you travel."

32

"What about my face? I just take it with me."

"Oh . . . but darling you can put everything into these little bottles."

"Terribly kind," said Emma, reflecting that the tyranny of being given something you didn't want lay heavy on the heart.

"After all . . ." Susan's glance went over her daughter with sudden accuracy; "you're not looking your best . . . have you got the curse?"

"No, Ma. I've just come a long way."

"You shouldn't let yourself be seen in public like that."

"Oh—in *public*. What does that mean? I've been acting now for nearly ten years, and I can still walk the streets of Chelsea without people queuing up for my autograph."

"Fame comes in different ways, darling." Susan was repacking her handbag. "Sometimes it comes overnight (and *that* isn't always the best thing). You've done very well in a quiet way, and now you've got your big chance—"

"Ma, please stop saying that: I feel terrible about my big chance: at this moment it looks like the Black Hole of Calcutta."

"Oh, Emma; you've been drinking."

Emma thought to deny it; saw the glass beside her, and judged that the smell of spirits must be on the air. "I had one scotch because I feel bloody scared, and also I hate arriving anywhere in the morning."

"But here you are with the best thing that could possibly happen, and you look as if you'd just buried your best friend."

Emma shivered. The air in the room seemed to grow thin, the air dark. "Don't say that either. I don't want to think about death."

Susan looked bewildered. "We're not. We're talking about the future; how good it's going to be." She glanced at her daughter. "I know you think I did the wrong things

33

when you were small—"

"Please, Ma; don't let's go back to the past. I haven't even unpacked."

"I wanted you to have your chance in Hollywood; it wasn't my fault it didn't work out. I meant it for the best."

"I know. I know."

"I never left you alone. . . . Where are Carey and Jonathan? Why haven't you brought them with you?"

"How could I? I had to leave in a rush. Besides, they're happy on the Vineyard." At once Carey came to her mind, screaming on the sands, and she shut her eyes. I don't want to remember that, she thought: I don't want to hear her say *Take Carey with you*; please, let me forget. . . . She said forcefully, "They're happy with Marguerite and she'll bring them over at the end of the summer."

"I'd've had them. You know I'm always ready at a moment's notice."

"Yes, I know."

"You're going to say they'd rather be with Marguerite."

This was most likely true, but not possible to confirm; nor to say that her mother's somewhat confused household wasn't the best place for children. She just said, "They like the Vineyard. It's marvellous for them. And they have Rick to play with."

"I can't see that there's anything so special about Rick Ashley—surely there are lots of other little boys."

"Maybe, but they seem to like Rick."

"Marguerite as well. . . She may be my niece, but would it interest you to know that sometimes I get very tired of hearing how good and unselfish and altogether wonderful Marguerite is?"

Emma gave a slight smile. "No."

"Carey and Jonathan are *my* grandchildren. And they seem perfectly happy with me. And you're happy to let

34

them come, aren't you?"

"What else can I do? I'm an actress and I have to go on tour: I can't drag two small children about with me. I see as much of them as I can."

"And when Marguerite brings them over from the Vineyard, shall I have them then?"

"Well, I guess so. I guess so. Marguerite and Lance will be kind of busy—"

"So I *am* of some use after all?"

"Oh, Ma, of course. Don't make me feel guilty; I'll need another drink."

"There's no need to feel guilty. I love to have the children. But it's no good denying that Carey misses you. Funny, because—"

"Why the hell's it funny?"

"Now, darling, don't lose your temper. You always could, and it's not good for your looks. I just mean you'd think it'd be Jonathan who minded most: boys usually turn to their mothers. But he never says much."

Emma took a drink from her glass. "What does Carey say?"

"Oh, goodness ... just a child's babble: 'When's Mummy coming back? This afternoon? *Next* afternoon?' I don't know why she always thinks you're going to come in the afternoon... Now what have I said to upset you?"

"I don't know... I can't help not being with her..."

"You wouldn't cry if you hadn't been drinking—"

"*Please*—"

"Darling, I'm trying to help you. You're my only child and I want everything for you—"

"You want too much."

"I want you to have everything you deserve—what's wrong with that?"

"No one gets everything." (Did some echo of Audrey Byers' voice touch her?) "And when I feel I've got to succeed, it frightens me... Why did you say that about Carey?"

35

"I'm sorry—oh, Emma, don't cry like that." Searching in her ungainly handbag Susan found a crumpled paper handkerchief and made efforts to dab at her daughter's face. "You know how much I love to have the children; buy clothes for them; do anything—"

"I can't help not having enough money. Whenever I earn anything, there's always this ghastly tax and I never understand it, or how it comes to so much, and when I don't pay it there's trouble."

"Oh dear; there's always trouble if you don't pay bills. Sometimes I can't pay them myself and *writs* come in."

"Bills are different." Emma blew her nose. "Tax is a great gloomy *nothing*. You don't get anything for it. Oh, I know about the Police and the drains, but there's nothing you can bring home and undo."

"Oh, poor Emma." Flustered, Susan searched for another handkerchief. "You must stop crying and believe in yourself, in all the wonderful things that're going to happen."

Chapter Four

At the read-through of *The Newcomer* the cast came together for the first time. Their meeting-place was a large and dingy room in Islington which had once, it seemed, been a gymnasium. Within the room was an air of caution, as if different breeds of animal life were to be brought together. Jeremy Hirst as their director had indeed the wary look of a lion-tamer; he prowled, tall thin and blond, script in hand. He was the first to arrive, which gave him time to prowl.

(There were those who looked on Jeremy as an unnerving director, since he had so many ideas, and was moreover so often in the habit of changing them. In his younger days he'd played Richard the Second, Constantin and even Hamlet, but though the critics were respectful the public stayed away. Failure, if such it was, had given him a tolerance of defeat. When he turned to directing—which, though he missed the applause, he found greatly more to his taste—nerves only attacked him on first nights, when he would walk the streets, hands in pockets and head down, until cold or curiosity drove him inside.)

His feelings for Emma were divided. He was enough a man of the theatre—forty next birthday and many plays, as it were, under his belt—to recognise her quality; he could also smell trouble. Though he'd never worked with her before, he'd heard all the rumours: unpredictable temperament . . . drinks too early in the day; how much more than rumours they were he'd yet to learn. The image of her came clearly to his mind's eye: haunting face; a voice which contained—what was it?—*lacrimae rerum*: the tears in things—

He tossed the script on to a table and lit a cigarette. Tears. Heartbreak. The language of too lush advertisement. That wasn't how Emma was. Emma had something within her tough, hard and difficult: she could whip with her tongue; she could sulk and cast a shadow over her companions, as if they'd been told of a time-bomb below the rehearsal room. He mustn't become sentimental about Emma; nor on the other hand must he be angry with her sometimes childishness. But he was aware of threat, of disproportion, as in an empty room of dignity with furniture polished and the curtains hanging in quiet folds, one is nevertheless aware that someone is hiding there.

He took up the script again and ruffled its pages. A good play, even a fine one. And *his* to mould. With the connivance of the cast . . . He reviewed the cast in his mind: Emma, Ben, Brenda, Mark and Juliet . . . Which, if any, would fail him? Or would he fail himself, missing some essential point in the production, some necessary emphasis? . . .

He prowled again. There always came a point such as this when he said to himself, "This isn't the Third World War; it isn't the bubonic plague; it's a *play*, which'll be forgotten in weeks or months; it's the usual mixture of high spirits and despair, talent and near-talent, electricians and stage-hands and props which go missing at all-important moments; a complex endeavour which in the end will leave, to coin a phrase, not a wrack behind . . ."

All the same, it was *his* play. Or rather, his production; and he would feel any final failure to be his own. What's more there had to be something to give hope, to lift the heart on waking. For what else was there? He believed in no God, and since women held no physical attraction for

38

him, he would have no children . . . There was this play. And Emma.

In the rehearsal room, Jeremy viewed his cast, which was now complete. Mark, Juliet, Ben, Brenda. And Emma. Most particularly he viewed Emma. It became clear to him that she contained within her that mixture of uncertainty and arrogance which bedevils so many artists in whatever form they practise. In the midst of triumph would come a thrust of doubt: did she stand with that most desolate company: those who have talent, but not enough, only the perception to see what they cannot do?

The rest of the cast didn't greatly trouble him—not so far. Mark Severn, an actor of fifty, who could not surely have been anything else (of Jeremy's own sexual persuasion) read with casual ease; Juliet Boyle, thirty-five, competent, with too sharp a nose, sat upright on her chair; Brenda, plump, fair, snub-nosed and over fifty, had, like Mark, the complacency of one who's travelled this way many times before.

And Ben? Ben Hardy was new to him: twenty-four, perhaps, with fair curling hair, the face of a Raphael angel and a trace of cockney accent which his drama school had not quite obliterated. His blue eyes had shadows beneath them, which didn't seem to belong to his years.

As they read, Jeremy's glance returned to Emma. It was not his imagination; something was wrong; from his hunched position on a broken-backed chair, Jeremy decided that Emma was losing her composure (if composure was what she had); her hands were trembling and she'd lost her place in the script. With one shaking hand she turned the pages of the script trying to find it, then said, "Oh, God."

Here we go, Jeremy thought, and without moving said, "Now then, darling; it really doesn't matter losing your place; just draw a deep breath and begin again."

"It isn't that." Emma drew her hands down her face;

39

the rest of the cast had the look of passengers just told their flight will be several hours delayed. Emma said, "I can't *find* her—Daisy, I mean. I don't know who she is."

"Yes you do, darling."

"I don't. I thought I did when I first read the script, but it's like meeting a person and thinking you've known them all your life, and then meeting them a second time, and they're a stranger."

Juliet (who had, Jeremy thought, the look of a dark Athene) said, "Have we got to have this?"

"Quiet, darling," said Jeremy. "If Emma's having one of her turns we must all try to be patient."

"I am *not* having one of my turns. I'm a professional—"

"Then behave like one, ducky," Jeremy said.

"I'm trying to. I've just lost this. I'm sorry. I can't help it."

Mark, Juliet and Brenda watched with differing aspects of boredom, but Ben with his seraph's face went and put an arm about her. "You'll find her, love," he said.

Jeremy caught the look which passed between Emma and Ben: the authentic spark of sexual communication, the swift acknowledgement that has no words and needs none. Jeremy shifted in his chair, not pleased with this either.

The moment quickly passed; Ben returned to his place and Emma said, "I'm sorry."

Maybe she was, thought Jeremy; at least one must hope so. He changed the position of his long legs. "Can we all go on as if nothing had happened? . . . About this girl Daisy . . . *you*, Emma: you're a catalyst (look it up in the dictionary, dear, when you get home); you've come into this family at a moment of crisis—no, wait, listen: you may have read this, but you need me to say it. You've come from the States because your father has died, and his greatest friend has invited you. (And you got the part, ducky, not only because you look like a catalyst, if ever I saw one, but because you can produce that rare thing, an authentic American accent: British actors who think they can simply don't know they can't.) All right: you come into this extremely English, on-the-surface ordinary family, where, as they say, unbeknown to you, the father is in deep financial trouble: and his wife, with the skill of Iago, Lady Macbeth and Machiavelli concealed within the person of a middle-class housewife has managed to get her (admittedly beautiful) son engaged to the daughter of a wealthy businessman who has no other children and will leave her everything when he slips on.

"And into this delicate tangle, ignorant as a babe in arms, you come and explode the whole works like a hand-grenade. *Not* because you're a tart, or a go-getter or anything at all but yourself, a mixture of Kate in *The Shrew*, and Mary Rose. (If you're old enough to remember who Mary Rose was, which I doubt.) Not only Ben, God save us, but his father falls for you. With the result that Ben's fiancée, and his mother, plan to tear you limb from limb. And on top of it all, you have to remember that you're funny: it isn't, after all, *King Lear*; you are a tough, funny, innocent (they do have them) American girl— Henry James brought up to date. If you know about Henry James."

Emma looked at him with dignity. "I know about a lot of things."

"All right, all right." Ben, dusty light on his curled hair, was turned to look at Emma; Mark, shirt open at his neck, lines on a still handsome face, one arm draped over the back of his chair, sat, an old professional, bored to the teeth.

Deciding to ignore him, Jeremy went on, "We haven't got till Christmas, ducky; in fact we've only got three weeks' rehearsal, which isn't enough. As you all know, we are not putting on *The Newcomer* by courtesy of any random millionaire, nor as an afternoon frolic for friends

41

of the family. We may be artists acting our heads off, but we're also involved in a highly risky commercial enterprise. We—or the management—have to pay a great many salaries and find a great deal of cash. Everything we do and all the time we take, costs money."

"Does that apply to your speech?" Mark said.

Jeremy controlled his temper. "Yes," he said, and no more. Emma was looking at him with the eyes of a worldly (yet other-worldly) child; a child who had darker knowledge than the adults around her; who had wept unseen for some misfortune yet to come.

She said, "All right. You don't have to tell me about *money*; I know all about it." (But not how to manage it, Jeremy thought; he kept silent.) "All right," Emma said again, "I wasted time—but not a lot of time. And every-one keeps telling me what a chance this is, and I wish they'd *stop*. Stop, stop, stop."

Jeremy kept his eyes on her. The words were not hysterical, but he smelt hysteria somewhere about. 'That something extra'—yes, it was there in Emma all right. But what else? . . . He recalled suddenly a dream he'd had, when he'd been given a priceless vase: he could see the gleam of peacock porcelain. He'd known a feeling of great excitement; and then as he turned the vase he discovered that one side of it was made of ash which crumbled in his hand . . .

"All right," he said. "Let's go back to page thirty-four. Your line, Emma."

He heard her voice. "*What a swell place. Why, it's kind of grand.*"

Mark now. "*It seems pretty ordinary to us.*"

Emma shook her head. "*No, it's not ordinary. Not to me. Not if you've been used to an apartment in downtown New York, measuring all of five foot by nine.*" Her head lifted from the script, and she looked at some imaginary room. "*We don't have anything like these back home.*"

Ben's turn. "*Well, we don't have anything quite like you*

over here."

Emma looked at him with drowned surprise. "*I like that. That's cute.*"

"*What an odd word to choose*," Juliet said with the required venom.

Jeremy let them read on. It was going well. Emma's small crisis might never have happened. Though perhaps he should have known better, he could already hear the crescendo of applause, see the rave reviews in the morning's press . . .

He listened.

Emma returned home by taxi. As she paid the fare and overtipped, she began to think about money: how was she going to cope with the expenses of the flat and the bills (there were always bills) and the extraordinary amount she had to pay for things like stockings, underwear and make-up? Money seemed to take the form of a large and threatening bird which would swoop upon her when she least expected it. Why was it so difficult? She had no idea what would be left of her earnings when she'd lived on them (and she had to live, didn't she?) and then the tax envelopes fell on the mat and she felt sick and needed a drink which she couldn't afford.

She shut the door. Strange how quickly the companionship of the theatre world could vanish, leaving a silence burdened with apprehension. She lit a cigarette and poured herself a drink. It was absurd—wasn't it?—to be alone at all; it was absurd to be filled with this curious dread. She had everything, surely, all the luck in the world. How many young women, just out of drama school, walking the city streets, waiting in bedsitting-rooms for the promised telephone call (which would not come) from this or that theatre management, would give ten years of their lives to be in her place?

Indeed, she could recall herself, that self of some years ago, a young actress auditioning before the faces of men

43

with beards, cigarettes and ashtrays: "What have you done?" they would ask, and she would reply that she'd been Assistant Stage Manager in rep. and played Goldilocks in pantomime in Scarborough. The sweat on her; her knees and hands trembling... "Very nice, dear: very nice indeed. We were all very excited." (You could have fooled *me*.) "It's just that we can't see a place for you in this particular show." Out into the cold London street (why did it always seem to be cold after auditions?), hands deep in her duffle coat, head down, kicking at the pavement as she walked. Dismissed. Not wanted. How did you ever get through the barrier of those who sat like dark angels at the gate of hope?...

She'd known all that, the dusty taste of failure, the casual but lethal words: "nothing for you in this particular show." Nor in any other show; always the same answer...

But now... Oh God, she was lucky. *Lucky*. She had everything which that girl who walked with rejection down the cold streets had wanted. And yet... The girl couldn't know that the golden future had its shadows: that one never stood, firm and assured and said, *"I'm there*: I've got it all." Doubts came in: had she done as well as she supposed? What were the shadows at her shoulder? Fear, guilt, self-distrust?... Perhaps that girl, workless and shabby as she was had at least been free of these. She'd been innocent, even virgin. Didn't drink; only smoked from a battered packet of Craven A. Hadn't yet married; had no children—

Emma took another gulp of drink. *The little princes in the Tower*. Why had the phrase come into her mind? Jonathan and Carey were boy and girl. And they had the best of things, surely? How many children crossed the Atlantic, spent summers on an island off Cape Cod; would be given the chance—when they were old enough—to see plays from the best seats, go backstage to the dressing-rooms—it was a fairy-tale life ... wasn't it?

44

Take Carey with you.

I don't want to remember that. If you were in a play you had to give it all you'd got; it did no good to think about Carey and Jonathan who were small and young, and barely knew the world at all (What's "tour"?); who were at this moment three thousand miles away.

But who were *her* children, born of her; who had been helpless and her own—

Oh, Christ, I must stop this. I must honestly stop this. They're all right; kids' memories are short. Carey won't remember what she said... (When's Mummy coming back? This afternoon? Next afternoon?)

I don't like this. I ought to be on top of the world. Why do I get things wrong?...

No, I won't think like that: it isn't true. It wasn't my fault Desmond got killed; it wasn't *really* my fault that Geoff and I parted. Well, I may have stepped aside once too often, but anyone who'd been married to Geoff would have stepped aside: he had about two ounces of humour, and looked as if he *slept* in striped trousers and a bowler hat.

All right, she said to some accuser who kept up a continual challenge: maybe I should've known that before I married him—maybe I *did*, but it was too late then; there were all those wedding presents (whatever happened to them?) and he seemed to worship me, and let's face it, I enjoy being worshipped, but it gets boring after a time.

Yes, all right, I know he suffered and I'm sorry—at least, I suppose he suffered: how was anyone to *tell* about Geoffrey? Oh, God, yes; he *cried*, didn't he: but I don't want to think about that—it was right out of character, anyway; he must have had too much to drink...

Perhaps she shouldn't have been an actress at all; perhaps those years of effort, the long hours of rehearsal had been after all a waste of time; perhaps she should have stayed as Geoff's wife (or at least *some*one's wife) and looked after her children...

45

No, she couldn't have done that. She saw a long dreary corridor of damp clothes, cooking and talk about such things as would bore the pants off her. She had to be an actress, however tough it was; she had to live with the distant throb of excitement; she had to do the work which, when she entered upon it, seemed to ease the burden of her fears and anxieties, to oil the springs of whatever machinery made her tick.

So that brought her here, to this moment when the devils came in. The devils had all forms and sizes; they could bring accurate memory of bad notices; the harsh words that stung like wasps. "Miss Emma Pride plays the part of Cordelia as if she had just failed her A-Levels and didn't want her father to know." "If we wept at Lear's *Never, never, never* it was nothing to do with Miss Pride who was better dead than alive."

How they could sting!

"Miss Emma Pride as Isabel accepts the news of her husband's death like a hostess being told that Fortnum and Mason's have run out of caviar."

Who the hell was that? One of the sharp clever new boys who were always to be feared. And now she had to face them again . . .

She poured herself another drink. The only palliative, to deaden regret and fear—

The sound of the telephone made the glass jump in her hand. Nerves. Silly. Wasn't friendship, conversation, love, what she was waiting for?

She answered the telephone.

Ben. Ben Hardy. "The marvellous boy", she thought, recalling the words from some old school desk.

He asked her after preliminary, rather breathless conversation if she would have dinner with him. She stood and ruffled her hair. What did she want to do about dinner? . . . She caught like a brief flash of light that moment of communication in the rehearsal room. She said, "I figured on having dinner in . . ."

"Oh . . ."

"Why don't you join me? There's cold chicken in the fridge. Or something in the fridge: it'll be cold, that's for sure."

A faint chuckle. "All right. That'll be fine."

"Get a taxi."

"It's been rather an expensive week."

"Oh, golly—*all* weeks are expensive."

When he'd rung off she wandered absently to the fridge. The telephone call seemed to have taken her out of despondency. She didn't know much about Ben, except that he was younger than herself, and that after their first meeting some question touched her, as if a bird's wing had crossed the light. Or as if someone had whispered a warning which she had not perfectly heard.

He arrived sooner than she expected. (He *had* taken a taxi.) From the window she could see him foreshortened, standing in the grey street, as he searched for the fare. People spied upon, she thought, had an odd vulnerability, as if you watched them asleep. Secret, unknown, yet in a way more true than when you faced them, when the mask was on. For there was always a mask, of some kind.

She thought about this as he sat on the sofa, drink in hand. The different background gave him a difference too; not the actor of the rehearsal, but a young man who had with surprising speed invaded her living-room. (At her own invitation, of course.) A good decision? She wasn't sure.

"I don't know much about you," she said. "I mean, as an actor."

"Not a lot to know. I only left drama school three years ago."

"After that?"

The seraphic face smiled; one hand smoothed the fair curling hair. "Oh . . . what happens to everyone in this game. Very little cash and lots of staircases. (Why do agents always live so high up?) A.S.M.-ing, understudy-

47

ing, a season of rep, at the end of the pier in Colwyn Bay. Quite a good shot at Mercutio in Bristol. With, let's say, gaps in between."

"How did you get this?"

"A wild piece of luck. It nearly always is, isn't it? This young man was being difficult to cast—plenty of war veterans all wanting to get back on the band-wagon, but they were too old. (Awful to be too old for anything, don't you think?) Then Jeremy Hirst came to the Lyric, Hammersmith where I had a small juvenile bit in an eminently forgettable play." He drank, while his eyes looked to this recent turn of fortune. "He asked me to audition, and of course I got a flu bug, but I went along, shaking with flu and fright, and read for him. I had that ghastly feeling all the time—you know?—'Oh, God, here's my chance and I'm missing it'—but some sort of bright angel was hovering over me (I rather like the idea of angels, don't you?) and Jeremy rang me two days later and said I'd got it."

"Pretty good—after not a lot of experience."

"Oh—experience. What everyone wants you to have had and no one will give you. Four years at drama school, but that isn't it, is it? Not having to earn your living; surrounded by people who want the same thing and are learning it with you. Cosy, warm, like being in an incubator. Then—bingo—you're out in the cold with the wind going through your feathers. And no one wants you. At least—" he smiled and lifted his glass—"until now."

She nodded and wandered to the kitchen. His presence had dissolved the dark mood; as she prepared a tray she felt light of heart. Returning, she put the plate of chicken before him and smiled, as if at some private joke.

"What's funny?" he asked.

"Cold chicken's all one colour. It ought to have something to cheer it up."

"You do all the cheering up it needs."

"*I* do? Don't believe it. I know what people say: Emma's having one of her 'downs': what shall we do

48

about Emma? ... Don't tell me you haven't heard them."

"I haven't been around that long in the theatre."

She wasn't sure if she believed him. "Long enough to have heard something."

"I've only heard—"

"Well?"

"That you're—loving."

"You mean I go to bed with everyone?"

"No—"

"I don't, whether you've heard it or not." A brief flash of anger. He looked up at her with awe, amusement and inquiry. "I've been myself," she said, more quietly. "And that self isn't a tart."

"Darling, I never said it was."

Anger slid away. The "Darling", so natural in stage talk, was here of a different tone.

She moved to him with easy perfection. Although she told herself she hadn't decided that this would happen, she let herself be received into his arms. She listened, pleased, eyes half-closed, to the words he spoke.

Once she withdrew her head to see in focus the young face with the fair hair and the deep blue so deep-shadowed eyes. She was lost now, drawing closer. How splendid youth was, male youth before the world marred it. She had loved older men, but youth had the true enchantment for her ... Would this always be so? Ben was younger than she; in a few years she would be over thirty: would she still need the young men, more than they needed her? She knew actresses like that, women whose perfection of skin and eye and breast was fading but who needed the warm physical perfection of the young men. ...

No need to dwell on that: now she was young enough to meet him, name enough to command his awe, his sense that he was the one who asked, she who granted. That was important: she needed to be the one who bequeathed pleasure at the same time as she received it.

His hands trembled as they sought her: only when his mouth and tongue found her responsive did he begin to lose his nervousness and take on assurance.

No, it wasn't a casual coupling. Her hands slipped over his fine skin, down to the hips and thighs and the strong emerging desirous flesh. The warm weight of his body; the movement inside her like a pulse of her own body—this was love, this was ecstasy; this for the moment was the whole of life. Galloping pleasure almost obliterated him as a person. This man who drove his love into her now was in some way other than the young man who had stood with such beauty in the rehearsal room; some other voice which whispered to her words which came as quickly as shreds of paper on the wind.

Oh, yes; yes, yes, she said, not knowing what she answered; I love you, I love you; while the heady delight swam from her loins like a whirlpool, and his own deep gasp of pleasure seemed to be part of her own joy.

When it was done they lay clasped together. Slowly time and reality returned. Here she was, half-naked with Ben Hardy, mostly naked too, clasped to her, their sweat mixed together. The deep sweet pleasure was done; the day was coming back. She could see the plate of cold chicken on the table beside them.

Ben lifted his head and smiled at her, drowsily, with the bruised sleepy pleasurable look which she knew well on the face of men when the act of love was over. "What a marvellous thing," he said, his voice blurred.

She shifted slightly; his weight, lately so pleasurable, was now a little irksome; her arm ached. He bent to kiss her bare shoulder; she watched with reserve, even detachment. He was still Ben, he was still as beautiful, but magic had passed. Did she wish it hadn't happened? No . . . but . . .

She half-pulled on her clothes, and saw that he was still held, as she was not, in the sensuous half-dream. "*Do* you love me?" He kissed her gently. "*Do* you?"

Had she said that? It was possible; it had seemed true, but she thought now it was not. Not love, that ache of the heart, that submerging depth which closed like waters above your head, blinded you to all else.

She didn't answer, and perhaps now a little puzzled he said, "You know we didn't . . . that is, we haven't . . . I mean precautions."

This too she received in silence. He looked down at her still, it seemed, with love. "It *could* be."

She pulled away from him, stood up and finished dressing herself. "No, it couldn't. Not after just once. I don't work like that."

"How can you be sure?"

"I tell you; I know myself." Her voice was rising.

"You can't know your own body. None of us do."

"Oh, stop talking nonsense. What d'you know about conception, anyway?"

"I'm not innocent. I'm twenty-four."

"Oh . . ." The words were oddly touching; she turned away and went to her bedroom. When she had repaired herself, she returned to him. He was fully dressed, except for his tie; he had become more of the young man who had so beguiled her in the rehearsal room.

His glance, youthful, uncertain, revived her affection. She said, "Hungry?"

"Not sure."

"You came for dinner."

He gave a smile of gentle amusement. Yes, he had a face of extraordinary beauty: she could imagine how he must have looked as a child, and the pride his mother must have had in him. Must still have, she supposed. She asked, on an impulse, "Where's your mother?"

"My *mother*? She died when I was six."

"Oh . . . Your father, then?"

He shrugged. "He married again. So I have a fairly glamorous stepmother. I don't see much of them."

51

She thought of Carey and Jonathan ... no, it wasn't like that for her children. . . .

He said, "You look as if something haunted you."

"Oh, I always look like that. It's got me as far as I've been."

"You'll go to the top. Right to the top."

"No one can know that."

"I can. My grandmother had second sight."

"Is that a joke?"

"No," he said. "She had a pack of Tarot cards, and she told your future."

"I don't know much about Tarot cards."

"Oh—they're exciting. They're very ancient—there's the Hanged Man, the Knight of Cups, the Sun, and the Falling Tower. Weird and spine-chilling. There's a book about them called *Ancien Tarot de Marseille*." He looked aside, as if to some mystery. "She got things wrong sometimes, of course. But ever since I was a child it was what I liked most, to sit beside her at a green-topped table while she put out the cards. There was always a table-lamp beside her which lighted the cards and put shadows on her face. She seemed to me very old, but I don't suppose she was really *that* old. She had thin hands with thick blue veins: I can see them now, putting out the cards. She wore rather old-fashioned clothes, long skirts, black mostly. When she saw something she didn't like in the cards she shut her lips together and said nothing. If you asked her she shook her head and muttered about the cards not 'speaking properly today'. But I always knew."

"Knew there was something bad?"

"Uh-huh. She went quiet like that before my mother died. I suppose it might have been a coincidence: she never *claimed* to have been right. But I think it all meant a lot to her; I mean she really believed it."

Emma sat, entranced. All things mysterious appealed to her: the predictions of astrologers; ghosts; any story that touched on forces beyond the material world.

52

"Go on," she said.

"Once when I was a boy—about seven, I think—I can't remember—I was hanging about in the hall. Grandmother had a friend with her, a woman about the same age. And I heard them talking in lowered voices, and you know how *that* hooks you when you're a child."

Yes, Emma said; she knew.

"So I hung around by the door which wasn't shut, though they couldn't see me."

She listened, chin in hand. She could see Ben, a small (even more beautiful) boy of seven, lingering in some darkened hall. All the curiosity, loneliness and duplicity of childhood seemed to be there.

"They talked for a bit, and I was beginning to lose interest when I heard my own name. Well, *that* as you know is totally riveting. The friend said, 'I understand Ben is very interested in the cards.' There was a pause, and though I couldn't see my grandmother, I could imagine her shuffling the pack. Then she sighed and said, 'Yes . . . Ben. Poor Ben.'" He smiled. "*That* got me even more. Why was I 'poor Ben'? Because of my mother? I waited. My grandmother went on, 'The last time I did the cards for him—' and her friend said, 'Well?' sounding just as eager as I was. 'This is something I haven't told to anyone. After all, who is there to tell? His father—more concerned with his new wife, and the stepmother herself not greatly interested.' I began to feel sorry for myself, but more than that, wildly curious. 'Not told to anyone' is another riveter, you'll agree. Then my grandmother said, 'When I last read the cards for him they told me that death walks very close to Ben.'"

Emma looked at him in silence, cold.

He smiled, as if deprecating the effect of his words. "Well, of course it wasn't true. Here I am, a big boy now. But at the time I felt both frightened and rather *grand*. Important. After all, it singled me out from everyone else, which all children want, don't they?"

53

She didn't answer. The cold held her, as when her mother had spoken of death.

"As I say . . . she was wrong. For quite some time whenever I had a sore throat I thought 'This is it, I'm going to *die*.' It was dramatic and I was only partly frightened. But when I found that I always got better and my temperature went down, I kind of forgot about it. In a way I was disappointed. I didn't *want* to die, but it was rather a let-down *not* to, if you see what I mean."

"Sure."

"Of course, when people aren't kind I remember what my grandmother said, and think, 'Well, soon they'll be sorry.' I don't know who would be sorry, because only a very few people are sorry when you die—*really* sorry, I mean, don't you think? One person, perhaps, or two, but the rest . . ." he shrugged and looked aside, still smiling. "I think what most people feel is partly a reminder of their own mortality, partly a twinge of excitement— drama, I suppose. What was the line? A poem I used to know. '*Oh, is he gone? they say*'—something like that." He glanced at her. "There's no need to look sad about it; I'm as strong as six horses, as you can see. As I proved."

She let him kiss her, but she wasn't comfortable with this evening . . . Too much, perhaps; rehearsal, lovemaking, and now this talk of death . . . No, not death; only the superstitious murmurings of an old lady who believed in cards and tea-leaves. And Ben, a child of seven, listening with unguarded innocence, at sea in a world of mysteries . . . All at once the figure of the child changed, changed from Ben to Carey, standing on the shore of Martha's Vineyard.

She turned her head sharply away.

"What's the matter?"

Still turned from him she said, "What d'you do when you think of things you can't bear to remember?"

"Oh . . . talk aloud to myself. Clench my fists till the nails hurt. How d'you mean—when you've made a fool of yourself—fluffed a line or something?"

"No. No. It's just something that's too much; that I don't want to remember."

"Tell me."

"No, I can't. I want to forget it."

He kissed her again, and this time she clung to him, for he was gentle and loving, and she needed all the comfort he could give.

Chapter Five

As before Jeremy was first at the rehearsal room.
Anxiety, he reflected, always made him impatient to
begin.

And anxiety, he said to himself, as he observed a piano
which stood forlornly in one corner, as if it had been
abandoned on some removal exercise—is what we have.
Absently he emptied an ashtray into an old paint tin
which served as a waste-paper basket.

Wondering why exactly the omens for this day seemed
doubtful, he looked up as the door opened. When he saw
Guy Forster, the author of the play, he thought perhaps
he knew.

This was by no means Guy's first play, and he surely
knew enough to be clear that authors at this stage could
do nothing but harm. More especially as he brought not
only himself as author but other disturbing factors into
the room.

Jeremy, after a guarded greeting, summed them up.
The wounds which Guy had received in Burma had so
shattered a leg that he walked with a one-armed crutch;
perhaps the bullet scar down his cheek was the more
arresting: his skin was brown, but the long mark showed
white and puckered. The face itself had a Mephistophel-
ean cast, with a downward smile and raised eyebrows as
if, Jeremy thought, he defied you to show surprise or
pity. The eyes, set wide in the ruined face, had once had
some beauty. Now they showed a tigerish glint, an im-

patience with prevarication or stupidity, or the easy counterfeit coins of conversation which passed for truth.

It was, Jeremy said, only the second day of rehearsal. Guy answered, "I know," and with difficulty lowered himself on to a chair. "I had a reason for coming. You'll remember that after Emma's audition you and I had an argument."

Indeed Jeremy remembered it; conducted over a dinner table, civilised and exhausting. The challenging glance went over his face. Guy said, "This play means a lot to me."

"It would be hard," replied Jeremy, "to find a playwright whose play *didn't* mean a lot to him. Or any artist and his work, come to that."

"Quite. However, this play took me longer to write than any other. It's been in my head for a long time. I don't want it spoiled."

"Nor does anyone else,"

"Ah . . . No. However . . ." Guy moved his crutch. "Reliability may not exactly draw audiences in, but *un*reliability keeps them out."

"Gossip about Emma—" Jeremy began.

"I'm not relying on gossip. I know about talk in the theatre: thick as weed in a stagnant pool. I daresay Emma's never finally let anyone down."

"She hasn't. And we've signed her contract."

"I'm not suggesting we break it. I just want to see how things are going."

"It could put her off. Authors—"

"Aren't too welcome at this stage; so you said, and so I know. However, a little pressure won't do Miss Emma Pride any harm." The eyes showed a glint, perhaps of malice; or perhaps anger because at some depth he'd not accepted his disfigurement.

"Not sure about that," Jeremy said.

"You want to protect her."

"Naturally. She's the lead. Everything depends on

57

her."

"So we're in agreement, more or less."

Jeremy didn't dispute it. Nor did he press Guy Forster to go. A man of difficult temperament, he wasn't one to tangle with. Jeremy said merely, "You won't expect them to know their lines?"

Guy said he didn't expect anything; he didn't care for actors who were word-perfect too soon; he'd rather they got the 'feel' of the play first. "I want artists not parrots," he said, propping his chin on his hand, and looking towards the door.

Unconscious of their doom, Jeremy thought, the artists were approaching.

One by one they came into the room. Mark Severn first, the lines on his Roman-coin face deepening as he saw Guy; Juliet Boyle, slim and dark in a green trouser-suit, standing for a moment ice still; Brenda Jones, plump and happy, suddenly rocking back on her heels.

"Just dropped in," Guy murmured.

Juliet appeared the first to recover. "Well! What a beautiful day. Hi to high summer: I don't know where that comes from, but I clearly remember saying it on some stage sometime: must be the Bard, I suppose—with all respect, he had some pretty corny lines, didn't he?"

"He wrote in a great hurry, dear," said Mark, dusting the edge of a table and propping his haunches against it. "I had a wonderful time in Hull once working out *exactly* how old Hamlet was, what with all that about Yorick bearing him on his back; we all got quite hilarious and rather drunk. However, it doesn't seem to have spoiled the play's chances, does it?"

Brenda had recovered too, and settled her round shape on to a small stool and took knitting out of her bag. "It soothes me," she said placidly to Guy, whose eye had fallen on it; "helps me to go over my lines."

Guy nodded briefly. Juliet paced back and forth. "Where are the shining ones?" she asked.

58

"Not late," muttered Jeremy, eyeing her with some distrust. Juliet's mood was sharp, which was not what he wanted. In spite of several good performances, even promises of greater things as Perdita in a production of *A Winter's Tale* when the critics had brought out their superlatives, Juliet hadn't made the top. At the sound of her name someone would look up and say, "Why, *yes*; she was so good. What happened to her?"

What happened to her was that the interest of managements cooled, for no exact reason. Perhaps because her next play was a flop, or because she struck a moment of truth in *A Winter's Tale* which like all such moments couldn't be explained or with certainty repeated. Nothing stood still, except in memory. And memory only had value when you were dead; no good being a memory when you were alive—that brought you back to 'whatever-happened-to-her-she-was-so-good-in-whatever-it-was'.

Not for the first time Jeremy was glad that his excursions on to the stage as an actor had come to nothing, or rather had led him to the other side of the footlights where he could work away from the public's view—

His train of thought was interrupted by the arrival of the Assistant Stage Manager, a dark young man with shaggy eyebrows, who seemed to have been running, and said he'd had to wait for a bus. He was 'on the book', and after one glance at Guy Forster, sat himself in a corner and opened the script.

Brenda, still knitting, said that waiting for a bus gave her time to meditate; and Mark said he'd rather have the bus.

Jeremy glanced at his watch. He'd called the rehearsal for half-past ten; it was twenty-five to eleven. Five minutes on the wrong side would not have troubled him had it not been for Guy who, while conducting a desultory conversation with the others in the room, kept his eyes on the door.

Ben arrived first. He showed no alarm on seeing Guy; merely blinked in a bemused, happy way; said, "I'm not late, am I? Oh, good;" and looked round the room. For Emma? Jeremy thought so. And there was something in the boy's manner that disturbed him: a dream in his eyes, as if his thoughts were elsewhere. And, today especially, Ben's thoughts must not be anywhere but on the play . . .

Steps outside. And Emma. Just over ten minutes late.

Trust Emma, Jeremy thought, to make an entrance, even here, which had everyone's attention. On seeing Guy, she paused for a moment; then gave an ecstatic smile which could *not*, Jeremy reflected, have been caused by Guy's presence . . . A mystery somewhere: he was wary of mysteries. Emma said only, "Sorry I'm late—not very late is it? Couldn't get a taxi. They kept rushing past with other people in them."

"It's a way taxis have," said Guy; his voice told nothing. "Ever tried the tube?"

Jeremy said, "Emma on the tube stands out like an orchid in a nettle patch."

"Ah—indeed," said Guy. "An orchid? So expensive, and in my view—like caviar—not really worth the cost."

In case Emma should take this as an affront Jeremy said quickly, "We'd better get started. We'll go from Act Two—" the young A.S.M. with shaggy eyebrows turned the pages of the script and said, "Got that, Mr Hirst."

Guy sat, his crutch beside him, the scarred face impassive. Jeremy tried to ignore him. "We're right into it now," he said. "The fat's in the fire. Let's go."

Knotted on his chair, he watched. He spoke little. Occasionally he pulled them up, asking for a quicker pace here, a lighter touch there; a movement upstage for Mark . . . Guy said nothing at all, but watched with haggard concentration. Making notes in his head, I daresay, Jeremy thought; but thank God he's not saying them aloud.

The even flow broke when Brenda spoke a line back to

front: "It's *funnier* like that," said Mark; and Guy said, "Maybe, but it wasn't meant to be funny in the first place." The brief relaxation of hilarity died down; the play in its rough early shape continued.

Jeremy listened to the cadences of Emma's American accent: as near-perfect as he could judge; and her playing too—surely Guy must agree with that? Her first tentative love-scene with Ben had an especial tenderness—

Of a sudden that moment of communication between them yesterday came into his mind: they hadn't fallen for each other, had they? Disturbed by this thought, he interrupted: Ben, he said, perhaps with more force than was necessary, needed to be *down*-stage at this particular moment; he was all-important—in *front* of the sofa (when there *was* a sofa). Frowning, Jeremy watched Ben obediently move. Did he sway a little, put out a hand as if to support himself and then, finding nothing there, withdraw it?

"You all right?" Jeremy asked, as if he defied him to say he was not.

Ben gave his sleepy smile. "Perfectly."

Perhaps he was. Perhaps the small mis-step had been nothing more than a momentary aberration. Had Guy noticed anything? Impossible to be sure. Ben was himself again; Brenda, Mark, Juliet and Emma appeared to gain strength from the challenge of Guy's attention. In fact, contrary to his first feelings of ill-omen the day seemed to be going well. He had the surprising sensation of a man able to get through a locked door without a key. *Why* were things going so well?

Now, he said to himself; if calm seas and prosperous voyages are going to make you nervous, you'd better get out of this business fast and go in for bricklaying.

Guy remained for the two hour rehearsal until the break for lunch. He had a few points, he said, which he'd like to put to them over the customary beer. The cast went ahead. Jeremy, the unlooked-for triumph still with him said, "It went well."

Guy manoeuvred himself upright, leaning on his crutch. "Yes," he said; and added, "She was ten minutes late. And I have a worry about the boy."

"*Ben?*"

"Yes," Guy said; "Ben."

Later that evening at a table in a pub not far from the rehearsal room, Mark, Brenda and Juliet sat together over drinks and cigarettes.

They had the tired air of conspiracy which all actors and actresses have when the day's work is done.

"If you ask me," Brenda said, "we're very lucky. Very lucky indeed. When you've been in the business as long as I have little upsets like authors coming when they're not expected mean *nothing*. Absolutely nothing at all."

"If anything," said Mark, "I've been in the business *longer* than you have; I've been putting on make-up for what seems like centuries."

Brenda observed him, cigarette dangling from a corner of her mouth. "Well, maybe; but you haven't my sunny temperament."

"And what would I do with that?" asked Mark, giving a random glance to a young man at the bar counter.

"Nothing bothers me," Brenda went on; "nothing less than the whole set catching fire ... not even that: I remember one *Othello* when I was Emilia and some damned fool in doublet and hose lost control of his torch and a curtain went up in a sheet of flame, but I kept absolutely calm—"

"Maybe you were some way off," said Juliet.

"Darling, I was nearest of all—we had to ring down the safety curtain and call the fire brigade. But that's not the point. We've a marvellous play here and a *very* nice director, even if he does—well—prefer the boys—" Mark's face took on a remote solemnity as if he were thinking of far lands like Tibet— "and there's no reason at all why we shouldn't have a very happy tour."

Mark said, "Have you ever known a *really* happy tour?"

"Oh yes, hundreds," said Brenda, settling herself more comfortably on the pub seat. "My philosophy is, if you think a play's going to work all right, it does."

"That seems to me," said Juliet, "the most unlikely piece of optimism I've ever heard."

"I'm all for optimism," said Mark, "if it isn't misplaced. I remember playing Parson Manders with a company who were *all* at each other's throats—"

"It's simply a question of how you look at it," Brenda said. "Never a harsh word, that's my motto. I'm naturally good-tempered and I behave as if everyone else was too."

Mark and Juliet looked at her as if she'd claimed the certainty of eternal life.

"No," Brenda said, meeting the brooding glances; "I am *not* Pollyanna. I simply have a theory that works."

"You think it's going to work this time?" Juliet asked. "With Emma; and Guy Forster looming over us like an eagle bothered about its eggs?"

"But that's what it's all *about*," Brenda said, blowing out smoke. "You have to sit back and let it all glide past."

"I remember once in Cardiff," Juliet began, when Mark interrupted. "Darling, we can *all* remember once in Cardiff, and points north, east and west: it does no good to revive past horrors. For the present we have to face facts. We all know about Emma; we all know about Jeremy as a director— and Guy Forster as a playwright—"

"Yes," Brenda said absently; "the only one we don't know about is Ben."

"The beautiful Ben?" said Mark, an edge to his voice. "He's just one of Nature's golden boys, and he'll be lucky if he doesn't get plunged into a 'beautiful relationship' (I quote) with Jeremy."

Brenda looked at him, her broad face smiling through cigarette smoke. "That's not the direction it's going: Ben's in love with Emma."

"But he's only just met her!" Juliet exclaimed.

Brenda looked at her with the superior knowledge of her years. "It doesn't take long to fall in love with Emma; if you don't know that you've been somewhere else for a long, long time."

"And where does *that* take us?" said Mark, still edgy.

"Well," Brenda said, "we know—don't we?—where it'll take them. As for us, we have to swim steadily on, avoiding the rocks. Like Scylla and Charybdis."

"I always think," said Mark, "that they sound like two tiresome women out of opera."

"There's just one thing," Brenda said, "Ben *is* an unknown quantity. He could surprise us."

Juliet said, "I thought your philosophy was for swimming steadily on."

"Oh, it is, it is. But one has to be prepared. One can't know exactly how he'll jump."

"For God's sake," said Mark: "you give us a Lift Up Your Hearts and then bring out a nasty little nigger in the woodpile . . . Prepared for *what*?"

Brenda remained unruffled. "I don't know. But whatever it is, there's no good in getting fussed."

"Seems to me," Mark said, "you'd better tell that to Emma."

"Maybe," said Brenda, looking thoughtfully aside. "Maybe. Perhaps Emma's in for a surprise."

In New York my father prepared himself to go to the Vineyard. There he would stay for a week before he, with Marguerite and myself, Carey and Jonathan, returned to England.

At that time my father was in his late forties: his thick dark hair showed no sign of grey, but glistened in the light: his large nose and full mouth were not unpleasing and spoke of strength. Though heavier than he had once been, he moved quickly and with impatience as if time threatened him. His hands had a long-fingered beauty which was at odds with his build: a woman sculptor had once wanted to make a cast of them: my father refused, saying he was too busy. Maybe he was right; maybe she had further interests than sculpting his hands. All his life my father drew women towards him. Sometimes he responded; sometimes not. As I look back, I think there were only two who really mattered to him: Emma and Marguerite. They were, in character, at opposite poles: perhaps this was their attraction.

From his apartment on East 52nd Street he looked down into the chasm of the traffic-laden street. The evening rush-hour from which he had mercifully escaped swept by like a continuing wind. His secretary, a middle-aged woman called Sheila Lines, with prominent teeth and much competence, had brought him the last of his letters to sign.

"You must be mighty glad to be leaving, Mr Ashley," she said, blotting his signature with a flourish.

He said he was.

"And Mr Forster's new play. With Mrs Pride in the leading role. You'll be just crazy to see that."

Lance said Yes, again.

"Mrs Pride, now..." Sheila Lines gathered the letters together and put them into her brief case.

Lance turned from the window. "What about Mrs Pride?"

Sheila Lines had a careful, no-expression on her face. "I just *hope* she succeeds." The words, it appeared, meant the opposite of what they said.

"Why shouldn't she?"

"Oh ... no reason at all." Sheila Lines had received the sharpness of his voice. "I know you have a great admiration for her—"

"I think she's a damn good actress."

"Why, sure; I know you do, Mr Ashley; I wouldn't disagree with that."

"What would you disagree with then?"

"Isn't she rather a *selfish* person?"

"Dear God, all actors and actresses are selfish, more or less; that's what makes them tick. They can at the same time be exceedingly generous; more so than others of the human race."

"There's no more to be said, then."

Moodily he observed her closed and offended face. He wondered when and how often Emma had managed to get on the wrong side of Sheila Lines. Her face, so set in disapproval, looked all of her forty-odd years. Briefly he wondered about her: she'd been his secretary in New York for more than six years. Secretaries sometimes (didn't they?) nursed unspoken passions for their employers. He didn't want anything like that; he had enough trouble as it was. She had shown nothing beyond a willingness to work; perhaps too great a willingness. He could remember saying once, "For God's sake, don't pick up *every* pencil I drop"; and she had gone in wounded silence from the room. Was she jealous of Emma?

That old love between himself and Emma was three years in the past, somewhere between the death of his first wife and his marriage to Marguerite. A mistake to let his thoughts turn to it. Yet at times they could do nothing else.

Emma, young, with two children and two marriages behind her, so that one faced a paradox—a child, no longer virgin: innocent, yet with old knowledge. She'd come to his office, having fallen out with her own agent; he'd been recommended to her, she said (as if he'd been a doctor or a dentist); would he take her on?

All too easy after that. He had been subject, he thought, to that same spell which she could cast over an audience: she haunted his mind and his body: there was no way, even had he wished to, that he could have escaped the beginning.

But the end? Well, in the end, he thought, she asked too much; he became aware of danger, of being pulled more and more deeply into a whirlpool—

The telephone ringing in his apartment brought him back to this present New York. Sheila Lines answered it, the disapproval not yet gone from her face.

"I'm not here," he said; "I've already left." He didn't want any more business now; he wanted to be free and off to the Vineyard, to Marguerite . . .

But Sheila Lines held out one hand; and he listened to her voice: "Long Distance . . . Yes, I'll hold on . . . Yes . . ." For some time she listened; then covered the mouthpiece with her hand. "I think you'd better answer, Mr Ashley. It's the director of Mr Forster's new play—"

"Jeremy Hirst? What does he want?"

"Something seems to be wrong with one of the cast—"

"Emma?"

She shook her head. "No; it's a young man."

Chapter Six

It was always a good moment when my father was coming to the Vineyard. A good moment, but shot through, as I remember, with a tightening of nerves, a raising of temperature. When I woke in the morning and thought "he's coming" everything was different, as if colours were charged with some electric substance, and sounds echoed with a boom like the sea.

I can remember that we all came downstairs to the familiar wood-smell of the house and the dazzling morning sea beyond the wide windows. Marguerite was already up, preparing breakfast in the sun-filled kitchen. A smell of coffee drifted to us. Marguerite wore shorts, shirt, and nothing on her feet for the day was already hot. I can remember how long and brown her legs were, as if they were made of some other substance than flesh, unstained and creamy.

Sitting at the table I could see the white sails on Menemsha Pond and as I dug into my egg, I thought about England and school. From here they seemed improbable; my world at the moment consisted of the house at Gay Head, the shape of its rooms, the sand, the hot unstinted sun. The cooler rainy streets of London, the unadorned corridors of my prep school, seemed to exist only in imagination, as if they were something I'd read about. Of course, when I was back there (for I knew, in spite of everything, that I would go) it would be this house which would belong to a dream. I hadn't time then to consider how little I wanted to go back to school; my father's imminent arrival obscured all else. And when we got to London, he would still be with us, working there, as would Marguerite. I remember once my father saying to Marguerite that I had 'continuity', and I can see now what he meant. It was true—for a time.

Back in England I should not however see so much of Jonathan and Carey, for they would go to Emma's mother, and Jonathan to a different school. It was fairly easy to imagine myself without Jonathan, who slipped through my life like a shadow; but Carey? . . .

She was of course too young to play games appropriate for a boy of nearly seven. There were times when she got on my nerves, because she knew so little (or at any rate so much less than I did), times when I was absorbed and her invasions made me shout at her to go away. I was always sorry afterwards; and there were other times when I was glad to see her because she seemed to think I was the cat's whiskers and greeted my arrival with a yell of delight and run and put her arms round my knees. Though I was so young I found this flattering, as one does when an animal shows a preference for you.

Sitting there at the breakfast table while Marguerite tied a bib round Carey's neck (sometimes it was best *not* to watch Carey eat) I wondered why I didn't entirely agree with a woman visitor to the Vineyard house who'd said, My, what a lucky little boy you are! Certainly my mother was dead, and I was brought up by Marguerite; but then as a stepmother Marguerite didn't run true to form at all, being kind and, it seemed to me then, interested in me. Whether she *loved* me or not I didn't at that time consider, for so long as people didn't shout at me or slap me, I took it that they were friendly. My father, it was true, could sometimes lose his temper with me, but he sometimes lost his temper with everyone. This could for the moment be distressing, but I accepted it as part of the fact that he *was* my father—blood being not only thicker but more turbulent than water; and that the spark of anger was also the spark of love.

'A lucky little boy.' *Why* did I not agree? Perhaps because, as I've since learned, the majority of people do not like to count themselves lucky: it seems to diminish their powers of endurance, or to suggest that they have been given more than their fair share. Certainly I can remember Marguerite saying once, after listening to a long spiel from some woman friend about what a terrible time she'd had when young: "Boy, am I going to give a prize to anyone who's had a *happy* childhood."

But as I look back it seems to me that in spite of summers on the Vineyard, a good-natured stepmother and a loved (if intermittent) father, there was a deep black hole of anxiety in the centre of my life, such as I understand scientists now say there is at the centre of the universe.

It was present, on that morning as I waited for my father's arrival. I knew that though he would embrace me and say that he was glad to see me, he would quickly become immersed in other plans, other people. How important was I to him? I suppose this was the uncertainty. I simply didn't know. My instinct told me that his pleasure in me was transitory and depended on good humour on his part, and some spark of originality on mine. I was alert all the time, it now seems to me, striving to make my mark, to gain his attention and his love.

When we had finished breakfast Marguerite shepherded us into her car. It was an old car, accustomed to the rough sandy road that led from the house to the mail-box at the end. As we bumped over the sand with the bushy green on either side, the thick wild roses and purple vetch, my excitement grew. Soon we'd see him, first in the sky (which seemed appropriate enough) and then down towards us in the midget-sized plane to the small rather ramshackle airport (as it was then) with its wire fence, blowing acacia trees and wooden check-out building.

We drove inland, through Chilmark and West Tisbury, along the Edgartown Road, and found the wooded places at the centre of the Island. As always, I relished the Indian names, and peopled the Island with splendid Indians of my imagination: I had invented a large crowd of them and they were called after the places I loved—Menemsha, Squibnocket, Nashaquitsa, and of course they took the Moshup's Trail: Moshup the legendary giant and Chief of the Island. My father, when he was in the right mood, would listen as I talked of them.

But I knew well enough that for the present he would have no time. Arrival was confusing, and would be made up of many voices: of Marguerite's warm American drawl, Carey's high-pitched exclamations, Jonathan's polite English sound, and my own efforts to be heard, known and loved.

At the pint-sized airport we got out of the car and waited with the other Islanders who expected visitors from Boston or New York. I cannot now exactly remember them, but I expect they were the usual casually dressed company; young men and women, barefoot and lightly dressed, tanned by the sun. Here and there you would see Indian stock in the formation of a face, and this beguiled me most of all. . . .

We could hear the plane now. The small company at the airport showed signs of renewed life, as if a wind had gone over them. I was still young enough (in fact I am still young enough) to find the enlargement and the noise and the landing of the aircraft a moment of excitement. I watched as the few passengers (not more than half a dozen) came down the small rickety steps.

My father was the last but one.

I started to wave and call out as I always did; then stopped.

He came towards us without any wave of his hand. He looked concerned and preoccupied. Though I had taken a

71

fall of heart as I saw him, I was struck by the energy of his looks. Lance Ashley, I thought: a man who dealt in the theatre, big names, a world whose dazzle only just touched the edge of mine: I wasn't old enough to understand the plays he was connected with; and when he took me to a star's dressing-room with its atmosphere of strong lights, make-up, face cream, sweat, and exuberance of 'after-the-show' I found it all a little frightening: a feeling of frenzy touched me like a live wire.

Now he gave us only the most casual of greetings. Dragging sulkily behind, tearful, without hope, I followed as he collected his case from the dump of luggage, and made, with Marguerite, Jonathan and Carey, for the car. When they had all climbed in I was still some way off.

"*Rick!*" My father's voice carried well in all circumstances. "For the love of Mike, hurry up!"

I came more quickly because one did what my father asked. He still looked impatient as I clambered into the back seat of the car beside Carey and Jonathan.

I sat, heavy with my burden, scowling in the back corner. I hoped that my father or Marguerite would feel the pressure of my disappointment but they seemed entirely absorbed. I couldn't hear, above the car's engine, what my father said, though I strained to listen. Jonathan was listening too. Only Carey was oblivious, keeping up a tuneless chant which I wished she would stop.

It wasn't till we got back to the house that I heard their voices clearly, and by then they had already been talking for some time.

They had wandered into the living-room, and from the open door of my bedroom I heard Marguerite say, "I suppose it was too much to hope for, that you should arrive here and we should *not*, within five minutes of your coming, be exercised about Emma.'

"I can't help—" my father began.

"You can't help anything, my darling," said Marguerite lightly.

72

"What could be wrong with the boy?'

"I've no idea," said Marguerite; "but in my experience of the theatre, something is nearly always wrong with somebody when it's most inconvenient. If you don't know that by now—"

"Oh, I do. I do. But this seems to be serious. Jeremy says no one's been able to see him."

"What's his name?"

"Ben. Ben Hardy."

"D'you know him?"

"Heard of him. I've not seen him play. But Jeremy says he was doing well. Particularly well with Emma."

"Ah. Maybe we're at the heart of the matter."

I dawdled into the living-room, Carey and Jonathan behind me. I was aware of complexities, of some duel whose nature I couldn't understand. I watched as Marguerite wandered back and forth, cigarette in hand. Odd, but I was on her side. I loved—and feared—my father; but Marguerite caused no fear. And when, as now, I saw distress on her face, I felt a pang of love for her. What Jonathan felt, I don't know, but I seldom did. Carey, a child's book in her hand, wore a look of anxiety, but this wasn't unaccustomed either. It occurred to me even then that Carey found life even more bewildering than I did, and being younger, had fewer resources to deal with it.

My father said, "What d'you mean?"

Marguerite shrugged. "What's eating you isn't so much this young man, who may or may not be seriously ill. It's the effect he could have on Emma. 'Playing particularly well'—that could mean anything, couldn't it?"

My father looked aside. He said, "Emma works on a knife-edge—you know that. If she makes a mess of this—"

"Isn't that up to her?"

"When she's in trouble—"

"She turns to you: understood. But that doesn't mean you've got to drop everything—"

73

"She rang me in New York."

"She did? Well, well. But Emma rings everyone: we know that one too—"

"She sounded," my father said, "pretty worked up. After Jeremy, this call came through from Emma."

"Had she been drinking?"

"I daresay. She'd tried to see Ben, but they wouldn't let her. She got hysterical—some sort of nonsense about knowing he was going to die—"

"It sounds true to form. However, it isn't really our problem. We've planned a week here—what difference does that make?"

"A whole lot to Emma."

Silence; Marguerite gave a small shrug. My father said, "I can go alone—you can follow. Bring the kids."

Marguerite glanced over her shoulder at us. Carey was crouched on the floor with her book—coloured pictures of animals—open before her, and I could see that she had torn one page across, almost from one corner to the other. I didn't think it then, but now it comes to my mind like the torn flap of skin from a sliced wound.

"Don't think that's the best idea," Marguerite said.

"Why not?"

"Seems to me—if you're going to cut this stay short, I'd best go with you. Which means taking the kids too."

I looked up at them both. I didn't like any of this: I had been looking forward to the week on the Vineyard, but I didn't want my father to leave us here alone. Whether he knew it or not, I felt myself bound to him by a cord of need and love; and having so recently greeted his arrival I felt a sharp fall of heart at the idea of waving good-bye. I made tentative steps towards him. I said, "If you're going to England I want to go with you."

His strong dark-eyed face looked at me as if what I'd said had puzzled him. With adult perception, I must suppose that he had no time—had never perhaps had time—to give me more than the fringes of his attention, of his love. He scarcely ever spoke of my mother; there wasn't even a photograph of her. Would she have loved me? I can only imagine so, but had no certainty. Within myself I carried the seeds of someone unknown, someone whom my father had been able perhaps to put out of mind. Marguerite could bind up my knee if I fell and dose me if my stomach ached, but her first concern was for my father, and now some strain lay between them which wasn't to do with me at all.

"I want to go with you," I repeated.

He gave an exclamation, half impatience, half pity. "Look, old chap, this is business—just let me think, will you?"

Stung with sorrow I turned away. Marguerite touched my head, ruffling my hair in affection, but this wasn't enough.

My father said, "I'm afraid for Emma—as an actress. Not as a person—"

"No?"

"Emma is—Emma. I organised this; I told her she couldn't fail—"

"Wasn't that enough?"

My father sat with his head down. I can see now, but couldn't then, the dilemma, and wandered away while the talk continued between them.

Through it all I heard Emma's name. Perhaps it was then that I first began to look on her with distrust; even as an enemy.

It was Carey who said from her bewilderment, "Are we going to see Mama?"

My father's abstracted glance turned to her. "Oh yes—we're going to see her. Your Mama," he added, "will always be a person to be seen."

Puzzled, Carey picked up a toy (a wooden Indian, with the paint scratched) and said, "Are we going today?"

"No, honey," Marguerite said dryly; "it takes longer than that to close up this house."

75

"Tomorrow?"

"Maybe the next day." Her voice was resigned.

"Are we going on a ship?" Carey asked.

"No, an aeroplane."

"An arrowplane?"

"We fly," Marguerite said, her voice still tight; "it's quicker."

"See Mama *sooner*."

"That's right."

Jonathan was looking with cool grey eyes at his sister. "See Mother! I'll bet. No one ever sees Mother for more than ten minutes. Least of all us." I can hear the acid in his voice, which surprised me even then.

Carey flung her toy away. Through piercing wails her voice came, shredded: "We're going to see her. We *are*."

"Now, honey—" Marguerite was wiping the small face and smoothing the blond hair, damp with sweat and misery. "Now, c'mon. You're going to see Mama; she'll see you all she can; she's waiting for you."

Carey's sobs became hiccups. "Waiting?"

"Sure."

She made it sound, I thought, as if the purpose of our return to England was for Carey to see Emma; and however puzzled I was, I felt certain this was not so. I wondered vaguely whether it was wise for Marguerite so to mislead Carey, but her words had at any rate quietened the yells, and Carey retrieved her toy, as if comforted.

But I was not comforted. I wanted to stay longer on the Vineyard, and I wanted my father to see me as someone of moment in his life.

The air was troubled, and the short time left on the Island confused with calls about airline tickets, sorting of clothes, and the tension between my father and Marguerite.

In the end, I was glad to go.

My father's London house was in north London, on the

76

edge of Hampstead Heath. (It would now be worth many thousands of pounds, but appeared simple if pleasant to me then.) Our arrival had the strangeness of all arrivals in places which are from time to time familiar. I padded about the house, trying to come to terms with it again, while images of the Vineyard still floated through my mind. No more of the dazzling blue water, the sand dunes and the Indian names. No more, for the present, of Carey and Jonathan, who had been met at the airport by Emma's mother, Susan Denzil. I could still see her untidy figure waving enthusiastically to Carey and Jonathan, who did not respond. Carey had trotted away with her head down, built of disappointment. As I'd watched her go, I'd known a pang of regret, not so much at losing her for she made so loud a noise when she cried, but because I'd not always been nicer to her. (I can remember, many years later, a friend saying once that that it was no use worrying: when you parted with anyone you always felt you'd either given too much or too little.) As she'd been led away by her grandmother she turned once and waved an arm in our general direction. Whether this was on instruction or showed any regret at leaving us, I could not then know. I knew only that I was glad not to be taken over by Emma's mother, and preferred the company of Marguerite and my father. Although I was still confused as to the reason for our sudden arrival, I began to feel better.

My father, though preoccupied, showed me enough attention to say, "Well, Rick; back to the London home!" and I said Yes; and that I liked it. Though the curiosity still ate into me I knew better than to ask questions. I went upstairs to unpack, and while I was there the telephone rang. I thought, Oh, it's begun; for the telephone was always ringing, wherever we were.

Then I heard my father's voice, carrying clearly with anger: "What d'you mean, you can't find her?"

Silence; then he said, "No answer from her flat? She

must be on her way."

Silence again, for however angry or distressed he was, my father could—most usually—listen. Then: "Oh, Lord. Three *hours*? She's never that late for rehearsal . . . Is there any more news of Ben?" (Who was Ben?) "Have you been in touch with the hospital? . . . Yes, I see. Well; we have a problem. Yes, we certainly do."

Riveted by the word 'hospital', drawn by still unsatisfied curiosity, I crept downstairs. I heard the sound of a number being dialled; then silence. As I reached the bottom of the stairs he said to Marguerite, "He's right; she's not there."

"And Ben?"

"Jeremy says No Change. Or As well as can be expected. Or one of those meaningless hand-outs that hospitals give you. And no one, but no one, can get hold of Emma." He moved impatiently to the window, as if Emma might be found there. "She *mustn't* do this. She absolutely mustn't."

Marguerite had an air of controlled sympathetic calm. "D'you want me to call the cops? Accident—anything like that?"

My father looked again from the window. "No, I don't think that's the answer. I don't think she's been run over. I think she's—"

"Sloshed?"

"I don't know. I pray not."

Marguerite lit a cigarette. "This seems to be your baby."

My father glanced round with a wry smile. "Sure."

Marguerite looked towards the Heath, whose green the London summer had tarnished. Different from the Vineyard, different from New York. Perhaps it was this, I thought then, that put sadness on her face. I know differently now.

"And how you deal with it," she said, "I haven't the least idea. I'd help you if I could."

"Yes, I know that."

The silence after this was filled by something I didn't understand.

My father moved from the window. "I'm going to the hospital. If you'd keep ringing Emma's flat."

"Sure."

"And if you get her, contact Jeremy right away."

Marguerite nodded, and pulled a page from the calendar which had hung unused since we had left for the States.

As my father prepared himself to go out I trailed after him, though I knew it wasn't a good idea. I didn't say anything; I knew better than that. I watched him change his shirt, comb his hair, check his wallet and go hurriedly downstairs. He gave me one brief glance over his shoulder and said vaguely, "Rick?" as if he were surprised that I should be there at all, but it was recognition, of a kind.

He said good-bye to Marguerite, who wished him luck. "Yes, we shall need that," he said, and was gone.

What happened next, I could not then know.

Within the hired car, Lance watched moodily as the London streets passed by. He seemed to have been travelling for ever, he thought: and why? Anger, intensified by the exhaustion of travel, flowed through him. There were, weren't there, plenty of people to look after Emma: why did he have to assume the role of her protector?

Well, you know the answer to that; he told himself: whoever Emma may have entangled herself with since, she sees you as someone who'll come to the rescue when the going gets too tough. And you go along with it because, in spite of being married to Marguerite, which is as good as anything can be, you haven't quite got Emma out of your system. And Marguerite knows it.

Oh, hell, he said aloud.

Accustomed to command and control, it irked him to

be driven by contrary winds outside his bidding. If Emma makes a hash of this, he thought, I'm not playing any more; she can make her own way without me, without telephoning me in the small hours, and bringing me back from the States to hunt her across London. . . .

Are you sure? the voice whispered.

Damn it; he said with the force of uncertainty; Yes, I'm sure. . . .

The hospital met him with vast and numerous corridors, lifts and contrary directions. He strode with increasing frustration through this alien country of the sick, the disabled and the old. There could not, surely, be much wrong with Ben; not something that couldn't be cured; Emma had flown into a needless panic and brought him to this tiresome chase. . .

He didn't like hospitals; he liked the theatre with its fever and obstacles and hard work; he liked the comforts which money could bring: good food and drink; easy travel; such clothes and presents as he would want to wear and give. These corridors and the hurrying nurses made all these things seem of small account, as if he were a child, playing with toys. . . . He said to a passing nurse, young, dark and pretty, "Can I see Mr Hardy?"

She said, "You'd better speak to Sister," and went skidding off. He thought perhaps she had disappeared for good, as staff were wont to do in hospital; but after some moments she returned and led him to a small room with a desk and a telephone. Sister was small and auburn-haired with good eyes; not much more than thirty. She glanced up at him. "Are you a relative?"

"No, I'm a theatrical agent." (In this place it sounded absurd as if he'd said he was an acrobat.) "Mr Hardy's in a play I'm concerned with."

Whether Sister had any idea of the demanding world of the theatre he could not tell. She said, "I'm afraid it's not possible for anyone except his family to see him just now."

80

"Then he's very ill?"

"I can only say, he's not able to receive visitors."

"Have any family been to see him?"

Sister gave a brief lift of her brows. "A young woman was here. She seemed very distraught. She said she was his wife—"

"His *wife*—"

"But we were able," Sister said ignoring the interruption, "to establish that he wasn't married."

Oh, God; he thought; Emma. Must have been Emma. Coming here, and trying to get away with nonsense like that. "Do you know where the young woman went?" he asked.

Sister shook her head. "We tried to calm her down and offered her a cup of tea, but she wouldn't wait."

No; of course she wouldn't wait; she was off to some limbo which could well put the kybosh on her career. He said, "This may sound very trivial to you, but I have to know what chance there is of Ben's coming back into the show."

"That's a question for the consultant, I'm afraid."

"And what are the chances of seeing him?" he asked, but could have given her answer: "Only if you're family, I'm afraid."

An implacable if courteous wall. As he might have known. She said, "I'm sorry, Mr—?"

He gave her his name, and turned away. As he strode back down the corridor he was still angry with Emma. Telling that absurd lie. . . .

Once again in the street he wondered briefly *why* Emma was so distraught about Ben. . . .

After all, casualties among casts—even serious casualties—were common in the theatre. The obvious answer occurred to him, and he thought We have, it seems, *all* the problems. In the street he hesitated. Where now? The tramp and roar of London dulled his mind, already weary from travel and this fruitless chase. Had

Emma perhaps turned up at the rehearsal room? He found a telephone box and called Jeremy.

Jeremy, whose patience also seemed to be giving out, said No; Emma wasn't there, and the rest of the cast weren't—to put it mildly—taking it too well (not to mention Guy Forster). Oh God, Lance thought; the author; that's all we need. Actors, Jeremy said, didn't like to be reminded at the same time of their mortality and indefinite delays in rehearsal. Only Brenda Jones seemed to be taking it calmly; she was knitting in a corner and dispensing such light as there was.

Lance said he didn't think that was any help at all; and rang off.

He then telephoned Emma's flat. The double-sound brought a maddening absence of reply.

So now? Nothing occurred to him, or nothing that seemed worth pursuing. It was a fool's errand, anyway. He hailed a taxi; he'd go home where he could think in peace with Marguerite beside him... Again he watched the passing streets, some still scarred from the war's bombing. How absurd to be in a fever about a young actress, when a World War had not so long brought death, misery, the macabre evil of the concentration camps... What did Emma matter? What did *any*thing matter, come to that?

Well, for as long as he lived, the theatre mattered. And Emma would not cease to trouble him. Had he been wise to agree to those holidays on the Vineyard; to let Emma and her children figure so largely in his life? Naturally not; but this wasn't the moment to draw back....

He was home. He called, "Hi," and strode into the living-room.

Then stopped.

Marguerite was standing by the mantelpiece. Her face was turned towards him with humorous, placid inquiry.

On a chair by the window he saw Emma. She looked pale and shiny of skin, not even beautiful. She'd been

82

crying. She held a cup of black coffee in her hand.

"Good God," he began.

Marguerite said, "It's no good being angry. She's in a bad way. I've telephoned Jeremy."

Lance stood, hands on his hips, observing Emma. It was a moment of decision, he thought fleetingly; he could if he liked make this a reason for washing his hands of her; a moment to tell her that actresses who were unreliable were no good, and he wasn't going to waste time on her.

It could be said; it was the time to say it; but—

Emma was looking up at him. "All right—I know. I know what I've done." (Did she?) "But Ben—I couldn't get over it. He looked so awful. And he had to have an ambulance—"

"My dear Emma," he said; "a great many people have to have ambulances."

"I know. But he's been in hospital three days now, and no one can see him. I tried today—"

"Yes; I know you tried," Lance said.

"They wouldn't tell me anything; they wouldn't let me see him; but they made me feel that it was something dreadful, so I went and had a drink."

"More than one," he said.

"Well . . . of course. When I feel terrible, it's the only thing that's any good."

He sat down. "You realise that we cut short our stay on the Vineyard; and then the *first thing* I hear is that you've defaulted on rehearsal—"

"Because of *Ben*."

"Look, ducky, life is full of happenings like Ben. Especially theatre life. If he's ill, I'm very sorry; it's tough, but you didn't even let them *know*—"

"I said," Marguerite repeated, "it's no good going on at her."

Lance looked about him. "Where's Rick?"

"In the garden."

83

"Has he seen Emma?"

"Sure he's seen Emma. She arrived about twenty minutes ago. And quite soon—almost now, aren't you, darling?—she's going to the rehearsal room, to pick up where she left off."

"If," Lance said, "there's anything to pick up."

Emma looked at him. "What d'you mean?"

"I don't have to spell it out."

"They couldn't—"

"Oh, yes they could. What's more, I'm talking about manners. What was to stop you letting Jeremy know?"

"I didn't think I was going to be late. I went to the hospital early; but then when they wouldn't let me see him and they all looked so prim and gloomy, I couldn't think about Jeremy; I could only think about Ben."

"Have you any idea what's wrong with him?"

"Not really. He just went this awful colour and kind of collapsed during rehearsal."

Lance said, "You—took a liking to Ben?"

He thought she understood the question and he understood the answer which she didn't give. She said, "He's a *person* for goodness' sake; a nice person; and I play opposite him . . . Lance, he couldn't *die* could he? He's so young, and he's never been ill—"

"He's not going to die, honey," said Marguerite. "And you promised to go back to the rehearsal room."

Emma looked large-eyed and dishevelled, such as a young ghost might appear to a disordered mind. She said, "If Lance will come with me."

Lance met Marguerite's eyes. Everything was said, he thought, in that exchange: her acceptance, her knowledge that whatever he might say in protest he would in the end go: which he did.

He didn't know exactly what he'd expected in the rehearsal room. Trouble; but not this emptiness, since the room contained only Jeremy Hirst and Guy Forster. The air was smoky, and held a drift of a woman's scent (Juliet Boyle's, perhaps).

He felt like a father bringing back a runaway child to school. Emma looked like an actress from a silent film, retrieved from disaster: an orphan of the storm. She said, "I'm sorry. I couldn't help it."

Lance took the measure of the feeling in the room. He explained as much as he could. Guy's scarred face was blank; Jeremy looked tired and harassed as if he'd been on a long and difficult journey. (But not as long as mine, Lance thought.)

Guy nodded. "Indeed, it's a sad tale. But it looks, doesn't it, as if we shall have to find two replacements instead of one."

Emma whispered, "You wouldn't do that. The Management wouldn't do that. Not for one rehearsal. I've never missed a performance—"

The Management, Lance recalled, was Reggie Graves. Reggie, though not then the name he is now, had a sharp eye for talent and what would "work" in the theatre. He had a clear head also for costs, for the addition sums which all Managements must make.

"The Management," Jeremy said, "is concerned with the backers, and the backers are men who more often than not know very little about plays and players, except what they're told. They ask simple questions. You know what men with money are like. Nice chaps, but above all they want to know what they're going to get in return for their investment. How much the whole thing is going to cost, and what are the expected profits? How much will come into the box office, and how much into the bar? . . . They may be gamblers (they have to be in the theatre) but they're not fools."

"Reggie doesn't know about this?" Lance asked.

Jeremy shook his head. Emma said, "Oh, please—please don't tell him. It'll never happen again—I promise it'll never happen again."

85

It sounded true, Lance thought. Perhaps she believed it herself.

"You'll have to prove to us, my dear Emma," said Guy, his face unsmiling, "that you're worth all the trouble you cause. You'll have to prove it one hundred and one per cent."

Emma nodded. She looked pale and obedient. No one so far had discussed the problem of Ben; that was still to come.

He had to remember, thought Lance, how good an actress Emma was; he had to persuade himself that today's default had been merely an aberration and would not form a pattern for the future. He had to forget that history repeats itself, that the human animal seldom, except under severe pressure or grief, and sometimes not even then, greatly changes.

He had to hope.

Perhaps it was a victory of a kind, Jeremy thought, as rehearsals continued over the next few days. Despite his misgivings, and Guy Forster's distrust, Emma was playing beautifully. Ben's part was taken by a young man called Paul Dane. He was a competent enough actor, but had none of Ben's looks. He showed no sign—perhaps this was just as well—of falling for Emma. Nor she for him. However, the balance of the play was altered, and he could only hope that Ben would return before it was too late. News from the hospital, sparse as it was, suggested that Ben was improving.

After one more incursion into the rehearsal room, when he watched Emma exclusively, Guy Forster had not reappeared. He couldn't dispute, he said, that Emma was perfect as Daisy. If . . .

No need to elaborate the If, Jeremy reflected. At heart it was his own opinion.

On one day when Emma was playing exceptionally well, Jeremy sat hunched on his chair, watching with the passion of exhausted relief. Those whom he watched were in their different ways day-worn: the women without make-up; Mark's grey hair ruffled, the lines showing deep on his face; Emma looking as if she'd been rescued from a river.

One part of his mind judged the performance, made mental notes to use later; another was taken by the extraordinary toughness of actors, the hard enduring professionalism which underlaid the childish confusion, the jealousies, the fun. This room lacked all charm, the table was littered with coffee cups whose cold dregs had formed a solid rim, overfull ash-trays and pages of the script. Artificial light made of all this a place of small comfort. The question of Ben still hung over them. Yet the company were playing to a fine pitch. This was the quality you could trust, he thought with a gleam of hope: the control that took charge, even at the worst moments, the application of men and women doing the job they'd been trained for. The company were not Mark, Brenda, Paul Dane; Juliet and Emma; they were the characters in the play, despite the casual quality of their dress.

He felt, as well as hope, a twinge of pride. How much did the men and women who had "an evening out at the theatre", who trod on carpet and sat on red plush seats think—or know at all—of these rough hours in an untidy room? Little enough, he thought: through all art and indeed all life, people saw and accepted the finished product: the book or the play; or the train that sped past the drowsing countryside. . . . Few asked how or when, about the work and knowledge and skill that lay behind the accepted thing.

Briefly he put aside the question of Ben. He must watch with the concentration of one who hopes to achieve anything at all in the harsh public arena. This production might be blessed or cursed; for the present the voices continued.

87

Chapter Seven

In her small house, in a side street off Chelsea Embankment, Susan Denzil was tidying the children's rooms. Though the task had no particular glamour she found pleasure in it: these early days of the children's stay with her always held comfort. The early days before one of them (usually Carey) had got on her nerves and she'd spoken sharply to her and smacked her; then been ashamed and sorry afterwards, for she wished the children to love her more than they loved Marguerite; more even than they loved Emma.

Susan paused with a pile of Carey's small pants and vests in her hand. Was that true? Emma was her daughter, her only child. Yet Susan couldn't deny this passionate desire that the children should love *her*; that she was jealous when Carey asked for "Mama". Susan could not help sometimes reflecting that Emma didn't deserve the devotion which Carey gave her. Emma did none of the hard work, she was for only short times in the company of her child, and often then preoccupied. Perhaps that was part of the allure: it was always a good thing to be unattainable, even when the lover was a child. You don't get what you deserve, Susan thought; life doesn't work like that. She must accept it.

But Marguerite, her niece, was another matter. Marguerite wasn't Carey's mother. Marguerite had nothing—except Lance Ashley; her stepson, Rick; and, of course, that splendid house on the far side of the Atlantic.

Susan thought about the house. This one was pleasant enough, but how could she compare it with the house on Martha's Vineyard? Nothing in this London street could compare with that strange and haunting island. Once she had visited it and, while admiring it, had not wished to go again. She didn't feel that she belonged there, not with Marguerite, nor with the wealthy Americans who lived for the summer in the other houses in the bushy parts of Up-Island, and who were so hospitable, and yet made her feel that they could see the circumscribed life which she lived here in London.

Marguerite was her brother-in-law's – Dan's – child, and Dan had gone far off: to the west coast of the States: an old quarrel had never healed . . . What had it been about? Something to do with money: quarrels nearly always were: Dan's brother (Susan's husband) had long ago claimed more than his share of an inheritance . . .

Her eye caught the photograph of herself and her husband, Martin, taken soon after Emma's birth, with Emma herself on her lap, not more than three months old. (How extraordinary old photographs were, as if one could arrest time at that moment when one was still young.) But now Emma was a grown woman, twice married, an actress on the fringe of fame, and with two children of her own . . . Where had the years gone?

There in the small garden Jonathan was hitting a ball with a tennis racket, and Carey in a blue romper suit was fumbling the catches he tossed to her. Something timeless about the children down there: Carey might have been Emma as a child . . .

Where had all the years gone? And what had she to account for them? Had they all been wasted?

The doorbell brought her out of this and sent her quickly downstairs, pinning up her hair.

When she opened the door she stood for a moment, struck into silence.

She had not seen Geoffrey Gardner, Emma's second

husband, for what seemed like years. "Good gracious," she said, making further efforts to pin up her hair, for Geoff Gardner, though he'd finally parted from Emma, was a man to be tidy for.

He took off his hat and said, "I hope I haven't come at an awkward time." He wasn't tall, but held himself with his chin lifted, as if someone had challenged him to be taller. Horn-rimmed glasses didn't obscure the fact that his eyes were good, hazel, if unsmiling.

She couldn't say that any time would be awkward to confront him without warning. He added, as if in excuse, "I had to see a client nearby, and I came on the offchance you'd be here."

She led him in, and pushed a pile of magazines under the sofa. I have simply no idea what to do with him, Susan thought. She could hear the voices of the children from the garden. And one of them *his* child, though her separation from him seemed to be complete.

She made a gesture to a chair, and he sat down. "Emma—" she began, but he interrupted.

"I haven't come to see Emma. I read she was in England, and I knew the children would be here." His glance slipped to the garden, then back to her.

She stood, still bemused, her thoughts flying down unlikely corridors: Had he come to take Carey away? Was he going to ask to stay the night? Mentally she explored the spare bedroom, which was filled with old boxes and trunks.

He said, "My wife doesn't know I'm here. I'd be grateful if you wouldn't tell her."

She shook her head. Was it likely she'd tell Geoff Gardner's wife (whom she'd never met) anything at all? What extraordinary—even unwelcome—things happened when you were in any way involved with Emma's life.

Geoff Gardner leaned back on the sofa and clasped one ankle on his knee. "Daphne's a wonderful girl—"

90

(Daphne was his wife, Susan remembered: the daughter of a Knight who had been honoured for his work in industry)—"but—of course it's understandable—anything to do with—with my first marriage upsets her. More than upsets her." He appeared to look aside to the occasions of these upsets.

Though a man of culture and intelligence, as Susan understood it, he seemed to speak as one under authority. Perhaps like some men of standing in their own professions, when it came to the home, he found it easier to give in. She had known such wives, who though of inferior intelligence, laid the rules down: No, they were *not* going out to dinner; no, they were *not* going to Rome in September; they preferred the quiet of the Dordogne. . . .

Still at a loss for comment, Susan waited. "Emma," he went on, "is a very disturbing person. I mean attractive," he added, taking his glasses off and putting them on again. "I don't want to go over the past."

Oh, good, Susan thought: she had no wish to recall that difficult time of Emma's parting from Geoffrey, here in the untidy sitting-room with the children outside.

"When I married Daphne, she—made it a condition that I shouldn't see Emma. And now that Emma's becoming more famous, Daphne feels more strongly still."

(Well, yes, Susan could understand that; not the easiest of conditions to know your husband had once been married to an actress of much sexual attraction and rising power. Even if Emma had brought the end of the marriage on herself . . .) "Unfortunately," Geoff Gardner went on, "the ban seems to include Carey." He looked down at his feet, as if expecting reproof, but Susan still gave no more than a sound of acknowledgement. "We agreed, as you know, that when Emma and I parted, she should take Carey. *You* were there, after all; and I offered help; monetary help, I mean. This Emma refused."

"Oh, well; yes," Susan said; "I expect it was her pride." She had in fact, no clear idea why Emma had

91

refused money from Geoff Gardner; unless perhaps she'd been taken by some unexpected sensation of guilt. "The trouble is," Geoff went on, "that Daphne is a bit *obsessional* about Emma, and she feels that Carey will remind me of her. Daphne and I," he added, "as perhaps you know, already have two small children of our own."

(Pretty quick work, Susan thought; perhaps the strong-minded Daphne had done her best to bring this about? *Her* children instead of Emma's . . .)

"But I do," he continued, "I can't help it—from time to time think about Carey."

"I suppose that's natural enough," Susan said absently, still wondering what he expected her to do. She was surprised to feel a pang of compassion for him. Daphne (in Emma's terms) sounded like hell-on-wheels; and Geoff himself one of those who had suffered from flying too close to Emma's sun.

"I've no wish to cause trouble in my present marriage; it's stable and very happy." Oh, well; perhaps it was: Susan thought; people have different ideas of happiness. "So I find it best to keep away from Emma, and anything to do with her. But this afternoon, finding myself so close to you—I had a sudden impulse—just to see the child."

Susan didn't know why she should have the sensation of travelling suddenly downwards in a lift. Why should Geoff Gardner not briefly see his child? . . .

Except that it had long been accepted that he would keep away: and she had a firm conviction that Emma would have said No.

But Susan was one of those who find saying 'no' difficult, especially to men dressed as Geoff Gardner was, in city clothes. So she called Carey in from the garden.

The child didn't at first respond and she called again, more sharply. At last, after crouching to pick grass from the lawn, Carey trotted in through the french windows saying, "Not time for bed, not time for bed—"

On seeing Geoffrey she became silent and stood still.

She didn't know who he was, Susan reflected; this moment should have some poignancy or drama or *something*; she had no idea how to promote it.

Geoffrey Gardner, however, took matters out of her hands: he said, "Hullo, Carey: I'm your father."

Carey continued to look at him with solemn mistrust.

"He's come to see you, Carey, darling," Susan put in, with some hope of putting things on an even keel.

Carey was shaking her head elaborately from side to side. "Don't know him."

Geoff Gardner had a puzzled sadness on his face, as if, Susan thought, he'd found a fault in a ledger. "You don't know me," he said; "but I know *you*." (This wasn't quite true, Susan thought, but the poor man had his problems.) He put out a hand to touch Carey, but she pulled sharply away. "Don't know you. Where's Mummy?"

"Mama's busy, darling," said Susan; and Geoff Gardner once more put out a hand to touch the flawless, miraculous skin—

At once Carey began to cry. Indeed, Susan could understand that it was disturbing for the child to be presented with a gentleman in a dark suit whom she didn't know and who said he was her father. "Don't *want* you," Carey said to him, between yells. "Want Mama."

"Now, quiet, darling," Susan said; "this really is your father—"

"Want *Mama*!"

The room was now full of noise. Interested Jonathan, racket in hand, had wandered in from the garden. "She can yell, can't she?" he murmured, as if to himself.

Through the barrier of sound Geoff said, "Hullo, Jonathan."

Jonathan said, "Hullo," absently, returning to the garden to fetch his ball.

Geoff Gardner got to his feet. "I'm clearly not doing any good here, am I."

Before Susan could reply, Carey said, "Is the man

going?" Her yells became quieter.

"Yes," Geoff said, "the man's going."

Flustered, torn between relief and a discomfortable feeling that she had failed him and he must be distressed, Susan saw him to the door.

In answer to her confused apologies he said there was no need to be sorry; the whole thing was his fault.

He bade her good-bye; and said as he turned away, "Perhaps Daphne was right all along."

Right or not, Susan reflected, Daphne, though not present, had had the last word. She watched him go, an anonymous man in a dark suit, for the moment defeated.

What extraordinary things do happen, Susan reflected as she went back into the house, hoping that the matter was now done with. But it seemed that Geoff Gardner's sudden arrival had disturbed Carey; she didn't want to play with Jonathan; no, she didn't want a glass of milk; no, she didn't want the bathroom. Though her yells had subsided, she now kept up a continual and formless lament, a general protest about everything.

This in the end frayed Susan's temper so that she finally smacked Carey's arm. The smack, though light, raised on the smooth young flesh a mark of red, instant and appalling.

Carey broke off and looked at it with her usual lost amazement at the things which could happen.

"Oh dear," said Susan; "I didn't mean to do that."

Carey seemed, by the events of this day, to have been shocked into a general silence. Impossible to know what she was thinking. Jonathan ate his supper and answered questions politely. He made no reference to Geoff, whom he'd known briefly as a stepfather. Though she was glad of Carey's silence, Susan found it disconcerting. "Have you got a pain?" she asked. Silent, Carey shook her head. "Do you want a story?" "No. Don't like stories."

That was all she said. She did not, Susan remembered afterwards, even say Goodnight.

Jonathan, alert for failure on his sister's part, said with careful accuracy, "Goodnight, Grandmother," and went to his room. As she shut his door, Susan wondered what his curious detachment concealed. Unguarded, his young face could show bitterness, even hatred. For whom she did not know.

Next morning, Susan woke early, as she always did when the children were with her. Usually Carey's voice sounded a tuneless clarion call about six o'clock: this morning she'd not heard it.

She put on her dressing-gown and went downstairs to fill the kettle. The gas-light sprang with its small signature of cheerfulness. Comfortable to know that the children were upstairs, though that abortive visit from Geoff Gardner still puzzled her—

It was not Carey's but Jonathan's voice she heard. At first she paid small attention; then caught a trace of urgency.

"*Grandmother!*"

What could be wrong? Tripping over her dressing-gown she ran up the stairs.

Jonathan in his pyjamas was standing by the open door of Carey's room. The small touseled bed in which Carey slept was empty. His pointed face had a controlled excitement. "She's not there—"

"I can see she's not there. Perhaps she's in the bathroom—"

"She isn't! I've just been there myself."

This is nonsense, she told herself as she went hurriedly downstairs, calling "Carey! Carey, where are you?" Jonathan followed on bare feet; she could feel his enormous but unexpressed interest behind her. Susan muttered, "She can't have gone far in her nightdress—"

"Carey isn't in her nightdress." Relish for drama in Jonathan's voice. "I saw; she's put her clothes on."

Susan felt a twinge of true panic. "Put her *clothes* on? She can hardly dress herself."

"Well, she has. The things on her chair have gone. I saw."

Yes, Jonathan would notice everything; no need to go back and see if he was right. She went through the small house, trying to tell herself that Carey had woken early, become bored (a grubby toy rabbit lay cast aside on the floor), wandered perhaps into the garden. . . .

But the garden, though she hurried there in her dressing-gown unmindful of the neighbours and the wet grass, gave her nothing. She said to Jonathan who, still in his pyjamas, followed her, "Has she taken her shoes?"

Jonathan scampered back into the house; returned and said, "No, her shoes are still there. But her bedroom slippers—those red fluffy ones with a duck's head on— they've gone."

Carey. In her clothes, put on somehow, slippers on her feet . . . Susan said, "Go and get dressed *quickly*, Jonathan; you'll catch cold . . . No, at *once*; I shall too; we can't do anything like this."

Stabs of fear became more frequent; dressing hurriedly, she tried to quell them; tried to put out of her mind the effect on Carey of Geoff Gardner's arrival, and her silence afterwards. What had gone on in Carey's mind? You couldn't possibly know. . . .

She told Jonathan to look everywhere in the house; he scampered off calling, "Carey! Hi, Carey—where're you hiding?" She herself went out into the morning street. How absurd; Carey was, as Jonathan said, hiding somewhere; she wouldn't have ventured into the vast complexity of London's streets . . . A picture of Carey wandering down the pavements brought the sweat to her forehead. Little traffic on the road as yet, but one car would be enough if Carey wandered off the kerb—

She wouldn't think like that. A road-sweeper harvested the first litter of leaves. She asked him if he'd seen a little girl; a fair child with red slippers. He looked questioningly at her (she had after all dressed very hurriedly:

96

perhaps she'd left something undone), and gave her no help at all.

She turned from him. Which way to go? Back to the house, in hope?

She went quickly there, but Jonathan was waiting on the front step. He'd been all over the house: Carey was "absolutely not anywhere". He added, "She's always asking for Mama. Perhaps she's gone there."

Susan looked at him. It was just possible. Emma's flat was within walking distance; Carey might remember the way. . . .

But to telephone Emma, who must be due at rehearsal? . . . It had to be done. Hand shaking, Jonathan eager and alert at her side, Susan dialled Emma's number.

A sleepy voice said, "Hullo?"

"Emma—it's me; Mother."

"Oh, Lord . . . children all right?"

"Yes—that is, well—what I wanted to know—is Carey with you?"

"*Carey?*" The voice sharp now, sleep falling away. "No, of course not; she's with you. *Isn't* she?"

"Well, yes, she was, but . . . she's wandered off somewhere."

"Wandered *off*? What the hell d'you mean?"

"Don't shout at me—"

"Of course I'm shouting! You ring me at some ungodly hour and tell me that Carey's *lost*—"

"I didn't say lost—"

"Yes, you did. And how the hell can she have wandered off as you put it—how can she have *got out*?"

Anger and distress made Susan's voice shake. "I don't know. She—she can just reach the door handle. It's never happened before. You know she's always been safe with me."

"How in God's name did she go? Carey isn't the kind of child to . . ." A gulp and a pause; Emma might be reflecting, Susan thought, that she didn't truly know what kind of child Carey was.

"Darling, I keep telling you. I don't *know* what happened. Except that yesterday evening Geoff turned up without any warning—"

"*Geoff* turned up? I don't understand any of this; Geoff never comes to see Carey, or me; Geoff is absolutely out as far as we're concerned; what the hell did he think he was doing?"

"I don't know," Susan said, feeling more and more distressed and incompetent; "he just said he was passing by, or been to see a client, or something. He didn't stay long—"

"I'll bet he didn't stay long. And he's not going to stay at *all*—ever: he's got his own life now which isn't anything to do with mine—d'you mean he's come back and scooped Carey up, or something?"

"No—no. I'm quite sure of that." (Indeed, remembering the defeated figure which walked away from her house, she was.) "But it seemed to upset Carey—seeing him, I mean—"

"Damn, damn, damn. Why the hell should he upset Carey?"

"Well, I suppose he is her father—"

"Not any more he isn't. When—when we've found Carey I'm going to ring him and tear him off a strip he'll not forget about—"

"Oh, Emma; I promised him not to let his wife know."

"Too bad. I'll be over right away."

"What about your rehearsal, darling?"

"Carey first."

As she put the telephone down, Susan said to Jonathan, "Go and look some more. Look *every*where."

He nodded. "Mama was cross, wasn't she?"

"Upset," Susan suggested.

"Oh, I see; upset," said Jonathan. How he felt about this Susan had no idea. He went away, calling for Carey again.

Within a short time a taxi drew up. Emma: tousled, bare-legged, dressed in a skirt and blouse that didn't match, a jacket slung over her shoulders. Susan's eyes went over her daughter with distrust and apprehension. Something wild in Emma's looks; this Emma could do anything. White-faced, she put an arm round Jonathan who looked at her with interest. "I'll have to ring everyone," she said, letting Jonathan go free, his eyes still alight with interest. "The Police," Emma said; 'and Geoff, damn him; and the rehearsal room.... We've got to find her; we've simply got to find her."

"Well, of course," said Susan. Anything else was unthinkable.

But, she reflected, looking at her daughter, thought of. Oh yes, thought of.

Emma had stopped running. She had run in the streets beyond the house, calling Carey's name. No answer anywhere. She walked slowly back, smoothing her disordered hair with a shivering hand. Words from the telephone went through her mind: the Police, who had been polite, asking for details which she had scarcely patience to give them; Geoff, who had sounded shaken and said "he had meant no harm". "Well, you've *done* harm," Emma had shouted at him, and put the receiver down. Last of all Jeremy, when she'd told him she'd be late for rehearsal. That voice became as cold as iced water. When she explained that Carey was *lost*, for goodness' sake, he said he was sorry, but children as he understood it often strolled into unlikely places and were quickly found again. She opened her mouth to speak in rage and anguish, then, as before, put the receiver down. With the sensation that she was putting down at the same time her chance in *The Newcomer*; for the moment it didn't seem to matter.

Back at the house, she searched Susan's room, opening cupboards. "Where's the booze?"

"Darling, it's too early—"

"For God's sake; don't give me that." She hunted in her bag and brought out a small bottle of tablets. She swallowed two and her mother said, "What are those?"

"Nothing much. A kind of put-it-all-a-little-way-off thing. They do no harm. You *must* have some drink in the house; it isn't civilised not to."

"It's in the kitchen. But—"

"No 'buts'," said Emma, on her way. She returned with a tumbler half-filled with whisky, and the bottle of tablets in the other hand.

Susan said, "You shouldn't mix—"

"Please, Ma, *shut up*. I don't know what to do. I just don't know what to do." *Take Carey with you*. No, she wouldn't think of that.

"If only it'd been you who came to see them and not Geoff," Susan said.

"Oh God, don't try to make me feel guilty; that only makes it worse. I thought they were all right. They always have been—you have, haven't you, Jonathan?"

"Yes, Mama," said Jonathan playing with a ping-pong ball.

"As for Geoff—he won't do that again; I can promise you that. He must have been out of his mind—"

Susan again saw the dejected figure. "He had a sudden impulse to go and see his daughter—"

"She's not his daughter; she's mine; we agreed on that. If you see him again, Jonathan, tell him to go away."

"Yes, Mama."

Susan said, "You shouldn't let Jonathan see you drinking so early."

Emma shook this away with a turn of her head. Indeed Jonathan appeared entirely unmoved by the glass in his mother's hand. Emma sat briefly on the arm of a chair, then rose and prowled near to the telephone. "Why doesn't someone ring? Why doesn't someone *say* something? I can't wait for ever; I can't even wait an hour; I

100

must *know*."

"Don't cry, Emma darling; it's the drink that makes you cry; I've told you before."

"I've got to drink; it's all too much—Carey lost . . . no, no, she can't be lost."

"Shouldn't think she'd go far," Jonathan said, retrieving his ball from under the sideboard.

"Why not?" Emma looked at her son, surprised out of tears.

Jonathan shrugged. "She clings a bit, doesn't she? Especially to you."

Emma looked at her son as if a trace of jealousy or malice had touched her. She said, "I see her all I can."

"I tell her that," said Jonathan; "but she goes on asking, just the same."

"You didn't have to say that!"

"It's true."

His detachment made Emma cry again. "*Any*thing could have happened to her. Anything at all—"

"We've told the Police," Susan said. "They take a missing child very seriously."

"So I should bloody hope."

"We're doing all we can—"

"We're not doing *any*thing," Emma wailed; "we're just sitting about talking. And waiting. Waiting."

It was Susan who said, "There's someone coming up the path."

Emma flew to the window. "It's *Carey*!" She was out in the hall, swamped, drowned in relief; to the front door which she opened. She bent and spread wide her arms and Carey tottered into them, wordless. Emma lifted her up and held her. The flood of relief was so strong that she didn't at first notice the young woman with blowing hair who stood a little awkwardly on the step.

"Oh, sweetheart,' Emma said to Carey, "where *have* you been?"

101

The young woman spoke for the first time. "She was walking along the Embankment by herself. I thought she was going to try to climb over the wall."

"Over the wall?" She put Carey down. "What on earth were you doing?"

Carey looked up at her. "Tried to find you. Went to your house. You weren't there."

"Oh—darling; you mustn't go out alone; you must promise me never to do that again."

Carey looked doubtful. Then, "Promise," she said.

Emma turned her smile, tears banished, on the young woman who waited there. "You found her? You brought her here?"

The young woman said Yes; and Carey had led her to this house.

"Oh Lord, am I grateful. Come in and have a drink."

The young woman gave a lop-sided smile and said, Thank you, but it was a bit early for a drink.

"But you brought *Carey* back! You *must* come in."

"No," the young woman said; "I do really have to be going."

"Then—what can I say? Thank you isn't enough. What can I give you?"

"Why . . . nothing, of course." She made a gesture to Carey, then let her hand fall. "I'm just glad I saw her. It was the slippers," she added inconsequentially; "it was the slippers that caught my eye."

"But—"

The young woman turned with the same shy smile, lifting one hand. The last Emma saw of her was her tall slight figure, head down, going along the path, out of her life. No time even to tell her that she might see herself, Emma Pride, on the stage of a London theatre in a few weeks' time. . . .

Emma shut the door. She had Carey; the terrible fears were dissolved; this world, of the children and her mother, stood where it did.

And now that other world, the world of the theatre, came back.

Chapter Eight

The first row took place in Reggie Graves's office in Henrietta Street. Reggie was a plump young man of thirty-six (not yet with the fame which would later come to him) but on his way up: already he had the assurance of a man who has a clear grasp of affairs, and a polite but inexorable way with those whom he conceived to be wrong.

Amongst these, Jeremy had no doubt, he was for the present, included.

Jeremy sat sideways on a small chair: Reggie leaned over his desk; on another chair Guy Forster turned his scarred face from the light, with his crutch beside him.

Reggie lit a cigar and said, waving the match, "Frankly, I'm not prepared to be buggered about any more. Guy's piece of work is the best he's done, and I'm damned if I'm going to have it wrecked by an actress who plays fast and loose. *No* one's worth that."

Jeremy looked at the floor. "I think Emma is."

"No good thinking," Reggie observed. "One's got to know."

"I agree," said Guy, turning his head so that light fell upon the long white scar.

Jeremy said again that they had a contract.

Reggie put a careful half-inch of ash into the tray. "She's broken that."

"Oh, God—" Jeremy thought that the chemistry between himself and Reggie Graves didn't work: he could feel, somewhere in Reggie, the strongly masculine man's distrust of those of a different sexual persuasion—"the poor girl had lost her child—"

"And whose fault was that?"

"The child was staying with her grandmother—it wasn't anything to do with Emma—"

"Emma's child," Guy Forster said with lifted eyebrow, "has nothing to do with *Emma*?"

Jeremy rubbed his forehead. When you were in danger of losing a battle, he thought, you chose all the wrong words. "She'd done her best—"

"As far as I understand," Guy said, "she doesn't do anything except leave her children in other people's care—either Lance Ashley's wife, or the children's grandmother, who by all accounts isn't entirely reliable—"

"What else *can* she do? She's got to work, hasn't she?"

"She's got to work, and manage her family so that they don't cause the kind of chaos we've just had." Reggie Graves leaned back in his chair. On the wall behind him were posters of productions which had proved successful. He had the air of one determined that whatever he did next was going to be successful too.

Taking strength from opposition, Jeremy said, "And if you get rid of Emma, have you the slightest idea who we should put in her place? Remembering that Daisy is crucial to the play; get her wrong and the whole thing's down the drain."

"No one's denying that." Reggie drew on his cigar.

"Well, have you any ideas? For Daisy?"

"I always have ideas." (Oh yes; swords were crossed, Jeremy thought.)

"An actress," he said, "who has Emma's quality, of the right age, looking right, and available?"

Reggie gave him a look of mild hatred. "Difficult, of course. But—yes, I have ideas. There are always more actresses than parts." He lifted the weight of *Spotlight* and plumped it back on his desk.

"Sure," said Jeremy; "I read that in the long winter

105

evenings. But the *right* actresses?"

"And the right actress," Guy said, "is one who can't manage her home life and her career at the same time?"

O.K.; this is a fight, Jeremy thought. For Emma. In spite of his own doubts, he was going to fight for her, and trust that she wouldn't let him down.

"You'll not find anyone like her," he said.

"Maybe not," said Guy. "But she drinks too early in the morning; she hasn't got control of her life—"

"Who has?" said Jeremy.

Reggie made a small acknowledgement of this with a narrowing of his eyes, as if he tried to see at a distance. "I'm not asking that an actress should be something between a Salvation Army lass and a games mistress. Though the qualities of both would help, one can't deny. All artists, so I understand, have difficulties in living. Too much sensitivity; too much depth of feeling—or at any rate, too much *something*." He shifted his chair. "Mind you, us coarse chaps who look after the money have our vulnerable areas too, though sometimes you won't get anyone to believe it. All right, Emma has that particular quality of understanding pain—whether it's her own pain or other people's I wouldn't be too sure. Perhaps it doesn't matter. The people out there *think* she understands them; I'm clear about that. What I'm also clear about is that I can't afford to take risks." He glanced behind him at the posters on the wall. "I've had my failures, of course. But I don't *invite* them. Do I make myself clear?"

Yes, Jeremy thought: all too clear.

The telephone rang: Reggie answered it with controlled impatience. Yes, he said; he was waiting for a call to New York. Yes, it was important. Person to person; Miss Andrea Forbes.

Jeremy looked up. Andrea Forbes—she might just be a substitute for Emma; she had some of the same quality, though not, in his view, the whole magic. She had, on the other hand, no such reputation as Emma's; Andrea had a fair English beauty, and a fair English name, more or less. She was married to a journalist, had two children, and had run into no outright scandal.

Jeremy said, "Give Emma one more chance. Doesn't she deserve that? This was an emergency—"

"Have you noticed," Guy said, "how emergencies seem in general to happen to the same people? Oh, I grant you that anyone is likely to be involved in a train accident or a road crash. But there's a pattern in some people's lives; they fall over, time and again."

"The jargon is 'accident-prone'," said Jeremy, beginning to lose his temper; "and we all know it. I simply say that you can't judge Emma yet."

"That's your opinion."

"Yes. But I am directing this play. And I suggest this. That we call a rehearsal tomorrow morning, early. I can get the Harvey Theatre. We'll have to put up with the set—one of those 'study with fake-books' jobs. Never mind. You can get a better view of Emma from the auditorium of a theatre than in that bleak hole of a rehearsal room." He swallowed his pride and his anger and said, "I do beg you to do this. Tomorrow?"

He waited. Guy and Reggie exchanged glances. At last Reggie leaned back in his chair. "Very well; we'll try once more."

Emma walked down the hospital corridor. Like Lance before her, she found this busy antiseptic world alien and uncomfortable Would she see the Sister she'd seen that other time, when she'd claimed (without success) to be Ben's wife? She must hope not.

However, this time she came lawfully; Ben, Jeremy had told her, was allowed visitors. Ben was recovering. Nevertheless, Emma trod with caution. Whatever they told you in hospitals, Emma had the sensation that they held something back; that they didn't tell you it all. I don't ever want to go to hospital, she thought; not ever. Whatever I get, I want to stay at home. But I'm young, and I shall be well for years and years.

She walked down the ward. Why am I afraid of seeing Ben? she thought. He's been ill, and he's getting better. It happens to lots of people.

Yes, there he was. She caught sight of him at the end of the ward before he saw her. He was sitting in a chair beside his bed, in his dressing-gown, reading a book. The contrast between him as she'd last seen him, his skin grey-white when he collapsed during rehearsal, was so marked that she felt a great bound of relief. Why, things *could* get better; you could come back from the abyss.

As she drew close to his chair, he looked up. A small shock here, for his face was thinner, much thinner, and pale, though some of his colour had returned.

But his smile on seeing her was joyful, all-embracing, and transformed his face. "*Emma*. How wonderful; how absolutely wonderful. D'you know there was a time when I didn't think I was going to see you again?"

Moved, she leaned over and kissed him; and felt the slightness of his shoulder under her hand. But he was better; *better*. She must keep telling herself that. "We've all missed you," she said, sitting on a chair before him.

"Have *you* missed me?"

"Oh yes . . . yes."

His beauty still endured, in spite of his illness; and he looked very young.

"When I first came here," she said, "I told them I was your wife—"

"Ah . . ." The blue, drowsy, so deep-shadowed eyes looked at her, it seemed, with love. "Don't I wish you were."

Movement and voices and clatter from a sluice, but she had eyes only for Ben. It was good to be loved; perhaps when he was recovered and out of hospital, he would make love to her again. She took his hand, and again felt its thinness. "What was it?" she asked.

He shrugged. "Oh, they never say much, do they? The big man told me I had a 'kind of anaemia that needed watching'. How d'you watch an anaemia? Sounds awfully dull, doesn't it . . ."

She couldn't answer his smile; the careful words of medical men had always frightened her. "Needs watching, what does that mean?"

"Oh, you know the way they talk. They gave me a blood transfusion at first: all that's a bit of a fog. Now they give me some pretty disgusting pills—'medicine now, Mr Hardy'. The pills make me feel terrible, but they seem to be doing their job. Last I heard the big man was 'pleased with my progress'. So that can't be bad, can it?"

"Jeremy says they're going to let you out."

He smiled and put his book aside. "Sounds like prison. Well, it is rather. A *kind* prison. But I want to be back in the play; back with you. Darling Emma."

"I want you too."

He put up the thin hand and touched her face. "You're lovely," he said. "Quite beautiful."

"No, I'm not. I just have this odd face."

His hand followed her cheek and her jaw. "Shall I really get out of here; even, perhaps, make love to you again?"

She put her lips to his hand. "Of course."

"Is there a lot more life to come? Good things, and fun, and love?"

"Of course," she said again; "you're young; there's all the time in the world."

"It seems too good to be true. You here; and still a chance of getting back into the play—"

"Well, of course you're getting back into the play. Anything else is unthinkable; that other young man isn't any good at all."

"He's not too bad," Ben said; "I've worked with him

109

once."

"Yes, but he isn't you. He doesn't look like you, for a start."

He was still smiling. "What do I look like?"

Emma said, "An Andrea del Sarto angel."

"What d'you know; an angel." He laughed and new colour came on to his face. "I've missed an awful lot of rehearsal time—"

"Never mind. I've had my problems too. But somehow we're both going to be in that play together. And after that—who knows? Wonderful things. All the world before us, as they say."

"All the world," he said. "That sounds nice. Plenty of room, plenty of time."

A nurse veered towards him, quickly on the move. "Your tablets, Mr Hardy. Take a good drink of water."

As he swallowed the pills and the water, Emma said, "He's coming out; isn't that good?"

The young nurse nodded, making a mark on the chart which hung at the end of his bed.

"You've got him *well*," Emma said.

For a moment the nurse's young glance slipped to her face. Emma couldn't read her eyes; perhaps they were concerned with her own thoughts, or registered only the neutral comment of all hospital staff . . .

"My father hasn't been," Ben said. "He's in Bermuda; too far away, I suppose."

"It doesn't matter about him," Emma said. "There's *us*. And the play."

"A whole future?" he said.

"Why, yes."

She kissed him again before she left. As she walked down the ward, she kept turning to wave to him. It was all right; Ben was (almost) himself again. Youth was on his side; he'd grow stronger and put on weight; and this time of imprisonment would be forgotten.

It was just that she didn't like hospitals; and the way

110

they kept their secrets; the look she had seen in the nurse's eyes.

She wouldn't think about that. Ben had smiled at her and loved her; and would soon be back. She must remember that when she had to prove herself tomorrow.

The Harvey Theatre was small, dusty, and at ten-thirty in the morning gave the impression, Lance thought, of something remembered from a troubled dream. Daylight filtering in touched the stage with different clarity. The auditorium spoke of absence, with each seat waiting for an occupant who wasn't there.

His eye ran over the few occupied stalls: Jeremy Hirst, Guy Forster and Reggie Graves. Reggie's jacket lay over the back of one of the stalls; the day was warm. The smell of his cigar touched the waiting air of the theatre.

And what I am doing here? Lance thought. He could as he waited hear in memory Emma's voice on the telephone: she needed him, she'd said; she needed someone on her side. Reggie and Guy Forster were angry, but it hadn't been her fault: how could she go to rehearsal when Carey'd run away? . . .

Please, Lance; you have to be there. I think Jeremy wants me to succeed, but the others don't. Please, Lance.

The old story, Lance thought. He was a busy man; he had an intelligent and compassionate wife, and a son. But he couldn't quite shut his ears to Emma, for she seemed to need so much, and to move so close to danger. Would his presence give her courage, as she'd said it would? He'd already spoken to her that morning; she hadn't looked hungover or even particularly nervous, except for small pulse at the side of her mouth. She'd talked of Ben, whom she'd seen yesterday in hospital. His recovery had, it seemed, uplifted her. The question of her relationship with Ben returned to him: but he knew well enough, whatever that had been, she still needed his (Lance's) comfort and strength. Which was why he was here; and

111

why she gave him the look which he knew so well—the child, perhaps justly punished, but now contrite and wishing to be loved again.

From the dusk of his seat in the deserted theatre, he watched and waited. Jeremy Hirst had vaulted his long length up on to the stage and, script in hand, was talking to the company: Emma, Mark, Juliet, Brenda; and Paul Dane, in place of Ben. Faintly from the streets outside came the rumble of traffic: but here, Lance thought, they were all encapsulated in the endeavour of this play: the early striving before lines were perfectly learned; before the audiences came in. . . .

Jeremy returned to his seat; light just touched his thin, intelligent face. He'd chosen—rightly, Lance reflected— the scene of Emma's first appearance, because everything rested on that: she had to show in those first lines that she could throw an invisible cord into the darkness before her, a cord which would tie the audience immediately in a noose of attention.

Lance kept his eyes on Emma. She was wearing a blue summer dress, the skirt loosely flowing, as the fashion then was. Her waist was slight, bound by a sash of grey-blue. She wore little paint on her face, but even in the crude light from the baton her eyes had enchantment, so large, so much aware of sorrow.

She moved on the alien set as if the nervousness which he knew must gnaw within her didn't exist. No ballerina, he thought, could have moved more exactly, with more control. He didn't look at the other three in the stalls. He could smell Reggie's cigar, and feel the movement of the seat as Guy tried to make himself more comfortable. Lance listened, entirely given to Emma.

Once Jeremy loped back on to the stage; and tried different movements, another pace. He returned to his seat; watched; then said, "Sorry, no, I was wrong; as you were. Do it again."

Lance felt a *frisson* of impatience: couldn't Jeremy have

112

let well alone? But the company, including Emma, made no protest. Indeed, Emma was playing as well as she ever had; the quality of her bewildered, sorrowing joy had never shown itself more clearly. You couldn't take your eyes off her, and even as she spoke the most casual lines something in your heart responded . . . And they can't be missing *that*, Lance thought, still not looking at the men beside him.

The early scenes of *The Newcomer* were played out before them. Jeremy made notes on his pad, but didn't interrupt again. The performance was still ragged, of course, with hesitations, wrong movements, lines fluffed, a failure on a laugh (though no one was laughing much, Lance thought; well, neither was he). But he could see the chrysalis there; somewhere in this imperfect construction lay the later performance, when the audience and the warm excitement would change the air.

But Reggie's verdict—and Guy's too—was still to come.

Had the morning gone so quickly? Reggie was glancing at his watch. Not possible to guess from his expression whether the rough performance had pleased him or not. Nor Guy, whose marred face showed no more than its usual impassivity.

They had come to the end of the scene. Like those who slip off clothing which has become too onerous for the day, the company drooped, relaxed, found places to sit among the alien furniture of the set; in Emma's case, on the floor. Silence slipped oddly into this place which was built for sound. Brenda was talking quietly to Juliet: Lance caught the word 'marmalade'; he didn't have to remind himself how quickly actors could switch off. And Brenda, of course, wasn't waiting for a verdict.

Reggie had risen to his feet and wandered towards the stage, hands in his pockets.

"That was all right," he said.

"More than all right," Lance muttered to himself.

113

"Some ragged ends, naturally," Reggie went on; "however, it's early days."

Emma sat on the floor resting on one arm; her breath came rapidly, as if she'd been dancing. Reggie's eyes rested on her. Indeed Emma shone on that blighted stage, as if she belonged to some different species. If she knew that she waited to know her future, whether she had swung Reggie's judgement in her favour, the only sign was the hand which rested on her thigh and shivered a little.

Reggie said, "Emma—come down here, please."

She rose obediently, like a schoolgirl summoned by the headmistress. Lance was beguiled by the complexity of one who could range from a virago to a girl with an almost Victorian submissiveness.

Reggie touched her on the arm and led her to a seat in the stalls. Bemused, Lance watched. The words 'Beauty and the Beast' came to his mind: Reggie looked over-weight and without charm: Emma touched with some unearthly gleam. Reggie said again, "That was all right." Emma waited. Her hand still shivered a little. Reggie went on, "You have a family. And many other problems beside, I daresay."

Emma still said nothing. The company watched from the stage.

"I don't deal in uncertainties," Reggie said.

Perhaps Emma lost a little of her colour. She didn't move. Her voice came quietly. "This is my part. I can play it."

"No one's arguing that, dearie," said Reggie. "Very nice that was up there, as I've said; very nice indeed. But—well, you know the But."

"It won't happen again."

Reggie drew on his cigar while he looked at her. As if, Lance thought, he was doing arithmetic in his head. He said at last, "I don't go much for promises. People make them, break them. I go by my own wave-length—

antennae: whatever you like to call it. Them. I don't often go against my hunches. And when I do I nearly always regret it."

Silence again. Lance thought that Emma now showed a true nervousness, as if she saw her hopes slipping over the horizon. She stayed silent, as if the moment were too much for her.

"However, Reggie said; "I'm going—for once—to put my trust in Princes. Or otherwise, since no one reads his Bible now—I'm going to believe that anyone who can give so much to the part of Daisy so early in rehearsal is too good to lose."

From impassivity, Emma moved with total speed: she leaned forward and flung her arms round Reggie's neck. Lance watched the soft hair fall over Reggie's shoulder and the graceful line of her arm. Nothing Emma did, he reflected, was ugly—except perhaps what went on within.

Chapter Nine

The out-of-town run of *The Newcomer* began in the autumn of that year.

Emma's son, Jonathan (like myself) went to school: he in Kensington and I in Hampstead. Carey stayed with her grandmother. Unlike the time on the Vineyard, I didn't see her. Nor did I think much about her: a boy of seven hasn't much time for a child of four who is out of his sphere.

Before the company left for Edinburgh I can remember a rare thing—an argument between Marguerite and my father.

I was home from school: I wore a green blazer and school cap, and was eating a large tea on the kitchen table. (I kept my cap on because it was new and I cherished it.) The door was open in the warm evening, and I could hear their voices clearly.

"Just for once," Marguerite was saying, "I'd like Emma to fight her own fight, whatever that is. You went to the rehearsal where she seemed to be on trial. O.K.; you're her agent. But that wasn't why she wanted you there, and you know it."

My father was silent, and, watching through the open door, I saw him move to the window where sun drenched the London green. He said at last, "It's not only Emma."

"If Emma wasn't in the play—"

"It's the whole thing. Emma *and* the play. And Ben too, of course. He's short on rehearsal time."

Marguerite lit a cigarette. "Just for once I'd like you *not* to go North; to stay home with me."

I had stopped eating. Though I wasn't old enough to understand, I could feel discomfort in the air.

My father said, "I've promised to go. It's all set."

"You could cancel. Wouldn't be the first time. How often have you called me on the Vineyard and said you were held up in New York? You could go to the first night in the West End—"

'If there *is* any first night in the West End."

Marguerite strolled into my line of vision. "I've gone along with a lot," she said. "Emma's everyone's problem, particularly yours. But I guess I've got to the point where I think it's someone else's turn to take the load."

"She needs me."

"Oh, sure; sure she needs you. But she's getting a big girl now, and she must learn to do without you." She drew on her cigarette, and I saw that her hand shook. "I don't want to break anything up—"

I saw my father turn with a sudden movement. "You know I should be lost without you."

"Lost?" The word, as I recall it, had the gleam of irony.

"You know what I mean." His voice was impatient. "The only peace I get in this pretty merry-go-round of theatre life is with you. And Rick."

I was surprised to hear my own name, and more surprised to know that I contributed anything to his peace.

"No peace with Emma?" Again irony touched her voice. "You surprise me."

I saw my father's glance slip from Marguerite to the open door, and to me. He changed his face and voice, a process of which children are from their earliest days aware, whatever their elders believe.

"Finished your tea, Rick?"

Yes, I said, though in truth I hadn't; but the talk disturbed me.

117

"Go and play in the garden, there's a good chap."

I went at once. Unreasoningly, the tears came to my eyes. I didn't like the conversation, but I liked less to be banished, implying that they had things to say which I mustn't hear. Such banishment could only mean that they spoke of things which, if I understood them, would be more disturbing than those I'd already heard. That uncertainty which lay at the heart of my life with Marguerite, who was not my mother, and my father so frequently absent, seemed to strike home. Perhaps it was those words: 'I don't want to break anything up.' Like most children, I didn't want change: I wanted the permanence of Marguerite who spread about me an atmosphere of care and good humour: and I wanted, at least, the impending presence of my father.

Without heart, I tossed a ball over the grass and ran to fetch it.

The substance of the voices in the room was lost to me, only faintly travelling on the air.

The great northern city seemed to Emma cold and grey; grey stone, grey streets and a grey sky. Where had the sun gone? It seemed to have been left behind in London, or even farther, on the Vineyard, or in New York: the stages of her progress.

The small hotel where the company were staying had an ancient musty air, as if it had been kept for a long time in a museum. Draughts triumphed over heating. The bedrooms had narrow hard beds and a small strip of worn carpet on linoleum-covered floors. A Bible lay on each bedside table.

The common rooms were darkish with old-fashioned furniture lurking amongst tall rubber plants. There was no bar.

Emma, sitting on the edge of her bed, with Ben in a prim armchair in the corner of the room, poured whisky from a flask and said, "For God's sake, darling, cheer me up." She took in the bleak room and the small short-hemmed lace curtain at the window. "If you *tried* you couldn't make a place more like all one's nightmares."

"Perhaps they did try."

"Oh, thank God you can make me laugh. Thank God you're here."

"I'm pretty pleased to be here too. Lucky as well, all things considered."

"Luck .... I suppose we're both lucky. Why don't I *feel* lucky? I was all right travelling up here, safe in the train, with all that country going past, watching the rain on the windows and the people getting on at the stations: people you didn't have to talk to; people you could just wonder about. Bliss. But now ... What's happened? What's happened, Ben love?"

He smiled at her. "We've arrived."

"Oh hell, yes; arriving. What that chap said; Stevenson or somebody. I wish he hadn't—because one has to arrive sometime, doesn't one?"

"Oh yes; one has to arrive." His glance turned aside, towards the window.

"What're you thinking of, when you do that?"

"Do what?"

"Kind of cloud over."

"Nothing much. Just dreaming."

"Dreaming of good things?"

"Perhaps. Dreaming of you."

She considered him, pleased as always with his attention and his looks. "You're better," she said, "but you still haven't put on enough weight."

He said, "If the food here runs true to form, I shall be swelling with suet before the week's out."

She said, "Come here."

He moved to the bed and kissed her. She could still feel the thinness of his body as she put her arms round him.

He said, "Supposing I can't make love to you—"

"Doesn't matter," she murmured. "Just kiss me as if

you wanted to."

"I do. Oh, I do."

She held him untidly on the narrow bed. She was glad of his mouth on hers, the increasing strength of his embrace. He was too young, he couldn't wholly reassure her; but this love was easing to her fears... "Lovely Emma," he said; and she gave him smothered words of answer, while she pulled at her clothes; and he said, "Oh, darling Emma; I *can* make love to you; I can; it's the most wonderful thing in the world;" and she received him with the deep pleasure that she remembered; saying, "Oh, it's good, good; dear Ben..." She held him as if she comforted him; his long absence made this the more sweet.

When the final shiver of love had gone through her she felt none of the detachment which she'd known before. This was Ben, with his beauty nearly restored, close to her again.

"Lovely Emma," he said again; "what a perfect thing to happen. I shall love you always and always... How long is that, d'you think?"

She stroked his hair. "No need to think about time. Lots of good things to come."

He kissed her. "Nothing better than this... Oh, I hope I can go on making love to you for a very long time ... I don't want to think of an end."

"No end," she said.

"None?" he said, kissing her.

"No, none. There isn't an end. There's simply now."

"Now," he echoed sleepily.

She felt him shiver and held him more closely. Beyond his shoulder she could see the small bleak room. "Wouldn't it be awful," she said, "to come to a place like this and be alone and old and not loved; not to be *anything*?"

He smiled and lifted his head. "That won't happen to you."

But when they came to the dress rehearsal, Emma found that the pleasure of this encounter had faded. The performance had the raggedness of dress rehearsals everywhere: the set fitted badly on to the stage; a door wouldn't open; Juliet was distressed about a hat she had to wear in Act Two—the assistant stage manager was sent scurrying to the shops to find one more suitable. When they broke for a rest, Emma's hands were trembling and sweat gleamed on her forehead.

"Not feeling well, dear?" Jeremy asked.

"I don't like this theatre. It's unfriendly, fighting you. I don't think it's right for this play."

"Too bad; we have to make the best of it."

"The whole point of being in our business," Brenda said, "is that you have to make the best of everything."

"A professional," Juliet added, waiting for her hat, "can play in *any* theatre. Even a log cabin on a mountainside."

"I've said before, I *am* a professional." Emma wiped her face. No good being angry. What did she need? Ben was looking at her with undefeated love; and the memory of Ben was to be cherished, however much these present events obscured it. But she needed more than Ben; more than the pleasurable comfort of his body. She needed someone to reassure her, to strengthen her resolve; she needed Lance. And, though he'd promised her, so far Lance had not come. He *must* come today. Perhaps he'd be waiting for her when she got back to the hotel . . . no, surely he'd come to the theatre? At least, tomorrow, for the first night.

The theatre . . . she looked out, and couldn't imagine that echoing auditorium filled with enthusiastic people (in fact she couldn't imagine it filled at all—would anyone come?)

Jeremy, crouched before his single-lighted desk in the stalls, was, even at this point, having new ideas. As a

121

result Emma dried twice in the first scene. She felt a rising surge of panic; swallowed it in the face of the rest of the company who remained patient; continued with the scene. But she wasn't timing it right; the flow of ease was missing. . . .

At the end of the scene Jeremy unwound himself and stood up. "We've got to do better than this—"

"Dress rehearsals," Emma began.

"I know all about dress rehearsals, darling; I ought to; God knows, I've watched them for what seems like centuries. We've got to do better; and what's more the lighting has too." He prowled towards the wings, with the A.S.M., small and dark, like a terrier behind him. "We don't want," Jeremy said to the electrician, a tall bent man with greying hair, "a cool English afternoon to look like a Florida sunset; can we bear that in mind? You'd better put in a steel."

Emma sat on one of the prop chairs. She was, she thought, empty of everything: fear, ambition, hope. She thought that the rest of them felt much the same. They showed a tired acceptance, edged with irritability. Her eyes went over them: Mark, Juliet, Brenda, and last of all, Ben.

Ah yes; Ben, though exhausted, was his usual self: the young man who loved her; his glance rested on her with its tranquil and loving smile . . . Was there something more in his face, as if behind the gentle young man, something looked out which she was afraid to see? . . . No, Ben was playing well; perhaps the best of them all.

"Now," said Jeremy, returning to his desk, script in hand, "we have to start all over again. And," he went on quickly as Mark turned, "if that's not clear to all of you, you just haven't been paying attention to the theatre in the last fifteen years, or however long you've been working for it."

Emma didn't speak. The A.S.M. appeared with sandwiches and flasks of coffee. She was still drained of feeling, but she knew that Jeremy was right: the thing had to be done better. The only shadow was the look of Ben: had Jeremy noticed him? If so, he made no sign. Perhaps like many of those concerned with the theatre in time of crisis humanity had deserted him.

Once more, then, after the coffee in cardboard cups and the spam sandwiches. Once more through the whole play: just over two hours. Better? Perhaps, Emma thought—though judgement was marred by weariness; better, though the lighting appeared to be under the same nervous pressure as the rest of them, and the pace of a scene with Mark was wrong. . . .

At the end they all looked, Emma thought, as if they'd been on an all-night train journey through cold country.

Jeremy, as drained as any of them, left his seat in the stalls and climbed long-leggedly on to the stage. There he sat on the floor, and shuffled through his notes.

"Thank you," he said; "you did your best." His voice, tired and without enthusiasm, seemed to suggest that their best wasn't enough. "It wants a slightly quicker pace, especially in the middle of Act Two, because we're reaching a climax and all those nice people out there have to know it. Ben, you need to climb a little faster at the end of Act One; you've fallen for Daisy *bang-splash*: O.K.?"

Yes; Ben said, it was O.K. He loooked paler than ever, but said nothing more.

Beyond that, Jeremy said, and the lighting, and a feeling that the play needed *more* from everyone, he hadn't anything further to say. Except, of course, to wish them all the best of luck.

The small company of his cast looked at him with dulled acceptance, as if he had put them into a trance. Shuffling into coats, running abstracted hands over their hair, they made their way, a forlorn group, it seemed to Emma, out of the stage door. The theatre showed no lights and seemed to offer no sort of gaiety.

The late air was chill, and Mark muttered, "Never

123

cared for northern parts. Give me the South of France every time: I'm a sybarite."

"Never known what that was," Brenda said.

"Someone who likes comfort, dear."

"What an odd profession to choose, then," observed Jeremy.

"It was laid on me," said Mark with dignity.

Once in the street, Emma said, "There must be somewhere that serves drinks; we can't go back yet."

But all of them, it seemed, wanted to go to bed.

"*Bed*," Emma exclaimed; "but I don't sleep when I'm in bed; I'm just there, alone with the dark. . . ."

She said to Ben who lingered beside her, "Won't you come with me?"

He slipped an arm about her waist. "Darling Emma, I'm played out. I truly am. I wish I weren't."

She glanced up at him. Under a street lamp his face showed with extreme pallor. Tired, like all of them, she told herself. But unlike the rest of them, she wanted as she always did, whether things had gone ill or well, to sit up and drink and talk, sometimes till the night was past.

"We're all close by, love," said Ben; and Brenda observed that she always slept for seven hours.

"Oh, God, seven *hours*," said Emma. "How does anyone sleep seven hours?"

With this they returned to the hotel. The hall was empty, and so it was not until she reached her room that she found the telegram. Someone had placed it on her dressing-table, between the pots of face cream and the spilled powder. She tore the envelope with a shaking hand.

She read: "Sorry, can't make Edinburgh. Letter follows. Lance."

She sat down on the bed. "But he *has* to come. He said he would." Absently she found her flask and poured herself a glass of neat whisky; and then another. "He promised; he can't opt out."

124

She drank more; then went to Jeremy's room. (No use going to Ben; she couldn't explain that she needed, in different ways, both of them.) Jeremy was in his pyjamas and dressing-gown, not yet in bed. In the flat light from the central bulb his face looked tired and pale. "Golly, darling, why aren't you in bed? It's late. And to-morrow—"

"Lance isn't coming." She held out the telegram with a shaking hand.

"Darling—*so what?* We all want to go to bed, and you *need* to go to bed, if you're to be the slightest use tomorrow: be a good girl and leave Lance and telegrams and everything else; do that for me, will you please?"

"But I need him—"

"And I, my darling, need an actress who can play Daisy before a first public tomorrow—"

"I know. But I need Lance to be there—"

"Well, you'll just have to manage without him, won't you?"

Emma went out and slammed the door, which brought an elderly woman's head in a hair-net round the door of her room in protest.

Emma fled downstairs. The hall was empty in the quiet of the small hours: a coin-box telephone was fixed to the wall. Impatiently she waited for the operator, and asked for Lance's number in London. She heard the telephone ring and ring; then at last, Marguerite's sleepy voice. "Who's that?"

Well, of course it would be Marguerite. Answering the telephone by her bedside. The bed where she lay with Lance.

Emma put the telephone down without speaking, and ran out of the hotel.

It was only as she met the night air that she realised how much she had drunk. She tried to run, away from the hotel, away from Lance's telegram, away from the rehearsal, but running was like the abortive effort in a dream.

She swayed, her head spinning with air and the drink. Frustration made her breathless, and she began to cry. The night sky revolving above her head, the pavement made of cotton-wool . . . she grasped the cold iron of a railing. She muttered, "Why can't he come? I need him; he knows I need him; he can't turn me down." And while she hung there, tethered to the railing, some thread of reason was asking "What the hell am I doing here, *me*, Emma Pride, the leading actress in a play by Guy Forster—I ought to be sleeping in splendid peace, or drinking champagne—oh God, I don't want to think about champagne. . ."

"Feeling all right, Miss?"

She had heard no steps. She turned a tear-marked face to see a young policeman. The *Police* . . . She saw a cell, arrest, headlines. . . .

She wiped her face. If only the dark whirling air would stay still . . . 'Yes, I'm all right. Thank you."

"Ye dinna look too well, Miss."

"I—I didn't feel well, and came out to get some air." (What did they call it? *Drunk and disorderly*. But she wasn't being disorderly; she was—within her powers—doing her best to be polite to him.) If only her voice would come steadily, that distinctive voice which could charm audiences, lovers, but perhaps not this young Scotsman who knew the effects of drink when he saw them.

He said, "Seems to me, ye'd better go home, Miss. I'll come with you."

She didn't want him to come with her; though he spoke pleasantly enough, he might be taking her to a Police Station.

"I'm all right, thank you. There's no need . . ."

But once she let go of the railing, she swayed again and the night sky and the lamp lights spun like a merry go-round.

He took her arm. "Now if ye'll tell me where you live. . . ."

(Coming quietly, wasn't it called? She felt cold and frightened, but she had no choice but to obey him: she needed the support of his arm.)

Silent now, she walked beside him, leaning on him. "It's here," she said, as they reached the hotel. Please let him go now, let there be no more about it: he mustn't know who she was; and no one from the company must see her, brought in off the night streets by a policeman, as if she were some drunken outcast: she wasn't like that, it was only Lance's telegram after the stress of the rehearsal, and the sudden night air. . . .

"All right, Miss. Take my advice and stay indoors."

"Yes," she gasped, grateful, relieved now; "yes, I'll do that, Officer." The shock seemed to have sobered her, and her voice came more clearly; she had stopped crying.

"Goodnight, then, Miss."

Bewildered, having the sensation of one who has narrowly escaped a road accident, she stood alone in the hall. All was quiet. Perhaps everyone was asleep. She felt the silence come down; the silence she most feared, when there was no one to speak to, no one to take her hand, or love her... She thought of going to Ben's room, but something remembered in his face prevented her.

Heedless of the time, which was now after one in the morning, she went again to the telephone.

The voice which answered her had the sharp wakened quality of alarm. "Yes? Who's that?"

Emma said, "It's me, Mother."

"*Emma*. What's happened? I was fast asleep. Is anything wrong?"

"I want to talk to Carey."

"*Carey*? You must be out of your mind; Carey's been in bed since seven o'clock; I can't wake her now."

"Ma—I do want to speak to her. I really do. I don't see enough of her; I can't see her till this tour's over; I want to know she loves me."

"Have you been drinking?"

127

"It's nothing to do with that; I'm just standing alone in this damned awful hall, and everyone's in bed—"

"So I should think."

"And there's no one. Lance isn't coming up—"

"Lance is a married man; you can't expect him to be at your side whenever you want it."

"Oh, please, Ma, don't be reasonable; it isn't the time—"

"It isn't the time to telephone—you never think what it's like at the other end—"

"I had to ring. I just had to. Geoff hasn't been to see her again, has he?"

"Geoff? No, of course not. Darling, you *have* been drinking; you must have been, to do this—"

"It's just been a hell of an evening; we've been rehearsing since forever, and I don't know if it's any good. Please, Ma; let me talk to Carey, just speak to her—"

"I've told you; she's *asleep*. If I wake her up it may frighten her."

"No, it won't. She hardly wakes up; I've been into her room and spoken to her, and she just says 'Mama' and turns over and goes to sleep again . . . *please*."

She stood in the cold hall, while she heard her mother's voice, turned from the telephone; Emma said, "What is it?"

"It's Carey. The noise woke her."

"Then let me speak to her."

After a breathing silence she heard Carey's voice, drenched in sleep. "Mama?"

"Carey, darling, I just wanted to tell you I loved you, even though I'm not there and I can't see you. I love you very much. Do you love me?"

"Yes."

"Say it, darling."

"Carey loves Mama."

"Very much?"

"Carey loves Mama very much." The voice still full of

128

sleep.

"Goodnight, darling. Go back to sleep now."

She put the receiver down. 'Carey loves Mama'. She needed it to be true; after all, in spite of Lance, in spite of Ben, Carey was the only one who could love her for the rest of her life, however long—or short—that might be. Jonathan from his earliest days had shown this unnerving detachment, but Carey was loving, like herself; they were two of a kind.

She went slowly upstairs. Her head throbbed with exhaustion and the drink, the long hours of rehearsal and the encounter in the night street; but Carey's words had comforted her.

She undressed and crouched in the warmth of the spartan but welcoming bed. Welcoming, because she was by now very tired, in need of sleep.

But instead of sleep, words of the rehearsal travelled through her mind . . .

Tomorrow. For the first time before an audience. Something she ought to be used to, but wasn't—never would be, perhaps. Someone had said, hadn't they, that no actress (or actor) gave a really great performance unless he or she suffered from nerves beforehand. Some were even sick.

An audience. Those people out there, comfortable in their seats, saying in effect, *Amuse us, or else* . . . You had to meet that challenge, get them as it were by the scruffs of their necks, and make them forget their preoccupations with their mortgages, their marriages, love affairs, children, jobs. You had to so move them that they came out of the theatre a little dazed, like people who had been swept into another world . . . *You* had to do that.

Tomorrow.

Chapter Ten

The bare tiled back parts of the theatre were full of movement, hurry and suppressed anguish. Jeremy moved from dressing-room to dressing-room, giving what were intended to be pep-talks, but had the overtones of a dirge.

He's lost confidence, Emma thought, as she faced herself in the looking-glass, with Juliet beside her. (No 'star' dressing-room yet; and certainly not in this theatre whose hind parts were as cramped, draughty and unwelcoming as she'd known.) The sun-hot sands of the Vineyard seemed further away than ever; success seemed far away too. In the unshaded light her face looked strange, eyes wide with apprehension, skin pale, lips pressed together as if she were afraid of being sick. "A face that can break anyone's heart." Lance had said that. (Damn Lance, who'd let her down.) At the moment she could see nothing but this staring lost face of a young woman without any particular charm. There was her voice—but this at the moment could be no more than a croak of fear.

She tried it out on Juliet. "How d'you feel?" (A hoarse whisper.)

"Terrible. Naturally. Why ask?"

Emma nodded. She saw Juliet's hand shake as she put eye-black on her lashes. Some of the mascara dropped on to an already made-up cheek and Juliet said, "Sod it." Emma felt a current of fellow-feeling.

The tannoy box on the wall barked into life. "Fifteen

minutes, please."

"Oh, God," said Emma.

"You're not on till ten minutes after curtain up," Juliet said, repairing her cheek.

"That makes it worse."

"You'll be all right. This is your evening, ducky; and if you don't know it you must be out of your mind."

"*My* evening?" Emma said, for by now the idea of Daisy as her great chance had faded, and turned into something nearer to the Inquisition.

"You know it," Juliet said, getting to her feet, and adjusting the belt of her dress, eyes still on the strip of looking-glass. "We all know it."

"And that makes me feel worse too," said Emma.

"Never mind."

Any minute the box would squawk again, and Juliet would go, out down the stone stairs to the draughty wings.

"Wish me luck," Emma said, as if she were drowning.

Juliet smiled, a tight smile as if she were afraid of creasing her make-up. "Of course. All the luck in the world."

The box, its voice like the rasp of a file, announced, "Beginners, please," and Juliet, casting one last look into the glass, went from the room.

Almost time. Emma put on more powder with a trembling hand, then dabbed it off with a tissue. Could she remember her lines? Could she remember her *first* line? Oh God, why do I *do* this? There must be easier ways of torturing yourself, like holding your hand over a naked flame . . .

Your evening, ducky.

But it might not be; nothing was certain. Was it raining? Glad of something to do in these last minutes (could the moments before execution be much worse?) she went to the mean window and pulled the curtain . . . No, the night was dry. A gleam from the front lights of the theatre touched the pavement. Men and women

131

walked there; men and women who had apparently *not* decided to come and see Emma Pride in *The Newcomer*; who were not concerned with her at all.

No more time. As Juliet had done, she stood once more before the looking-glass, seeing what the audience out there would see. Only—I trust—better lighted, not this over-painted image seen apparently by a flash of lightning.

Down the stone seps. Through the heavy doors, labelled NO SMOKING, as if one entered prison. The young A.S.M. in the wings; no sign of Jeremy. The A.S.M. gave her an encouraging smile (nice but all very well for him; he hasn't got to go out there, alone, on to the stage, before all those people.)

And yet, in those few moments before her cue came, she suddenly knew, frightened as she was, that there wasn't anything else she wanted to do. She wanted to show that audience out there what she was made of; the glittering promise that lay ahead.

A few more seconds now. By some command of which she was almost unaware, she controlled the trembling of her hands, and a nerve in her cheek.

Now. The last of the private dark, and into the light.

From the moment she started to speak, the trembling and the sickness within her fell away. She was Daisy, the young American: the accent came as easily as if she'd spoken it all her life. What about the laughs? They were all-important: the quickest signal that the people were in tune with you . . .

Even while you played Daisy to the full, there was a part of your mind which judged the response from the people out there in the dark; which could feel like the vibration on a nerve the momentary inattention, the drop in belief. Nothing now but this: Lance, Ben, Carey and Jonathan were all lost; there was simply this imperative: that she should bind all those people out there to her by some alchemy; that they should go home, speaking of her, haunted by her; that they should all (or almost all) fall in love with her . . . Nothing less.

Why, they had come to the end of the first Act. The curtain sliding down on the stage where she faced Ben after their scene alone . . . whispering down, making a draught with its movement.

The applause? Solid; did it reach that intensity which every artist knew was necessary to call the thing a smash-hit? Not possible yet to know. . . .

The dressing-room once more. Nothing now but the limpness after great effort; Juliet said, "O.K.?" and Brenda looked in from what she called a cupboard under the stairs and said it was splendid; but Emma muttered, "Yes, maybe"; she had no will to talk, and leaned on the shelf before the looking-glass. The person there was changed, because the first Act was done: she had faced the lions in the den and survived. Much as she would have liked a drink, she knew enough of the demands of a performance not to take one. When it was over, when the taut spring could uncoil . . . not yet.

Once more on to the stage. The curtain rose upon her alone. (Was the lighting correct? She could hear some whispering from the wings: would they *shut up*, please.) Her heart thumps were heavy, but she felt a surge of confidence. . . .

Now, Emma knew that things were going well. Laughter came readily; in the moments of pathos, silence held the house as if the people there had been forbidden to move. Nearing the end. And now she had a sensation of rockets going up in her head; or as if she galloped with the wind behind her—

One had to be careful, she warned herself: triumph was for later.

They were coming to the end now. This moment in whatever play—comedy, classic or modern drama—had a sameness about it: unspoken knowledge, here on the stage and out there in the dark that this interval of illusion

133

was nearly done; that whatever magic had been dispersed within these two hours or so would not long after drain away.

Yes, it was done. The last line spoken (by Ben) and right on cue—no hang-ups, thank God—the curtain was slipping down with quiet heaviness; she could feel the wind of it, and even as its golden fringing touched the boards, she could hear the applause. Shivering now, she left the stage, and waited while Mark, Brenda, Juliet and Ben took their bows; then she came running on, even as she'd run over the sands of Martha's Vineyard.

The applause grew more intense; it was like hearing a car's engine accelerate: she bowed, felt the tears behind her eyes (but they mustn't fall); bowed again and heard, amongst the clapping one or two voices raised in a cheer; she heard her name. . . .

They called her back, she didn't know how many times. She could feel as she stood there the waves of love coming towards her—why, nothing but this mattered; no one else; simply those people out there, for whom she'd worked, all her life; for whom she lived.

Shivering, but now with triumph, with the giddiness of achievement, she found her way to the wings, head buzzing with sound and acclaim.

They were all there. Their voices merged into one voice: "Told you so, ducky"; "Well done"; "Very nice, darling"; Brenda kissed her, Ben kissed her with gentle intimacy; she could feel the sweat on his face. Elated, she looked about for Jeremy. Had he been there for all of the play, or had he followed his habit and walked the streets, only appearing at the end?

She stood before him, expectant, draped in glory.

"Yes, darling," he said; "it was all right."

"All *right*?"

"I saw it," he said, as if she asked him the question. "I heard that nice reception. Very pleasant—"

"Pleasant!"

"You have to remember, darling, that this is only a beginning. A *good* beginning, I grant you. Don't want to prick your balloon. But we've got to get to London. Like I said, it's a beginning."

Emma stared at him. For a moment she could have slapped his face. Then the logic of the theatre took hold: what he said was true. She had a long way to go; one night when the gods touched you on the shoulder was not a promise of endless triumph. But it *had* been a night of good fortune; no one was going to take that from her.

"We're going to celebrate," she said. "We're going to celebrate on *me*." Never had she been more sure that she must be the giver, the one from whose pockets golden coins dropped; if there was still a long way to travel, all the more reason for making the most of tonight.

When she faced herself in the harsh-lighted looking-glass again and wiped make-up from her face, it could have been another person she watched there: someone who had been through the fire; the fears over, leaving only a light-headed exhaustion which was more pleasant than vigour.

"*Now*," she said, "I can have a drink . . . who's for champagne?"

"I guess we all are," Juliet said. "But mind your bank account."

"To hell with banks. I'm going to make money. Did you *hear* them tonight?"

A small smile from Juliet as she too dropped smeared tissues into the waste-paper basket. "You can never say To hell with banks. There's always tax at the end of the tunnel—"

"Oh, blow tax."

"You can't say that. They hunt you down like bloodhounds. Like the Mounties. They always get their tax."

"This is a *good* moment, for heaven's sake." Emma was beginning to lose her temper. "Why does everyone want to spoil it?"

"They don't, ducky. Simply that being—let's say—a *little* older than you, I've learned some of the things you haven't. And tax is one of them."

"Tonight's not for learning."

"Maybe not. But one day will be."

Word of mouth spread quickly, fuelled by notices in the local papers, and one in the *Daily Telegraph*, which Emma had read at least eighteen times: "*Fine New Play by Guy Forster*—Last night saw the best of this playwright's work, and a personal triumph for Emma Pride as Daisy; Miss Pride has hovered on the fringe of success for some time, but this marks her breakthrough to larger things. She has a quality of pathos mixed with humour, and her voice is irresistible. The rest of the cast . . ." It took her some time to get to the rest of the cast: though when she did she was pleased to see that Ben had his share of admiration, not least for his looks: "Keatsian, fair young Adonis . . ." These Ben accepted with quiet amusement; a wry mockery. "Anyone would think I was part of some ghastly beauty contest."

The tour, mostly triumphant, moved on, punctuated by the Sunday journeys which offered few comforts (so soon after the war trains were spartan); and, when they reached the new theatre—in Manchester or Cardiff—the problems of lighting and scenery and the occasional performance which failed to catch fire.

One couldn't, Emma found, keep that first pitch of elation throughout a whole tour, but mostly the audiences gave her the response she so much needed, and had now come to expect. She was drinking less; only the need to sit up late after the performance and talk through the small hours stayed with her.

Only two developments touched her with misgiving. First, beyond a telegram of congratulation, no word had come from Lance. In the end, not being to help herself, she had telephoned him.

"All right," she said, "I'm doing fine: I'm God's gift to the theatre. But I want you to see me. Damn it, you are my agent—"

"And a lot of other people's too."

"But I am—let's say—at least a little different from the rest?"

She heard a sigh on the wire. "Yes—oh, yes; quite a lot different. But I can't come now."

"You could come up for the weekend. Catch the Saturday night performance, go back on Sunday. *That* wouldn't interfere with your work, would it?"

"No . . . not with my work."

"You mean Marguerite?"

"She is my wife. And I have a son. We're going to Paris for the weekend."

"Oh, isn't that splendid," said Emma, putting the receiver down.

The other perplexing circumstance was Ben. Though he didn't fail in tenderness towards her, though he played as well as ever in their scenes together, he did not make love to her again; and he never sat up late with her after the performance was done; he kissed her and went to his room. He looked sad when he left her, and she couldn't reproach him, for love was there in the face which, though beautiful, looked thin and pale, drenched with exhaustion.

But at the performance the next night she played as well as she ever had; the audience rose to her, and she thought, "*This* is what being an actress is—riding over the top of everything, and I can do it; I don't need anyone; I don't need Lance; I don't even need Ben; I'm me, myself, and this is my world: I can *do* it."

When she met Jeremy in the corridor backstage he paused and said, "Thought you'd like to know—I'm very pleased with you. If you can go on like this—"

"Of course I can go on like this!"

He smiled, a little dryly. "Hold it. I'm just saying that

you're being a very good girl, both on and off the stage. And I think we've got a hit here—"

"We *have* got a hit! We can't lose—"

"We've the West End to come."

"The West End! What's that?"

"You know what that is. Everything to play for. Make or break. Becher's Brook."

"We'll be the best thing that's hit them since what the last best thing was."

"Trust so. But don't stop being a good girl."

She had no intention of it. She'd got into her stride, and the world was before her, despite Lance, despite Ben. Even when Jeremy became dissatisfied with the pace of a scene, and called a rehearsal early in the morning, watching them with moody distrust, as if they'd never played this scene before, Emma remained calm. And when Jeremy said, "I don't want to depress anyone—" it was Juliet who interrupted: "But you do, darling. We've all done our damndest; *and* had what in my childhood was called a rousing reception: actors (and actresses) need praise, or hadn't you heard? We need some warmth to help us face the cold winds when they come."

Even this, Emma let go past her. It was Jeremy who looked as if he was wondering how cold the winds might be.

Brighton was the last stop before London. The town always lifted Emma's heart: the mixture of elegance and vulgarity; the end of season spaces on the sea-front; the turning and glittering sea itself.

Sometimes she would rise early and walk along the shingle of the morning shore, where this October sea had the delicacy of unstained fabric, lipping the stones and the scattered drifts of sand. One morning she stood there, coat about her shoulders for the air was chill, watching the calm but steady incoming tide. The multiple blues of the water, the sky an acid green, misted with saffron. The two piers marked their territory out into the sea.

No one about save herself, and some way distant a man raking the rubbish left on the shore. Far out to sea the small image of a ship just discernible. Flutter and lisp of water, and the dazzle of morning that might perhaps turn to grey this afternoon but just now was rainbow-coloured, feathered with gaudy light. . . . So quiet, that enormous sea, as if it could never drive its waters high in spray above the stone bastion of the front; never wreck ships or men: a whispering, deceiving quiet. . . .

The man who scavenged on the shore moved slowly towards her. What was it like to work like that, scraping rubbish, alone on the early shore? Not to have the world before you; to be young and with beauty and loved?

But these things would not last. The old man with his workman's clothes seemed now like a dark bird on the brilliance of the morning, an omen of dread things.

She turned her eyes from him. Here she was, Emma Pride, her name in lights on the façade of the theatre; young, loved, to be envied. . . .

But the morning had briefly turned sour. It was as if a hand had touched her shoulder, a voice whispered, like the sea, in her ear. The beauty of the morning had an ache at its heart, the loveliness spoke of passing things, of a pinnacle that would never be attained, of the loneliness which in spite of all triumph, all companionship, followed you like a shadow. Was there an element within her which would in the end fail and falter; was barred from the final gate of paradise?

She saw how she must look at this moment, the figure of a woman on the shore, looking out to the tamed sea; coat about her shoulders; anonymous, slight, not tall; above all, alone. . . .

Of a sudden the sea appeared not a thing of beauty but a force having menace, its depths which lay beyond the sun's light; those dark deeps an analogy of the unknown deeps within herself . . . Had she not read that the depths of the sea were black with a night darkness, ice-cold, and no man knew what life lay there; only the sunken ships and the drowned knew that place, the rusting eaten remains of structure and men. . . .

She turned away. She did not look again at the scavenger, nor turn to see the peacock brilliance of the morning sea. Her steps came loud on the shingle like the crash of falling coins, and this sound too was lonely. The shingle sloped upwards, and she was out of breath when she reached the promenade. There she turned and looked once more behind her . . .

A deserted shore, except for the scavenger, and the wide brilliance of the sea.

Before they had finished the week in Brighton, the first shadow came.

To begin with, Emma paid no attention: too much was happening: she had no time for any vagaries of her body. The delay could be accounted for in so many ways: overwork, excitement, the continual change of place and air. It was nothing to worry about; nothing at all. She mustn't let her mind dwell on it, for nothing must get in the way of the play and her performance.

Then one night she woke at half-past two (exactly by her clock) and fear bit into her, like an injection of fluid which runs through all the veins.

What if it *was* so? It might be. Now in the silence of the early hours, with no company, no action, no human voice close by, she remembered Ben: those two easy occasions of love-making; she remembered her exclamation, half in anger, that she knew her own body.

Did she?

Well, of course not; no one did; no one could be sure.

She sat up, shivering. Suppose it was true? *Now*, when they were soon to open in London; when she'd had the best notices ever, such words as one only dreamed of.

And the whole thing could turn to ash because of those

140

easy moments of love with Ben. . . .

No. Nothing could be as cruel as that; not after the way I've worked; not after waiting so long. . . .

Perhaps it wasn't so. Perhaps not. Why, it could easily be all right . . . Sitting there in bed, she felt the full flood of relief, as if she'd been given certainty. This run of good fortune could continue, unflawed. Like the end of toothache, the tide of relief coming in.

Except that uncertainty remained.

She needed to talk to someone; she needed help badly; she thought she had never so much been in need of help. . . .

But there wasn't anyone. You didn't know whom you could trust in the theatre: theatre people could be splendid and kind and generous, but they *talked*, for goodness' sake: how they talked; gossip was their natural coinage; no one—could they?—could resist it.

So what, then? If she *were* pregnant? Abortion at that time was illegal; she'd heard of women who'd had them, but she had no idea how to go about it. And wouldn't there be a risk? She'd heard of a young actress who'd died, for heaven's sake. . . .

Perhaps she wasn't as late as she thought; where was her diary? Shivering, she got out of bed and scrabbled through her handbag. She found the diary at last and turned the pages, her throat dry. Monday to Monday, *one* week; Monday to Monday *two* weeks; hell, now she'd turned two pages at once. . . .

Could she pray about it? She felt doubtful that God, who had always seemed to her remote, august and difficult to please, would pay attention in such a case; but one could always try. She muttered, Please let it be all right; please, please . . . I won't take any more risks if it can be all right now.

At rehearsal next morning (Jeremy despite his usual outward calm was showing pre-West End nerves by picking small flaws in the performance) Emma was held

141

in a fog both of too many sleeping pills and this continuing anxiety. While Jeremy discussed with Mark some emphasis on one of his lines, Emma sat on the floor, head down, lost.

"Silent, ducky?" Brenda asked.

"Thinking," Emma said. Could she, when they were alone, speak to Brenda? The temptation was strong, but doubt persisted. Suppose it was a false alarm, did she want Brenda to know that she'd made love to Ben, and feared she was pregnant?

The answer was No.

It was, she supposed, this deep abstraction that prevented her from paying full attention to Ben. Indeed, she had a desire to keep her eyes from Ben.

But suddenly while he was playing a scene with Brenda and Mark, Ben sat on a chair with his head in his hands.

Everything stopped. Even Emma's preoccupation for a moment stopped. Jeremy walked up with his loping stride; Brenda became at once solicitous, the epitome of a maternal woman ready with bandages, Emma thought; Jeremy said, "All right, old chap?"

Ben raised his head. His face was dust-pale and glistened with sweat. "Shall be," he said.

"You don't look it, dear boy," said Jeremy sharply.

"Giddy for a moment," Ben muttered, wiping the sweat from his face. "It'll go. Sorry."

The A.S.M. had produced a glass of water. "I'm afraid the bar isn't open," he said.

"Doesn't matter." Ben sipped the water. "I'm not allowed drink anyway, because of these pills."

"What a terrible bore," said Mark.

Emma stood still. Of a sudden the triumphant cavalcade of this tour, so near to its climax, had come to a disturbing halt. She felt a tide of misfortune coming towards her cancelling all the glitter that she'd known.

She heard the confusion of voices: "Doctor . . ." "No, I don't want a doctor. Just rest for a little: I'll be all

142

right." "Anyone can feel ill during rehearsal. In fact *every*one feels ill during rehearsal. I knew a girl once . . ." No one, Emma thought, spoke the words that must be in all their minds, that Ben had been ill before.

By the time they broke for lunch, Ben had, it seemed, somewhat recovered. "Sorry," he said; "sorry to cause all this trouble. I'm all right now."

Was he?

Though after the lunch break Ben was back on his feet, playing as well as before, the question stayed with her.

On the last night before London, after the final performance, after the confusion of dressing-room congratulations, the mixture of gin, make-up and hot lights, Emma slipped away with Ben.

The night was cool but fine; street lamps cast a dry gleam on the roads as the cloudless moon made on the sea. A sea-town by night, she thought, contained some mystery. She took Ben by the hand and they walked down to the pebbled shore. The harsh drawn breath of sea on shingle was louder than the traffic of the town which—with the last cheers of the audience and the lighted stage—seemed lost behind them.

Was she going to speak to him of her own fear? She didn't know. Words from *The Newcomer* still went through her head; she was not yet free from the part of Daisy. Here, it seemed, time was suspended. There was simply herself and Ben, both under a shadow.

Ben put an arm about her as if to protect her from the night wind which smelt of the sea. He kissed her cheek and said, "Why did you want to come here? You usually want lots of talk and lights and drink."

She drew herself closer to him, glad of the warmth of his body. "Tonight I wanted to get away from them."

"Just to be with me?"

"That's right."

He looked at the dark mystery of water which had no horizon. "Sometimes I'm afraid of the sea."

Between the wash of waves, Emma thought, their voices were hushed, as if they trod enemy country. "Afraid?"

"All round the world; the oceans and the sharks—so much depth of water."

"There's more water than land."

"I know." He tightened his arm about her. "I'm glad you're here. One needs someone. There has to be someone; love somewhere."

"Oh, yes, there has to be love. But—"

"But?" he asked, turning to look at her.

No, it wasn't the time to speak. Not yet. Here they had a quiet comradeship in the sea-scented dark; it seemed that all problems could be solved in such quiet escape; perhaps fear could be lost too.

She said, "I was thinking—about you. If you're all right."

"Oh . . . yes; I think so."

"No more than that?" Their voices were still hushed. "Aren't you sure?"

His face, looking to the dark sea, had some expression she couldn't fathom. "Just that sometimes I feel so suddenly exhausted. And at night I get into these tremendous sweats—have to change everything and dry myself."

"Have you been to the doctor?"

"Oh—what doctor? We move at the end of every week."

"You can't be seriously ill, Ben; you can't be."

He kissed her once more. "No, of course not."

But she wasn't entirely comforted. London was to come, and she hadn't spoken to him; and the threat was still there.

Chapter Eleven

On her return to London Emma made for her flat. It met her with its usual silence and a smell of tired carpet. Her mother had put a small bunch of chrysanthemums in a vase; some of the petals had already fallen. "God, I hate *arriving*," Emma said; "there ought to be some way of getting out of it." None of the pile of waiting letters looked of much interest: coloured postcards from friends abroad in the sun; more menacing, envelopes marked Inland Revenue or Electricity. She wouldn't open them yet.

Here in the quiet room, her fear returned. She wasn't going to count the number of days; that would only make things worse. She had simply to hope. She read the note from her mother: "... so delighted to hear of your success, darling; you must be so terribly happy; I've put some things in the fridge, but of course I hope you'll come to us—the children are longing to see you: Carey asks for you about every ten minutes ..."

Emma sat on the bed with the note in her hand. Clearly she remembered the night when she'd rung her mother and insisted on speaking to Carey. Oh yes; she wanted Carey's love. Simply that, just at this moment Carey's love wasn't the most important thing: she had to be sure she wasn't pregnant; she had to be sure (as far as one could ever be sure in the theatre) that *The Newcomer* would repeat its success in the West End: London audiences were different; more sophisticated, more demanding, the highest and most dangerous fence of all . . .

And she had to be sure about Ben.

She thought of the possibilities open. She could, of course, go and see her mother and when the children were out of the way tell her of what she feared about herself . . .

Instantly an image of her mother's response, which would be fluttery and near-hysterical, made this unwelcome. No, she couldn't talk to her mother . . .

Before she'd unpacked she took bottle and glass and poured herself a drink. There; that was better; the sliding warmth touched a nerve somewhere in her midriff, dulling the edge of fear.

She drank easily and quickly; took a second and a third. Oh yes; much better now; she felt powerful, not afraid of anything—or *nearly* unafraid . . . A fourth? It could be a mistake, but she didn't want to lose this sense of good fortune and high spirits . . .

When the door-bell rang she was sitting, tousle-headed, glass in hand, her suitcases unpacked.

She rose and felt herself sway (damn; supposing it was Jeremy, with some new idea for rehearsal tomorrow?), steadied herself with one hand by the wall, while the other held the glass.

As she opened the door she had the impression of a small animal bounding in and jumping at her knees.

Carey.

Carey, with Emma's mother behind her, and Jonathan standing aloof, expectant, in shorts and a blazer.

Carey began to shout. "Mama! Mama! Carey loves Mama! Mama's come back! Can I stay with you? Want to stay with you."

Oh God, Emma said to herself; I can't take this now; I can't give what's needed; I haven't got it . . .

Carey's voice persisted. Emma took a step backwards, swayed, and put the glass down with care on to a small

146

table.

She said, "'Lo, darling; don't make too much noise; Mama's got a headache."

By now they were all in the sitting-room, and Susan, Emma guessed, since she had her shrewd-look on, was pretty clear about the drink. Jonathan, as if he'd been instructed, said, "Hullo, Mama; have you had a nice time?"

"Marvellous time, darling; Mama's had a sim-simply marvellous time; just now I've got a headache." She sat heavily on the sofa and Carey began to crawl on her, trying to kiss her with wet appreciation. "Carey, darling, just leave Mama alone for a minute... Just give me a chance to *breathe*, please..." She made an attempt to move Carey away, but Carey persisted, saying "Tickle Mama; make Mama *laugh*..."

"I said *stop*."

"Emma, darling, you shouldn't speak to the child like that; she's only—"

"I know she's 'only'; I just can't take it now."

Carey let go and moved a little distance off, pink-faced, legs just reaching the edge of the seat, mouth beginning to square.

"Oh *please*," Emma said; "please don't cry. I was just trying to tell you; Mama isn't well; she's got a *headache*; can't you understand?"

"Carey loves Mama.'

"Oh... Jonathan, take her into the kitchen and find something for her to eat."

"Don't want to go into the kitchen! Want to stay here with you—"

"Darling—*please*."

Jonathan took Carey by the hand, without any enthusiasm. As the kitchen door closed her voice came: "Don't want the kitchen; don't want..."

Susan looked at her daughter, "How *could* you? She's been longing to see you—"

147

"Please, Ma, *shut up*. I didn't know you were coming; I didn't know you were going to bring Carey and Jonathan—"

"They wanted it to be a surprise. Carey said—"

Emma covered her face with her hands. "I don't want to hear what Carey said—"

"You wanted to hear her on the telephone at one o'clock in the morning."

"That was then; now's different."

"Darling, I don't understand. You've had the most wonderful tour, and then you come back here and shout at Carey . . . What's the matter?"

The temptation to tell her was strong; Emma resisted it. "Pre-West End nerves."

"Is that all?" Absently Susan was plunging through her large handbag in search. "I thought I'd brought a little present but I seem to have left it behind." She suddenly looked at her daughter, and Emma turned away. Susan might not command great intelligence, but she *was* her mother, and mothers had perceptions which went beyond intelligence. "You don't look well," Susan went on. "Oh—I know you've been drinking—that's obvious; but you've lost weight—"

"Tours—" Emma muttered. "Different theatres; travelling on Sundays in trains that haven't recovered from the war . . ."

"Nothing else?"

"No. No."

Susan didn't look as if she believed this; but before she could say more, Jonathan and Carey returned, Carey's face marked with tears and chocolate. "I found some biscuits," Jonathan said.

As she looked at the children, she felt some deep apprehension as if she'd dreamed some disaster which had happened to them. She made a movement towards Carey, but Carey turned away. "Don't want you," she said, "Don't *want* you." She went to her grandmother and struggled

148

on to her lap, as if sanctuary were needed somewhere.

"I'm sorry," Emma said, "oh God, I'm sorry; I didn't mean to be angry. But I feel terrible, and worried about a lot of things..." No good talking like this to Carey. Carey, who so short a time ago had been the only person whose love she needed. But now... Dangers and anxieties bound her in, and she could only see Carey as from the other side of these, knowing that sometimes later the backlash would come; that she would regret with anguish what she had done this afternoon.

Before the opening of *The Newcomer* Emma telephoned my father, who was at home. (I was at school.) Marguerite, Lance said, was out; she was working on designs for a play at the Old Vic. Lance was waiting for a telephone call.

The gods, Emma reflected, were sometimes on your side.

"I need to see you," she said.

"O.K. Grab yourself a cab and come along. So long as we're not going to argue as to why I didn't come North—"

No, Emma said; she wasn't going to do that.

She arrived at the Hampstead house within the hour. Lance greeted her with a warmth which seemed to her a degree or two less than usual. She glanced round the room, with its evidence of Marguerite and Lance himself; the room of two people who knew when, not so much the next meal, but the next planned piece of living was coming from: despite the exigencies of the theatre, an ordered life. Emma looked at it with brooding envy.

Lance said, "You need to leave that look of quiet desperation in the wings, darling. Daisy's a sunny girl."

Emma let this go by, and Lance, sitting himself firmly in an armchair, looked a little puzzled. She said, sitting opposite him, "I've not come to talk about Daisy."

"All right, fine. No Daisy. You seem to have done

149

pretty well by her, anyhow."

Emma said, "When does Rick come home from school?"

"About half-past six, I believe. He's caught up in a school play—"

"He's not *acting*?"

Lance smiled. "No, thank God. He's got a gift for painting and he's helping with the scenery. If helping's the word."

"Then I've time to talk to you?"

"Well—sure." There was a question in his voice.

Emma looked again round the room, as if it might offer help. "I've simply got to talk to you."

"That sounds like trouble." Lance's voice suggested that trouble was not what he most wanted.

She said, "When people say they want to talk to you, it's nearly always trouble.'

"Um," said Lance, shifting his position in the chair. "One of the reasons, Emma dear, why I didn't come North to see you was that I promised Marguerite—"

"I don't care what you promised Marguerite. This isn't anything to do with her. I'm not asking you for anything except—"

"Except what?"

She faced him in the comfortable room. "I think I'm pregnant."

Lance closed his eyes. "Oh, no. Not *now*." And then, "Who?"

Nothing for it, Emma thought, but to tell him—perhaps he'd already guessed. "Ben. Ben Hardy."

"Oh dear, oh dear, oh dear. Does he know?"

Emma shook her head. "I tried to tell him. But it just wasn't the time. He'd been ill—"

"Not as ill as you're going to be, my darling—"

"It wouldn't be any good, telling him. I've got to do this on my own."

Lance had risen from his chair and was pacing the

150

room. "Could you marry him?"

She hugged herself, as if she were cold. "No. Not possibly. He's too young. And what on earth would we do—he and I, with a family? No, it wouldn't work."

"Then—"

"I can't mess up this play. It's the best chance I've had. Everything going right . . ."

"Have you told anyone else?"

"No."

"So why me?"

Emma looked at him. "You know why. I trust you. There *isn't* anyone else."

Her eyes followed him as he visited different corners of the room; absently picked up an ornament from a table. He said at last, "There has to be someone else."

"You mean you won't help me?"

"Help you! How, in heavens name?"

"If I *am* pregnant—"

"You're not sure?"

"There's still a hope things might be all right: I've been having hot baths and jumping off tables and drinking gin; it's supposed to—"

Lance gave an exclamation, half pity, half exasperation. "Oh . . . honestly. Emma.'" He flung himself back into his chair. "You seem to have been remarkably careless in this . . . encounter."

She looked at him as if he were a master who rebuked her for not learning her lesson. She said, "It was—unexpected."

He said dryly, "It very often is. Ben's a young man, and looks pretty innocent. But you—you've been married, had two children . . ." He shrugged, as if reason were an implement of no value here. "Are you in love with him?"

"I don't know. He's sweet and loving and very beautiful: it was reassuring and—"

"Yes; you can skip the details; I can imagine them well

enough. I'm sure Ben is all you say, but if you go to bed with every young actor with looks who's reassuring and kind, you know where that'll get you, don't you?"

"It isn't every young actor; it's Ben."

"Plenty of time for you to meet other Bens."

"Lance, I don't want a lecture."

"I'm not lecturing; I'm only giving a general warning."

"I don't want that either. If you can't help me—won't help me—"

Lance clasped his hands between his knees and looked at them with absent interest. "I didn't exactly say that—"

"Yes, you did."

"What I mean is this. If you *are* pregnant, I'll do what I can. Whatever that is. I'm not a doctor, God knows; but I daresay I can make some contacts. *If* you have an abortion, if that's what you truly want—"

"I don't know about want. There's just no other way."

"I'd suggest you think about it, long and hard."

"I have. I have."

He made a gesture with one shoulder. "One thing I do know: it'll cost money."

"Oh . . . *money*. Does money have to come into everything?"

Lance made a grimace. "It seems so. And if, as I suspect neither you nor Ben have enough—I'll, let's say, subsidize you."

She looked at him, beaten, grateful. "But," Lance went on, "it'll be the last time."

"You don't think I'm going to get into this kind of mess again?"

"No—maybe not; but I mean more than that. We were lovers once; that's over. What's over too—or must be—is this father protector role. After this you've got to make it on your own."

She hugged herself again as if his words had chilled her. "You mean you're going to ditch me entirely? No more Emma—never at *all*?"

"Oh—" she caught again exasperation and pity. "Nothing's as iron-fast as that. But you could be a danger to everything, not least me and Marguerite. Marguerite's too good to lose; I'm not going to risk that. I guess I'll always be around. But in ordinary friendship—not more."

"That makes me feel lonely."

Lance looked at her with an upward glance and a slight smile. "Oh, Emma my sweet, you'll never be lonely. You never can be. Perhaps that's your problem. There'll be other Bens."

"Are you jealous?"

He smiled and made a sudden movement in the chair. "Oh ... jealous. No, I'm not jealous. Except that nothing, I suppose, is lost: we have our memories; they leave scars: everything does. Let's say that your dalliance with Ben—or whatever it was—marks a turning-point. Whatever may or may not be the result, it changes things."

"Why does everything change?"

He looked at her again, she thought, with compassion. "For you, Emma, darling; things will always change. All I can wish for you is that you get all you deserve as an actress—that nothing happens to spoil it."

"An actress, yes; but what about me? *Me*, Lance?"

"You ..." His glance remained on her. "I'll make a change in a life's habits and pray."

It must have been about here that I returned from school in my green blazer, covered in paint and filled with excitement. I had no idea then what had been going on; I saw merely my father, whom I expected and Emma, whom I did not; but they were adults, out of my sphere. I chattered on about the school play (*The Tempest* which I didn't understand except that it had a shipwreck) and how I'd spilled a paint pot, and how the mistress who took us for drama had been *very* cross. . . .

153

They met this with contrived interest, and my father told me to go and wash before I touched anything. It is only now with hindsight that I'm aware of an air of strain in the room, and Emma's look of one who has been overthrown.

The Newcomer opened in London's West End the third week of October. The first night had a gleam of expectation; advance rumours had spoken of triumph. So soon after the war, dress was muted, but a sprinkling of evening gowns, expensive scent and dinner jackets gave to the auditorium, even before the play had begun, a touch of celebration.

The dressing-rooms were not much better than those on tour: West End glamour stopped short of the front of the house. But Emma had her own, for which she was grateful. She could prepare for the evening's trial without having to talk to Brenda (too friendly) or Juliet (too sharp). She had only to respond to Jeremy as he swanned in saying, "I know—we all know—you'll be splendid, darling. Remember *every*thing I've said." (Emma looked at him blankly; she could, she thought, remember nothing at all he had said, ever.) "Guy's very pleased with you," Jeremy went on. So's everyone who loves you." She thought, Who are they? but didn't say it. "Not scared, are you, ducky?" he asked.

"Of course I'm scared."

"Ah, yes, well: West End nerves." He kissed her, taking care not to spoil her make-up. "They'll dissolve when you get on stage."

She said, "How's Ben?"

"Ben's fine."

When he'd gone she faced her image alone. More than West End nerves, if he only knew. Her conversation with Lance stayed with her; she didn't know yet what the outcome would be.

With an effort she made herself travel into the part of

154

Daisy once more, after so many times—but the first time for these people here in London, for the critics who would sharpen their pens in the national papers tomorrow. For Reggie Graves and Guy; Lance and Marguerite ... All of them waiting there, for the play. For her.

Never mind the large question mark that hung over her, never mind Lance, or even Carey weeping at her rejection.

All that must be, for this present, forgotten: now was nothing but the play ...

Fifteen minutes ... Beginners, please ... Ten minutes, Miss Pride ...

No more time.

Very early on, she knew it was going well. The silence and warmth that reached her from the darkness out there, the laughter with its edge of conspiracy, as if she and they were in some plot together: these things told her that she had command of them. Not just a play for the out-of-town places, but a play for London, the capital, where she needed to be.

The end was noisy, as noisy as any she could remember; she was tearful as they stormed at her with applause, as they handed her flowers; as Jeremy joined them on the stage (Guy Forster would never take a curtain call: by the time he'd crossed the boards, he said, the temperature—whatever that might be—would have dropped to zero). As Jeremy joined them she clasped his hand, felt the sweat on it mixed with her own, and for this moment of triumph forgot all else.

Impossible not to sit up and wait for the reviews. They sat, drinking champagne and coffee and smoking cigarettes; all of them, even Ben, whose face, Emma thought, had taken colour from the excitement of the evening. Sometime after three o'clock the A.S.M. came streaking in with the papers, his face alight.

"They're splendid," he gasped, and they all fell upon

155

them, greedy, their hands shaking.

Emma read them carefully while her hands steadied. There was another side to triumph, she found; the quiet after storm, the fullness of achievement.

There wasn't a bad notice, not one—a cautionary word here and there about the play itself; or the rest of the cast; but for herself a continual sound like the blowing of trumpets; the entry into a golden lighted place, where voices chanted 'Emma Pride! Emma Pride!' like an opera chorus. Extraordinary the sensuous pleasure of reading one's own name, in praise. She read the sentences until she knew them by heart: "Quality not found, in my experience for many years ... Emma Pride is rare, exciting, unforgettable ... She takes the part and misses none of its subtleties, none of its power or humour ... Like watching a skater whom you feel must fall because he turns and twists and such heights, but he doesn't, he lands safely, every time ... *Welcome, Emma! We love you!* (Not one of the 'top' papers, but gratifying just the same. People would read it.)

It was all there. Won. This round, at any rate. And where might she not go from here?

Not till she returned, in the small hours of the morning, to her room, did the question mark come back.

She made herself undress and go to bed, where she lay awake till light thinned the dark.

For two more days the play continued in its triumph. Though she was still under threat, though she knew that (if it had to be) a late abortion could be a dangerous thing, Emma drew from the applause and excitement strength to keep anxiety at bay. It would be all right. Everything was too good; the gods were with her.

And then the evening came.

It began like any other. She arrived at the theatre, taking one deep glance of pleasure at her name, glowing now, from the façade (*my* name), went to her dressing-room, having been greeted by the stage-door-keeper with his mark of admiration and collected her mail (there was always mail now: old friends, lost for some years, suddenly came to life and sent cards and letters of congratulation). Her dresser who was a small cockney woman of sixty or so was moving with appropriate speed, preparing Emma's changes of clothes.

"Nice dry evening, Miss; seems to be a lovely house tonight." Mrs Crashaw, the dresser, had been a musical comedy actress many years ago and knew all the right phrases. She did not however, Emma sometimes reflected, know when not to voice them.

"Fine," Emma said.

"Friend of mine, an old trouper like myself, was out front last night, and she enjoyed it ever so much. Said it was the best show she'd seen since *Trelawny of the Wells*."

"Fine," said Emma again, stripping open the envelopes.

"O'course she's a bit older than me."

"Of course," Emma said absently.

Mrs Crashaw hung up Emma's dress for the first Act and gave it an admiring, even protective sweep of her hand. "Ever so pretty this: suits you no end."

Emma said "Mm," as she read a letter written in a large enthusiastic hand: "Darling—how *wonderful*—Freddie" (who the hell was Freddie?) "and I are absolutely thrilled; can't wait to see you again and talk—" Think *I* can, Emma observed to herself, seeing the signature 'Muriel' and recalling a plump young woman last seen in Scarborough.

"Lot of trouble in the wardrobe room tonight, quite a to-do; Miss Juliet's change for Act Two not back from the wash, or not properly ironed, or something . . . you know how it is."

If she did, Emma thought, she didn't want to hear about it. She must learn to shut out the sound of Mrs

Crashaw's voice, while appearing to give polite attention. She felt a trace of guilt, however, when she didn't listen, for Mrs Crashaw was lonely; her husband had died ten years ago, and her life now was in the powder, sweat and scent-smelling dressing-rooms, and in the actresses who occupied them. She had endless stories of these occupants, and strong likes and dislikes: "Treat you like dirt some of them, as if you were some sort of skivvy; I shall never forget when so-and-so played here..."

It seemed however that she took to Emma; she called her 'love', and chattered maternally, her talk sprinkled with compliments.

One could, though, have too many of these. Especially when, to play Daisy to perfection, she had to bury the growing dread...

"Um," she said abstractedly to the continuing talk; and "Yes, how awful." This was a safe bet with Mrs Crashaw whose stories were nearly always about disaster, rudeness or death.

At last Mrs Crashaw moved on saying, "I'll call back love, when I've done the rest of me chores."

"You do that," Emma said.

Blessed quiet as the door shut. Now she could face her image in the glass, thinking only of Daisy. Putting away the fear. I *am* an actress, after all; I'm on the way up, and it's going to be all right—

It was, it seemed to her afterwards, just at this point that her door flew open with scarcely a knock to herald it.

Jeremy. Looking as he seldom did: dishevelled, off course and breathing fast.

"Ducky—"

"What's up?"

"Ben's up."

"*Ben?*" The first little drop in her heart, the first fall from the high tower.

"You'll have to play with his understudy."

"Oh God—"

158

"Now, don't make a fuss. You know him; we've rehearsed with him; he's all right—"

"He's hell: what about Ben?"

"Same as before. He just keeled over. But worse this time. We got an ambulance and he's gone straight to hosp."

Emma was on her feet. "Why didn't someone *tell* me?"

"No time, ducky. And it was important to get him there fast. Anyway, there was nothing you could have done."

"I could have spoken to him, for goodness' sake."

"Don't think he'd've known, darling. He seemed a long way off."

"But I didn't even say good-bye!"

"Don't think it's time for good-bye. Just that he's ill. The hosp'll get him better. That's what they're for."

She faced him in the small heated claustrophobic dressing-room. "*Why* did this have to happen? Why, when things were going so well?"

"That's always when things happen," Jeremy said dryly.

"I can't play without Ben!"

"Now, come. It's bad luck, but—"

"Bad *luck*. He must be so . . ." What was he? She could remember his voice: *I shall love you always—always . . . How long is that, d'you think?* Ben by whom she might be pregnant. . . .

"Poor lad," Jeremy said. "It's tough. But just for the present, ducky, you've got to put him out of your mind."

"I can't."

"Yes, you can. You know you can. Johnny" (Johnny was the Front of House Manager) "will have to make that daunting little thrust between the curtains and say that Ben Hardy's indisposed, etc. They'll be sorry. But it isn't Ben they've come to see; it's you. The play's all right, and the rest of the cast are all right, but just now you're the talk of the town. Or most of it."

She looked at him. It was true: all the things you'd hoped for came at the wrong time. Jeremy, who guarded his words, saying this . . . But perhaps he said it only to bolster her courage because he needed her.

She felt herself shiver. Ben, in a hospital bed, surrounded by the clinical world he detested; entirely removed from the lighted counterfeit of the stage.

Jeremy was standing there, as if he waited for judgement.

She said tiredly, "All right. I'll play with Paul. I'll do my best."

Harassed but relieved he kissed her and was gone.

No good thinking beyond the next two hours. For those two hours she would reproduce the enchantment; she would persuade those people already gathered out there that she *was* Daisy, and that nothing beyond the confines of the stage existed, not fear, not illness, not the final darkness which waited for them all . . .

Death walks very close to Ben.

Chapter Twelve

Ben barely recovered consciousness. He lay in the large London hospital, his beauty still apparent, but almost drained of colour and life. In the long ward his curtains were mostly drawn, and quietly but persistently nurses, housemen and doctors clustered there.

A tall man, brown from a Bermuda sun, was allowed within the curtains. He had the look of mixed bewilderment, guilt and fear which a father who had given little overt love to his son must feel at his son's death.

The hurrying and busy hospital staff paid him small attention. If they knew that he had scarcely seen Ben since he went into the profession of the theatre, they made no sign. Not theirs to judge. Ben's father found the tears coming to his eyes as he saw his son, bound like some innocent captive by the wires of drips and blood transfusion. And none of these, they had told him, were enough; they were trying all they could, but... Acute lymphoblastic leukaemia—which Ben had been suffering from—was nearly always fatal. He heard the difficult words: leukaemic cells replacing the normal cells in the bone marrow ... anaemia producing excessive fatigue ... final and fatal shortage of red blood cells....

When he asked how Ben had been able to go on with his acting career, they spoke of remission; the use of powerful drugs (again the words meant nothing to him). Cause? No one knew. Except that exposure to radiation ... the survivors of Hiroshima and Nagasaki... But

Ben had not been one of these; this was merely the meaningless malignancy of some casual and inhuman power.

He moved away from the curtained bed, for he couldn't too long stand and look at that sculptured face which didn't belong to the world any more; the face of a young man who had once played with him on a nursery floor; on the sands of some summer place, crying, "Daddy! Daddy! Look at my castle; come and look . . ." Had he gone?

That was lost; guilt and regret stood with him now like dark attendant angels. Please God they would go away . . . indeed the sooner he could get out of here the better. Maybe it was a shameful thing, but he didn't want to stand by that bedside and watch the inevitable and terrible process of death. And the death of his own son . . . *Ben*, whom he'd once held in his arms, and later quarrelled with—or rather chosen to quarrel with, for Ben had little animosity within him. The boy he'd pushed on one side, as it were, for the sake of Deborah, his new wife, who was waiting for him in some other part of the hospital.

A nurse's voice from between the curtains. Oh God, let this be over soon: let the dark angels vanish; let him get back to Deborah, and the life that had nothing to do with this benighted place which let his mind loose upon mysteries. He wasn't one for mysteries; he wanted the solid enjoyments of the world: a woman and food and drink; and no feared finger pointed towards him from such a bed as Ben's was now.

Nevertheless, he went in. There was no great change, to his eye. The multiplied mechanical devices obscured the truth of what was happening within those curtains. The nurse on the other side of the bed covered Ben's free wrist with her fingers. A sound from Ben, from the mouth that was still so young, that he could remember from childhood. Then silence, except for the little distant noises in the ward: the wheels of a trolley, the rubber-soled hurrying of feet.

162

But here it was over. He could see that: he had lived through the last war, so recently ended; he had been with those men who had surged up the long leg of Italy; he had seen death often enough not to be deceived.

Something seemed to be expected of him, though he wasn't sure what it was. There was the sensation of a hand clenched in his chest, but no true anguish yet; perhaps that was to come. He leant over with difficulty and kissed the young forehead, which was still warm. He couldn't remember when he'd last kissed Ben. He gave one final look but there was nothing more to do, only this great need to be back in the living and lighted world.

He turned away.

The day Ben died Emma went to her mother's house and took Carey with her.

It wasn't difficult to do. Susan was busy in the house, Jonathan indoors; Carey playing alone in the garden. Emma went quietly in through the back way, keeping an eye on the house. She didn't want to see her mother, nor even Jonathan. She simply needed Carey, blindly, in shock and misery. Did Carey need her? Well, of course; Carey always needed her.

Indeed as she crept into the garden where the warm October day with its ripened leaves belied the news she had just heard, Carey came running towards her, arms outstretched.

Oh, thank God, Emma thought; thank God there's something good, some love somewhere. For in a world where Ben with his youth and beauty could die, she had suddenly found herself adrift, shocked and afraid. She had thought of telephoning Lance, but she didn't want to revive the question that hung between them: talk of doctors and nursing homes. No one now could be of true comfort except Carey who loved her with blind acceptance. (She had put out of her mind that moment when Carey had turned away and said *Don't want you*.) Carey would always want her; would accept her, however she behaved.

She took Carey into her arms, and said "Hush" as Carey began to shout "Mama!" with expected joy. She walked softly on the bright fallen leaves, having put Carey down. "Where are we going, Mama? Where? Grandnan's indoors. So's Jonathan." "Never mind. We're just going for a walk together. I'll give you some tea." "Cream buns?" "Anything you like—oh, anything in the world you like." A small silence, while Carey trotted beside her, hand in hers, looking up. "You've been *crying*." "Got a kind of cold." "Looks like crying," Carey observed with adult judgement. Emma said, "Colds always do."

They were away from the house now. She had left a note, clearly to be seen, inside the back door; she didn't want the kind of panic there'd been last time when Carey'd taken off on her own.

The river ran heavy with the October light, and the buildings on the other side were defined with a bloom of amber which transformed them into beauty. All this, the splendid dying of the year, the Indian summer, and Ben couldn't see it; would never see anything again. She grasped Carey's hand more tightly. Ben's death threatened everything, even Carey... No one was safe. How did you accept that? Tears came to her eyes and she wiped them away. "Mama *is* crying." "No—not really." "Why's Mama sad?"

Impossible to talk of Ben to Carey; she just said, "I'm all right so long as you're there, darling." Carey screwed up her face, puzzled by this: then did a small skip and pointed. "Pussy cat on the wall. Over there. Can I stroke him?"

Of course, Emma thought, when her mother read the note she might—though asked not to—come to Emma's flat. Perhaps it would be better to take Carey to a teashop. Outdoors with Carey she was safe. Safe, yet frightened, overthrown. *Ben*. Beside her on the stage through all those nights of warm applause; Ben who had been her lover . . .

It was at once too much, incomprehensible and only too well comprehended. She felt lost, without bearings; seeing the men and women who passed her, the balm of this year's late sun, the pavement under her feet as things newly constructed by some malevolent hand.

Only Carey could offer comfort because only Carey loved her enough.

She took her to a tea-shop. Emma looked round at the pretty aprons and small tables with vague surprise: not her usual haunt. Carey sat on the chair with her short plump legs not reaching the ground apparently pleased with all about her, interested. "Not tea at home?"

"I thought this'd be more fun."

"More fun," echoed Carey, making no judgement.

Emma sat and watched Carey who was now drinking a glass of orange juice, holding it with both hands. Emma herself took nothing. She fed on Carey's face; saying to herself, This is my child, and she's living, and will live for a long time. And she will love me, she won't leave me as Ben has, as Lance has; as everyone does, in the end . . .

She needed a drink, but there was none to be had here. She glanced at her watch. After five. Plenty of time before she had to be at the theatre . . .

But of course they wouldn't have a performance tonight; no one could have a performance of a sharp satirical play on the night of Ben's death.

Ben's *death*. No, she thought; I still don't believe it; I shall walk into the theatre and he'll be there, moving with that easy grace; the gentlest of all of us; too young to be lost . . .

No. It was true. Death. Final. Not ever again . . .

"More cake," Carey said.

"O.K.," Emma said. "But you have to say please."

"Please, Mama."

165

Yes, it was all right so long as she could sit here with her child opposite her, and see love and the future there. She didn't want anyone else; except that more and more she needed a drink. Shock was coming home, driving deeper into her being, and she began to shiver.

Ben.

No, she must think only of Carey, who was innocent of death, all evil, all darkness.

"Does Grandnan know where we are?" Carey asked.

"Yes; I left her a note."

"Why didn't you talk to her?"

"I only wanted to talk to you."

Carey wiped the (probably ersatz) cream across her face and seemed bewildered by this also. "Finished my orange juice." She held the empty glass upside down.

Without reproach, Emma righted it. "Best come along now, darling."

"Back to Grandnan's?"

"No."

"Want the bathroom," Carey said.

"All right." Emma took her hand. "We'll go to my place."

Once in the flat, and Carey attended to, Emma poured herself a glass, full to the top, of whisky.

"Mama taking medicine?"

"You said it." While she drank, she absently fondled Carey's fair head. The child clasped her knees. "Are we going to stay here?"

Emma drained the glass. "Not here. I don't want people—not even Grandnan. She might come and look for you here."

Carey gave a heavy nod, which perhaps was to show her understanding, or merely that she accepted all that was happening to her.

Emma took her hand and they were out again in the street. The rich light had quietened; the water was scalloped with shadow, and a small wind turned the leaves of

166

the plane trees, causing some of them, toast-brown, to fall.

Opening time now; she found a pub with tables outside and sat Carey on one of the seats. Emma bought her a lemonade and herself a double whisky. So long as she could go on doing this, her senses dulled by drink, and Carey with her, promising life, she need not look too deeply into the thought of Ben . . .

Life and death. Therefore choose life. She couldn't remember where that came from, but she'd heard it somewhere. And Carey was life.

So long as she could sit here.

It was ten past seven when Susan found her. Emma was on her fourth drink, and Carey was beginning to be tearful because she was cold. It isn't all right any more, Emma thought. All the dark things are coming in; Carey's unhappy and the drink isn't working—

She looked up, drowsy, to see her mother, with Jonathan beside her.

Emma said, "Oh, no."

"I've been looking *every*where for you. They've been telephoning from the theatre till I've been nearly out of my mind; asking for you, where you were—"

"The theatre? But they can't be having a performance to*night*, not with what's happened to Ben—"

"Well, they are; Jeremy Hirst says he's talked to Ben's father, and he says Ben would have wanted them to go on. They're going to have a kind of two minutes' silence before the curtain goes up in Ben's memory—"

"Oh, how terrific, how splendid; if I were dead, I'd be over the moon about that; how *can* they?"

"Well, they are, and they want you; they're all frantic."

"Let them be frantic, damn them; what do they expect me to do—"

Carey began to cry in small snuffling snorts. "Carey's

cold and Mama's cross."

Emma said, but without emphasis, "Oh, shut up. Ma, I'm not going to that theatre tonight, not tonight—I can't—"

"Oh yes, you can," said Susan, with unaccustomed force. "You have to. Jonathan and I came by taxi; it's parked over there—"

"You mean you're taking me to the theatre *now*, like this, without even having a chance to—"

"Emma, it is twenty past seven. If we go there now you'll have about five minutes to make up and change and be ready for your entrance."

"You *want* me to go? You must be out of your mind; I can't go on tonight like this; everyone'll know I've been drinking—"

"You've got to come *now*."

Carey gave a large wail. "Don't like it when Mama's cross."

Distraught, Emma looked briefly at her: a small noisy burden which had such a short time ago been a source of life. "Oh, heavens," she said: "don't cry; I can't stand it. I've had enough."

She stood up, swaying a little. The sun had quite gone from the street and she shivered in the chill wind. Carey was still tearful as Susan with the energy of the desperate and exasperated, moved them all into the taxi. Jonathan said to Carey, "I should shut up if I were you." To his grandmother he said, "Are we going to the theatre?"

"We must."

"Oh, I like the theatre," said Jonathan, giving only one quick glance at his mother who, unsteady and with hair awry, was being pushed into the taxi by his grandmother. He wore an expression of shamed surprise.

In the taxi, Emma sat silent, looking from the window at the passing streets. She had none of Susan's anxiety that they should go faster; she felt dulled from all sensation now—certainly a little drunk, but without acute

168

feeling of any kind. She only knew that this was a bad day; that she had never gone to the theatre with so little enthusiasm, so little hope . . .

At the theatre, Jeremy waited by the stage door. His face said all that was needed. Taking one look at it Emma said, "I didn't believe you'd play tonight. I didn't see how you could."

"You might have taken the small courtesy of finding out." His voice was steel-thin.

"I'm here now." She stumbled on the way to her dressing-room, and he said to Mrs Crashaw who opened the door, "Black coffee, fast. I don't know," he added with a glance at Emma, "what this performance is going to be like, but we have to do our best. You're stoned out of your mind, ducky, but perhaps you can get through."

Emma drank the coffee, splashed cold water on her face, put on her make-up with a shivering hand. She saw Susan take Jonathan and Carey, like ghosts departing, from the dressing-room. Mrs Crashaw refilled the coffee cup with the expression of one who's seen this sort of thing before . . .

When the evening was over, Emma didn't need anyone to tell her that her performance had been a disaster. Back in her dressing-room she sat facing the wan and shiny image which didn't look beautiful any more.

Mrs Crashaw fussed behind her.

"Keep them all out," Emma said. 'I don't want to see anyone; I don't want excuses or raps over the kuckles; I just want out. And fast."

It was a beginning, of a kind.

I had some idea of this even then, for I was woken in the Hampstead house by the telephone; and after that the voices of my father and Marguerite. I couldn't hear all they were saying, but I caught, in tones of exasperation and anxiety, Emma's name.

Part Two

Chapter One

I first went to New York when I was sixteen, nearly seventeen. It seemed strange that I had been so many times to the Vineyard, and never to New York. But of course the Vineyard was for summer holidays, and New York in those days was almost deserted in the steamy oppressive heat. (Now, with better air-conditioning you can find a lot of people still there, even though the pavements scorch your feet and the nights are loaded with neon-lighted warmth, and the warble of police cars has the same effect as the cicadas of the Mediterranean, emphasising the long hot hours.)

I went because of a letter which came to my boarding-school from my father. "My dear Rick," it began. My father was still married to Marguerite (which in the theatre world was unusual) and in the years which had brought me from childhood to adolescence he had accumulated success: he had larger offices in New York and London, and the names which came up in his conversation grew larger and of more dazzling impact.

Not that his conversation now played a great part in my life. I went to boarding-school in Somerset when I was eight; and the holidays were at rare intervals spent on the Vineyard, but mostly with friends and friends' parents in places like the Isle of Wight or the Lake District. It was not that I didn't enjoy these excursions; merely that I felt that I was there on sufferance, that I didn't belong in the way that my contemporaries belonged to their parents.

Perhaps it was this that sometimes sent me off on my own, and brought protests from the said parents that I was 'difficult' or 'sulky'. Certainly as puberty caught up with me (or I caught up with it) I had moods of silent hostility; I was unco-operative; occasionally rude. My boarding-school was progressive, co-educational and generally dedicated to the arts. It was no spartan public school, and certainly no 'blacking factory'. The surroundings were beautiful, especially in the summer term; the children, though no more compassionate (nor no less) than others were often the children of parents who had made their mark in the world and therefore trailed clouds of glory, as indeed I did myself. From time to time I would boast of actors and actresses I had met—Brenda Jones, who had acted with Emma in *The Newcomer* had now retired and lived close by: sometimes I had tea with her and she talked—endlessly but fascinatingly—about the past.

But I was lonely there. I had not then the insight to explain my loneliness, for was I not surrounded with children of both sexes, and teachers who were known by their Christian names? (There were Bob and Bridget and Alexander: available at all times for consultation on anything from spots to birth control.) But despite all this I walked by myself; read poetry or smut, as schoolboys do; fell in love with a girl with long black hair and blue eyes who found me—not surprisingly—dull, and preferred the son of a musician who despite his uniform of jeans—which we all wore—looked like Shelley.

It was this tendency to go off by myself, to rebuff friendship, or to seek it where it wasn't forthcoming, that first caused the Headmaster, whom we called Grundles, but whose name was Groundsman, to write to my father.

I can imagine how little pleased my father was to get such a letter in the midst of theatrical confusion; of telephone calls from across the Atlantic as common as calls from a nearby street. He was fond of me, but he'd sent me to a good (and expensive) school; he (and Marguerite) always remembered my birthday; that done, they pursued their peripatetic and busy lives. Marguerite didn't fail in her friendliness towards me; but she was my father's wife, and I was not her son. Perhaps when I was a child they'd both felt more responsibility for me; perhaps Marguerite's maternal instincts, such as they were, dwindled as I grew older and I daresay less appealing.

But when months went by and I didn't see them, not for holidays or half-terms, I had a sense of belonging nowhere. I once, on a summer afternoon while we learned to build a log cabin (though it was unlikely that we would ever, being urban in our roots, have much use for one) said to Deirdre, the girl I was in love with, something about 'not belonging', and she laughed, swung her black hair, and stood, hands on hips, the young breasts just showing under her shirt. "Oh, Jesus; none of us belong; what d'you think we are, pet poodles? We're ourselves, and we do what we want. What have parents to do with it? Sure, they begat us, or however you like to put it; they changed our nappies and pushed our prams; but after that—it's our business. They're *boring*; even when they're intelligent, they're boring; they don't know about us or how we feel. So stop being sorry for yourself."

"I'm not! I was simply trying to explain—"

"Ain't nothing to explain," Deirdre said. "You're getting a big boy now, and parents don't matter any more. They're for the scrap books (just look at Auntie Maud) and paying bills."

Though this struck me as harsh, it didn't destroy my devotion to her, or infatuation, or whatever it was. She was nearly fourteen but looked two years older; we all grew up fast at Lonsdale. Since there were plenty of girls about we didn't fall much for our own sex (though this could happen); but the girls, when they were as pretty as Deirdre, commanded court; and on the fringe of this court I lingered, darkly adoring, and without receipt of anything in return.

I could see the force of her argument, but it didn't convince me. There was a subtle difference in the way those parents who took me on holiday talked to their own children, and talked to me. They were generally kind, and polite if they asked me to do something; and mild in reproach. (I sometimes wished they'd yell at me, the way they did at their own children.) But love, of course, was absent: couldn't be anything else. My failures and triumphs, such as they were, couldn't be of great interest to them; though they did their best to pretend they were.

Jonathan, also at boarding-school, was half of England away. His school, though more conventional, had this in common with mine: they were both expensive, and betrayed our parents' greater readiness to spend money on us than time. When my father and Marguerite, with Emma and Carey as well, were in the States, Jonathan and I sometimes stayed for half-terms with those anonymous parents whose faces I cannot now remember.

I recall particularly one week spent at Freshwater in the Isle of Wight. This was at Whitsun, and I couldn't help comparing the cool sea-washed pebbles of this shore with the baked sands of Martha's Vineyard. The sea drove, grey and roughish on the shingle, and, June though it was, the winds on the cliff tops forced us to wear sweaters, and no one bathed. The parents were vegetarians, walked strenuously, sandalled and bare-legged, and had a learned interest in Tennyson, in whose steps we travelled as we walked on the wind-blown cliffs and visited the hotel which had once been his home. In spite of myself I found their enthusiasm, if in advance of my own, at least catching: I was able to see the image of the fine-faced old man as he climbed the few steps to his library, or at the end ('Sunset and evening star') walked with his nurse, wearing a large black hat (how did it stay on in the wind?) on the cliffs. We toiled up to the monument in his memory and looked out over the rough grey green Channel, which took occasional cool glints of sun as the clouds parted. The other two children, a boy and a girl, seemed to have an old-fashioned regard for their parents, and the interests they pursued: they explored the grounds of Farringford (Tennyson's house) and asked pertinent questions about him.

Jonathan, however, would have none of this. Tennyson was out of his ken, an old man who'd written poetry which he read to Queen Victoria: enough said. Like many delicate-boned people he shunned the cold and was forever winding a scarf round his neck, or stamping his feet and asking to go home. Once back at the hotel he disappeared, and after long search was discovered in the kitchen parts chatting up the prettiest serving-maid.

The parents, though dedicated to tolerance in all fields, found this uncongenial, and there followed a brief set-to while they explained that Jonathan was their responsibility; while he was on holiday with them he kept out of the kitchen and walked on the downs.

When this was over, Jonathan wandered with me into the table-tennis room. Lightly bouncing a ball with a hollow click on the table he said, "At least Mr and Mrs God can't object to a game of ping-pong—can they?"

"Other people's parents—" I began; he interrupted. "Oh, I know, I know. They belong to another world. You can't be yourself. Or if you are, there's trouble." He bounced the ball again; the sound comes back to me now. "Carey, of course," he went on, "goes to school in the U.S. of A., and has the time of her life."

"With Emma?" I asked.

He glanced at me, as if the doubt in my voice came through. "Oh, sure. Ma must rock the boat. But at least she's there—Carey, I mean. Where it's all happening. Where at least in the summer it's warm. While I moulder in the draughty corridors of my school, or shiver on the cliff-tops with this homespun couple who in spite of having produced two children seem to have taken against

177

sex."

"They're a bit earnest," I said; "but I've known worse."

He glanced at me again. "Of course you get pushed around too, don't you?"

I could have agreed, but was reluctant to admit it. "I see Father and Marguerite when he's working in London."

He shrugged as if he knew how little this meant. "D'you know, I think for long periods at a time Ma entirely forgets that I exist? At *all*? Every now and again I get a present or a postcard—'Heaps and heaps of love from Ma'—just as if nothing had happened. I suppose as far as she's concerned, nothing has."

I looked at him with curiosity. He was as far as I could judge a good-looking boy—even a young man—and it crossed my mind that a mother might have been proud of him. Such a thought could not of course be expressed to Jonathan himself: he would have shot it down with accurate fire. But for a moment I felt a surprising pang which might have been pity for Jonathan, who would again have scorched it away.

The week ended, and we left the Island on a fine day. As we travelled by ferry across the still water of the Solent, Jonathan looked back to the misted downs and said, "I rather like islands." These were the first words of admiration which he'd spoken on the holiday, and the last. Then we lost each other again.

When I did see my father, I felt a difference in his manner towards me. Some affection remained, but I could tell that I irritated him; perhaps (now I look back) he saw me, as fathers are said to see their sons, as a rival; resenting the growing virility which would strengthen as his own diminished.

So I didn't agree with Deirdre; I wanted a father who was concerned with me. A great deal of this, perhaps, was the ordinary egotism of the adolescent, the need to be noticed, even if what is being noticed is bad behaviour. I had the feeling that I could do anything, seduce a girl, hit someone over the head, and apart from the natural processes of law—or the girl's parents—no one would greatly care.

One evening, when we were free to do what we liked (which was often) I wandered away to the depth of the trees which bordered our grounds. I walked with my hands in the pockets of my jeans, my head down, dark hair flapping about my ears. I was, I'm sure, scowling, for my thoughts were generally sombre now. I went more deeply into the tree-laden quiet, seeing myself as some dark wanderer, perhaps out of Edgar Allen Poe. On and on, lost in a muddle of thought.

The sound of a voice stopped me.

A girl's voice, giggly, muffled.

Standing there, still among the leaves, I knew it was Deirdre's voice.

At first I couldn't tell where the voice was coming from. Then I heard a boy's voice, answering, though I couldn't hear the words. His voice too was hushed and amused . . . was it amused? I couldn't think of the word.

Then I saw them. I hadn't moved, except for my head, and they didn't see me. They were lying together on the earthy floor; her shirt was somewhere near her neck, her breasts naked. The long dark hair was spread about her on the ground, and her face smiling and heavy-eyed. In that moment of watching I knew how often I'd dreamed of holding Deirdre like that; and how little likely it was. I had just time to see the boy: the one who looked like Shelley, before I turned away and ran.

Not that I was shocked. Lonsdale claimed 'no pregnancies so far' and maybe that was true; but a lot of what we called snogging went on, and a great deal of talk about it too. But Deirdre was something else.

I walked with the half-pleasurable misery of all adolescents; black at heart, yet in some way enjoying it. On and on, out of the school grounds. This was easy enough, for the last things Lonsdale went in for were barbed wire and guard dogs. There was some sort of counting of heads by ten o'clock, just to see that no one was lost in the woods or in someone else's bed.

I wandered down the country road. It was some time after six, and the summer green was abundant, frothing like a sea. I went on, telling myself that I was despised and rejected (Lonsdale didn't go in much for scripture, but my father and Marguerite had instilled me with some of its knowledge). The nearest village was Camsdowne, and I didn't linger there, for boys from Lonsdale were known among the villagers. I walked further until I came to a lonely pub. It was called, appropriately enough, *The Black Horse*, and didn't look inviting, as pubs usually do.

But it had the advantage that people I knew wouldn't frequent it, and I went in. I went into the Public Bar, where a few old men sat producing a cloud of smoke. I counted on the fact that I was tall for my age (taller than my father) and that my voice was fully masculine. Digging in the pockets of my jeans I asked for a pint of bitter. I asked as if I expected nothing else but the glass on the wet-ringed counter before me; but I thought the landlord, a lean man, as unappealing as his pub, was eyeing me with caution, as he drew the beer handle. "Not seen you around before."

"No. I'm—I'm staying with friends."

"Ain't you at school?"

"I've left school."

"You eighteen?"

"That's right."

I retired to an empty, none too clean bench and drank the beer. Beer may sound mild stuff to the young of today, but I wasn't used to it (Lonsdale for all its tolerance didn't go as far as liquor) and I quickly felt the warm glow spreading through me. Good. Never mind that I was unloved by Deirdre, and that my father and stepmother were far off: I was a person in my own right, and I could do what I wanted. When the glass was empty I returned to the counter. "I'll have another," I said.

Again the sharp unfriendly look. But I was now more of an adult than before, because the drink had given me confidence; he shrugged and refilled my glass without comment. The old gaffers in the pub eyed me once or twice, then lost interest. A couple playing with greasy cards paid me no attention at all. I drank the second pint. I asked for a third because I was feeling so fine, so entirely removed from nagging thoughts of Deirdre, and of my father.

But that third pint was a mistake. I knew it half-way through because the walls of the smoky bar began to swing and the old men sitting there faded out of focus. With difficulty, I finished the glass. I waited for some moments before trying to get to my feet. Was the landlord watching me? With caution, holding on to the table, I rose, and saw him look my way with dubious inquiry as he polished a glass.

But he said nothing and with an effort I walked on a sliding floor out of his pub.

Oh, hell. I had only one longing now, to get back to school without anyone seeing me. I hoped I wasn't going to be sick, but the warm air gave no comfort. I staggered, wondering if I could make the walk back to Lonsdale without falling down. I *did* have to stop at one point to be sick, which I hated. Watery-eyed, nose running, I stumbled on. Just to get back, unseen; to get into bed and sleep till this swaying nausea had passed. All my command and confidence had left me, and I was worse than I had been when dark with gloom, rejection and jealousy—but sober—I had walked away from the school.

The earth spun, but I struggled to stay upright. I wiped my face with my handkerchief. I didn't like myself at all; I felt stupid and messy and ashamed. Please God, I could get in without being spoken to; I could wash, wash my mouth out, plunge into what would be my first drunken sleep. At that time—like all those who've drunk too well—I swore it'd be my last.

The country lane was quiet, and in those days saw only the occasional car. Lighting-up time had come and when I saw the headlamps I pulled myself (as far as I was able) against the hedgerow, waiting for the car to pass.

But it drew up beside me. And at the wheel I saw old Grundles. Well, of course he wasn't old by adult standards; he just seemed old to us. He was, in any case, the last man I wanted to see.

He was alone. He wound down the window and peered at me through the failing light. "Good Lord! Rick Ashley. What're you doing?"

I mumbled something which he couldn't hear. He leaned his head out, had a good look at me and no doubt met a smell of beer.

"Good Lord," he said again; "you're drunk."

Useless to deny it. White-faced and swaying I stood at the side of the road. He opened the door. "You'd better get in."

I don't remember much more about that evening. Grundles, his blunt profile and grey moustache just visible beside me said little as he drove me through the darkening lanes. The lurch of the car made me groan quietly to myself. When we reached the school Grundles sent me off to bed, saying over his shoulder, "I'll see you in the morning."

The words were spoken without threat; we weren't in Dotheboys Hall (far from it); but while my bed seemed to be sliding backwards like a trolley, I wondered what would come of this clownish escapade.

The next day Grundles was moderate, casual, sitting on the edge of his desk and smoking a cigarette. His blunt face was inquiring and amiable; he did his best, and I was the one who failed. "Silly thing to do, wasn't it?" he asked; and with my head down (crowned with the father and mother of a headache) and my hair falling over my face, I agreed. "Any particular reason?" he asked; "for in my experience people usually have a reason for getting drunk. As early as sixteen, anyway."

It was impossible to say anything about Deirdre. I mumbled something about feeling depressed.

"Work going badly?"

I shrugged. Work was not so much going badly as not going at all; I was opting out of nearly everything I could. "So-so," I said.

"Hear much from your father?"

I gave him a glance. "Not a lot, no. He's busy."

He nodded. "Most parents are. However..."

He hadn't much more to say; nor had I.

But as a result, it seems, another letter went to my father; and so the letter beginning "My dear Rick," came to the school. By then I'd seen a psycho chap who appeared as puzzled as I was. "It seems," my father wrote, "that the best thing you can do is to come over here. We have to be in New York; no bad thing for you to come here: it is, if not the eighth, maybe the ninth wonder of the world. Tickets and times will follow."

He made no mention of my escapade, nor what might have caused it.

So it was that I travelled alone across the Atlantic and arrived at what was then Idlewild.

Some of my confidence returned as I made my way through passport control and baggage check-out. Even today I find that travel, if it goes smoothly, eases the soul.

And there was Marguerite, waving. I was both glad and sorry that my father wasn't with her.

As I walked towards her, case in hand, I looked steadily at Marguerite. She was one of those women who appear to be the same age for a long time: good bones, and a high lift of her head; she hadn't put on weight, and the long slim legs were as good as ever.

She embraced me as if she were truly glad to see me, and perhaps she was.

She slammed the boot of the car with my case in it, and gently pushed me round to the right side of the car, because for the first few minutes over there I always forget. "Not going to drive, are you?"

"No," I said, comfortable with her.

"Been having trouble?"

"Kind of."

"Tough," said Marguerite, manoeuvring her way through the long dingy district of Queen's; "but there's always trouble when you're sixteen. And after," she added. "However, that, as they say, is another story."

"Where's Pa?"

"Oh—working. Most of the time he's working. He's up amongst the big ones now."

"I know."

"Is that your problem?"

"Don't know that I've got a problem." I looked through the car's window. The streets held none of the towering excitement which I had expected. "Is *this* New York?" I asked.

Marguerite smiled. "Sure. But not Manhattan. There's an awful lot of Queen's. Give it time."

I watched as we drove nearer to the heart of the city. Over the Queensboro' Bridge, into Second Avenue—yes, here was the city I'd read about and was excited, even on this dubious arrival, to see. Here were the cavernous streets and topless towers, sheeted on one side with shadow, on the other with light. Marguerite said, "We have to stay for a few days in New York, at the apartment. Then to the Vineyard."

I said, "Fine." It seemed to me that Marguerite was debating whether to say something more. The unfamiliar New York streets slipped by.

Then she said, "What have you heard about Emma?"

184

"*Emma*?" For the moment I could think of no answer. What had I heard about Emma? Publicly, as it were, quite a lot: privately, little. As an actress she'd gained ground, both on the stage and in films; she gained rumours also. The racier papers from time to time had articles about the switch-back career and private life of Emma Pride. Failure of *The Newcomer* all those years ago had not been lethal; like most courses in the theatre, Emma's journey had been unpredictable, and the triumph of its opening had given her enough impetus for a re-flowering as it were. Indeed, perhaps her indiscretions may have helped to keep her in the public eye, if not always in Management's good books. "It doesn't matter what they say so long as they say something": certainly they said things about Emma, good and bad: her name became news, because she could play superbly at one time, and fall heavily on her face, metaphorically speaking, at another.

One more marriage came and went, but it all passed me by: I didn't see her; nor Carey, and little of Jonathan. Emma was a figure remembered from my childhood: it was occasionally surprising to read her name and recall that time past when I'd known her. Sometimes I boasted about it.

I said now, "Only what I read about her."

"And that's been plenty," said Marguerite, changing gear. "The going's been pretty rough: she isn't all that young any more."

I supposed not. It seemed surprising, for people stayed in your mind at the age when you last saw them. "Our contacts with Emma—Lance's and mine—have been off–on, like a faulty switch. But I think I should warn you that she's back in the picture now. There comes a time," Marguerite said, "when you have to help Emma: there's no other way ... Here we are," she said in a different voice; "East 52nd Street."

Emma was banished from my mind: it was hard to

185

think of any place more unlike Lonsdale School; the pavements between the towering structures seemed to be made of hard hot light, I couldn't see a tree anywhere and the traffic ripped and thundered past, a bemusing band of colour with the predominance of the yellow cabs. An awning of striped red and white led to the entrance of the apartment which was suddenly as cool as November. It was my first experience of New York's savage contrast between sun and air-conditioning.

Marguerite didn't say much more than the usual commonplaces of arrival, and for this I was grateful. I could look around the twelfth-floor apartment, which had a small terrace (a luxury in mid-town New York, I later learned), and furniture of scarlet on cream rugs. My own room looked down into the cavernous street below with its flashing cars, and as I unpacked my case I was glad not to be alone in this place which, exciting though it was, showed no sign of personal interest.

I wandered back into the living-room, where Marguerite was on the telephone. She glanced up as I came in. "Yes, he's here. Pretty well on time, no problems. Well, none to do with the flight. He's right here with me in the room. Looks O.K." She said to me, "Lance. Have a word with him? Just to say 'hullo'?"

I took the receiver, not without a throb of misgiving. "Pa?"

"Hullo, Rick. Welcome to New York. How d'you find the heat?"

"It's O.K."

"Marguerite taking care of you? . . . Yes, I'm sure she is. See you soon."

I thought as I put the receiver down that I hadn't said much. I was still vaguely ruffled, for 'taking care of you' sounded—didn't it?—as if I were six instead of sixteen. And hadn't his voice had a ring of counterfeit jollity? As if all the months of absence were of no account, and everything was the same as it had been?

I turned to see Marguerite's eyes on me. "Want to talk?" she asked.

Certainly while I sat high above the Atlantic my head had been full of self-justification, I daresay self-pity. But now none of the words seemed ready. I said, "Don't think there's much to say. I went out on a binge and Grundles found me lurching in the lane."

Marguerite had put a glass of iced coke beside me, and given herself a gin and tonic. "You're happy at Lonsdale?"

It would be absurd to say No; for Lonsdale had everything to make you happy—perhaps too much. I wasn't going to talk about Deirdre; that was private. All the same, it would be untrue to say I was happy at Lonsdale for I was not. I muttered, "It's O.K."

"Not more than that?"

I shrugged and was silent. She took a sip of her drink. "Maybe one shouldn't ask people if they're happy at sixteen. What's known as the gloom of youth. Hard work, being young. Hard work, come to that, being any age ... However, every problem is different." As she rose to put more ice in her glass, I wondered what problems attended her at forty-plus. As if she caught my question on the air she said, "Being married to your father has its complications. Now that he's so way-up in his profession, we don't seem to stay anywhere for long. Or if we do, it's like living in Grand Central Station."

Was this an apology, an explanation of their absence?

"Yes, I suppose it is," I said, reflecting that there was a dimension where other people's lives turned on mysteriously, out of one's sight, and one was a stranger there.

A little while later my father came in. I observed him closely, for he seemed to be at the root of my trouble; but he was almost his usual self, skin tanned, dark hair going grey; further marks of age on his face, and perhaps more weight on him than before, but still the sense of vigour and liveliness; a man going places and fast. He gave me a

187

firm clasp of the shoulder and threw himself into a chair. "So, Rick! Letters from the Headmaster. What's it all about?"

Marguerite was fixing him a drink; I could see this ritual being performed each evening, on his return. Bourbon on the rocks. He said absently, "Thank you, darling," and waited for me to reply.

I stared at the floor. Here in New York the whole of Lonsdale and whatever had ailed me there seemed a long way off; not easily explained. I said, "I wish he hadn't written to you. There wasn't any need."

I glanced up to see my father looking steadily at me. "I think perhaps there was," he said. "Nobody minds about your getting drunk—there has to be a first time—but he's been worried about you for some while."

"They worry too much at Lonsdale," I said. "Digging around into the psyche—you can do too much of that."

"No one's unkind to you?"

"Golly, no." (Was Deirdre unkind? But that wasn't what he meant.)

"Groundsman says you don't seem to have a lot of friends. That you wander off by yourself."

"I like walking alone."

"Problem, then?"

I drank more of my coke. "There isn't one, really."

My father crossed his legs with a trace of exasperation. "You're not helping me."

"I'm sorry."

Marguerite said, "Maybe it's a bit early for this. Too soon off the aircraft."

"I don't think so." My father was smoothing the plentiful and greying hair. "Never too soon to get to the root of things. If I didn't believe that I wouldn't be where I am now."

Marguerite smiled. "And where's that?"

He answered her smile, a little wryly. "I'm a successful man."

"Sure. But what we have to find out right now is whether you're a successful father."

I felt my face go red. It sounded childish; I was, after all, sixteen, and tall for my age.

My father made a face at this. "Ah—well, that's another story. I suppose, since we have Rick here and letters from his Headmaster, I must have doubts. *Am* I a good father, Rick?"

An impossible question. "Well, yes, sure."

"You don't sound very certain."

"He isn't meant to be certain," Marguerite said, perhaps trying to lift the embarrassment from me.

My father got to his feet. As he prowled about the room I could feel the force which always came from him, the tightening of the air: a man to be reckoned with. What love he had to give me, I couldn't know. He said, "I have to earn a living. Lonsdale's damned expensive. I suppose that's not what we're talking about."

Marguerite said, "No."

"All the same..." my father said; and I could only allow that if you were going to be at boarding-school, Lonsdale was a pretty good place. The fault wasn't Lonsdale's but mine. If it was a fault, to want to be important to someone, which I believe now it is. Or at any rate, a dangerous desire.

"We'll do everything we can for you," he went on; "Give you a good time—"

I was about to say, perhaps ungraciously, that a good time wasn't exactly what I wanted when the telephone rang and my father grabbed it, I think with something of relief. I heard him talking about out-of-town productions, dollars and contracts: his world, of which I had no part.

Marguerite stood up and took me with her into the kitchen, where she began to prepare a meal. I made clumsy efforts to help her, and she said with sympathy, "I guess you have to take your father as he is, or not take him at all. He does the best he can."

This I was beginning to understand; even to feel a little sorry for him. What could a busy man say to a large adolescent son who was by no means ill-treated, but appeared to be nursing some unexplained wound?

The days when as a child I waited with excitement for his arrival on the Vineyard were gone: you couldn't bring the old life back. Things were changed now.

I didn't then know how much.

It was when we were half-way through dinner that the bell of the apartment sounded with its suppressed buzz. My father said, "People always come at the wrong time;" and Marguerite got to her feet without fuss, putting down her table napkin.

I listened to the voices in the hall, not best pleased with this incursion (whatever it was) since the evening had begun to feel friendly and, despite my earlier misgivings, something of the old warmth had returned. My father's head was lifted as if he recognised a voice, which I did not.

Marguerite returned with that look of amused inquiry which I knew so well.

With her was Emma.

I did several takes. This was Emma Pride, whose name flew like a flag across the entertainment cities of the world. This was Emma, who had been part of my childhood, of summer days on the Vineyard. And this was someone new.

The haunting beauty of face was the same: the large sorrowful eyes, the even, gentle line of jaw. But it was as if someone had scrawled upon that face with an unkind pen. Though always slight, she was thinner, as if something had been burning away at her. She had a cigarette in her hand, and looked as if she always did. She wore a scarlet evening dress that showed the thinness of her breast. Her scent was strong in the room.

Her glance fell first upon me. "Good Lord. It's Rick."

I got to my feet and knocked a knife on to the floor. "Hullo, Emma. (Should I still call her Emma? I couldn't think of anything else to say.)

She gave me a comprehensive look, neither friendly nor unfriendly, and I remembered that her attitude to me had always been ambiguous; I never quite knew why.

Dismissing me, as it were, she flung herself into a chair. "I just walked out on a dinner—"

"Are you hungry?" Marguerite asked with quiet innocence.

"No, darling; just *furious*. I could use a drink." Marguerite wordlessly rose and poured a whisky. Emma took it with a brief acknowledgement. "There were these high-powered chaps, and they were telling me as nicely as possible—I mean with vitriol spread thin, or whatever you do with vitriol—that they don't want me on Broadway in the fall. I was all set for a large-scale revival of *Man and Superman*; and now they say they've already cast it; they suggest either Hollywood, or some experimental nonsense out-of-town. Neither's what I want to do, and I told them so." She stubbed out her cigarette, and immediately lit another.

My father rubbed his chin. "They may be right. Revivals on Broadway can be hazardous, as I don't need to tell you. And Shaw ... A great man, but he does go on rather."

"But they're *doing* it. With someone else. Lena Carlin. Whose experience in Shaw must be minimal, if not less." She looked from my father to Marguerite. "All right, she's maybe fifteen years younger than me, but *I've* had the classical experience: I've played them all or nearly all: Ibsen, Shaw, the Bard—haven't I?"

"Yes," my father said; "and played them very well."

"So then—"

My father lifted the pepper-pot, then put it down in a different place, as if he were playing chess. "I don't have to spell it out."

Marguerite was watchful and silent; she gave me a second helping of vegetables and poured wine into my father's glass. Emma leaned her chin on her hands. She looked both younger and sadder, more as I remembered her. She said, "There's no reason why they can't rely on me."

No one answered her. She said, more desperately, "I've *worked*, haven't I? Oh God, I've worked. And if I sometimes need a drink or pills to get me through the night, what's that to them? Providing I come up with the goods in the end?"

Again my father was silent. It occurred to me that Emma had entirely taken over the evening; no one was getting much of a word in, and if they did it was about Emma.

She said, "All right; I had a bit of trouble on Broadway last season—"

"Let's call it that," my father said. I think they'd all forgotten about me.

Emma turned quickly to him. "I'm not going to quarrel with you."

"That's just fine," Marguerite said; "what I like best is when no one quarrels with anyone."

Emma said, "I was playing Beatrice; it was a hard grind, and Benedick had about as much charm as an anteater; we were losing money and—" She caught my interested glance—"Oh, Lord; do we have to have the kid with us as well?"

I flushed, and Marguerite put out a hand and touched my arm.

Emma subsided. "Sorry. Poor old Rick." She lost interest in me again. "Like I said, I've walked out on them."

"Wise?" my father asked.

"My sweet Lance, whenever in my life have I done things that were wise? If I have, you could count them on the fingers of one hand."

I saw a look of affectionate amusement go over his face; and I saw Marguerite notice it. This was the Emma who charmed, whose honesty overcame the chaos which at most times attended her. "And which exactly of Broadway's great men did you walk out on?"

Emma's glance said, Need you ask? "Jo Hornsby and Martyn Belgruber."

"Only just about the two most important men in the New York theatre."

"Well, yes," Emma said, "otherwise, what would have been the use of walking out on them?"

Again my father showed that trace of half-weary half-affectionate amusement; and even Marguerite laughed. Oh yes; I could see why Emma, in spite of the rumours, still commanded affection; was even now—as Marguerite had warned me—able to find welcome with them.

My father said, "And where do you go from here?"

"God knows; a nunnery, I should think."

"That'll make the headlines," my father allowed; "but might not be in the best interests of the nunnery. Or God."

Emma pushed her glass forward in mute request for more drink. She looked tired and sad, and not at all the edgy and brittle person she had appeared when she first came in. She ruffled her already ruffled hair, and said, "I wish I wasn't wearing this dress; it was all right for walking out on them, but it isn't right now."

This made Marguerite laugh again. Emma went on, "But I've jolly got to work in *something* because there's a ghastly mess of Internal Revenue that I don't understand, and don't want to understand, but my accountant tells me I've got to pay." She lit a cigarette and coughed. "Fancy working to pay tax."

"One of the rules, ducky," my father said.

"Why are the rules so difficult?" Emma asked. "Why can't there be *nice* rules?"

193

I remember thinking she had something there.

"Oh, but there are," Marguerite said. "Things one takes for granted. Like finding a stamp when you thought you'd run out."

"Well, maybe; but I need more than a stamp, God help me. I need a whole new life, and a whole new bank account."

"And," my father said, "running out on Jo and Martyn isn't going to help you with either."

"God, I know. I know. But it had to be done. Well—all right, I'd had plenty to drink and I lost my temper. But they asked for it. Lena Carlin. What does Jo think he's doing?"

My father said, "He's directed more hits than any man this side of the Atlantic."

Emma looked at him with sorrowful acceptance. "Well, it's gone to his head. And he lectures me as if I were some Victorian daughter who'd gone to the bad and come home with an illegitimate child."

She bent her head. For a moment I didn't know what was happening to her. Perhaps she was going to laugh? But then I saw the change in her face, and she began to cry, quite noisily.

I felt disturbance rather than pity. Lonsdale had accustomed me to more emotion perhaps than other schools would have done, but Emma in her scarlet evening dress crying at our dinner table was something more. I couldn't think why in the midst of a fiery speech she should suddenly cry, unless it was because she'd had too much to drink.

Marguerite put one arm across Emma's shoulder. Lance looked steadily at her, his face to me unreadable.

After this outburst of weeping, the ragged evening brought itself together again. At least it did for my father, Emma and Marguerite. Whatever problems I had brought with me were sunk out of sight. As they talked about Jo Hornsby and Martyn Belgruber, and the prospects of out-of-town plays, I felt the isolation of all the young when the conversation travels beyond their world.

I got up, without anyone appearing to notice, and wandered to the window. It was dark now, and into this darkness the city towers rose, built of patchworks of light. Below in the canyons of the streets traffic moved like threads of speeding gold. The scene was at once exciting and fearsome, as if one looked into some glittering aspect of hell.

After Emma'd gone, I went to my strange bed. I heard my father and Marguerite talking late into the night, but I don't think they were concerned with me. The sound of the city, modern, powerful and dangerous, like a mechanised sea, at last blurred into sleep.

Chapter Two

The next morning my father went to work in his office on Madison Avenue, and Marguerite, showing no signs of a late night (she had retained the capacity to look good on all occasions) was on the telephone. She gave me a wave of one arm and went on talking.

I helped myself to coffee. An echo of Emma's scent hung on the air, mixed with my father's cigar. Sun brimmed at the window and I could hear the noisy flood of the New York day outside. Marguerite put down the telephone and said, "Hi. I have plans for you. No, don't look as if you were going to the dentist. We have to see Emma."

"We saw Emma last night."

Marguerite gave a lift of one eyebrow, as if she took the protest in my voice. "Your father wants us to see her again."

"Why doesn't he go himself?" I asked, mouth full of toast.

Marguerite got to her feet. "Well, there you have a question. Take too long to give all the answers. I did warn you that Emma had arrived, with full orchestra and chorus, back into our lives. Anyhow, Lance is opting out of this one—for the present. I have the pretty task of persuading Emma to apologise to Jo Hornsby and Martyn Belgruber. Not a chance, I'd say: but we go together."

I thought it sounded a grown-up thing to do, and brought me into the scheme of things, whatever that was;

and I felt a lift of spirits as we left the apartment and Marguerite hailed a yellow cab. I said to myself, Here I am in New York, on my way to see a famous actress. Never mind that she'd been drunk last night, and in tears. We flashed through the streets, up-town to Emma's place on Riverside Drive. This appeared grander—or any rate greener—than my father's apartment. The house looked out on to the Hudson, and the water was blue and touched with blades of hurtful light.

Up in the elevator, to the ninth floor.

I don't know who I expected to greet us. A maid; a butler, perhaps; even Emma herself.

Certainly not Carey.

I didn't at first recognise her. She was just fourteen now, and though not tall, and slight like her mother, her figure was sketched in, as if an artist had tried his hand at the transition from childhood to adolescence. Her fair hair was long and she was dressed in a thin blue sweater and skirt. She said, "Why—it's Rick. Rick Ashley."

I looked at her for a moment in silence. She had grown very pretty, and something touched me: perhaps the past, that child on the island shore; perhaps a question mark about the present; perhaps the future. . .

Carey returned the look, brows lifted as if I'd said something to her, though I had not, beyond a bare greeting. Then she kissed Marguerite and made an adult and sweeping gesture to the room. "You'd better sit down. Ma's not up yet." Her accent, which I remembered as being like my own, now had strong American overtones.

Marguerite said, "How's Emma?"

I saw a drift of shadow over the eyes which were so like her mother's. "A bit hung-over, I guess."

Marguerite nodded. "That figures," she said, as she sat down.

"Was there trouble last night?" Carey asked.

"Kind of," said Marguerite. "What we have to do is to try to persuade your mother that if she still wants a future

197

in the theatre, she has to play ball. If, as I say, she wants a future, and I think she does."

Again the shadow came on Carey's face; every now and again she seemed to withdraw from us. In the strong light I could see how pale her face was; not an unbecoming pallor, for she was so young, but unexpected.

Her eyes caught mine, then slipped away. "A future . . . well, yes, I guess she wants that. Could you use some coffee?"

Marguerite said she could, if it was to be a long wait.

Carey went into the kitchen; my glance followed her, for she was something new and strange, and to be noticed. I heard her putting out cup and saucer with a child's enthusiasm; after a moment or two came a crash as she dropped something. "Sorry," she called. "Clumsy; always was. . . ."

The noise didn't seem to be very loud, but I heard then the sound of Emma's voice as she flung open her bedroom door. "What in hell's name's going on?"

She came into the living room, wrapping a robe about her. She was tousled with sleep, and angry. I stared at her, for even last night she hadn't looked like this.

"I'm trying to *sleep*, for God's sake!" Abruptly she stood still, seeing Marguerite and me for the first time.

"What on earth. . . . It must be the middle of the night."

Marguerite gave a placid glance to the blazing window, but said, "Well, yes; guess it must seem like it."

Emma turned to Carey again. "Why the hell didn't you tell me they'd come? Instead of crashing about in the kitchen like a demented hurricane?"

Carey became still. Remembering her as a child I wondered if she would cry, but her face showed only pallor and control. This disturbed me more than tears would have done. She said nothing, but put the coffee pot and cups on the table. Emma began to speak, but Carey said, without expression, "I'm going out."

"Don't be an ass—" Emma began.

Carey took no notice. She said good-bye to Marguerite, and went out through the door.

A brief silence held us all. Then Emma, taking a cigarette and folding her robe about her, said, "For God's sake, Rick, go after her. Bring her back. I'm not having her walk out on me like that."

After a glance at Marguerite who nodded, I went after Carey. It seemed odd, like an adventure. The elevator had already gone down; I waited for another. The day seemed to have changed very rapidly; perhaps days did, in New York.

When I came to the street I hesitated for I couldn't see her anywhere. Absurd—this was Carey, whom I remembered as a child of some four years old; who had drifted without remark from my life. . . .

I felt a flood of relief when I caught sight of her on the other side of the road, walking with purpose south along Riverside Drive.

I began to run, calling "Hey! Carey! Wait for me."

She didn't hear (not surprising through the traffic) but at last I made my way across the road, ran and caught up with her.

She looked at me with enclosed inquiry, without pleasure. I felt clumsy. I might have known the Carey of the past, but this Carey was unknown, her face secret and unreceptive. "Did Mama send you?" she asked.

"She wants you back."

"I'll bet. Not going yet."

I stood, perplexed. "But she'll wonder—"

Carey turned to walk on. "No, she won't. She knows about me. Coming too?"

Again I hesitated. What sort of reception should I get if I arrived back alone? "O.K.," I said, and began to walk beside her, trusting that she wouldn't go far.

She moved in silence, head down, as if her thoughts possessed her. I wasn't comfortable in the silence and said, "Do you often walk out like that?"

"Now and again."

"Isn't it worse when you go back?"

"Sometimes."

"Does your mother often—"

The head now turned with a flash. "You be careful what you say about her."

"Well, hell!" I said.

"Hell what?"

"She's just shouted you off the scene, and you walk out, and then you tell *me* to be careful!"

She looked ahead, chin lifted. "I don't like people talking bad about Ma."

Exasperated, I said, "Well, what d'you *expect*? She was drunk last night at our—"

"*Shut up!*"

"I don't think I like being shouted at, any more than you do."

"Too bad."

It was the moment to leave her; to turn and go back to the apartment. But I didn't. Far off was the memory of the child who had clung to me on the shore of the Vineyard; here now was also a child, older, but one who as far as I could judge was in need of help. Or in need of something. Perhaps I could provide it.

We walked further in silence. I thought she was just moving aimlessly, but then she said, "Know what we'll do?" The recent passage of arms might not have happened; her voice was even. "Go for a boat ride."

"Boat?"

"Yeah. It's the thing to do. Besides, it's pretty. I like being on water. No one can get at you. Like a dream."

"But how long'll it take?"

"You can be *boring*," she said.

I stood still. "I simply don't know why you have to be rude to me."

Though not looking at me she smiled slightly. "No—I

don't either. But it's boring to ask how long things'll take. What's it matter?"

It seemed to me that it mattered a good deal if Emma was going to fly into a rage when we returned late, but I didn't say so. I seemed to have set my course for this day, which was already out of control.

"O.K.," I said. "Let's make for the boat."

When we came to the pier head she asked, "Got any dough?"

Yes, I said; I had some dough. I pulled a couple of dollar bills from the pocket of my jeans. "Not enough," Carey said; "but I've got all we need. C'mon; the next boat's just leaving."

She bought the tickets and we ran forward together up the small gangplank on to the pleasure steamer. (I think it called itself a cruise yacht, but it looked like a pleasure steamer to me.) Carey went with assurance to a couple of wooden chairs. They were almost the last two left; the boat was crowded with men and women in light summer clothes, most of them with cameras.

Slowly we moved off from the pier, down the Hudson River. From somewhere over our heads, apparently disembodied, a male voice began a commentary—a jocular monotone pointing out the famous towers of Manhattan to our left (a great swing of cameras) and the green of New Jersey to our right.

Carey paid no attention to this, but stretched out slim bare legs into the sun and lay back in her wooden chair. "Want a hot dog? Or ice-cream?"

I said No.

She watched the slow water as the boat travelled smoothly forward. "Kind of nice, isn't it? I often make this trip."

"On your own?"

"As a rule. I like being on my own."

"Why did you ask me to come, then?"

"Oh. . . well. You're part of long ago. I used to like

you."

"*Used* to?"

"Well, I don't know you now, do I?"

The commentary continued. ". . . approaching down-town New York; Battery Park and of course, that great girl, the Statue of. . ." Carey made a face and said, "I've learned to shut that voice out; it makes all the same jokes. . ." She stood and leaned on the rail, very much at home. Her skirt blew in the slight wind off the river. I stood beside her. She said again, "I like water. Deep. Hardly any noise. D'you think it would ever be possible to drown?"

"Out at sea? Of course—"

"No—here. In water like this." She leaned further over the rail, looking deep into the silk-smooth blue ship-shadowed water.

"No," I said sharply, because I didn't like the way she was leaning over.

She said dreamily, "I've sometimes wondered. How you'd go right down and not come up again. People do. They throw themselves off Brooklyn Bridge, practically all the time."

"I don't think it's a good idea to throw yourself off anything."

She turned sideways to look at me, still leaning over the rail. "You take things awful seriously, don't you?"

This I thought made me sound boring. I denied that I took things seriously, but said that I didn't think drowning was funny. I then caught sight of a woman in a yellow dress with bare fat arms who was reading a brochure. In the brilliant light I could read words on it; and I turned with alarm to Carey. "It says this trip takes three hours!"

She smiled at me, chin on the rail, hair blowing. "Of course it does; what d'you expect? We go all round Man-hattan Island and come back to the starting-place."

"But there'll be one hell of a row when we get home."

"There was one hell of a row when we went out."

202

"That doesn't make it any better."

"Guess not. But no worse. Ma's used to me going off. She won't get the cops out. She'll know that I'll be back."

I had my doubts, but protest would clearly be profitless. While the boat slid quietly on, Carey bought two ice-cream cones, and I watched the sun flash from the windows of the city towers, flash and change as we passed by. Carey licked her ice-cream, quickly melting in the heat, and said, "It's odd seeing you again. Sometimes I've wondered about you."

"*Have* you?" It seemed flattering.

"Yeah. I thought of you in England, being well-ordered and well brought up."

That, I thought, sounded patronising. "Don't know who I was brought up *by*," I said, countering this. "Father and Marguerite aren't around all that much, and they don't exactly bring you up at Lonsdale."

"No one brings you up, I guess," Carey said, taking another lick of her ice-cream. "It's been a pretty odd life here. Especially with Ma."

Yes, I could imagine that. School days, with intermittent visits to theatre dressing-rooms; a home invaded by theatre fever, late telephone calls and many drinks. I said, "I don't know what to say about Emma. She shouts at you and you walk out, and then you won't hear anything against her."

Carey seemed to consider this. "That's how it is. It doesn't make much sense. But then I don't think things make a lot of sense. Know what I mean?"

"Yes," I said; I knew. I did, too.

"Ma and I—" Carey looked dreamily ahead to the dazzling distance—"(there's Ellis Island)—Ma and I have a kind of nutty life. You've heard things about her?"

"Yes," I said cautiously, and no more.

"Well, they're all true." She finished her ice-cream and wiped her hands together. "She mixes drink with a whole lot of pills, and then sometimes she can't get up."

203

"Out of bed?"

"Off the floor," said Carey dispassionately. "I came in early one morning to see her, and she was just lying there. I tried to get her back on to the bed because I didn't want anyone else to see her like that. But I couldn't; she was too heavy."

She spoke as if all this were nothing extraordinary, but I could see her, slight and unable to lift her mother from the ground. I asked, "Were you scared?"

I expected a flash of anger, but she considered the question, looking ahead to the great span of Manhattan Bridge. "Yeah. A bit. For one awful moment I thought she was dead. But then she moved. In the end I called the maid, a nice coloured lady called Sabrina. She's one of those people who always look the same, whatever happens, whether there are eighteen to dinner, or Ma's passed out."

The great bridge shadowed us as we pulsed evenly beneath it. Carey's story sounded at once ordinary and frightening. I said, "How can she go on acting?"

"Well, she does. And it's O.K."

"All right," I said. "I can't say anything about her that you'll agree with."

She let this go by. "She's O.K. on stage, once she's there. At least, I *think* she is. I'm not there all the time; I only see her now and then. I believe there have been times. . ." She broke off, and began to bite her nails. "You get to hear things," she said, pulling at the bitten thumbnail with the other hand. "But when I've seen her, she's been all right. She likes me round in her dressing-room afterwards; she calls me her mascot."

"D'you like going to her dressing-room?"

Carey looked again to the slow-moving, blue-grey and gilded towers. Her face had a look of her mother's: large-eyed, haunted, withdrawn. "Sometimes. When there isn't a row and it doesn't feel too hot. And the dresser doesn't say, 'My! Isn't she like her Ma! Going to be an

204

actress one day, are we, honey?'"

Yes, I could understand that.

The boat was turning round the tip of Battery Park, swinging slowly into the East River. The sun had the kind of force that suggests inhuman strength. Carey said, "Wouldn't it be nice to stay like this for ever? Just travelling over water? Then nothing awful could happen."

"How d'you mean, awful?"

"Don't you feel that something kind of frightening is around the corner?"

I didn't ask her what she was frightened of. I began to see that, though she had shown an adult certainty in getting aboard the ship, she wasn't truly in command.

Tentatively I put a hand on the back of her head.

She looked at me then in surprise: I can see her face clearly now: a child's face, but shadowed and inquiring. She put up a hand and took mine, but whether to push it away or to make some acknowledgement, I wasn't sure. I let my hand fall. She said, "You think I need taking care of?"

"You said you were frightened."

She glanced over her shoulder at the sweating crowd of passengers, whose faces and arms were scorched by the sun. "What d'you think of when you see a mass of people like those?" She made them sound as if they belonged to some other species.

I looked at them: men with shirt-sleeves rolled up; women in summer dresses, bright as petals. "Not much. I think they're all separate. That I couldn't talk to them."

Carey eyed them carefully as an artist might. "I think, when I see them all together, about how one day they're all going to die."

"You think *what*?"

"Well, they are, aren't they? All of them. There's no one gets out of that."

I was silent as the boat swung slowly down the East River. I couldn't say that it was a thought which I gave much time to. But the words if they hadn't changed my view of the crowd (whom I couldn't really see all rushing to their tombs) had changed Carey.

As if she knew this she said, "You think that's kind of grisly?"

"Yes."

"Well, maybe. That's how I am. That's what I dream of. Bones and witches and death." Then she laughed. "Oh, c'mon, it's not as bad as that; I'm not some kind of nut. Look, there's Long Island. And round the top of Manhattan we come into the Harlem River. I'm always sad when we get there, because it's nearly over."

"And when it's over," I said, "we go back home."

She made a face. "Sooner or later you always have to go home. It'll be all right, you see."

But she was wrong.

When at last we had rounded the whole island of Manhattan, when the commentary had covered everything from Grant's Tomb to the Bronx, from Wall Street to the Chrysler Building and Greta Garbo's apartment ('we'll leave her be; she wants to be alone'); and we'd disembarked at the Pier, full of sights and dazzle and sun, we made our way back to the apartment.

Where Emma, now fully dressed, was very angry indeed.

"What the hell d'you both think you've been doing? For nearly *four hours*?"

"We took a trip—" Carey began.

"I want to know," Emma said, with new fury, "what two children—with one who isn't a child any more—think they're about in—in leaving me without a clue as to where they are."

I could have said that Carey had persuaded me that this escapade was routine, and there wouldn't be any trouble, but I had no heart.

Carey had changed from the child who thought about

death to a girl who looked as if she'd been slapped in the face.

Emma said, "You may like to know that I've spoken to Marguerite. She went back to her apartment, in case you turned up there."

Carey was leaning with one hand on the wall, as if she needed its support. "What d'you mean, spoken to Marguerite?"

"We agreed it was best," Emma said with an edge to her voice, "for you to go to England. You can travel with Rick."

It didn't at the time occur to me that it was unflattering that Carey should on hearing this cry, "Oh, *no!*" and burst into tears.

"Don't cry," said Emma sharply; "it won't help."

Carey looked up, eyes brimming. Though any girl in tears embarrassed me, I felt a pang of pity, even of possession, as if those hours on the boat had brought her close to me.

But I was a listener as they spoke—or fought—each other: I was out of my depth; there was something here that I didn't understand.

"Why've I got to go to England?" Carey asked. "How can you decide something like that, all at once, without asking me, without—"

"Because I've had enough. Because you sweep out of here like a prima donna, when I'm in all sorts of trouble—"

"I don't want to go. I don't want to leave New York. You said it was good to have me here; you said I was your mascot."

"I say a lot of things."

"You mean it wasn't true?"

"I meant it at the time—" Emma looked at Carey's stricken face, then turned sharply away. "Don't look like that."

"England's so far off."

207

Emma's hand was shaking as she lifted a glass. "No, it isn't. People go back and forth like it was the subway."

"It's far off."

"I've got to have some peace—I've got to take myself in hand, can't you see that?"

"I don't stop you having peace!" Carey said as if she cried to heaven.

"Please," Emma said, "just leave me; just don't say any more. It's best for both of us if you go. Go with Rick. To Marguerite. Maybe she can help you. Take a cab."

Carey was looking at Emma as if at some lost depth of unhappiness. All I could see was a woman of marred beauty in a fine fury with a glass in her hand, and had she been my mother I would have been out of the place like a scalded cat. But Carey only turned with reluctance, shoulders drooping. At the door she halted. "I haven't any dough."

Emma with a small exclamation went to her bag and drew out a wedge of dollar bills.

Carey accepted them in silence. Head down she asked, "How long have I got to stay with Marguerite?"

Emma said, as if she meant it: "I can't talk any more! Just *go*."

Clearly, no more to be said. We came out into the blaze of sunlight. Carey's face was marked with tears and I was somewhat ashamed to be walking beside her, for every now and again people looked our way. Yet I still felt a bond between us. Though we had spent only a few hours together, the past and present seemed to have merged, and Carey was someone I had known for a long time.

After a silence she said, "It isn't a good thing for me to leave her."

I couldn't answer that; I couldn't say that she seemed to me to have an exaggerated idea of how much a child of fourteen could mean to a woman like Emma. Carey said, as I didn't answer, "Guess you're pretty fed up."

"Why, no," I said; and suddenly, without warning,

she put her hand in mine. It felt warm and moist, and I held it hard, for she seemed to be asking for something.

"We'll go together," I said; "to England."

She nodded, and waved down a yellow cab. We scrambled in and sank into it, on our way to Marguerite.

If you discount the time when she was four years old, it was our first journey together.

Chapter Three

From there, things moved fast. Marguerite took us to the Vineyard; my father stayed in New York. Marguerite gave me the occasional word of encouragement, but seemed mostly concerned with Carey, who was so often silent, and would disappear to be found at some corner of the bushy hill, looking out to the great swathes of water which surrounded us.

One day I couldn't find Carey anywhere. I looked all over the rough garden, and climbed down the steep pine-smelling sandy path to the quiet shore of Menemsha Pond, where she often liked to go. No sign of her. I climbed back again, wearing only my bathing trunks. I wandered barefoot along the sandy path that led inland away from the house towards the mailbox, but an afternoon quiet hung over the island like warm smoke and only distantly could I hear the sound of a car on the empty road. Pines, purple vetch and wild roses, unstirring in the heat, formed a place of enchantment, as if a spell had been placed upon it. Had I not once heard that Martha's Vineyard had been suggested as the source of *The Tempest*; and that in the taverns of London, Shakespeare listened to the stories of the voyagers, drawing from them the spirit of Ariel and the darker form of Caliban?

I turned back to the house. Silence; Marguerite was in her study. I searched further. The house had a room below ground-level where Marguerite kept her canvases. I went, still barefoot, down the stairs.

It was there I found Carey. She was curled up on the floor in a dusty corner of the large shadowed room, cool, away from the heat. She looked up as I came in. Though we had shared much time together, and laughed as the waves threw us rudely on to the Atlantic shore, I thought I still didn't know her; she kept something of herself apart, so that each time I saw her I wondered which Carey would present itself to me.

She had about her a mass of what seemed to be papers and photographs. As I came nearer I saw that they were old theatre programmes, press cuttings and photographs. The photographs were mostly of Emma. They had all come, it seemed from a large and ancient tin box, of the kind which I understood that sailors took in the old days on long voyages.

As I stood there she clasped some of them to her as if she feared I was going to take them away. I was going to do nothing of the kind; I just said, "How did you find those?"

"Prowling around. They're all about Ma." She scooped up the programmes and the photographs, the yellowing newspaper cuttings. "I've never seen them before. I don't know why. People hide all sorts of things, don't they? And she's kept *everything*—good and bad; why's that, d'you think?"

"Some people can't throw anything away." I forebore to add 'about themselves', which seemed to apply to Emma; I could see her harvesting this patchwork, jigsaw puzzle of her life.

"Suppose not," Carey said. "But why should they be here?"

I shrugged. "Marguerite's family, isn't she? And Emma couldn't travel around with that enormous tin thing."

"No, I guess not." She looked at it doubtfully, as if she tried to imagine Emma dragging it behind her. "There are letters too. Some of hers, some from other people."

211

"You mean you've read them?"

She looked at me, wide-eyes. "Yes, of course; why not?"

I began to say something about reading other people's letters, but then two things occurred to me: one, that Carey needed to know everything she could about her mother; and that—given the chance—I would read letters if I thought they were going to yield something of great importance to me.

Carey went on, "I hoped there'd be something about me, but they're mostly about rehearsals and directors; lovers and husbands. Well, one husband—the one that happened when we weren't seeing you."

"I never met him."

"He was a movie actor. Not a very good one. Name of Colin Brent. And he was *boring*. He kept looking at himself in the glass. They lived for a time in California, when Ma was making movies too. I was glad when it came unstuck."

Yes, that I could believe. Carey wouldn't want a step-father who monopolised Emma and had manifestly taken no notice of Carey herself.

I crouched down beside her. The theatre programmes had that look of pleasure gone which all such mementoes have; the cuttings had the dust, not of fact, but of time; these triumphs and disasters were past; new actors trod these stages now. I picked up one of the photographs. Emma, playing Peter Pan. She looked young and suitably boyish, hair cropped short, figure androgynous. How long ago? I said, "She doesn't look much older than you."

"No." Carey looked with intent devotion at the photograph of her mother. "Everyone must have loved her."

I didn't argue, but I had that image of Emma as we had left her in the New York apartment, filled with drink and anger. I thought, but did not say, "None of it lasts." Nothing; not the slight and eager Peter Pan, not the

212

Emma who had come running across the sands of the Vineyard; not even Carey, sitting there with her legs curled under her, hair spread about her shoulders, a child with a dangerous devotion.

She said, putting the photograph down, "There's something in one of the letters I don't understand."

I looked doubtfully at the sprawling words on the thick paper. I knew Emma's hand well; perhaps it was this that overcame the distrust which filled me as, over her shoulder, I read the words she pointed to.

Emma had written (to Marguerite): "Well, it's done now. It was the only possible thing—wasn't it? For God's sake say it was; I need someone to reassure me. Lance helped me, if that's the word; but I can't forget it; can't get over it. I dream it's all as it was; and then. . . Guilt, perhaps? To whom? I don't know. To whatever it was going to be, perhaps. Maybe some people can get away with it, but I can't. Yet it's *done*. Nothing can change that. And pretty beastly it was, too. Am I wrong to think that there's some kind of curse laid on me (no joke intended) because I've done this? That the furies will pursue me. . . All right; I can hear you saying, 'Come off it'. I try to. But I can't. It was the worse thing, worse than having a flop when you'd worked your heart out, and the first night had gone well. . . All right, I take everything too seriously; I know that; you've always told me so. But I'm me; I can't help that, can I? And I feel—oh, doomed; as if a huge curtain had closed behind me that I can't get through again. . . Write to me, please. Give me something."

I looked for a date on the letter, but Emma, as was her custom, had only written 'Friday', as if there was no other Friday but this. The paper however was discoloured and the ink old.

Carey said, "It was with the programmes of about ten years ago."

I nodded. Ten years. The ink dried; perhaps in spite of

213

all she'd written, the sorrow dried too. But old anguish still spoke from the scrawled words: I was dimly aware of the alchemy of time which at once put a distance from such a pain as Emma had spoken of, and yet brought it with immediacy into this present.

Carey said, "What d'you think it means? What was it about?"

"The end of a marriage, perhaps."

"She wasn't married ten years ago. You remember."

"The end of a love affair," I said, feeling grown-up and knowledgeable.

Carey gave me a glance, careful and wounded at the same time. "There've been lots of those."

I nodded. At Lonsdale there was much talk of parents drifting apart, and drifting towards other parents. We made what were I suppose crudely innocent jokes; but at heart we were disturbed, for it shifted our certainties. I said, "Do you mind?"

She pushed her hair from her face. "It isn't any good minding, is it? I mind when she tries to cover it up; I don't like being lied to."

"We all get lied to," I said.

Carey returned to the letter. "She says something about your father. He must know. So must Marguerite."

"We can't ask them."

"Some day I might... I want to know." She sifted through the papers again. Amongst the many photographs of Emma, one other slipped before us.

It was of a young man with extreme good looks (even I could recognise that); a newspaper photograph, with a caption beneath it. *Tragic death of young actor.* "Ben Hardy, currently playing in *The Newcomer* with Emma Pride, a new star, died yesterday in hospital. He was twenty-four." There followed a brief resumé of the career of this young man whom I had never known, or even heard of.

Carey stared at the picture with deep puzzled concern.

"Twenty-four. That's only eleven years older than me... Ben Hardy. Mama never talked about him, never said anything at all... D'you think she was in love with him?"

"Could be."

"Why do I feel as if I'd known him?"

"Perhaps you did, when you were small."

"No—I don't mean like that. A different kind of knowing."

I glanced at her. She looked mysterious in the shadowy light of the submerged room. Was she going to claim second sight? I didn't care for that sort of thing; my world in those days was four-square and solid; I had no time for the half-light of telepathy, card-telling or ghosts.

"*Why* didn't she talk about him—" Carey was saying, when the step brought both our heads up. Marguerite stood in the door, dressed in shirt and slacks, looking placidly at us.

Though Marguerite was not a person to be afraid of, I didn't like it, being found there with Emma's letters and photographs spread about us, the lid of the tin box betraying and open.

"Well now," Marguerite said, "do you make a habit of digging into other people's belongings?"

Carey's eyes narrowed. "Yes. If they belong to Mama. I want to know everything about her."

Marguerite lifted one eyebrow. "That would take a mighty long time. And not get us very far." She began to gather the programmes and letters together, putting them back in the box. Carey watched her with sadness, as if she saw treasure slide away. She said, "It was me that opened the box. Rick came and found me.'

I looked at her with gratitude, but she was still gazing at the box.

"Fine," Marguerite said; "I think you'd better come upstairs and talk."

She took us out into the rough garden where we could

look down on the water all around us. It was not yet evening, but a breeze ruffled the grasses, and dimmed the day's heat. Marguerite lay back in her low-slung chair, and we sat on the ground. Carey looked pale, obedient, containing her thoughts. There was something lost about her, as if she'd been washed up on a strange shore; and perhaps Marguerite was aware of this, for she spoke evenly, going easy on the words of censure.

"Looking through other people's papers is kind of mean," she said. "You can get to know things about them they don't want you to know. And that's not fair to them, is it? However much *you* want to know."

Carey made some sort of acknowledgement, head down, one hand pulling at the rough grass. She said, "Who was Ben Hardy?"

"Ben?" I saw the small change in Marguerite's face; she didn't often look disconcerted. "If you saw the photograph of him I guess you know all there is to. He was a beautiful young actor who died."

"What of?" Carey asked.

"Leukaemia—a kind of cancer."

"Was Mama in love with him?"

"Honey, I haven't the least idea."

I saw Carey look up at Marguerite as if she tested her truth. She went on, "There was something in one of the letters. Where she asked you to help her. Where she sounded kind of scared. She wrote 'Give me something'."

Marguerite said, "Your Ma wrote a lot of things like that." (And this I thought was the first time that I had known her to prevaricate, for I was pretty sure she remembered the words exactly, and what they referred to.)

I wondered if Carey would question further, but she only muttered "Maybe," and went on pulling at the grass.

"I have something else to tell you," Marguerite said, as if glad to leave the subject of the letter. "About school."

216

Carey looked up. "Not in England?"

"'Fraid so. Lonsdale. Where Rick is."

My surprise was lost in Carey's protest, "But that's boarding-school!"

"Guess it is," said Marguerite.

"I don't want to go there!"

"Sorry, honey; it's all tied up."

"How can it be? Isn't there a waiting list?"

"If there is," said Marguerite, "it seems that Lance has been able to overcome it."

"What's Lance got to do with it?"

"Seems he can pull strings," Marguerite said. "He generally can."

This I thought was true enough; but Carey said passionately, "It won't work! Why should I go?" and without waiting for an answer got to her feet, and went running away from us.

After a moment I followed her. She was scrambling fast down the sandy road to the shore of Menemsha Pond, slithering and gasping, losing a sandal and recovering it. Though older and taller, I had a job to catch up with her. I only reached her when she was down on the hot sand, by the green fringed shore, with the white sails skimming against the sky.

She gave one turn of her head, but made no other acknowledgement of me. She sat on the sand, arms round her knees, sandals kicked off.

I knelt down beside her.

Scooping at the sand she said, "They do everything without telling you. People ought to *tell* you things, even if you're young. Marguerite wouldn't answer my questions about the letter—"

"Perhaps she'd really forgotten."

"Don't think so. And I'm to be wrapped up like a parcel and sent to this school in England, without anyone asking me—"

I said, "Lonsdale isn't too bad."

She gave me a brief glance, as if she acknowledged that I was trying to comfort her. "But it won't be like life over here, mixing with theatre people; talking to Ma about the show—"

"No," I said; "it won't exactly be like that. But no one'll shout at you, either. And we'll be together."

She looked at me with inquiry then, as if she tried to read something there. Her face with its sadness and trace of apology slid something sharp within my breast; and there on the sand, with the steep piney path above us, and the water slipping in with grace of a woman's turned wrist, I leaned over and put my mouth to her cheek.

Before we were posted back to England, Marguerite took us to New York.

Emma was playing off-Broadway in the experimental play which she hadn't wanted to do; Carey and I were bidden to the first night. I saw this as a gesture from Emma; a palliative for the decision to send Carey to yet one more school. How Carey saw it, I wasn't sure. Though we spent our time together she kept her thoughts to herself.

We stayed in my father's apartment, for we would soon be *en route* for England, with our bags and passports and plane tickets. This made the brief stay in New York transitory as if it were a place already diminished by distance.

On the morning of Emma's opening night Carey went out and bought flowers. "For Ma," she said, sounding a little breathless, though whether because she'd been hurrying in the heat, or because she was apprehensive about seeing Emma, I didn't know. "D'you think she'll like them?" she asked, holding the amber-coloured roses towards me. I said Yes; of course she would, because Carey, breathless, with the flowers in her hand looked at once young and vulnerable; in need of protection.

However, there was nothing I could do for her now, for she said, "I'm taking a cab;" and clearly Emma's apartment on this day wasn't the place for me.

Carey was gone a long time. In fact my father and Marguerite were already dressing for the theatre when she returned. She came through the hall, and I said, "All right?" and she said, "Fine," white-faced, not looking at me, going like the wind to her room.

When she reappeared, dressed for the theatre she was still pale but a little more composed. I knew better than to ask questions. She wore a long-skirted cotton dress, which made her look older. Though she said little as we travelled to the theatre I had the sensation that she mutely asked for help. I didn't know how to give it her, except by staying silent beside her. What had Emma done, or said? I remembered the roses, and Carey saying, "D'you think she'll like them?" I had a sudden vision of those flowers scattered on the floor, petals torn.... but this was absurd. I must wait.

The theatre was in Greenwich Village, small, a little shabby. Carey and I went to our seats; my father and Marguerite were talking to new arrivals in the vestibule. Men and women drifted in to their seats; Carey occasionally turned her head, as if she were expecting someone, but I didn't think she was.

Still we were on our own; my father and Marguerite hadn't joined us. It seemed to me that time was lengthening—surely they should be in their seats by now? I glanced at Carey, who was still turning her head over her shoulder. Suddenly she said, "I don't like this. It isn't going right." Her face was still pale, her eyes troubled.

Two minutes before curtain-rise; still no sign of my father and Marguerite. The wash of voices with the occasional spring of laughter continued. Carey bit her thumbnail. Time for curtain-up; past time; no dimming of lights; nothing was changed. Except that within the surge of voices a different note sounded: the beginning of a question, even of protest.

Carey turned to me, face stricken. "Something *is*

219

wrong."

Indeed, the two empty seats beside us seemed ominous, but I said that probably some essential prop had gone missing, or the lights had fused.

Mutely she shook her head. She said at last with difficulty, "When I saw Ma. . ."

"Yes?"

"I asked her about the letter. The one I found."

I felt a small drop of the heart, but said nothing.

"I asked her what it was about. I had to know."

Useless to say that it was the wrong thing to do, and the wrong time to do it. I asked, "Did she tell you?'

Carey nodded; she looked paler than ever. "Yes. In the end she told me."

"Well. . .?"

She shook her head. "Sorry. I can't tell you. I can't tell anyone. I shouldn't have asked her. It's best to leave things alone."

I could only agree, but it was too late for that. The voice of the audience had now entirely changed. The note of protest over-topped all else; I could hear a subdued muttering instead of the carefree talk; here and there a call: "Let's get started!"

I felt the resentment of the crowd as if it were a wind on my neck. But they weren't, as far as I could tell, yet angry: the taunts were cheerful: an outlet only for impatience.

The slow hand-clap began gradually. Only a few at first, because the curtain was not so very late.

But this demonstration like all such was catching; more and more people were joining in, until the voices were silenced, or overlaid by the rhythmic derisory sound.

I took Carey's hand in mine. "It'll be all right," I said; "you see, it'll be all right."

She held my hand firmly, as if she tried to believe me. "Please, let them stop. Make the play begin."

If I could have done it, I would; but the seats beside us remained empty, the curtain stayed as it was, and the hand-clap grew in strength.

"I shall have to get out," Carey said; but before she could move, the curtains parted and a small man in a tuxedo, whom I took to be the Front of House Manager, stepped forward. The audience cheered; irony informed the cheer.

The young man gave a smile that covered, I surmised, apprehension, and said, "We're sorry, folks, for the delay; we've had some technical problems backstage. They're over now; we're all set to go, if you'll just have a few minutes' more patience. Thank you." He slipped back between the curtains like a fish; and I could feel how glad he was to go.

Apart from a murmur, muffled laughter, the audience was quiet now. Waiting. As Carey and I were. But the seats for my father and Marguerite still remained empty.

Like a quick-falling day, the lights in the theatre died. A sound came from the audience; a sigh of relief perhaps at the end of frustration. Carey didn't move, except to grasp my hand more tightly.

The curtain whispered up. The set was simple: table and a few chairs: an undefined darkness.

Into this barren set, Emma came. A flutter of applause sounded, but did not grow. The audience had waited a long time.

At first I thought it was all right. Emma stood, back to the table, frightened, listening to the anger of men's voices off-stage, mounting to a crescendo. She put one hand to her mouth. A spotlight like a coin illuminated her, and I felt again the sensation of power which came from her; you had to look at her, and go on looking.

Off-stage, the sound of a shot.

Emma gave a scream. A good enough scream; it was followed by the entrance of a young man with blood on his shirt. He staggered, and fell to his knees.

For a moment Emma stared at him, horrified. That was all right.

221

But then she moved. And swayed, and stumbled.

Even then, it might have been all right. The swaying might have been part of the script, but when she spoke her voice was slurred, inaudible. Still, perhaps... But she stumbled again, nearly falling over the body of the young man; and her next line was slurred too.

The audience, which had for a few minutes been quiet, began to mutter again. The sound went like a drift of wind over our heads; it must have reached Emma.

The two seats beside us were still empty; Carey gave an exclamation and scrambled past the knees of the already protesting audience. I followed her. I wasn't going to be left alone, watching Emma humiliate herself in front of a crowd of strangers; and I wanted to be with Carey, whatever was going to happen now.

Did eyes follow us as we scrambled up the aisle, Carey tripping over her long skirt? I kept my head down, following her. She fled out of the theatre into the warm street, round to the stage door.

The door-keeper (in shirt-sleeves and reading a tabloid paper whose headline screamed of some New York catastrophe) was at first uncooperative, but finally gave way to Carey's desperate determination.

We ran up the bare stone stairs, and came to the dressing-rooom.

This, when we entered it, had the true confusion of nightmare. My father was turning in the narrow space; Marguerite sat on the arm of a chair; a flustered young woman was pulling up the zip of her dress. Emma's make-up lay on a shelf below the bright mirror; shoes were kicked aside. Emma herself wasn't there; she must still be on stage. Our arrival was scarcely noticed: before we could say anything a young man with a long nose and wearing a damp red shirt added to the constricted crowd and said to the young woman, "It's no go; you'll have to take over, honey; like it or not."

The girl he spoke to was having trouble with her zip;

222

absently he helped her. "C'mon, honey; get going; you're our only hope—"

She looked as if she were being taken to a prison camp. "They don't want me; they want Emma."

"Not now, they don't," the young man said. "Just now Emma is number one disaster."

"They'll all go home!" the girl wailed.

"No, they won't. They've paid for their seats; we've got to give them something—" he gave her a little shove between the shoulder-blades as if he were pushing her into a swimming pool.

With one anguished look she turned to go, to be nearly knocked over by Emma who came at us with a rush and sat before the looking-glass with her head in her hands.

"*On*," the young man said, ignoring Emma, and pushing the girl in front of him. The door shut behind them; I could hear her protests dwindling as she was manoeuvred towards the stage.

We were left in the still crowded dressing-room, with my father and Marguerite, and Emma silent before the looking-glass.

"Mama," said Carey.

Emma swung her head. In spite of blurred make-up I could see beauty there; the likeness to Carey. "What in God's name are *you* doing here?"

Carey made a sudden movement and put her arms round her mother. She said, "I'm sorry. I'm sorry I asked about the letter. I'm sorry I made you tell me. It was all my fault. I'm sorry."

Without anger, despairingly, Emma pushed her away. "No," she said; "no, please—I can't take any more."

"Don't send me to England—let me stay with you—"

"For pity's sake," Emma said. "Will someone please take her away?"

My father put a hand across Carey's shoulders; Marguerite got to her feet.

"Time to be going, I guess," she said. "Let's get

223

home."

In the end Marguerite travelled with us to England, and sent us off to Lonsdale together. No more was said about my own problem, which seemed to have dropped out of sight; and we didn't see Emma before we left. Carey never spoke of the evening at the theatre, as if she wanted to clear it from her mind. Emma telephoned once, just as we were preparing to leave. Marguerite passed the telephone to Carey, who lifted it as if it were fragile. I don't know what Emma said. Carey listened for what seemed to be quite a long time; then she answered quietly, obediently: "Yes, I'll be good. Good-bye, Mama."

When she put the telephone down, she said, "Ma sounded kind of odd;" but no more.

My father came to the airport to see us off, and I saw this as an unspoken gesture towards me; it was all he could do.

But when Carey and I were settled at Lonsdale I couldn't help thinking that, though my journey to the States had been pretty negative in results, it had at least brought Carey back with me. And that was something stranger and more magical than I could explain.

Though at first she fitted in with the atmosphere of Lonsdale better than I'd expected, we were both solitaries, thrown together. And perhaps because we had both witnessed Emma's humiliation at the theatre, she turned to me as if for comfort.

She wasn't entirely out of things, at the school. Lonsdale went in much for drama, and to this Carey gave all she'd got. And, being Emma's daughter, she had plenty. She could move with easy grace and her voice was already low-pitched, like Emma's. She could dance, and even sing. Excellence has its own attractions; and gradually Carey found that other children came to her side just because she was good in the plays.

Good, yes. But even then, though I was no expert, I

had a hunch that she wasn't quite as good as Emma. Emma had some quality (damage it though she might) which was beyond Carey, and I thought always would be.

But for the present, Carey was pleased with her triumphs, and we wandered together, talking the world over. We sat on the autumn grass, Carey lying propped on one elbow; myself sitting with my arms about my knees, looking out through the fringe of my dark hair not to the quiet distances of the country about us, but to the perplexing aspects of life, and the future, whatever that might be.

"What d'you think they're doing?" Carey asked: "Ma, and your father and Marguerite?"

"Getting on with their lives," I said. "What else?" Even now, Carey never spoke of the letter we'd found, and to which she'd found the answer.

"They don't write much," she said, chewing a piece of grass. "If I have children I shall take them with me everywhere. Absolutely everywhere—"

"I thought you wanted to be an actress?"

"So I do."

"Going to be difficult, then."

"Not really. I shall have someone to look after them while I'm in the theatre, but the rest of the time I'll be *there*. I mean I shall come home—home'll be where I am."

There was a lot more to say against the idea, but I didn't say it. I'd learned by now that Carey didn't deal in facts as they were: she dealt in her form of facts. This sometimes let in a shaft of insight; but most of the time it was best to let things be.

"D'you mind not hearing from them?" she asked. "Not getting long cosy letters about all that's going on?"

I smiled. "Sometimes. But it isn't any good minding. Marguerite writes; and my father sends a message."

She rolled over on to her stomach, put out a hand and covered mine. I didn't want her to feel sorry for me, but

225

the touch was pleasant, making me want to kiss her cheek, so close to me. Uncertain whether she would welcome it, I said, "I do like you. I like you a lot."

She smiled, the smile that had even now sadness in it. "I like you too. You're the best person here."

Pleasure again touched me; it was after all a badge of achievement: by now Carey was known as Emma's daughter; and her excellence in drama put her in the limelight, even if this limelight was no more than the sun across the grass at Lonsdale.

Perhaps it was this that drove Deirdre who—though she'd shown no interest in me, was maybe put out because I no longer sought her company—to do what she did.

One evening while a rather earnest lecture was going on about ethics, I opted out and found a warm corner of the grounds. There I sat and read *The Adventures of Sherlock Holmes*, lost in a far luminous world of hansom cabs, murder and cocaine.

So lost I didn't at first hear the step on the grass.

I looked up to see Carey coming towards me. She came barefoot (this was encouraged, physical enhancement running in harness with intellectual and artistic) and wore a light sweater and a brief skirt. I had time to notice that the sweater showed the small breasts, and the skirt well-shaped bare legs. She held a newspaper in her hand.

She flung herself down beside me and tossed the paper towards me. "I found this on my bed. Someone had put it there. Kind of nasty, don't you think? Not even the courage to give it me."

I picked up the paper, an American tabloid, such as the stage door-keeper had been reading in New York. It was folded back at an article, with a heading about two feet high: "CAN EMMA SURVIVE?"; below this two photographs of Emma: one of natural perfection, the other taken off-guard, when she looked drawn and heavy-eyed, slack of chin.

226

Carey sat tensely beside me while I read.

"Remember Emma Pride, folks? That beautiful girl who was just about the most sought-after and talked about actress in town? Well, just now she's talked about all right, but not in the way she'd want to be. Just now Emma lies in a nursing home, after a collapse on the first night of an off-Broadway show. Rumour has it that she'd taken too many pills and mixed them with alcohol—that's murder; that's really murder; no one can get away with that, and no actress for more than two switches of a cat's tail... Emma Pride has three marriages behind her; all finished; and the estimated number of her 'friendships' varies from a lot to, let's say, more than a lot.

"Emma Pride has plenty going for her in an industry full of beautiful women and star personalities. We've all watched her, in a movie or on stage, and in spite of ourselves, we've wept and cheered, because Emma packs a punch like a heavyweight's arm. Or she did. But what happens now? Audiences are generous folk on the whole, but they won't pay out dollars to see an actress who lets them down.

"What's your guess?

"Emma, by the way, has two children, a boy and a girl; both in England; maybe being a mother isn't Emma's best role..."

I flung the paper aside. "Just a lot of muck," I said.

Without a word she turned to me, put her arms round my neck and held me close.

I responded clumsily but with pleasure. This was Carey, whom I'd known so long ago; and the girl who had travelled with me round the sun-bright, tower-crowded island of Manhattan. I kissed her face and felt the beat of longing in my loins. But I had enough sense to know that it wasn't sex she wanted but comfort; the kind of comfort I understood.

Still holding me she muttered, "You won't go away, will you, Rick?"

227

"Why, no—of course not." Indeed as I held her I had no wish to do anything else, not it seemed for ever. Just now wasn't the time to give her more than the comfort she needed. But there was time to come, plenty of time; all the years of the future, and I thought, but did not say: Carey, I love you. I love you more than anyone, and I always shall.

This might have been the easy exaggeration of an adolescent, but it stayed in my mind with a solemn elation, and I thought it was true. I couldn't then know how this love would develop or form; nor how the years would deal with it.

I stroked her hair, and she looked at me with the puzzled inquiry which I'd seen before when the ship circled Manhattan. I smiled at her, accepting this strange and unlooked-for moment: the sensation of love which till now had been denied me.

As she lifted her head her eyes fell upon the paper which I had tossed aside. She said, "Why would anyone leave it on my bed?"

I thought I had a pretty good idea. Deirdre had an American boy-friend; Deirdre had the turn of mind which would enjoy testing Carey.

"I'll be back," I said.

I found Deirdre at last with a group of boys and girls in the music room. A piano and recorders and guitars were in evidence. Deirdre was queen of the group as she always was, her dark hair falling back from her face, her fine teeth showing as she laughed.

I called her out.

"I'm busy," she said.

"No, you're not."

Perhaps anger has a force of its own, for she rose and came towards me. She wore jeans and a check cowboy shirt, and slightly swung her hips. "Well?" From some distance came the sound of what I took to be Vivaldi; there was usually someone playing high-class music at

Lonsdale.

I said, "You put that paper on Carey's bed."

"What paper?"

"You know damn well. That American rag, with the story about Emma Pride."

"Don't know what you're talking about."

"Yes, you do!"

Perhaps, tall and dark as I was, I had something of my father's strength without knowing it. Deirdre shook back her hair and tilted her chin at me. "Well, what if I did?"

"It was a mean thing to do."

"Oh, don't be so po-faced. It was a joke, for goodness' sake."

"Carey didn't think it was funny."

"She takes everything too seriously."

"That was a lousy article. Wouldn't you've taken it seriously?"

"I've told you: parents don't mean anything. I wouldn't mind if some paper said my mother lived in a Chinese brothel: what's it matter?"

"It matters to Carey," I said.

"Oh. . . Carey." She spoke the name with mockery. "Can't keep away from her, can you? Instead of trailing after me, it's her now."

"You can bet it's her."

"I wish you luck," she said, turning away.

"Thanks; I've got it," I called after her. I was trembling after the brief and silly confrontation, but this I thought was because of those moments when Carey had held me close.

I ran back across the grounds, but Carey wasn't where I'd left her. I wandered on; evening had come now, and the grass smelled of old summers and the trees had put on quiet like a frost. I found her at last by the pond which lay furthest from the school. She didn't at first see me. She was kneeling amongst the reeds and moss, and with intense concentration tearing the newspaper into small

229

pieces and dropping them into the water. For a few moments I watched her. Crouched, intent, ripping and ripping the paper, eyeing the pieces as they floated away on the grey skin of water.

As I stood close beside her, she looked up. She said, "I had to get rid of it. I know it's nutty because you can't get rid of all the copies of a newspaper; but I had to get rid of this one."

I said, "Sure," and sat beside her. The water put a slight reflection of itself on her face, and in the grey eyes. She said, "D'you remember when we were on that boat? When I told you I wondered what it would be like to drown?"

"If you're thinking of trying to drown in this," I said, with an effort to lighten things, "you're on your own. I'm not going into all that weed."

She gave a sketch of a smile. "Neither am I." She watched the pieces of sodden paper as they drifted away. "You can get rid of things, you see."

"Of course."

"But not the things inside you. What you feel." Her eyes were on the green-skinned water. A bird fled to the bank with a dry drift of wings, then was away, leaving silence. Carey said, "In a way, that crummy article was right. Except that it didn't say anything about her guts. How she's pulled herself back, time and again. Whatever happens, she dusts herself off and starts all over. Doesn't she?"

Yes, I said; she did.

"Nursing home," Carey said. "It's no nursing home; it's a psycho place in New York. She's been there before. It costs like all-get-out, but I suppose that doesn't matter. But it won't do her any good, staying there. I know it won't."

We were spying it seemed to me on dangerous country, for which of us was free from the accusing questions of well-meaning men who dealt with the mind?

"She'll be all right," I said, more to comfort her than in conviction; and again Carey turned to me, and I held her, as if against all danger, in my arms.

Chapter Four

Emma turned in the narrow bed. Light in the room was dim. She felt drowsy, not with the natural drowsiness of sleep, but with a heavy loss of energy as if her veins were filled with lead.

She lifted herself on her arm. She had no idea of the time. Except, she told herself through the fog in her mind, that it was time someone let her out of here. "I don't want this any more. I don't need to be here."

The door opened. Emma said, "Oh, Lord; it's you."

"Known warmer welcomes," said the young man, who wore a white coat and had a tailored brand of American good looks: broad cheek-bones, well-carved mouth and good teeth.

"It's not meant to be a welcome. I don't want to answer questions."

The young doctor pulled up a chair beside her bed. "Guess no one likes it much."

"Then why not leave me alone?"

"We're supposed to help you. Get you clear of problems."

"I don't like shrinks."

He remained unruffled. "No, people either love them or hate them, like snails or avocadoes. But for better or worse, we're here."

"I want out of here."

"So does everyone. We're trying our best to get you out. If you'd co-operate—"

Emma gave him a glance of drowsy hatred.

"For one thing," the young man said, "you ought to be out of bed—"

"I'm tired."

He clasped his hands beneath his chin. "Maybe. But not too tired to talk."

"Oh God, why do people want you to talk? How does that help? I'll talk if I want to; not before."

"The idea is to get you out of here, better; to take up where you left off."

"Where I left off was terrible."

"Maybe; but you want to pick up the threads again—"

"What does *that* mean? I'm an actress—"

"Sure," the young man said.

"I *am*. I don't want to argue."

"I'm not arguing."

Emma turned again to look at him. "I don't need to be here."

"Think you do, ma'am."

She didn't know why that made her cry. She pushed her head into the pillow, then turned savagely, wiping her eyes. "You don't know what it's like to be me."

The young man gave a faint smile. "Well, I guess none of us knows that. But I'm trying to find out."

"When I tell it, it comes out different."

"Try."

She looked across the dim room to the window. Outside was the world of New York; of Broadway; of men and women pursuing wealth or sexual satisfaction or just the problem of travelling by subway in the rush hour. Here she was removed from all that. Here she was in a half-light of mind that was companion to the shadows in the room. She said, "It was always difficult. From the beginning. I don't remember a time when it wasn't difficult."

"Your mother—"

"Oh, Jesus, I'm not blaming her. All right, she took

233

me to the States when I was small and tried to sell me to the showbiz boys and failed. So what? It didn't do me any harm. Trouble was..." Absently she took a brush from her side table and dragged it through her hair. "Trouble was, I knew, quite early on, what I'd got. What kind of talent. The question was, would anyone *else* know? Oh, you won't understand."

"Go on."

"It's like shouting when no one will listen. What did someone say about actresses? That they need the courage of a lion, strength of an elephant and the hide of a rhinoceros. Don't know about courage and hide, but I had strength—sure, I've flopped now, but early on I could work till every cow came home."

"Sure you could."

"But now ... someone told me once (can't remember who) that I wanted too much: fame and marriage and children. That you can't have them all." She fiddled with the brush again. "Maybe you can't. For a while it's all right, and then the decisions come in. Decisions are frightening. They get more frightening as you get older ... that doesn't seem fair, does it?"

The young man made a brief sound of agreement. He was listening. It was as if he was only a listener; that he himself had disappeared. Emma went on.

"I suppose it's not so bad when you get to something like eighty-four—if you ever do—because whatever you decide can't affect you for long. But in the middle of life—if that's where I'm at—they're murder. Either the ones you have to take; or living with the results of the wrong ones you've taken. And oh boy, have I taken the wrong ones."

The young man was silent; for Emma he might indeed have disappeared. "No one's fault but my own, and that makes it worse. Oh, much worse. There was this young man, you see." Somewhere in the room a fly buzzed, a vibrating string in the air-conditioned quiet. "He was very beautiful. Of course I slept with him. That's not the problem ... It's so long ago; there've been quite a number since. Everyone knows that."

She paused again. It wasn't really like talking to a person at all; it was like travelling in some other time; in the painful and unalterable past. "But Ben—he died. Whom the gods love ... Maybe the gods loved him; maybe it's the best thing that can happen. Anyway, he died. Right after we'd had this smash hit in an old play— oh, so long ago ... what does the play matter now? He had a cancer thing, of the blood—"

"Leukaemia."

"That was it. We thought he was going to be all right, but it wasn't in the end ... nothing is, is it? Or not much. And nobody helps you. They try; they try like crazy, but it doesn't work; it isn't enough ... I don't mean I'm sorry for myself; I'd just like to be different; to be rid of this great dark thing inside me, like a weight; like a dark heavy weight; like a child that'll never be born..." She found the tears coming again; it didn't matter. This was what he wanted; let him have it.

He still sat quiet. She said, "A child that'll never be born. D'you know anything about that? No, I bet not; how can you; no man does. They talk; Jesus, how they talk; but they don't know... It's the worst thing. For me it was the worst thing. That's what I mean about decisions. You make the wrong ones, and *nothing* can undo them. I still dream about it. I dream the child's inside me; that it's going to be born, and I have this great happiness and excitement, everything's in bright colours and I feel fine, and it's *all right* ... and then the colours fade and I seem to grow thinner; and I wake up. And there's no child; it's gone ... like it went, when I had the abortion. I wish I'd said No; I just wish someone had made me say No!" She wept noisily then. "But even if they had, I wouldn't have listened. I wanted to get back to the theatre." She wiped her eyes again, and her voice

235

steadied. "I told someone once, an old lady who was a kind of fan, and she said that Ben would know his child and his child would grow up with him, but I don't believe any of that. Ben's dead, and dead means dead: underground, not breathing any more. And the child was . . . wasn't even a child. I don't know how it looked: I've thought about that sometimes; I've thought of everything, but it isn't any use. It can't change anything. Whatever that child was going to be, it's gone, like something you throw out in a dustbin; and I shan't even know whether it was a boy or a girl; I shan't know anything, except it would have been beautiful, like Ben."

"You have two children."

"I know, I know. But Jonathan's as far away from me as could be; and Carey's . . ." Emma pushed the damp hair from her forehead. "I'm not sure about Carey. I've got it wrong: I told her about Ben and the baby: that was wrong—she went on at me, and I lost my temper. But perhaps . . ."

"Perhaps?"

"Perhaps, in spite of everything, she loves me. I think she does. But I get angry with her, and I can't help it. And I've sent her away. I don't know why I sent her away. That's what I mean: I don't *know* why I do things; why I make the decisions I do. They're wrong; they're always wrong. And in the night I remember them—"

"And then you need something to get you through."

"Well, sure; I need a drink and I need something to make me *sleep*. The nights are the worst of all—how do people get through the night? If they're alone? There's this dark and this quiet, and *no* one to help you, unless you telephone them—"

"Which you do—"

"Why not? They can go back to sleep afterwards. Why did God make the dark? The night?"

"You don't believe in God."

"Maybe not, but that's what people say; that's what the

236

Bible says; I read it at school: God divided the light from the darkness—something like that. And it's the worst time. Night is the time for fear, for dying."

"So you've wanted to die?" His voice was quiet, even conversational.

"Hell, who hasn't? Sometime or another. Somewhere about three in the morning—whether or not you're going to fail, whether you're loved; whether you love; all the mistakes you've made that can't be undone..." She turned her head to look at him. "Well, you got me to talk, didn't you? And it isn't any good. Because you can't say it all; you can't get out the truth of what's inside you—people don't understand."

"We try," he said; "we try."

When she looked up again, he'd gone. After the flood of words and the outburst of weeping, exhausted she slipped into sleep.

The voices woke her, slowly at first.

A nurse, the dark one she didn't like; and behind her two figures, dim as yet.

"Visitors for you, Mrs Pride."

When she saw that the figures were Lance and Guy Forster moving with difficulty on his crutch she grabbed her powder compact and comb and said to the nurse, "Why the hell didn't you let me know? Give me a chance to..." She dragged the comb through her hair. The nurse made no answer, but turned and went out, shutting the door with her usual maddening quietness.

Lance and Guy Forster. They looked strange in this room, out of context. She was still not recovered from her session with the young doctor, nor from the drugged sleep. Their figures as they pulled forward hospital chairs were not quite in focus.

She said, "I need a whole hour with the make-up girl before I see gentlemen callers like you. And I've had one hell of an afternoon."

237

"We've come to make it better," Lance said, as he sat down. She looked at him, through a blur of sleep, with mistrust. He's the person I can't forgive, she thought: he'll come when the going gets too rough, but the link that held us has gone; he belongs to Marguerite.

She shifted her position on the bed, catching the gleam of light on one naked arm. How long since she'd seen Guy Forster? . . . He brought back recollections which she wanted to obliterate. He had, she thought, changed little; the scarred face and the ungainly movements seeming to serve instead of age.

He said, "We've brought you a script."

"A *script?*" More and more she felt she hadn't fully woken from sleep. "I don't get this. I honestly don't. D'you know what this place is? I'm not here for a broken ankle or tonsillitis. I'm here because they think I need someone to muck about with my mind—"

"We know why you're here, Emma dear," said Lance. "But you've been here some time."

"Seems like centuries."

"And—" he lifted the bulk of the script from his lap— "Guy has written this play."

Bewildered, she looked from one to the other of them. "Guy has written a play? But the last play of Guy's I had any part of was *The Newcomer*, and none of us want to remember that—"

"It was a long time ago," Lance said. He was in clearer focus now; dark, with more flesh on him; still with an air of command. "I've read this—" he tapped the script— "and I've talked to Guy about it, and we've agreed that there's only one person to play the lead."

"Play the *lead?*" She rubbed her face, as if to rub the sleep and the bewilderment away. "Great heavens, I'm not playing anything, except a woman surrounded by shrinks in what they call a funny farm."

"But that's coming to an end," Lance said.

She began to wake up; to see this visitation as some-

238

thing more than a dream. "Who said?"

"The chief boy here—Dr Elmsley—says he's very pleased with you. No drink, and only the drugs they prescribe. He believes you're ready to leave within a few days."

"You mean you've been *talking* to him about me?"

"In *loco parentis*," said Lance.

"I don't like sessions about me when I'm not there."

"But those," Guy Forster said, "there will always be, as long as you're in the theatre."

"Maybe—but coming *out*. No one *told* me."

"In my experience of hospitals," Guy Forster said, "which, in its way, has been extensive, no one tells the patient anything except the time of day or the weather. And sometimes not even that."

Emma looked at him; his face now more clearly defined; the scar speaking silently of some past savagery. She said, "I still don't understand. I've always been afraid of you—"

"Afraid?" Guy Forster said: "how interesting; I hadn't thought of that—*are* people afraid of me, Lance?"

"Sometimes."

"Ah . . . not intended. No one, my dear Emma, has any illusions about you—no, don't get angry; it isn't worth while. Lance, whom I trust, persuaded me that you were the actress to play this part. He argued—and you may recall that he's a good arguer—that this spell in purdah could give you a new start."

Emma gave a small smile. "I've had an awful lot of new starts. As you must know."

"Oh yes, I've heard. But I believe this *is* your part. If you can pull yourself up by your boot-straps. And this is the time—isn't it, Emma dear?—to do just that."

She felt the mixture of excitement and apprehension. "You mean it's now or never? That this is my last chance—"

"Nothing's as final as that," Guy said.

239

"We simply mean, Emma darling," said Lance, "that there's a tide in the affairs of men. As you will have heard several actors of varying competence say. And this point for you, with Guy's play, is your tide."

Emma pulled a sheet up. She wished she could focus fully on this, for it seemed to be important. "What you're saying is that I've nowhere to go but up."

"A turn of the tide," Lance repeated. He rose to his feet and put the script on her bed. "I suggest you read it."

"And," said Guy, rising also, with difficulty, "give us your decision, as soon as you can. You will, of course, have to read for the producer. The matter isn't sewn up yet. But for the present, it's with you."

She watched him go with his lurching walk to the door. Lance lingered. She said, "I still feel I'm dreaming this. 'People don't do such things'—hell, I was a good Hedda; a damn good one . . . But I thought it was going to be such a fight to get back—"

Lance smiled. "No one's saying it won't be, ducky."

"But *Guy's* play. After all that happened."

Lance shrugged. "Leave the past alone."

"You can't."

She saw the glance he gave her then, which seemed to contain all the years of the past; the time of love, the dark decision over Ben's child; this present, where he'd brought hope and opportunity: she wasn't sure if she wanted them. He said, "You have to. Pack the past in, and move on." He leaned over to kiss her forehead. "One more fresh start. With any luck."

"Luck . . ." she said; and he turned to go.

Then she was alone with the script, a small weight on the bed-clothes.

Lance caught up with Guy in the corridor. "Quite a lot of people," he said, leaning on his crutch, "would say we're crazy."

"Everyone's crazy in this business, one way or

240

another," Lance said.

"We'll have our share of opposition; backers aren't fools."

"We've got your name—"

"And Emma's."

Lance made a grimace. "I think I can sell Emma."

"They do say," Guy replied, "that you could sell frozen fish to an Eskimo. You certainly sold her to me."

"Gentlemen, can I have a word with you?"

Lance turned to see a young man in a white coat. Lance said, "Sure. But we've a lot on hand—"

"I shan't keep you long."

Lance exchanged a glance with Guy. Hell, Lance thought, I don't want any hiccups now. Guy gave a shrug of a misshapen shoulder. The young man seemed to take this as agreement, and led them into a small office. A desk bore several files and a telephone. How different was this from his own office, Lance wondered, where the calls were not to do with the frailty of the mind, but with the frenzy of the theatre? Perhaps they had much in common.

He and Guy sat down; the young man leant on his desk and picked up a pen. "I'm afraid this is a bit out of order," he said.

Lance waited uneasily. He didn't look at Guy.

The young man said, "My name's Longman, by the way. Dennis Longman. And I know who you are; I've been told by our senior consultant. You've been seeing Mrs Pride. She's my patient."

Unease strengthened in the room. Lance said, "Well?"

Dr Longman turned the pen upside down and beat it once or twice on the desk. "I understand that you've given her a script to read."

"Yes," said Lance, with an edge to his voice.

"I'm talking out of turn, maybe," Longman said. "But she *is* my patient. And I've observed her very closely. Listened to her. A great deal of our job is listening." He gave a faint smile. "And though I say it myself, I'm a pretty good listener."

"But for the present," Guy said, "it's us who are listening."

The young doctor acknowledged this. "I'll make it as short as I can. I believe Dr Elmsley told you that Mrs Pride could be out of here in a few days? . . . Yes .. And that she'd be fit to work again?"

"That what we were told," Lance said.

Another turn and jab of the pen. "And I have one serious reservation."

Damn your reservations, Lance thought. Hard enough to persuade Guy without reservations from young doctors who looked as if they were scarcely out of school.

It was Guy who leaned forward and said, "Yes?"

"I think Mrs Pride needs longer treatment. I think she's suffering from a severe depression. While she's been here, she's had no alcohol, and heavy sedation. The results have been fair. But the worst isn't over. Far from it. I think there's a suicide risk there."

Lance crossed his legs with impatience. Guy said, "I would have thought that was true of a great number of people who made their living by the arts. As well as those who don't."

"Quite. But in my opinion—and I *have* had the most to do with Mrs Pride—she's still at considerable risk. She needs supervision for longer than a few days—more like a few months—"

"A few *months*?" Lance exclaimed. "You'd drive her completely nuts if you kept her here that long."

Longman's young face looked stubborn, as if he knew that his youth didn't carry enough weight. "I can only give you my opinion—"

"How is it," Guy said, "that Dr Elmsley says one thing, and—"

Longman shrugged. "Experts don't always agree." He brooded for a moment, as if disagreement in this case had left its scars. "I haven't the last word on this. And—" his

242

smile was a little sour—"I could be wrong. Surprisingly, medical guys do admit to being wrong, sometimes. But —"

"All you're saying," Guy broke in, "is that there's a risk in letting someone like Emma Pride out of professional hands. Both Mr Ashley and I are clear about that. In fact, there's a risk in Emma Pride being *any*-where, in my view. Do we need to say more?"

The pen tilted, balanced on an outstretched finger, then fell. "Maybe not, Mr Forster. But I shouldn't be doing my job if I didn't give you my opinion, for what it's worth. After that, it's up to you. I simply make my point." Regret seemed to be mixed with the stubbornness on his face, as if he knew he was on the losing side.

"And," Lance said, "you've already put your point to Dr Elmsley?"

"Oh, yes. He disagrees with me, as I've told you." He flicked the pen, so that it rolled on the surface of the desk. Before more could be said the door opened, and a nurse's dark head intruded into the room. "Sorry, Doctor, but I think you should come and see Mrs Arnody—"

"Right away." Dr Longman rose to his feet. He was a small man, Lance observed. Perhaps he didn't like being overridden by Dr Elmsley who was six foot and more. Longman leafed through the files on his desk, found one and put it under his arm. "I guess there's no more I can say. Good-bye, gentlemen. You know you way? Good-bye."

None of that did I want, Lance thought, as with Guy he made his way out of the Clinic. Had Guy been impressed?

"He didn't," Lance said, "tell us much that we didn't know."

"Not much," said Guy, giving little away; "not much."

Chapter Five

News didn't come fast to us at Lonsdale; but after a time Carey had a letter from Emma.

She came running to me with it, not barefoot, for it was autumn now: but the day was fine, with the gold-winged drift of leaves spiralling and here and there touching the water, at whose edge I stood. It was the same water on which Carey had cast those torn pieces of newsprint.

She came to me because by now this had become a habit—perhaps more than a habit. It seems to me now that, cut off as we were from our parents, we drew most naturally together. It was as if the easy affection of adolescence was put under a forcing sun of disadvantage, and my love for her (which grew deeper all the time) was more adult than it would otherwise have been. For the present I didn't ask more of her than that she turn to me—as she did—with news or fear or excitement.

"Here," she said, holding out the letter with a shaking hand; "from Mama."

"You want me to read it?"

"Sure. Nothing private."

I looked at the letter, written on blue airmail paper. The handwriting was large and enthusiastic, and the words spoke of a new play, first on tour in Cleveland, Buffalo and Baltimore; then Broadway. The letter included a press cutting from a Cleveland paper: "Welcome back, Emma! Emma Pride after—let's say—her fair share of ups and downs, is back, and how. She's in wonderful form; like someone given new life, new wings. Of course the *character* in Guy Forster's new play goes to pieces; but Emma doesn't. Is there an Oscar for those actors or actresses who can kick the devils that were haunting them, and come back on top? If so, vote for Emma—she should win it every time . . ."

"Of course," Carey said, "critics in places like Cleveland aren't as tough as the ones in New York. I can remember Ma saying that the New York critics were the most scary of all. But that one's good, isn't it?"

I agreed that it was good. It would have been unkind to say 'Too good' which were the words that came to me.

Carey went on, "The only thing is she doesn't ask me to come over for the New York opening. She just says when it is, and how she hopes I'll be thinking of her and wishing her all the best."

"Don't see what else you can do; after all we're in the middle of the term."

"The *term*."

"You can't just walk out."

She gave me a sidelong smile. "Want to bet?"

"No, you can't. Carey, you absolutely can't. You haven't got the money or a plane ticket—or anything." I spoke passionately because I wasn't only afraid that she might make a fool of herself; she had become important, the most important person in my life, and the thought of losing her brought a sudden darkness into my day.

She drooped a little. "No, I guess not." She took the letter and scanned it again. "But she doesn't even say she wants me there—she *must* want me; she always said I was her mascot—"

"She's too excited," I suggested. "After all, the last you heard she was in a nursing home. And now she's on her way to an opening night in New York. You can imagine what that's like."

"Sure I can. People around all the time, telling her she's the greatest. Except when she shuts them out and

245

wants to be on her own. And then..." Carey stood, biting a thumbnail and staring at the water. "Then she wants me. Because the other people don't *know* about her. They truly don't."

"There's my father," I said.

"Yeah—but he's a man."

"What's wrong with that?"

She gave a slight grin. "Oh, nothing; there have to be men. But Ma needs a woman who knows how she ticks." I didn't dispute Carey calling herself a woman. But I felt a spasm of jealousy for this bond with Emma; it excluded me, and I didn't want to be excluded.

"When she doesn't sleep..." Carey fell silent, picked up a twig and tossed it into the water, where it drifted with wayward calm. "She takes all this stuff to make her sleep. Once I got scared and filled one of the bottles with aspirin instead."

I had a picture of Carey, resorting to this subterfuge; young and frightened and doing her best. I put an arm round her, and she looked at me in vague surprise. "It didn't work," she said, as if she knew the end of all such endeavours. "Ma found out they were aspirin, and knew I'd put them there—I suppose because no one else would have been fool enough to try. But she didn't *say* anything. She was silent with me, which is the worst thing. I'd rather she'd been angry. But Ma can be silent—oh, boy, can she be silent. It's like walking in an ice-field."

Useless to protest that Carey's devotion was misplaced (much as I wanted to); I'd learned enough by then to know that it isn't always the people who deserve love who get it.

"D'you think she's written to Jonathan?" Carey asked.

I had no idea. Jonathan at his public school was far from my life and my mind.

When he came back into our lives, the manner of it seemed surprising; but perhaps should not have done.

246

Towards the end of term, from his long silence, Jonathan wrote to Carey.

As always, she showed it to me. (Another letter; but the writing this time young, not yet formed, on paper from an exercise book.) We were sitting together in the music room, where someone was playing a gramophone record of a Bach chorale. Outside the weather was already unfolding the discomforts of winter; rain curtained the windows and it was already growing dark.

Carey said, "Jonathan's in trouble," and handed me the page.

"... been a bit awkward here, as a matter of fact. We had these lousy exams: I'm no good at them—or maybe I just can't be bothered to do the work; I find it boring, and I don't like to be bored. So I worked out a ruse (good word 'ruse' isn't it?) of putting these few facts on a piece of paper and wrapping it in my handkerchief."

"Silly goof," I said; and went on reading.

"... I thought I'd get away with it easily enough, but blow me this tiresome chap: maths master with a nasty mind (must have to be a maths master) had his eye on me, can't think why (or can I?) and before I'd got an inch of info. from my scrap of paper he swooped like a vulture and grabbed it."

"Poor old Jonathan," I said; and went on.

"And at my school (unlike, I should imagine yours, dear sister) there was all hell to pay. 'Thou shalt not cheat in exams.' Doesn't come in the Ten Commandments, as far as I can recall, but from the way they carried on you'd think it was top of the list. At first I thought I was going to be exorcised, as it were, with Bell, Book and Candle; but after a number of excruciatingly boring confrontations with practically everyone, including the Headmaster who thinks he's God—perhaps he is; I've few ideas on the subject—I'm being allowed to stay on. Branded, of course, but still around. One thing is, they're a bit foxed as to who to write to. When your mother's lost in the razzamatazz of the New York theatre and your father's dead, what do you do? In the end I believe they wrote to Grandmother: about as much good as hitting a ball into a snowdrift: you know what she's like now.

"However, that's where I go for Christmas. I gather that you and Rick will be there too. Some time since I've seen Rick—how's he now? Thin with glasses, or broad and full of self-confidence? . . . Well, I shall find out." He added as a postscript, "It seems that our mother is storming through the States on a wave of acclamation: might we not have been asked to join her? Apparently not."

I knew about Christmas: my father was much encumbered (when was he not?) but not Marguerite who was in hospital for a minor operation: it would be best, he'd written to me, if I stayed in England with Carey and Jonathan, with their grandmother. He didn't tell me what the operation was (perhaps delicacy prevented him) but I felt the letter was short on information.

"So we have Christmas with your grandmother," I said, giving Jonathan's letter to Carey. "What does he mean 'you know what she's like now'?"

"Kind of odd. Sometimes she goes to sleep in the morning. Doesn't always make the beds. Puts things in the oven and forgets to light it."

"Sounds kind of nuts."

"She's getting old."

"She can't be *that* old," I said. "Emma isn't forty yet."

"Well, she seems old. Or something. You'll see what I mean when we get there."

That's what I did. I arrived in scratchy humour, for in spite of Carey's presence (which could make all things bearable) I was still smarting from a brief letter from Marguerite which said, "Your Pa's terribly busy, so I'm writing to wish you a good time, Rick, honey. Could be quite fun with the three of you. Christmas presents

248

follow; hope they'll get to you in time and unmangled by surrogate postmen."

Nothing from my father; I judged that the pressures of helping Emma back to the top absorbed him. The presents would most likely arrive; but presents were easy, I knew that. A secretary (or perhaps Marguerite, if she wasn't too busy) would go to Saks or Macy's and spend a great deal of money. There had always been expensive presents; and I supposed it was the same for Carey too.

The holiday began in confusion (apt enough, now I look back). Jonathan, coming from the Midlands, arrived at Euston; Carey and I at Paddington. Our instructions were to make our way to Euston and meet Jonathan there.

This we did, and spent much time wandering about the sombre liveliness of this place of transit, for stations have always seemed to me to contain a mixture of pleasure and doom, which some people may feel on the outbreak of war.

Cases in our hands, Carey and I searched among the peripatetic crowds. No sign of Jonathan; only train whistles and porters crying "Mind your backs!'

We must have looked lost and shabby, for Lonsdale allowed—in fact encouraged—the kind of clothes which made us look as if we were refugees.

Carey returned from a sortie round a newspaper stand. She looked weary with travelling, and I felt a spasm of irritation. "It was a silly idea to meet Jonathan here," I said; "why didn't we go straight to your grandmother's?"

Carey wiped a face smudged with train dust. "That's what I mean about adults," she said, as if we'd been talking about them. "They get ideas that aren't any good."

She looked so tired that I took her into the buffet, where we sat together over a wet and crumby table with cups of tea and a bun each.

From time to time we glanced about for Jonathan, but less and less expected to see him. I looked at Carey across

the messy table, and thought that there was no one in the
world I would rather be with. She looked tired and shiny
from travel and there was a crumb on her chin, but I
wanted nothing but to stay close to her: for me she contained all the magic in the world.

As she met my glance, I saw the colour come on to her
face. She wiped the crumb from her chin and smoothed
her hair. She said, "I wish we didn't have to arrive." (I
didn't know till much later that she echoed her mother.)

"At your grandmother's?"

"Yeah. I like it here."

I gave a glance at the unprepossessing buffet with its air
of steamy, traveller-filled rush. "Here?"

"Here with you."

I touched her hand on the table. "Maybe we could just
stay here," I said; "camp out, get food from this place."

She smiled, with pleasure, with regret. "Someone'd
come and find us. They always do. I like places where no
one can get at you. Where you don't have to explain;
where you don't have to say all those boring things: about
how you had a good journey and how you *feel* about anything."

I understood that. I wanted to know what she felt about
me, but that was another matter. I wouldn't ask her. I had
the sensation that, though she was glad to be with me,
there were difficult paths to cross before I could truly
reach Carey, as I longed to.

We finished our tea, made one more tour of the station,
then gave up. In the taxi Carey watched the passing
London streets. "Different from New York, isn't it? I
remember Ma saying once that she had transatlantic
schizophrenia. I think I know what she meant. Whichever place you're in, you want to be in the other. *Why*
d'you think she didn't ask me to spend Christmas over
there?'

I didn't want a return to Emma. "Too busy," I said.

Her head was down; the long hair fell about her face

and she was biting a thumbnail. "Guess so."

I said, "You oughtn't to bite your nails; it spoils them."

She took her hand from her mouth and gave me a drifting smile. "But Christmas is a family time, isn't it? Don't people all get together round a huge table and eat masses of food—"

"And some time later," I said, "quarrel like mad."

"Maybe. But don't you feel sometimes that there's a pattern of life that you've missed, like missing a train? And you've got on the wrong train, the one that's going to stop everywhere and break down; and you've no idea where you're going to end up?"

"Yes," I said. And I did. It was some comfort that whatever Carey said, I knew what she meant.

The taxi lurched round a corner, and she said, "We're nearly there." She put out a hand and took mine. "I hate this," she said. "I really do hate it."

"Just arriving?" I grasped her hand hard.

"Meeting people head on."

"But it's only your grandmother and Jonathan. If Jonathan's there, and not pacing about Euston."

"I know. But it's new. I'll have to be someone else. Say different things. Answer questions, like I said."

I paid the taxi, refusing her offer of crumpled notes. "I've enough."

"One thing," she said, "they may not see us, but they give us plenty of dough, don't they? And yet Ma's always having a money crisis; something about Federal tax."

"People who make a lot of money always have trouble with it," I said. "It's best not to have too much."

With this piece of adult wisdom I picked up our luggage and faced the house, which looked blank and unwelcoming. No sign of Jonathan. More and more I was glad of Carey beside me.

"No flags out," she said. "Guess Grandnan's got the day wrong."

I remembered what Carey had said about her; and waited.

My few memories of Susan Denzil were of a rather untidy lady, given to sudden spurts of enthusiasm. These memories were intensified by the woman who opened the door.

She wore a dressing-gown and her grey hair looked as if she'd been lying on it. However, after one surprised look at us, she opened her arms wide.

"Carey, darling! How kind of you to come and see me. And who's this young man with you?"

Carey gave me a brief glance as if to say, I told you so. She said, "You're expecting us, Grandnan. And this is Rick—surely you remember him? Lance's son."

Mrs Denzil looked at me with dawning, if puzzled, recognition. Though I was sixteen and she seventy or more, she made those few gestures of vanity which any woman makes before any man, pushing back the straggly grey hair, and straightening her dressing-gown. "Good gracious, so it is. But I remember him as a little boy?" (Why did I find this often repeated comment tiresome? All men were little boys once.) "And this," she went on, head to one side, "is a young man—rather a good-looking young man." I blushed, for 'good-looking' was not the adjective I would have applied to myself; and it was the more embarrassing from what appeared to be rather a dotty lady in a dressing-gown. How extraordinary to think that this was Emma's mother.

Carey accepted all this with calm. "He's O.K.," she said evenly. "And we've come for Christmas; Ma must have told you."

"Christmas!" By the surprise in her voice, it might have been July. "Oh ... perhaps she did. I do forget things now. But I'm very glad to see you ... I expect you're hungry," she added doubtfully as she led us into the house. The house smelled of cabbage and neglect. "I expect there's something in the larder ..."

We were now in the living-room. Dust lay here, sliding piles of magazines; a discarded and grubby piece of knitting which had fallen to the floor. Most prominent of all, pictures of Emma: Emma as a child (looking very like Carey); Emma at about eighteen; Emma as Portia; Emma taken in a dreamy light, looking out on to some unimaginable future: Emma everywhere. Mrs Denzil made flustered efforts to tidy the knitting, and pushed the magazines into order.

Carey looked round the room with her usual acceptance. "Is Jonathan here?"

"Jonathan? . . . Why, no, darling; I haven't seen Jonathan for quite a long time."

I began to feel that we had wandered into Wonderland. I said, "But we were supposed to meet him at Euston."

"Oh . . . Euston." She made it sound far and unimaginable, like Tibet. "I don't think I knew anything about Euston."

Carey explained.

Mrs Denzil blinked and fussed more about the room. "It's a long time since I've been to Euston. Jonathan . . . d'you think he could have gone to Paddington to meet *you*?"

"If he did, he's out of luck," Carey said.

Carey's grandmother began to look distressed. "Things do happen so oddly. What are we to do about Jonathan?"

"Wait for him," said Carey. "Jonathan's not the kind to get lost."

Mrs Denzil frowned. "There was something about Jonathan . . . something not very nice . . ."

"I heard," Carey said.

"He'd done something wrong at school. Oh, dear!" To my deep embarrassment she seemed to be on the verge of tears. "I don't know why things should go wrong . . . with one's children . . . one's grandchildren. Emma . . ." Her eyes went over the photographs, one by

253

one. The tears started. "It doesn't go as you hope," she said. "I don't know why, but it doesn't . . ."

I remained, held in my embarrassment, but Carey said, "Things'll get better, Grandnan; you don't have to worry. Jonathan'll get out of his scrape, whatever it is; and we'll all be here for Christmas."

Mrs Denzil was wiping her eyes with the wreck of a paper handkerchief. "Darling Carey; it's so lovely to see you; I didn't expect I would. I get lonely, and I thought you'd always be in New York or somewhere . . . and now you're here . . . and with Rick, too. How dreadful of me not to be ready for you."

"That's O.K.," Carey said; she was gentle, reassuring, as if she and not her grandmother were the elder here. "Maybe we could go to our rooms?"

"Oh! Your rooms . . ."

"If they're not ready," Carey said, as if she'd known all this before, "we can make up the beds ourselves."

"Oh . . . *sheets*," Mrs Denzil said, as if these were forces of unknown influence, unlikely to be where they were needed, and went hurriedly from the room.

I said to Carey, "Is she always like this?"

"Most of the time. She could always be a bit scatty."

"Yes, but . . ."

Carey picked up one of the photographs of Emma. "There's Ma, you see."

"You mean she worries about Emma?"

Carey gave me a glance as to say Who wouldn't. "I think Grandmother misses her. So do I, come to that."

Emma. I too looked at the photograph, for it was beautiful and young and untroubled by disaster, drink or failed love affairs . . . As I thought of Carey tearing the pieces of newspaper and casting them on the water, and Mrs Denzil in a confusion of anxiety and loneliness, it seemed to me that Emma had a lot to answer for.

Before I could reply the doorbell rang.

"I'll get it," Carey said; and then was back in the room

254

with Jonathan behind her.

I hadn't got my bearings yet, but Jonathan I could recognise at once. Not as tall as I was, but in spite of trouble at school, sure of himself as ever.

"Rick," he said. "Long time . . . I've been lurking at Paddington. However, in the end I gave up. Someone got the wires crossed, I suppose: they usually do." I thought he looked older than his years; his fair head, downslanting grey eyes and narrow face might have belonged to a boy of eighteen. "Grandmother's in her usual tangled mess, I imagine."

"Shut up!" said Carey with sudden anger. "She can't help it."

Before Jonathan could answer, Mrs Denzil returned. She had put on a dress and made not very successful efforts to pin up her hair. Out of breath she exclaimed, "There are enough *sheets*," as if she'd been promised eternal glory. Then added, "Why, Jonathan! What a lovely day, to have you all here." Jonathan leaned forward as she approached him, more to avoid her than to give her a kiss. "Hullo, Grandmother."

She stood, looking round at us all, Jonathan, Carey and me. "You don't know how lovely it is to have all of you here. For Christmas! I must think about turkeys."

"I shouldn't do that for too long," said Jonathan. He hadn't lost, I observed, his note of mockery.

Mrs Denzil appeared not to notice it. "Isn't it awful to forget everything? There was a letter about you, Jonathan . . . something from your school . . ."

His face was still closed, amused; he was summing her up, wondering what he could get away with. "I had a bit of trouble with my exams."

"Oh . . . *exams*. Such beastly things. I think they ought to do away with them . . . What kind of trouble?"

"I tried to give myself a bit of help. Necessary, because I don't work for exams, but not allowed."

"Oh . . . cheating," Mrs Denzil said with unexpected

255

accuracy, as if a poor opponent at tennis had made a fine passing shot. I saw the colour come on Jonathan's face; she went on, "It's always a mistake; I expect someone's told you that. Have you been expelled?"

"Certainly not." I thought Jonathan was now angry, as Carey had been; and wondered what kind of Christmas this was going to be.

"Oh well, that's a good thing," Mrs Denzil said, moving towards the door. She paused, looking as Carey had done at the photograph of Emma. Her face slipped into sorrow. The back of her dress wasn't done up, and her hands twisted together. Though still embarrassed, I felt a shaft of pity for her. I said, "Emma's having a ball in New York; she's right back at the top."

She stared for a moment at the photograph as if she hadn't heard me; then said, "Oh, yes. I've read about it. I don't get to see her very often; she's either busy or she's . . ." She didn't finish her sentence. "I'll see what there is in the kitchen." With a kind of touseled dignity she went from the room.

While we prepared for Christmas it seemed to me that Emma haunted us all. Both Jonathan and Carey, in their different ways, could suddenly remind me of her; more disturbingly, so could Mrs Denzil herself. Would Emma be like that, when she was old? (So long ago, a memory of Emma's voice in the house on Martha's Vineyard, saying that she was afraid of being old . . .) But of course she wouldn't be a lonely and confused woman whose mind had slipped: Emma had surmounted her problems, and was a star again: echoes of her triumph reached us in newspapers and on the radio; she would, moreover, I felt certain, have a man somewhere about who was ready to love and spend money on her.

Meanwhile we only heard from her indirectly, through Marguerite. As the posts brought their multiplying Christmas cards, I saw Carey sorting impatiently through them for a letter from Emma. When she didn't find it, she tossed the cards down and wandered away, silent.

One day amongst the cards, we found a discreet reproduction of the 'Virgin of the Rocks'. Over Carey's shoulder I read the inscription: "To Carey from her father with love." A cheque fell out, which Carey picked up without unfolding it.

"Your father . . .?" I said.

"Yeah. He writes, birthdays and Christmas. But I never see him." She appeared to accept this, like all else.

"D'you know where he lives?" I asked.

"Oh yes. I write to say thank you. Quite difficult, because I've no idea really what he looks like now. I've seen a photograph of him when he was young. I guess he wouldn't know me, either."

At least, I thought, my father knew what I looked like. I thought Carey's father was missing a great deal, and said so.

She gave a small, deprecating smile. "There's a kind of ban. Pa's wife is so scared of Ma—or was—that the portcullis came down."

"Must be kind of odd, to have a father who doesn't know you."

"Well, everything's kind of odd, isn't it? That's what I mean about explaining—you can't. People lead kind of nutty lives."

She looked once more through the cards. "Still nothing from Ma," she said.

I said something about the posts being all over the place at Christmas; she nodded, and wandered off.

It was a cold winter, with the first drift of snow on the city streets. Little sun showed itself; a greenish light hung above the street lamps before darkness came. On one such afternoon, I looked for Carey, but couldn't find her.

"She's gone out," Jonathan said; "she put on those great wellingtons and that duffle coat and refused the offer of company." His eyes showed a trace of malice, as if

257

he knew I'd've liked to have gone with her; but I was giving nothing away.

Left alone, Jonathan and I played a game of cards in the firelit, lamplit room, while Mrs Denzil laboured confusedly in the kitchen.

His pointed, intent face was concentrated on the cards. "I don't know why Carey gets so chewed up about Ma not writing," he said. "What does she expect? Ma's in a splendid whirl in New York. We're problems, like too much furniture: we have to be slotted in somewhere." Though his voice was quiet, I tasted bitterness in it. He glanced about the untidy room. "I bet she's not sitting in a place like this. And not with someone like Grandmother, either."

I felt sorry for Mrs Denzil, out there in the kitchen. "She does her best," I said.

"Who's arguing? But she's a rather nutty old lady; not really able to face all the facts of Mum's life."

"That's what Carey said."

"Well, it's true. She doesn't want to know. And not knowing makes her brain like a bunch of feathers."

I thought about it. Jonathan had a way of convincing you, since passion was absent from his voice. "How can you go dotty on purpose?" I asked.

"I suppose you can't. But there's the subconscious," he said, as if it were in some way his property. He tapped his cards. "Your go."

We played in silence for a while. Jonathan got up to put more coal on the fire, since Mrs Denzil had let it go down to a depressing ashy gleam. He said, "You have girls at your school, don't you?"

I said we did.

"Must be kind of fun. In my school chaps fall in love with other chaps. Better than nothing, I suppose; but not really my country."

Observing his face in the lamplight I could believe that Jonathan would attract his own sex. I wasn't surprised to

258

think he responded; nothing about Jonathan was surprising.

After a time I said, "Shouldn't Carey be back?"

He looked up. "Carey? Does she have to be anywhere by any time?"

"It's nearly six. She went out when it was still light."

"She's probably taken herself to the movies as she calls them. Gone very American, hasn't she? Sometimes I think she puts it on."

"No, I don't think so. I don't think Carey puts anything on; she's just herself."

He was looking at me with a trace of mockery, as if I'd given away more than I intended. "Shouldn't get too mixed up with Carey, if I were you," Jonathan said. "She's too like Ma."

"She's not!"

"Well, well . . ."

"And I still want to know why she isn't back. I don't believe she's gone to the flicks. She's seen this week's, anyway."

"What am I supposed to do, then?"

"I don't care what you do," I said, angry for giving myself away. I got to my feet. "I'm going to see if I can find her."

"Out into the night? Out into the snow-laden dark?" Jonathan looked the more amused the more angry I became.

I didn't answer him, but looked into the kitchen where Mrs Denzil was lost in a confusion of steam and pieces of dough. I told her I was going to look for Carey, and she turned, wiping a damp piece of hair back with a floury hand.

"Look for Carey?" she said. Disquiet drifted over her face, "Isn't she with you?"

I told her, No.

She picked up the spoon and put it straight into whatever mixture she was cooking on the stove, stirring absently. "Look for her? Oh, well, yes; perhaps that's a good idea." She blinked through the steam, looking to the window. "Carey... It's dark; she should be at home."

Something in the air (apart from the smell of cooking) which I didn't understand. I was glad to get out of the house.

I met the sharp cold of a December evening in the city; the dark air pooled with street lights, the iron-damp smell of the river. Snow had ceased, but the pavements were skiddy, and a tattered garment of white lay over the town gardens.

What was I doing? For of course there was no sign of Carey, and I had no idea where to look for her. My hands deep in the pockets of my duffle coat, I made for the embankment. Here lights from the bridges plunged like cold spears into the icy depth of water. I crossed the road where the thin layer of snow quietened the traffic, and looked down into the river. It flowed, slack and sinister, sucking against the shore. My ears began to hurt from the cold, and I moved on, with the traffic on one side and the almost silent river on the other. With my mind's eye I saw again the Hudson and East Rivers flanking Manhattan, and tried to recall the heat and blue water of that day. I found how difficult it was to recall in one season the climate of another: I could see that hot day with my mind's eye, but I couldn't feel the warmth, or truly believe that there was another air than this cold city which smelt of the river.

But then as I walked on, losing heart in this enterprise, I remembered how Carey had leaned over the side of the pleasure boat and talked about drowning. Well, that was all nonsense, I told myself; of course it was nonsense. But with the cold and the dark and the merciless river slipping so quietly by, I felt a plunge of fear in my chest. To an impartial eye I must have seemed absurd; a tall adolescent figure, duffle-coated, dark hair blown in a cold wind, searching in love and fear for a girl who'd slipped away from him: an *Albertine disparue*. Somewhere in the non-rational part of my mind a long and improbable tale spun out, wherein I saw a police car and an ambulance, and a limp figure by the river's edge . . .

I was by now very cold, and my concern for Carey was changing to anger: *why* was I wandering about the dark in search of her? It seemed now to be her fault: I had not then learned that love more often than not drove one to absurdity.

I was about to turn home when I glanced towards the Albert Bridge. Lights dazzled there, but after some moments I saw the shadow of a figure looking through the ironwork to the water below. The figure was in darkness, but then a car's lights clothed it in full and momentary light, and I saw that it was Carey.

I ran up to her. There was no need to feel alarmed, for the structure of the bridge was high, and unless Carey climbed on it—which she showed no sign of doing—she couldn't possibly fall. I was out of breath when I reached her.

She looked at me with total surprise, her face pale in the dark, hair aslant in the cold wind that seemed to drive from the river.

My anger still held: I said, "You've been out a hell of a time."

She looked as if she had to translate the words in her head. I couldn't think what was the matter with her. At last she said absently, "Have I? I went for a walk."

"A pretty long walk. It's freezing."

She put her hands on the barricade of the bridge and looked down at the water. "Have you been looking for me?"

"Yes," I said; "and I'm freezing too."

As if she caught the anger in my voice she gave me a pleading glance and said, "Oh, Rick; I've done such a stupid thing."

At once my anger fell away; I moved closer to her.

"I don't know why I did it," she said. "I just wasn't liking it at Grandmother's any more; and there wasn't a letter from Ma; and I felt angry and I went out—"

"We could have gone together!" I protested with all the force of neglected love.

She gave me a brief, acknowledging smile. "I know. But it seemed like something I had to do alone. I went to see my father."

"Your *father*? But you don't know him."

"That's right, I don't. But, like I told you, I know where he lives in Kensington and I thought ... no, I didn't think: I just took off and went to his house."

I thought Hell, *no*; but didn't say it. "You should have warned him."

"Yes, I guess so. But I didn't. I just went. I thought maybe I could say Thank you for my present, instead of writing. It made an excuse, anyway."

"If you'd asked me, I'd've said Don't go."

Another small smile. "Maybe that's why I didn't ask you. It was an impulse—the kind of thing that Ma can do, and I suppose Grandmother, in her day ..." She looked down at the shining black water.

"What happened?"

"Everything and nothing, you could say. I walked about the street for some time before I pushed the bell. The moment I'd done it, I knew it was wrong. But it was too late; so I waited." (I could see her standing there, and felt a mingled exasperation and pity.) "Of course it was like all those dreams when you're in in the wrong place at the wrong time. One of his children answered the door— a girl of about nine. I thought it might be a butler or some- thing, but this kid just yelled back, 'Mummy, there's someone here'; and one of those stream-lined ladies with *every*thing in place: hair just out from under the dryer and a very expensive sweater and skirt, came on clicking heels into the hall. I wanted to chuck it in then and run, but

262

hadn't quite the nerve. She looked at me as if I were collecting for something, and said 'Well?' Not a very enthusiastic Well, at that."

I tossed a bit of paper from my pocket to the water below, living this with her.

She went on, "Then I heard a man's voice call, 'What is it, darling?' and she said, 'There's a girl here; I don't know if she's carol-singing.' I don't know why that made me mad: I said quite loudly that I wasn't carol-singing, and my name was Carey Gardner, and the man in the other room was my father. By that time he'd come into the hall and we all stood there in a sort of frozen silence as if we were forbidden to speak. Then another kid, a younger girl, came running into the hall and said, 'What's happened?' I could have told her what'd happened; I'd made a first-class hash of everything."

"Your father?" I said.

"Oh, he seemed a pretty nice guy, but of course he looked too as if something had just exploded in his face. There he was with his wife and kids—and a pretty tough wife, I'd say—and here was I, like the girl from the wrong side of the tracks. I couldn't get out fast enough. My father tried to say something (guess you have to try to say something to your daughter, even if she is a non-event in your life) but I turned and ran down the steps, and went on walking and walking, while it all went through my head and I felt hot with shame; and kept thinking *Why* did I do it."

I put my arm round her, because I could see that it had been one of those disastrous events which the mind finds too difficult to carry. "Why did you?"

She drew close to me. "I don't know. I was thinking about Ma, I guess; and I thought he'd once been married to her; and he *was* my father . . . I had a sort of fantasy of him being pleased. But of course he wasn't, and it's just turned into one of those things one doesn't want to remember."

"There are lots of those," I said, holding her more tightly. "And I suppose they get more as you grow older, because you've more time: like building up a library."

She smiled and leaned her head against my shoulder. "You mean it gets more and more difficult?"

"I shouldn't be surprised," I said.

She chuckled as we turned to walk home. I was glad of the weight and warmth of her body for the streets didn't seem so lonely, nor so cold.

Then as we walked the snow-stained streets she said absently, "I wonder why Ma *hasn't* written."

I felt a spasm of annoyance; like all lovers, whether sixteen or sixty, I wanted her to be concerned with me and me alone. "You know why," I said briefly. "She leads her own life, and leaves you to lead yours. Well, she does, doesn't she?"

Her face, lifted to the cold wind, looked sorrowful. "All the same, she needs me. I understand her. I understand her better than anyone."

"How can you know?"

"I just do. I'm her daughter, aren't I?"

I suppressed the impulse to argue; this wasn't the time, when she'd just faced the absurd encounter with her father. But it crossed my mind that one day I might argue with her; and it could be quite an argument.

I said, "What were you doing on the bridge?"

"Just looking at the water." She glanced at me, friendly again, perhaps teasing. "I told you once, I like water."

I grasped her more firmly. I wanted her with me, and I was frightened for her, though I had no more reason for my fear than some hazy talk about drowning, and her doomed effort to make contact with her father on this winter's night.

I looked up at the sky, which was scattered with icy stars. I was too young to have read Pascal's 'The eternal silences of these infinite spaces fill me with fear' but something of that touched me now as I walked in that cold air with Carey beside me, protected for the time being by my arm.

Neither Carey nor I made any mention of her escapade to Mrs Denzil; and Jonathan asked no questions. But, I thought, unease stayed with us, as if we were waiting for more than Christmas Day.

Certainly a large parcel arrived from New York, with presents of clothes for Carey; and leather wallets and such for Jonathan and me. I watched Carey as she tore at the wrapping paper: she found a scrawled card from Emma: shiny, gold, with 'All my love, darlings', written in her large unmistakable hand. Carey put it carefully on the mantelpiece, making no protest that it wasn't more personal. Jonathan accepted both the presents and the card with his usual reserve, only remarking, "Mama's handwriting gets larger the more successful she is." Certainly the scrawl allowed scarcely more than a word to a line.

Christmas Eve contained the usual confusion, and more that we didn't expect.

Mrs Denzil, still dusted with flour from making mincepies, said suddenly that we were all going to Midnight Mass.

Jonathan at his public school, was used to such celebrations, whatever he privately thought of them, but Carey and I made demurring noises, saying that we didn't go to church, no one at our school went to church, and we'd rather stay at home and wrap up our presents.

I expected Mrs Denzil to agree to this, since she showed few signs of opposing us. But she wiped her forehead with a floury hand and said, "Oh! But you *must* come—"

I said, "But I don't know anyone who goes to church."

"You do now," said Mrs Denzil with unexpected asperity. "I go regularly to the church along the road, and it's a great comfort. The Vicar's a very nice man, and sometimes he comes here for tea." To my embarrassment, she again showed signs of tears. "I don't know where I'd be without it. For I'm alone a great deal—it isn't often that I have the house full of children, like this. And Emma . . ." She turned her head away. Her voice was muffled. "I don't know whether Emma goes to church . . ." (I made no comment, but thought this improbable.) "But I pray for her," Mrs Denzil went on; "I pray that she'll be all right, because . . ." She blotted her eyes with a crumpled handkerchief, and I looked the other way. "I pray that she'll go on being a great success, and that some time I'll see her, because I don't see her now; I just hear things about her; and she's my only child . . ."

It was then that Carey surprised me. I should have been used to surprises from Carey; but I was not, and while Jonathan and I stood, held within our differing embarrassments, Carey plunged towards her grandmother and put her arms round her, flour and tears and all. "She'll be all right, Grandnan. She always comes fighting back; you know she does; we both know she does." She spoke passionately, and though her passion was concerned with Emma whom I saw as an adversary, I could not but admire the impulse which drove her to comfort her grandmother; and I loved her for that rush of compassion which I myself could not have made.

So we all went to Midnight Mass. I expected the church to be a bleak place, a sanctuary for lonely and odd old ladies like Mrs Denzil, and others who'd no where else to go on a cold night; but in fact the church was brightly lit and decorated with the green mackintosh and sealing wax of holly, and the bloom of chrysanthemums. The altar blazed, white for this festival, and the pews (it was not a large church) were crowded.

Mrs Denzil had put on a drooping black hat which looked as if it had been retrieved from a cupboard after long disuse, an old fur coat and several scarves. Before taking her place she genuflected deeply, and one of her scarves fell off. I was still embarrassed by her, but Carey scooped up the scarf and seemed untroubled. She made an effort to genuflect, though I doubt that she knew what she was doing it for. Jonathan merely inclined his head, as if he'd seen some acquaintance far off, and I did the same, not wanting to be left out.

I had small exprience of church services and was at a loss to know when to sit or stand, but the colour and the music and the smell of incense (the Church was, Jonathan informed me, 'High') all combined to give me a sensation which had little I daresay to do with faith or God, but which was pleasing none the less. I glanced at Carey beside me to see if she felt the same. Certainly, she was looking about her as if the place had some magic in it; her chin was lifted and her eyes bright. When all was in full flood, the priest in white vestments, incense drifting upwards, choir giving 'The Holly and the Ivy' all they had, she whispered to me, "Ma'd *love* this; it's like the best kind of theatre." I agreed, though I wasn't sure that the priest and his followers up there were performing principally for Emma's sense of theatre.

However, my embarrassment was not yet dead, and when Susan Denzil sang 'While shepherds watched their flocks . . .' in a piercing soprano which made heads turn, I felt the colour ride on my face. Jonathan stood with his head down; only Carey showed no sign of being abashed, singing cheerfully and in tune. The Vicar spoke of the birth of a Child, and how this time brought new hope for everyone, even the most sorrowful. Mrs Denzil wept quietly, Carey listened with apparent attention and Jonathan was looking at a pretty girl in the pew opposite. The Vicar was younger and generally more acceptable than I'd expected; he didn't intone or (except for his dress) look much different from some of the masters at school. "Rather a nice guy," Carey whispered to me, and I gave a brief nod.

When it was over we came out into the snow-footed and

icy quiet of Christmas Day. Mrs Denzil was alight with tears and goodwill: "There!" she said, as if she'd given us a promised treat; "wasn't that beautiful? Didn't you enjoy it?"

"Yes, I did," said Carey, walking with her hands in her pockets, solemn, head down. "But it isn't always like that, is it? I mean, when all this is over it'll be quiet and then I bet only a few people come: like a theatre when a show's coming to an end."

"Oh, you don't want to think like that," Mrs Denzil said; "Church is *always* beautiful. What a pity *none* of you've been baptised!" she added, as we went through the late night streets, huddled into our coats, under the distant stars. She dropped another scarf, which Jonathan retrieved. "*I* was," he said. "My father believed in it. And I was confirmed at school . . ."

"Oh . . ." Mrs Denzil looked at him doubtfully, as if she wondered whether this inoculation had truly taken.

We came into the house, out of the cold. The Christmas tree leaned sideways, and some of the decorations had fallen down, but a touch of celebration lingered even here. I wandered into the kitchen, where the floor was scattered with flour and a naked turkey stood on the table amidst the general confusion.

Then the telephone rang.

Mrs Denzil gave a small scream, as if the telephone like telegrams of old could only mean disaster, but before I was out of the kitchen, or Jonathan could do anything, Carey had flown to lift the receiver.

I watched her. I think she'd known almost before she spoke who it was; I saw her face colour and heard the delight in her voice. "Mama! . . . yes . . . yes . . . we've been to church—yes, *church* . . . with Grandnan . . ." A long space while she listened and I could faintly hear Emma's voice, so strangely from the other side of the Atlantic. I couldn't hear what she was saying, but Carey became more and more excited, pushing her hair awry and changing the telephone receiver from hand to hand. "Why . . . *yes*," she said at last; "Yes, yes, yes; I'm sure I can. Of course I can. Nobody'll mind; it'll be perfectly O.K. . . ." She listened some more, her face transformed, flushed, absorbed by the voice from so far away.

Mrs Denzil moved distractedly at Carey's shoulder, but Carey was unaware of her. "Of course I'll come!" she said loudly, and put the receiver down before her grandmother could take it.

Mrs Denzil gave a loud wail and took off her hat. She was at once absurd and pitiful. Carey turned, putting her hand to her mouth. "Oh . . . Grandnan, I'm sorry; I'm really sorry . . . but it was so exciting, and I forgot everything else."

Mrs Denzil was slowly unwrapping herself from scarves and coat, letting them fall where they would. She said, "Emma's my daughter."

Carey looked aghast. "I know, but—"

"I wanted to speak to her. It's Christmas Day."

"Oh, I'm sorry. Truly I'm sorry." Again she put her arms round the sad and shabby figure. "But it's so exciting—Mama wants me to go—as soon as I can, as soon as I can get there—"

Mrs Denzil looked bewildered. "Go?"

"To New York. Before I go back to school."

"But you can't! How *can* you? Tomorrow's Christmas Day—no, to*day*, and after that it's Boxing Day—oh, it's not possible; everything's shut—"

"But she wants me!"

"Emma always thinks she can have everything she wants." Mrs Denzil absently retrieved her coat from the floor. "She always did and she always will." (I thought that for someone usually dotty, she was talking sense.) "What d'you suppose we can do? I've got everything ready for Christmas—"

Even I knew a touch of pity then, remembering the chaos and the naked turkey in the kitchen.

269

"—and how are we going to get you on an aeroplane?"

"Ma said after Boxing Day. She said she'd send the money; she's got plenty of money now—"

"She won't have it for long." Mrs Denzil seemed to have moved into some area of perception and sanity. Carey by contrast looked stricken. "But I must go. I've never not gone if Ma wants me—"

"She didn't, I suppose," Jonathan said dryly, "ask for me too? No, I didn't imagine so. True to pattern." For a moment the closed expression of his face showed a flicker of wounded hatred. I found it uncomfortable.

"But *why*," Mrs Denzil was saying, as she gathered her coat and scarves together and put them haphazardly on to the sofa; "why does she want you? Now? I don't understand—"

But, I thought, I understood only too well. I could see Emma before the performance in New York, picking up the telephone on impulse, and tossing this small bombshell into our household.

Carey's excitement was now perhaps cooled by contrary winds. "She said I could come on the day after Boxing Day, and see the show, and stay till I had to go back to school. There's nothing wrong with that, is there?"

No one answered.

"I shall be here for Christmas Day," Carey protested.

Mrs Denzil in a moment of abstraction put on her hat again, then took it off. "It isn't the same," she said, but sadly, accepting. "Of course, I can't even promise that we'll be able to get a place for you on the aeroplane—"

"Oh, please!"

"I don't see how I can if there isn't room. There isn't always room."

"But you'll try? Please say you'll try!"

Mrs Denzil gathered up her clothes once more, scarves trailing, and made for the door. "Oh yes," she said; "I'll try. Emma always gets people to do the things she wants

270

... I'd like to have spoken to her. But then...." She was gone.

Jonathan yawned."Quite a Christmas Eve. I'm going to bed. "Happy Christmas, everyone; if that's possible."

"Ma sent her love to you!" Carey called after him.

He slightly turned, slightly smiled. "*And* a present! Almost too much," he said, and shut the door.

I faced Carey alone. She seemed torn by her excitement and the reception of it; and I might have felt sorry for her, but I did not. I was (inappropriately enough after the Midnight Mass) blazing with anger, the childish anger of disappointment, of loss.

"You should have said 'No'," I burst out.

"But she asked me!"

"She can't do just do that—ring people up after midnight and ask them to come to America."

"I'm not 'people'; I'm her daughter—"

"You could have said no, you could have thought of us—" but of course I meant 'me', and knew for the first time the furious injured pride, the balked longing of one who's been turned down.

"But Ma wants me—"

"And if she wants you so much, why didn't she ask you before? And what about Jonathan?"

"I don't know. I mean, I don't know why she didn't ask me before, and I don't know why she didn't ask Jonathan. Except that she knows I want to see her more than he does—"

"And you go at the drop of a hat?"

"Why not?" Her anger was matching mine.

"Because it isn't fair to any of us. Everything's changed—you were going to be here until we went back to school, and now—"

"But seeing Ma's the best thing! Just about the best thing there is!"

"Better than being with me?"

She looked trapped now, her colour and excitement

271

gone, anger in its place. "Different," she said. "You're different. I can see you when I'm back at school."

"And that's enough? That's all you want? You don't mind leaving me here in this—this extraordinary house where everything looks as if it's come out of a jumble sale, with Jonathan who couldn't care if I dropped dead; and your grandmother—"

"*Shut up!*"

"I won't shut up. You've made a mess of Christmas; it was good in that church just now, before we came home and the telephone went; and then . . . oh, hell, you *must* see!"

"But I've been waiting to hear from Ma!"

"And now you've heard, the rest of us can go to hell?"

"That's not fair!"

"I didn't say it was fair, I said it was true. How d'you think *I* feel? My father hasn't rung up from New York and asked me over; nor is he likely to. I'm just here with *your* grandmother, and what d'you think that feels like?"

"It's not my fault. I'm going—"

"You may not be able to. Get a flight at the last minute just after Christmas? I shouldn't think you had a chance." I'd found a means of hurting her, which I wanted to do; it was the only way I could hit out from my own hurt.

"I have—I have. There must be a chance. Somehow I'll get there."

"And come back? I wouldn't even bet on that."

Her tears were half distress, half anger. I leaned forward and grasped her wrist. She looked at me, frightened. I pulled her towards me and kissed her, clumsily but with force. She didn't pull away from me. I kissed her again, then let her go.

I said, "You liked me to kiss you."

She made no answer, but looked at me with drowned surprise.

I said, "You did. But you're still going?" We were not

272

only alone in the room, we seemed in the small hours of that morning to be alone in time.

She said, her voice thin, "Yes. If I can."

Then she went quickly out of the room, and I was alone with the slanting tree, my despised love, and the snow-quiet of the Christmas streets outside.

Part Three

Chapter One

You can't go back. I've learned that now. Not long ago I wandered down the Embankment, and stood looking at the house where I had spent that Christmas. I went there, not expecting to find anything, merely to savour a time which was irrecoverable, which had, I suppose, left a scar. But even the scar, I thought, was better than what I had now. The past was always acceptable (apart from the pain you'd given) because it was over, and you had lived through it and survived, to be the person you were.

The house had been repainted, and was occupied by strangers. What else did I expect? Susan Denzil had died; in fact that Christmas had been her last, with the drooping scarves and her sadness about Emma. Not long after she began to have severe headaches, and the medical boys found that she had some sort of growth in the brain; they operated, but it wasn't any good. I stood looking up at the house, remembering her. So many years—how quickly the dead faded from your mind if you weren't greatly involved with them. Her dottiness, it seemed, wasn't just caused by her concern for Emma; it had a hard, true physical reason. As I thought about her, I wondered if anyone else were doing the same. I doubted it. Certainly, at the funeral Emma had appeared distressed, but I daresay that was guilt, a common cause of grave-side unhappiness. It seemed doubtful that now, nearing her fiftieth birthday, Emma was thinking of her mother.

Though one couldn't be sure. I could remember from

so long ago, when I'd been a small boy on the Vineyard, in the summer's sea-washed heat, hearing Emma's voice (a young Emma then) as she talked to Marguerite in the kitchen: Emma's voice saying she didn't want to be— what was it? Old and stringy and lame... Well, fifty wasn't old: but it wasn't young any more; and Emma must be afraid. Perhaps when one's afraid one remembers one's mother. I couldn't know, not having had one that I had any picture of in my mind.

Why did I want to go back? My last memory of that house was of Carey leaving for the States, because through one of those contrary miracles, she had got a flight, and she'd gone to Emma.

And, as opposed to what I'd expected, she'd returned. She'd come back for the beginning of term, and I had known the deep relief of seeing, when you had feared not to, the person you loved. Through the early months of that year, while the February skies showed that marbling of light and dun-coloured clouds which despite its look of storm, promises spring, we made up our quarrel, and wandered again together. Sometimes it would surprise me that the small child who had screamed on the shore of the Vineyard should now be the centre of all my hopes and desire.

There was a time when we were happy. Or so it seemed, standing here now. I suppose we quarrelled, and it was a long time ago: Carey was a child, and I not much more than one, tall though I was, and much though I loved her. But she'd returned from Emma; she was with me, and when I kissed her she wrapped her arms round my neck, as if I were a token of rescue in a storm. Perhaps I was, for a time.

But that call from Emma on Christmas Eve was, as I might have guessed, only a beginning; and within a year Carey had returned to the States because Emma, now on the West Coast, had seen a chance for Carey in films. Not much came of that; but she stayed there, in a so-different life.

For myself, I took my stand in England. I'd been to school there; the house in Hampstead remained for the times when my father and Marguerite were working here. Perhaps what seemed to me their casual unconcern enforced my decision to make my way as a theatrical designer in my own country, rather than the States which lingered in my mind as a place of holiday.

And for a long while, despite letters, despite rumours of a love affair which had turned sour, I saw little of Carey, living as we did in different continents.

But she still haunted me. And between the lines of those letters I sometimes glimpsed a regret for the time that was past, the new distance between us.

And then came Carey's twenty-first birthday.

Preparations for this were more than usually extensive, for the party was being held in Marguerite's house on Martha's Vineyard. (One pattern, it seemed, endured—that Marguerite opened this house to all who came.) "You will, of course," my father wrote, "come over: and just for once accept from me the money for your fare." This was a reference to my—perhaps stubborn—refusal of his help; a determination to make my own way and earn my own money. (I hadn't done very well so far; young theatrical designers couldn't number themselves among the prosperous; sometimes it was hard to pay the rent.) It would have been ungracious to refuse; and in any case, I much wanted to see Carey again.

So Jonathan (subsidized by Emma) and I flew to Kennedy; and thence to the Vineyard.

From the moment of arrival on the island my heart beat with the expectation of seeing her; but the meeting as it turned out was oddly casual. She had been down-island shopping with Marguerite; and I met her, burdened with a larger paper bag filled with food for the party, outside the house. She put the bag down and ran towards me with

279

a grin of happiness and kissed me. "Why, Rick!" She looked pleased, friendly; I couldn't tell whether my arrival meant more than this. She was dressed in island uniform: shorts and a T-shirt; open sandals. Her skin was already brown.

I tried to see her with detachment: Carey at twenty-one. She still wore her hair long, but it had darkened a little; her figure was like Emma's, slight but alluring with small high breasts and slim legs. The grey eyes were like Emma's too; pale in the sun-tanned face. She had much of Emma's magic, and to look at her was to want her: to slide your hand down her neck beneath the drift of hair, touch the small breasts. And I knew, with one sight of her, that for me nothing was changed.

We were in July, and the day of Carey's party was deep blue and blazing with heat. The party was to be held out of doors, in early evening. To quell the bugs which would otherwise have plagued us, Marguerite had men come with a tractor and spray all the shrubs and trees, right down the slope, with insecticide. I wandered to the window, and said, "How's it feel to have the whole place disinfected for your benefit?"

She smiled. "Kind of grand."

Was there reservation in her voice? It became clear to me that amongst the preparations for this party (supervised by Marguerite, with a company of young people from the Vineyard) lurked a question: would Emma turn up? She was, we were told, flying in from New York: the skies were clear, so there would be no hold-up at the airport, as there sometimes could be when the island was wrapped in fog. But Emma didn't need a fog, as we all knew, to keep her from an appointment.

Though I worked in England (when work was to be had) in out of town rep.—places like Birmingham and Bristol—I still heard rumours of Emma; the same rumours there'd always been. There were those who called her 'a legend in her lifetime'; and those who said she was 'poison at the box office'. But she managed still to be a name—a name bedraggled with the weed of disaster—but a name, none the less.

Preparations for the party seemed to go on all day; boxes of vodka and whisky and gin and crates of wine lurked in the kitchen; Marguerite directed us, as we set up chairs and tables in the garden; plates and plates of food within the house. In these last years Marguerite's hair had turned almost completely white; this was becoming, for her face was still young, but surprised me, as if she'd put on a wig.

With Carey beside me (dressed now for the party) I set up a table, and put out cardboard plates. The blazing day was on the turn; the old breeze from the sea bent the grass and the pine branches swung. Down there was the water, bearing the sun's dipping light. The wind blew Carey's long blue skirt against her legs, and the white blouse against her breasts. Standing there with the wind against her, looking to the sea, she had something of all youth, with its expectations, its hopes and the shadow of its fears.

I put my hand on her waist for I needed to touch her, and asked, "Who's coming? Apart from us and Jonathan?"

"Oh, people from the Vineyard. And the theatre. Friends of Mama's."

"Why didn't she have it in New York?"

"Too hot. Anyway Marguerite does these things better than Ma. Ma's working—"

"In New York? In July?"

"She's doing a one-woman show at the Lincoln Center. It's going fine."

A challenge in her voice. I didn't take it up. I wanted to win Carey back—if winning was what I had to do—not argue about Emma. I said, "How do things go for you? I mean work?"

"I get by."

281

"No more than that?"

She shrugged. "It's not a good time for the theatre."

"It's never a good time for the theatre."

She smiled. "Television's hit it hard."

"You're telling me. Tried television yourself?"

She made a small grimace. "Oh, yes. I've tried everything. My voice comes over badly. Everyone says the same thing: 'Not as good as your mother's'. I never play on Ma; I call myself Carey Gardner, but they all find out in the end. People say '*You've* got a head start'—but it isn't like that. All right, you get noticed, but they expect a pocket edition of Ma, and of course they don't get it, and they mark me down. If I was Carey Bloggs, daughter of a real estate man, they'd see me as I am."

'A real estate man.' I said, "Your father? Is he coming?"

Her glance was accepting, showing both sorrow and regret, but overcome by neither. "My father? Why, of course not. He wrote an apology and sent a cheque. What else would he do? . . . How's it in England?"

"It goes," I said. "I get design work from time to time."

"At other times?"

"I do all sorts of things. Waiters, working in parks, even building sites." I was, I found, proud of this.

"Doesn't your pa offer help?"

"Not the kind of help I want."

"That's how I feel about Ma. I want to be *me*: Carey Gardner. Not Emma Pride's daughter." She looked at me with sudden passion. "That doesn't mean I don't love her. And go for her."

Yes, I said dryly; I believed that.

Her head drooped a little, while the voices and movement went on about us: preparations for a party, I thought, were like preparations for a war. She said, "I guess you hear rumours. Talk about her."

"Now and then."

I expected her to say they were exaggerated, but she went on, "They don't know the half of it."

I looked at her, for now the shadow was on her, the shadow I'd seen earlier, and knew well from the past. "Rows—oh, boy, really first-class rows—mental homes—and a number of pills you just couldn't believe anyone could take and live. And the Press—you don't have to forget the Press. I've seen Ma have hysterics because rumours had got out that some management had fired her and the Press were banging at the door. Like a siege."

Strange to hear these words in this paradisal place, and from a girl with beauty who was twenty-one. It was as if a child described a nightmare. But, I thought, Carey had been describing nightmares since I could remember.

"The best thing is," Carey said, "that she comes back. She comes right back. And somehow she finds someone to put up the money. Because she doesn't let go. And she still needs me."

I glanced at her. "Aren't there other people?"

"Men? Oh . . . yes. Lots of those. There have to be. It's all right for a time, and then there's a row; sometimes Ma threatens to commit suicide. Once she *did* try—"

"You mean when you were there?"

Carey's head was still down. "Yeah. It was a bad evening. She wasn't working, and she had this row with Don Parkes—he was a kind of crummy actor—and she'd been drinking. I was in the room where I sometimes stayed in her apartment, and I heard them shouting, and then the front door slam. Ma started flinging things about the room—she broke quite a lot. I tried to stop her, but it wasn't any good. Then she went upstairs like the wind; she was calling Don names, and saying that she didn't want to go on living, and that she'd never act again. But she'd done that before."

I remembered Carey, all those years ago, telling me that she'd put aspirins in the pill bottles; and I wondered what went on beneath the quiet voice that wasn't right for television. Indeed, as I watched the young face with the light on it, I became aware of darkness, dread beneath the lightness and the beauty. I remembered the child on the Manhattan boat who'd said 'I think about how they're all going to die'.

I said, dodging a young woman who was bringing out more chairs, "What happened?"

"I heard glass breaking, but I thought at first she was just throwing things about again. But then she screamed and I went up the stairs, fast as I could, and there was Ma in the bathroom with blood all over her hands." Though she still spoke quietly, her face had grown paler, as if she saw it all again. "It looked frightening, but I wasn't frightened at the time: I felt cold and detached, and I told her to lie down, and I called the doctor and fetched a towel. She'd broken a tooth mug, and tried to slash her wrists. At least—well, it seems kind of mean to say it, but I don't think she *meant* it to work. I don't think so. Otherwise she wouldn't have screamed for me so soon—"

"For you?"

"Well, yes; I guess it was for me. Because I'm better with her than anyone, like I told you. The doctor came and they took her to hospital, and for a time she wouldn't see anyone—not even me."

"And where in all this," I asked, "does Jonathan come in?"

"He doesn't—sure he's here now for the party; but most of the time he's in England. And even if he wasn't . . ." She shrugged. "He wouldn't be part of it. It isn't his scene. He hardly ever sees her. He says he's too busy working on his damn' paper." The flash of anger surprised me, for I didn't think Carey really cared what Jonathan did or didn't do. He had started as a journalist on a small provincial paper, but now worked in Fleet Street.

"Maybe he is," I said. As I remembered it, Emma had

shown small wish for Jonathan's company; and Jonathan himself had shown a wounded bitterness at this neglect. "Anyway, he'll see her tonight."

"If she comes," Carey said. She said it without expression.

I would like to have said, Of course she'll come! but I could not. I said only, "I miss you, there in London. I think of you."

Her face was turned to me. "Honest? In swinging London, with all those chicks?"

"I don't go much for chicks," I said, sounding, I thought, pompous.

"Don't tell me you don't have girl-friends. You're not the monk type, and you're not queer."

I shrugged. "Well, of course there are girls—"

"Nice ones?"

"You make them sound like an army. One or two. Yes, they're nice."

"And accommodating?"

I didn't want this; we were verging on a bantering battle about sex, which wasn't at all what I wanted. For the sight of Carey, there in the Island garden, made it more and more clear to me that I had never freed myself from that childish love. Standing there in the evening wind from the water, I thought you could find a great many reasons for this—all the past; the knowledge of Emma; the childish embraces at Lonsdale; the anger and the early passion. But love is not, in the last resort, composed of reasons, and to list them was as absurd as to list the qualities of such an evening as this in the high garden with the sea about us.

"If you don't understand," I said.

"Understand what?"

"How I feel. That I don't want anyone but you. That I never have." I spoke quietly, for people were beginning to swarm about us now, and this was not the time to make one's declaration of love, but I saw her face change from mockery to a serious wonder. She put out a hand and touched my cheek, and I thought, Why, it's here; everything I've wanted; I have Carey, and nothing else matters—but then the party began to swarm more closely about us, and my father was at my shoulder: "Come along, Rick! Strong hands needed; help us with these bottles;" and Marguerite was speaking to Carey, and the garden, so recently haunted, became full of voices, and Carey was swept from me as a swimmer is pulled away by a strong current, and amidst all the gaiety a shadow crossed my hope.

Colour and drinks; laughter going up in the evening air, gradually cooling after the blaze of day; the long skirts of women soundless as they brushed the grass, and beyond all this, the circle of quiet water far down; the distant Atlantic whose depths made puny the voices and the laughter here . . .

More and more guests wandering into the garden: all embracing Carey till she became caught up with them, her face flushed and her hair drifting in the wind, the centre of all attraction, apart from me. A pretty brunette with a cream-smooth tan and a scarlet dress which showed as much of her as it possibly could wandered to my side. I was glad of this, but only because I hoped that Carey would see me; I don't think she did. The brunette, perhaps disappointed, was pounced upon by a tall fair young man with a skin coloured even deeper than her own.

"You don't want to let things like that go." Jonathan was beside me, glass in hand. I made some sort of reply. I tried to sum him up, recalling what Carey had said. He was tall and slight with controlled movements that might have been effeminate but were not; his glance rested on the bosom of the brunette who had deserted me.

"Mingled with all this *jeunesse dorée*," he said, looking about him, "are quite a number of the famous: enough to make a story."

"You mean you're going to write about it?"

He shrugged. "The paper I work for has readers who like the 'big names of stage and screen'. Or that's how they put it. So I give them what they want. See that chap over there?" He made a gesture with the hand that held the glass. I saw a wreck of a man being helped to a chair; he moved on crutches, and his scarred face was seamed with lines, and crowned with a shaggy crop of grey hair. "That's Guy Forster," Jonathan said; "have you met him?"

"I think so—with my father, years ago." I was sure I had, but I remembered him with dark hair, and the face, though scarred, without lines. Threading the youth of this party was the streak of age: Marguerite with her hair white; my father more heavily grey; his jaw slackened: a man nearly sixty. Carey and I and the rest of us were young, but age like an unseen sorcerer moved among us, touching men and women with his hand. No one spoke of him; we all pretended he wasn't there.

Jonathan and I watched Guy Forster as he struggled into his chair. "Quite a playwright," Jonathan was saying, "in his time. Survived all kinds of ups and downs—including our dear Mama."

I glanced at him, catching the usual note of mockery. "However," he said, "they do say he's losing ground: we're in the age of the angry young men, and audiences don't want his kind of plays any more."

One more touch of the scorcerer's hand; one more change.

The garden was filling now: Carey was lost to me in the crowd. Someone filled my glass, and a plate of canapés was thrust with absent-minded vigour towards my chest. As the drink ran, laughter grew louder, then drifted away on the sea-quiet of the evening. Someone had put on a record player within the house, and music drifted out among us. I caught sight of the swing of Carey's blue skirt; it seemed she was dancing. I saw a bronzed young man with his arm about her waist, and knew a thrust of jealousy, powerful as a throb of blood. To rid myself of it I looked again to the water which was almost colourless now with evening, white touched with amber, as if the day had drowned there.

"Carey's enjoying herself," Jonathan said, his glance on me, as if he tested my need of her. "Well, it's her party, after all."

I agreed it was her party, and looked over the crowd once more. I could see famous faces; actors and actresses whom I knew only from the boards of a stage, or the coloured image of a screen. But . . . I said, "Emma?"

Jonathan looked at me with amused pity. "My dear Rick, if Ma had been here, we'd all have known it. There would be the equivalent of a red carpet, and a grateful cheering populace."

No Emma. My eyes went again in search of Carey. Perhaps her wild dance had something of desperation in it. I left Jonathan and made my way through the crowd. Voices clapped against my ears like wings and music threaded it all. Carey had paused in her dance; the young man still stood beside her, lightly but affectionately holding her hand. I said to her, "If you're dancing, it's my turn."

In the fading light the blue of her skirt had taken on a deeper, more vibrant colour. Her eyes, catching light from the sea, looked into my face from some depth of curiosity. Did she remember the words I'd spoken as the guests swept us apart? I didn't know. I was aware of the young man who had been her partner: tall, very brown; that breed of American male who seems to be built to some standard of strength and excellence denied to the rest of us; perfect teeth, hair of crackling vitality; a manner of cheerful indestructible command. Carey said, "This is Hal. Henry Bowring, Junior." (I never knew why American men had to be known as junior; I was not prepared to like any aspect of Henry Bowring.) He said,

288

"Hi. Carey and I are old friends; we were dancing—"

"But now," I said, "she's dancing with me."

Childish, perhaps; certainly Henry Bowring showed by his smile and the way he let go of Carey's hand, that he thought so. But I didn't mind. I had Carey now in my arms, and the music still drifted among us; others were dancing too; and we moved over the grass, soundless, like ghosts of ourselves. I had been afraid of Henry Bowring, but we had lost him now, and Carey held me close, so that I could believe again as I slipped one hand beneath her hair, lifted on the wind, and felt the slimness of her neck. She said, with her head against my shoulder, "She hasn't come."

'I know."

"Perhaps she missed the plane."

"Perhaps."

We were moving away from the crowd, to a place in the wide garden where the sea wind blew more strongly, and the music made less sound. I kissed her cheek and said, "It doesn't really matter whether she comes or not. I'm here. Isn't that enough?"

She looked up at me, as if she saw not only me, but all of the past, the desperate times with Emma, and the good ones too. She said, "I don't know."

"It must be," I said. "It must." Perhaps we'd all drunk a good deal, or the music and the crowded evening garden with the emptying glasses and the paper napkins blowing from the tables set us in a place outside the confines of time; I felt strong and sure of myself in this world of sea-smelling magic, with Carey in my arms.

I said, "I love you, I always have. No one—no one like you." I began to kiss her more deeply, finding her mouth, wanting her. "Forget Emma—she's no good to you. She never has been. There's the future—you and me. You can come back to England, and we can get married—it doesn't matter a damn what Emma says—"

I hadn't heard the steps on the grass. I hadn't heard

anything, with Carey so close to me, and the wind, and the singing of desire in my head. I hadn't even heard that the music had stopped. I just looked up and saw Emma standing there, a small distance from us.

I didn't know what she'd heard. I'd not been speaking loudly (had I?) but Emma was very close. And her face— that face which I knew so well, both in public and private—had the lines of anger on it, as well as the other lines.

For a moment she just stood there. A little murmur of talk came from the crowded party, but the loud laughter and the traces of song were silenced.

I don't know how long we faced each other. When you're shocked from the dreamy waters of dance and desire into the cold reality of hatred, your senses grew numb, and your sense of time too.

Emma spoke first, that well-remembered voice husky with anger. "So it doesn't matter a damn what I say?"

I had time to take in the picture of Emma as I realised that I'd spoken more loudly than I knew. She wore a flame-coloured dress which blew in the strengthening wind, so that she might have been some goddess or figure-head. The beauty was still there, though the harsh years had scrawled more of their writing upon it. She stood now, shoulders braced, as if she faced an enemy. Which I suppose she did: I suppose the enemy was me.

Before I could make any reply Carey had pulled away from me and run to her mother. She put her arms round her neck and said, "You've come!"

Angry myself, deserted, I saw Emma put an arm round her daughter's waist. Her eyes were still on me. "Sure I've come. I was late getting to Marine Terminal, that's all." Her voice was a little slurred; I couldn't tell how much she'd drunk. She glanced over the party as if she challenged them to whisper or comment about her.

Jonathan, suddenly beside me, murmured, "Doesn't anyone clap?"

290

Arms wide, Emma embraced them all—my father and Marguerite—and began to take on the role, learned over a lifetime, of the Most Important Person in the Room. Or garden, as it might be. She ignored me after that first comment, but this wasn't difficult, since there were so many people waiting to greet her—out of friendship, out of curiosity; here was *Emma Pride* who had survived more shipwrecks than anyone could count, had more love affairs, jumped through all the flaming hopes of publicity and emerged, scarred and scorched, but still standing and now moving with the scarlet dress through the garden, her face having in this dusk some of the lineaments of youth, so that she was beautiful again, and it must seem to her, loved, loved, loved.

Someone had restarted the music and Emma had a glass in her hand filled with champagne (how much more of that could she take and get away with it?) Carey had left me and was shifting through the crowd, trying to keep pace with Emma.

I made no move to follow her. I was still angry at her desertion, angry too with a fate that allowed Emma to hear the words I'd spoken. Jonathan lingering beside me said, "Quite a party. You don't seem to be the most popular boy in the school; why not?"

I didn't tell him, but just shook my head.

"Maybe Ma's jealous, seeing you dance with Carey like that—"

"Like what?" I snapped.

He glanced at me as if he acknowledged the unwonted irritation.

"Well, like you were drowned in each other. Ma comes and goes out of Carey's life like a disappearing rabbit—now you see her, now you don't. But Ma doesn't like anyone else to take Carey over, to be Top Person. Absolutely not."

He wandered away. I watched Emma's triumphal progress; now she was talking to Guy Forster and laughing

291

with him, leaning over his chair.

Not far from me stood a young couple: the girl (perhaps the brunette who'd spoken to me earlier; they all looked alike in the growing dusk), her skin gleaming in the half-light; the young man in white trousers and flowered shirt.

Their voices came to me, cool, American, detached.

"Like watching someone come back from the grave," the girl said.

The young man nodded. "She must be older than God. Time to bow out—but they never do, do they?"

"Not if they can help it. All that sex-symbol, 'don't you-all-love-me-and-want-to-go-to-bed-with-me' stuff at her age—it's yukky."

"Enough slap on her face to paint a yacht. Don't they look in the bathroom mirror? Or does the eyesight fade?"

"Everything fades, I guess," said the girl, and they giggled together.

Their judgement chilled me, even as the party gained pace again, and light slipped away leaving only a steel-shine on the water about us... Now my father, on higher ground, was calling for silence, asking us to drink Carey's health. I couldn't hear everything he said, for the wind blew much away, but I caught words about "... youth, its beauty and its hopes ... especially Carey's, whom we all love; who deserves the best of things... She'll need courage, but she has that; and we hope the world will be good to her. It's not kind to all of us, but..."

They drank to her, calling her name into the now quiet garden.

I stood alone, and spoke it quietly, for I wasn't, I told myself, part of the crowd: Carey, even if she'd run from me when Emma appeared, was mine, privately mine; and the future my father was speaking of was in my hands...

Oh yes, I loved her. It was like a pain beneath my breastbone, as if a muscle were twisted there. Of course I

292

wanted to make love to her, and I thought of her body, with its slight breasts and narrow waist; thought of it naked beside me—but this wasn't enough; I wanted Carey for my wife, for the long future.

In the midst of this dream I caught the sound of her voice. She was standing beside my father. In the blurred dusk she looked lovely and timeless, with the long blue skirt, the white blouse and her hair adrift on her shoulders. But as she spoke I could feel sadness on her; though she tried to answer my father's toast her voice which I knew so well, sounded thin, and although she smiled it wasn't a smile of true happiness: every now and again her glance slid to Emma who stood below her on the slope.

"It's been a wonderful evening—" Carey was saying: a voice (male) from the guests called "It isn't over yet!"— "I shan't ever forget my twenty-first birthday," and she turned and kissed my father, as if she feared to say more. Did she kiss Emma? I couldn't see, because once again Carey had slipped into the crowd, and little by little the sounds of gaiety returned. The music renewed its beat, and Emma's glass (like others) was filled and refilled. At one moment I found myself close to her. She stood alone, swaying a little, glass in hand. The lines on her face seemed to be of sadness rather than anger; and as I looked at her I remembered all the other times: on the shore of this island in the blazing sea-dazzle of light; in her dressing-room in New York after the audience had slow hand-clapped. This person beside me was not the public Emma, but Carey's mother; someone who had been interwoven into my life from the beginning.

On an impulse I said, "I'm sorry—"

She turned quickly. I saw then that she was less sober than I had believed, and she said, her voice both slurred and cold with hatred, "Sorry for what, Rick?"

"For saying what I did. For talking to Carey—"

The slap of her hand on my cheek came as such a total

293

surprise that I took a gasp of breath like a swimmer, rising from the cold. "Nothing you say to Carey matters a bloody curse—it doesn't matter—d'you hear; Carey's *my* daughter and you don't matter a damn."

She was shouting, and this brought a humiliating silence about me.

Perhaps stupidly, I stood my ground. "Carey may be your daughter, but that isn't any way to behave at her party—"

Confusion, then. Emma turned from me; my father thrust his way towards her and steadied her (for she stumbled); I had one glimpse of Carey's blanched face, but before I could get to her Henry Bowring put a possessive arm about her waist: "Come along, honey," he said; "let's go for a swim. Get away for a bit; this'll all die down."

I had reached them now. "Sure," I said, "this'll die down, until something else starts." I could feel the sting and colour on my face where Emma'd slapped it; fury filled me: I was angry with everyone. "D'you *want* to swim, Carey?" I asked her.

She looked bewildered, sad; but said, "I guess so. It'd be fun." She didn't look as if anything at the moment was being much fun, and my heart ached for her, while my anger endured.

Someone in the party had caught the word 'swim' and I heard the voices: "We're going for a swim"—"A swim"—"The water's warm; boy, that'll be good."

A scurry of preparations; of search for bathing trunks and towels; I saw the colour return to Carey's face; Henry Bowring, triumphant, took her hand, and they began to run down the slope of the garden; others followed, some pausing to take one more drink. I heard Marguerite say "Keep to the pond; don't go to the shore," but I don't think anyone heard, or if they did, paid attention.

They went running, towards the Atlantic shore.

My father stood, watching them; Emma on a chair

beside him, her face markedly turned from me. He said, "They're not going to the pond. But there's plenty of them; they can't come to much harm."

"We don't want," Marguerite said, "them to come to *any* harm."

"They can all swim," my father said. "Everyone on the Island can swim."

I heard Guy Forster say from his chair as he shifted a crutch, "What an extraordinary thing to be young and *want* to swim after a party—perhaps I did once."

My father said, "Not going, Rick?"

"Perhaps," I said. I thought he was going to say something about me and Emma, and I didn't want that.

I wandered away from them all. I took another drink, and remembered so long ago that first drunken walk home to Lonsdale school. I could take more than that now. The garden was ghostly with the murmur of voices, now that nearly all of the young had gone to the shore. I didn't much want to join them, but I wanted less to stay within earshot of Emma, and I went into the house and found my bathing trunks and a towel, and wandered slowly down the way they'd gone. My cheek still stung as the sea-wind touched it. Indeed, the wind had increased as evening came, and wrestled with my hair as I walked.

It was a long walk to the Atlantic shore (in other times we had gone by car on the Island Road); as I went I could taste the scent of wild rose and vetch; and overriding it all the salt of the sea. At last I came to the beach. Dimmed by the wash of waves and the huge silence of the sky, the voices of the party seemed small; no one could make his mark against that vast conspiracy of sea and sky. In the strange evening sea-light they all looked like figures on uncoloured film. Not all of them were yet in the water. In fact, though they had undressed (the girls to bra and underpants) some of the couples didn't look as if they were going near the water at all; I caught sight of them, bodies close together, in the shelter of rock or sand dunes.

High above us climbed the Gay Head cliffs. The sea was rougher than I'd supposed; the waves coming in with dim thunder, and the surf swarming, dull white, on the shore.

Now I was looking only for Carey. I didn't want to see her in Henry Bowring's arms; and I walked, having kicked my shoes off, barefoot over the sand. If I turned my head, I could see the lights of the house above us. They seemed far off.

Where was Carey? Some of them were now swimming, calling to each other in the great sea-washed silence, their voices thin and snatched away. I had pulled on my trunks behind one of the sand dunes and felt the wind on my naked skin. A girl, lying on her stomach, drenched by the incoming surf, lifted her face, laughing. I said, "Have you seen Carey?" but she shook her head. A young man swam up behind her and caught her feet and she screamed in mock fear. I waded into the water where the surf boiled about me. I could even now feel the strength of the waves as they dragged back, hissing, pulling like a strong man . . .

Then I saw her. She was swimming far out, steadily, as if she wanted to reach some distant place where the party with its stain could be forgotten. Swimming steadily . . . how good a swimmer was Carey? Pretty good, I supposed, for she had spent much time on the Vineyard, and as my father said, everyone on the Island could swim.

Where was Henry Bowring? Then I saw him, swimming inshore. As he stood up I was aware that he was even taller than I; he stood, brown and dripping, and reached for a towel. His thighs were hairy and wet, and the brief trunks barely covered his crotch. I didn't want to think of him with Carey, close to her, possessing her. I said, "Carey's a long way out."

He turned his head, towelling himself. "She's coming in. She said she'd follow me." A girl called to him and he wandered across the sand. Some aspect of this gathering

296

by the sea that I didn't like; perhaps it was just the aftermath of the scene with Emma, but I felt some disproportion, something out of the true, in this adventure by the shore.

I looked again out to sea. I expected to see Carey's head as she swam back to the shore, her fair hair streaming and darkened, but her face unmistakable because I knew it and loved it so well.

But I did not. I could see other heads, bobbing amongst the waves.

But no sign of Carey.

I shouted her name, and one or two heads turned; but voices made little impact, and I daresay they thought I called in fun.

I didn't wait any more. I strode into those heavy surf laden waves and dived, and began to swim as fast as I could.

And I knew at once that this water wasn't easy, that as one drove outward a strong current pulled you. Not too strong for me, but I was a man, nearly six foot, and a fair swimmer. But I couldn't see Carey, and I swam with a desperate vigour, as the waves pushed roughly over my head, and into my eyes and mouth. I turned and saw that the shore and the people on it had grown suddenly small. I turned back, lifted my head and called, "*Carey!*" again.

No reply; or if there had been, could I have heard it with the relentless water in my ears?

Something within me was deeply afraid, but I wouldn't let it come to the surface; I drove on, with the crawl learned long ago on the shores of this very Island; further and further out. The vast sea before me, steel-grey with breakers of dull white, seemed empty. I would not be frightened; I would not believe that anything had happened to Carey; not in these waters, so near home . . .

By now, I thought, they must know on the shore that something was wrong, but I didn't turn. I drove on, pausing only, as I trod water, to call her name with all the breath I had.

On. A vast empty sea, dulled with evening; a sea that might have no mercy. Carey was a good swimmer, but I thought that maybe she'd drunk quite a lot, and it wasn't a good thing to swim when you'd drunk well . . .

Further out. Searching with desperation now; afraid, because I could hear Carey's voice from long past; see her on the Manhattan boat, and by the school pond . . .

I drove more fiercely with my legs. I could feel the current pulling at me. I said, Please let me find her; but to whom I spoke, I did not know.

Further and further out. Could she have come so far? If my limbs were tiring I scarcely felt it, since my need and my fear were so great . . .

And then, a little distance off, I saw a break in the waves. It might have been nothing. Or it might have been a swimmer's head . . .

Driven more fiercely now, I swam towards it. Waves dissolved my sight, and hid it from me.

But then I saw it again. Clear, above the surface, just above, washed by the waves.

Carey. I yelled to her, and swam furiously now as if I swam to beat an enemy.

When I found her, she was almost exhausted; her teeth chattering, her skin marked with blue shadows, her body limp as weed.

"Oh, God," I said; "what were you doing?"

She couldn't answer at first. Then she gasped, "I thought I could do it . . ."

I didn't say 'Do what?' for I needed all my strength to bring her back.

As we reached the shore it became clear to me, through the triumph and the exhaustion and the tireless movement of the sea, that someone had indeed raised the alarm. They were all standing there: even the lovers had parted. I saw my father, and Marguerite who had come with a rug and brandy (I wondered briefly when Mar-

298

guerite had not come up with the practical necessities for any emergency); and Emma herself, shocked, I could already see, into sobriety.

Lifting Carey in my arms, I stood breathing hard, while the water dripped from us both. Carey's body, white and chilled, near naked, was taken from me: Marguerite wrapped her in the rug; my father put a hand on my shoulder and said something like "Well done;" but the words were lost in excitement. My father had driven to the point in the road where it skirted the shore, and he with Emma and Marguerite hurried with Carey towards it.

I stood and watched, exhaustion beginning to make itself felt through my limbs. Henry Bowring, close beside me said. "Quite a rescue. What was she doing?"

Towelling myself to restore warmth I muttered, "There's a current out there. She was losing strength." No need to say more.

Quiet had come down on us all now. The sea looked colder and fiercer, an enemy perhaps. I stripped my sodden trunks from me and pulled on shirt and trousers. I felt the flatness which comes after any strong endeavour; the party was over, Carey was safe, given into other hands, and those few of us left here by the cold shore were touched by the near escape from disaster. Like sleepwalkers, we gathered towels and clothes; some of the girls in bikinis shivered, and the young men put their arms about them.

I didn't hurry back to the house. I didn't want to talk about Carey, or the rescue, if such it was. I wanted only one thing. I wanted, when she had recovered from this evening, to make sure of Carey for myself; to get her promise to marry me, and come to England. There was life there, I thought, for both of us. Life without Emma.

I became aware of Jonathan, as I climbed slowly, weighted with exhaustion up the hill. He said something about Carey, but I shook my head, watching my feet as I plodded up the sandy road.

"No awards for bravery?" Jonathan asked; and I said, "Don't be an ass."

It crossed my tired mind that Jonathan might write this up for his newspaper, but I couldn't be greatly concerned with that.

I came at last to the garden. Everyone had gone, and only the debris remained: a mass of crumby plates, empty bottles, paper napkins like fallen petals after a storm. From this height the sea was quieter now, but I could still hear its rhythmic pursuit of the shore.

I stood alone there, in the blue dusk. I could see lights from other houses and smell the strong scent of the pines. I was glad of this respite; I could hear the revving of car engines, the muted good-byes. All over, all gone. The garden empty but for the echo of voices, and of the dancing, and of Emma's anger.

Where was Emma now? Doubtless with Carey, which was why I lingered here, glad of the debris-strewn garden, and the lonely sound of the sea.

Later I slipped into the house. I could hear voices, my father's and Marguerite's, desultory after-the-party, after-disaster talk. Silently I went to my room. I took a shower, washing the salt from my body and my hair; put on pyjamas and bath-robe. I lay on the bed and tried to read, but the words dissolved in the events of this evening; now I was dancing with Carey in the garden; now facing Emma in her scarlet dress, and feeling the slap on my face; now—most vividly—swimming out into the rough steel-white sea . . .

I flung down the book and moved to the window. Nothing but lights on the Island and far down a white garland of foam on the fringe of the now-dark sea. The sea from which I had taken Carey, limp, exhausted, near-naked in my arms . . .

Was she asleep?

300

I knew where her room was. I moved silently along the passage. Some greenish light, like phosphorescence from the sea, hung on the air. The house seemed now drowned in silence.

I gave a light knock on Carey's door. A sound? A brief questioning answer?

Gently I opened the door. I could see her fair head on the pillow. "Rick?" Nothing in her voice, not even surprise.

I came to the side of the bed. "I wanted to see you. To know if you were all right."

In the mysterious sea-lighted glance I could see a faint smile. "Oh, yes. Thanks to you. Silly thing to do, wasn't it?"

"You swam out too far."

"I thought perhaps . . . I'd go on till I couldn't swim any more—"

"*Why?*"

"I just wanted to get away. But it isn't that easy. And then I found all my strength had gone." She turned her head. "Sorry. Stupid. Too much drink, too much party. Too much everything."

I sat on the bed and stroked her bare neck. She looked up to me, eyes gleaming in this strange light, large with inquiry.

I said, "This isn't about making love. Much though I want you." I briefly kissed her mouth; there seemed some tang of salt there, as if the sea had not all been washed away. "I wanted to see you. Talk a little. Everyone moved in after—after we came back. But Marguerite took care of you?"

"Sure. And Ma, too, of course."

"Emma must have had the fright of her life. And that's saying something."

Distress went over her face "I think Ma's sorry about—about what she did."

"Big of her."

301

"No, truly, Rick; she is. You know what she's like—"

"Ah. Yes, I do. I think by now I do."

"She was fussed about being late for my party. She got the time wrong of the flight and had to wait for another. And while she waited—"

"She had a drink to pass the time," I suggested.

Again her glance went to me, as if she pleaded. "She was grateful to you—she said so—"

"Fine. Fine. But this isn't about Emma, however grateful she may be. This is about you. You and me."

She was looking at me now with perplexed inquiry. I didn't want her to be perplexed about anything; I knew what I wanted, what was best for both of us, what must happen. I said, "You know how much I love you?"

She could have demurred; talked of the sentimental image of a girl known from childhood, but she did not. "Yes."

"In a few days' time I'm going back to England. That's where my work is. I want you to come with me. And marry me."

Perhaps all proposals come at odd times; at the corner of a city street where the traffic lights show red; in a train carriage; in the confusion of farewell. This could well be the wrong time but it was, I seemed to know, my only time, and it was made.

As she didn't speak, I felt the racing of my heart, for though I had spoken easily, the words had not been easy to say. "You will, won't you, Carey? Promise me. You're twenty-one now—"

Again the smile. "I'm certainly that—"

"And you can do what you like. No one can stop you."

She lifted one hand and moved it over my face, as if she tried to learn the contours of it. "No one; but . . ."

I didn't like the 'but'. I said, "D'you love me?"

Hardly any hesitation. "Yes. Yes, I do—"

I kissed her again, holding her slight shoulders against me. We could have made love, but this wasn't the time.

302

"Then you have to say 'yes', that's all."

She was silent and I could feel the increased knocking of my heart: and I knew that I had come into her room with an overwhelming hope, which now had a shadow on it.

"Say you will, Carey. It has to be done—"

"Has to?"

"You know what I mean. I don't just want an affair with you; I want us to get married. Old-fashioned, perhaps; but that's what I want. Trace it back to having a peripatetic father, if you like; unravel whatever Freudian tangles you can find—I don't care. It's what I want; and I believe—oh, God, I hope—it's what you want too."

Now the distress was clear on her face, which wasn't what I wanted at all. She said, "Yes, it is, but . . ."

"Don't like all these buts—"

"Rick, please. Please help me."

"I am helping you. Or trying to."

"I can't—Rick, darling, I can't leave Ma now—"

"*Emma*? What's Emma got to do with it?"

"She's my mother—"

"When it suits her," I said.

"No—no—don't. It isn't any good. She can't help how she is."

"None of us can help how we are. But we try not to slap people in the face, and drink ourselves silly and make life generally hell for everyone around."

"Rick, Rick, please—that's no good. It doesn't help to talk like that about her—"

"I don't care whether it helps or not. It's true. Emma's got plenty of people around to pick up the pieces, whatever they may be—"

Carey put her hands over her face, and I could see that this had gone wrong, and I couldn't think why exactly, except that Emma had come into it and I wanted her away, because anger was coming back with the memory of that sting on my cheek in the garden. Carey said,

"Don't—don't—talk like that about her. Can't you see—she's getting older now, and the good things are falling away—"

"Is it surprising?"

"No—don't. It's hell for her; she isn't strong enough to take it—"

"Too bad,'" I said; "and I suppose the rest of us are?"

"No—no, please. She gets lonely and frightened—"

"She's not the only one."

"She'll feel awful about this evening—"

"Oh, she will? Too bad—"

"She heard you, Rick: that it didn't matter a damn what she said—"

"Well, it doesn't."

"That hurt her—"

"And how often has she hurt *you*? What about filling bottles with aspirin, and finding her with her wrists cut—?"

"Yes, but don't you *see*—it's not her fault: it was a good thing I was there—"

"It was hell you were there—"

"No—please—please try to understand. I know what frightens her; I know why she's like what she is—"

I grasped her shoulders. "Carey, darling, you are *yourself*: you're young and you haven't got to spend your life playing nanny to an ageing actress who's on the skids and won't want you around when the next lover comes along—not till he gets fed to the teeth—"

"No—no—no." She was protesting, with her hands over her mouth, sitting up in bed. "Don't say things like that about her; please don't."

"She's nothing to do with us. *Nothing*. She can make her own way downhill without your help. I just want to know: are you coming to England with me? Are you going to marry me? That's all that matters—"

She looked small and white, sitting there, the tears close; and I felt a pang of pity, because it had been such a

304

hell of an evening; but the pity wasn't enough to staunch my anger or my love.

She said on a whisper, "It isn't all. I can't leave her, Rick. Not now. If you'd heard her this evening—"

"I did."

"No; I mean afterwards, when I was back here; when she talked to me. She was so glad to get me back; she'd been so frightened—"

"She wasn't the only one."

"But she needs me, Rick; truly she needs me—"

"Balls!"

"Oh, God; she does; please try to understand—"

"Are you coming with me?"

Her hands were shivering, and again I felt the thrust of pity; but the fear and anger were stronger. "Because," I said, stupidly, recklessly, "it's now or never; if you can't leave Emma now, when you're grown up and in love—"

"I can't. I can't. She needs help—"

I stood up in one movement from the bed. "She needs help like a boa-constrictor!"

I would have been wise to pause, to reason, to give her the understanding she pleaded for; but I could not. Exhaustion, rage and what seemed to me like the rejection of love, sent me swiftly out of the room, without even touching her, without turning my head. I thought as I shut the door I heard her voice, but I paid no attention. I just went back to my room, like a rebuked child, or an animal. And there, perhaps, because of the long wild evening, the desperate swim; the hope of her promise and the bitterness of defeat, I hid my face and wept.

Of course it was badly done. I knew that when I woke after a few hour's sleep the next morning.

But it was too late then. With Marguerite I moved about the garden, collecting the debris of the night before. It looked sordid in the strong light; bottles and smeared plates, dead cigarettes. I slung cardboard plates

305

into a trash bag, gathered up crates of empty bottles. If Marguerite noticed that I was lost deep in silence she, with customary tact, said little.

Soon no trace of the party remained: the garden was itself again, as if nothing had happened there, neither the dancing, nor the angry slap of the face, nor the danger in the sea below. The sun grew stronger, and this was like any other Island day.

Except, of course, that all was changed, and I moved with a solid defeat within me.

I scarcely saw Carey, nor Emma. Emma, with Carey and Jonathan were packed before I'd spoken a word; Marguerite was driving them to the airport. From there they would fly to New York, to Emma's apartment.

Emma, in a white summer dress, gave me the briefest of good-byes. When Carey came out of the house I felt a shiver of heart; but then nothing, since it was only as I had expected: we were strangers. She looked pale, and as if perhaps she'd wept too, but she was quiet, entirely in control.

I didn't even kiss her. Perhaps we just touched hands as I said, "Good-bye, Carey."

She lifted her glance to me for a moment, and I think it was still pleading; but I had nothing to give.

"Good-bye, Rick."

Quickly she got into the car with Jonathan beside her. I watched the car out of sight, but it was only Jonathan who waved to me.

Marguerite, my father and I were due to follow, a few days later.

"If you want to talk," Marguerite said, on our last evening in the garden as she lit a cigarette, and I could hear echoes of the party which had ended in defeat, the music which was silenced; but I said No; it was over now; there wasn't anything to say.

Once in New York, I had days mostly to myself in their apartment; time to think. I tried to write to Carey; tell her that I was sorry about the evening in her bedroom and all the things I'd said; that if we could meet... But the words always came out wrongly, and I tore the letters up and threw them away.

One afternoon, on impulse, because the next day I was to leave for England, I telephoned Emma's apartment, hoping that Carey might answer. But both Emma and Carey were out; Jonathan too; the maid answered. I left a message, as it seemed that Carey was due back soon. I said I was leaving for England the next morning, and I'd be at Greenacre Park between four and five that afternoon if she'd meet me there.

Greenacre Park is not really a park. It is a small retreat off East 51st Street. It is built of granite, brick and steel, with a mass of rhododendron, azaleas and Japanese holly to give the feel of growing things. A synthetic waterfall streams down the furthest wall, which drowns the persistent sound of the New York traffic on Second and Third Avenues. Tables and chairs are scattered about, and the city people come here for breakfast rolls, iced tea or just space to breathe. Carey and I had been here before, and I knew she liked the place with its air of an oasis in the midst of sound and the canyons of city stone.

I bought myself an iced tea and sat there. The time was dead on four. I watched the people who came: some sunbathing in the dazzling heat; others seeking shade. Couples sat, heads close together. Old people, alone, read newspapers or slept. I drank my tea and waited, looking up each time someone entered the park, but it was always a stranger. Something mesmeric in the plash of the waterfall, indeed of comfort as if it washed everything away, even the weight at my heart.

Half past four. No reason why I shouldn't sit here till evening, but I had said between four and five, and some obstinacy within me made me stick to that. On the fringe of the fall of water I could hear the wail of police cars, of ambulances; the bleat of horns.

307

A quarter to five. Less and less likely that Carey would come, but I still looked up at the sound of steps on the granite floor.

Not much time now. Whatever reason might say, I knew I would go at five o'clock. Suppose Carey came five minutes after I'd gone?

But she knew where my father's apartment was; she must know that I was due for England; she could telephone me.

No clock striking could make itself heard above the plash of water, and the city traffic. As the hand of my watch pointed five I got up from my metal chair, tossed my cardboard cup into the trash bin, and walked the hot city streets home.

I didn't hear from Carey, and I left for England the next day.

Chapter Two

As I say, you can't go back. Once I'd returned to England I went to look, as I've said, at Carey's grandmother's house. Having lost her, I was trying to reach something from the past, from that Christmas long ago, but there was nothing there. Carey as a child and Carey as a woman were both lost to me; wandering to places of the past could do no good at all.

I picked up life again. I had a job, designing for a revival of *The Admirable Crichton* at a small theatre on the fringe of the West End. I found this fun, though I doubted whether in the climate we had now the play would draw the crowds. (It didn't.) But work of any kind was a panacea, and the company of the young men and women of the theatre, all lively and strenuous, full of ambition, was consoling. All of them, it seemed to me, were free from the weight of lead at my heart. But I could be wrong; no man truly knows another, as someone once said, and how right he was.

I heard nothing from Carey. As before in New York I tried to write to her, but I couldn't get the correct words on to paper, and again I threw the unfinished letters away. My father and Marguerite were still in New York, making visits when they could to the Vineyard. The Island seemed far off, like a bright fading dream, as it always did when I was back in London. Sea-sounding, magical; and now, perhaps, cursed, for it was there that I'd lost Carey . . .

I turned away; back to work.

Strangely, it was Jonathan whom I saw now. He was back in London, working on his paper, and though we'd always eyed each other from a distance, he seemed to me a link with Carey, and I kept in touch with him. We would meet in a pub at the end of the day and talk over a beer. We had bedsitting rooms in different parts of Kensington, so it wasn't difficult to meet on common ground.

Sometimes he had a girl with him; not always the same girl. Sometimes I did too; but for me it *was* always the same girl: a pretty, dark one who was A.S.M. for *The Admirable Crichton*. She seemed to have taken a shine to me, and while I could not get Carey out of my mind, an attractive girl who showed a readiness to stay by my side offered comfort. Her name was Barbara, and she wore slacks and cotton tunics, and did a funny take-off of Bette Davis. Good, cheerful company, and I wished I could love her, but I could not.

One evening, Jonathan and I met alone. We stood at the bar of the pub, which was warm with the last of an autumn evening, and drank our beer. Jonathan looked about him. "Where's the charming Barbara?"

"Gone to wash her hair," I said.

He lifted one eyebrow, and reminded me of Marguerite. "You want to watch that one. Usually means they're off with another bloke."

I felt a small pang of jealousy; irrational, since I wasn't in love with her. But . . .

"Never mind," I said.

He made no comment. I found that when we were together I eyed his face every now and again to find a likeness to Carey. If Jonathan perceived this, he made no sign. He never talked about the party on the Island; whether this was tact or general lack of interest in anything but his own affairs, I couldn't know.

"What's happened to your harem?" I asked him.

He smiled. "Oh—they don't always have to be around.

Sometimes I get bored with them and want peace—such as this."

I would, I thought, remain puzzled by Jonathan for as long as I knew him. Whatever secrets he had—and I suppose, like most of us, he had plenty—he managed not only to conceal them, but give the impression that they were of greater importance than anyone else's. He said, "How's the rest of your evening placed?"

I shrugged. "No plans. A movie, maybe."

He said, "Come back and try my cooking. I'm rather good."

I'd been to parties in Jonathan's one-room flat; it was—unlike mine—extremely tidy, and he managed to produce a great deal of food and drink from the stamp-sized kitchen. "Why not?" I said.

When we came to the flat, I looked about me. A green carpet, unspotted, stretched from wall to wall; in one corner of the room stood a small desk with a typewriter; and beside it a file, no title on it, anonymous, containing a bulk of paper.

"Looks as if you've been working," I said.

He gave a discreet glance over his shoulder. "Oh, yes, well—it's my job. I work quite hard, as a matter of fact. This air of a young man cruising through life on gilded feet is all a blind. When there isn't—" he made a gesture to the divan bed—"company here, I work far into the night. No complaints from the neighbours so far."

My eye rested a little longer on the anonymous file, thick with typewritten paper; then I forgot about it. For the time I forgot about it.

Jonathan gave me a sherry and worked with quiet efficiency in the kitchen. No, he didn't want help. There wasn't room for more than one at a time.

He reappeared with a pleasant mess of meat and mushrooms, and I congratulated him. He shrugged. "I like food. Seemed a good idea to learn how to make it. Seduction comes easier if you eat at home."

"I suppose it does. I hadn't thought about it."

"No, dear Rick; you wouldn't. You haven't my enviable capacity for thinking ahead. Can't imagine where I got it from, unless my father, poor chap, had that sort of mind. Shan't ever know."

"Do you ever think about him?"

"Not much. How can you think about someone you never knew? Even if he did, in the first instance, give you life. He was killed so long ago, in a war I don't even remember. Besides, Mum provides all you need to think about as a parent." He filled our glasses with red wine and looked dreamily to the typewriter. "Poor Mum. It must be terrible to be Mum. Having had so much; fighting to hold on, and losing bit by bit."

The subject of Emma was still a sore one to me. I said, "I thought she'd pulled herself back; on top again."

He looked at me placidly, giving nothing away. "One step forward and two back," he said. "And the backs, if you follow me, get longer every time. One day she'll run out of lovers, and what then?"

I said awkwardly, "You've no feeling for her at all?"

The question appeared to deepen the caution on his face. "I've never been much of a one for strong feelings. When I was a child I used to enjoy things with her. When she was in a good temper. She looked nice, and I was pleased when she was famous. But it became clear early on that I came a poor second to Carey every time."

I glanced at him, for bitterness came through the name. He went on, "And then she just wasn't around. That's not a mother is it, whichever way you slice it?" He took another mouthful of food, then said, "I wonder how she'll take the news about Carey."

I felt my heart slip. "What d'you mean?"

"Not heard? Carey's got herself engaged to some all-American chap, all chest and teeth, called Henry Bowring—"

"She can't have!"

I'd spoken without thought, from the shaft of pain, as Jonathan would not have done.

"News tells us otherwise," Jonathan said; and I became sure that his whole reason for asking me to dinner had been to tell me this. Out of—what? Jonathan had no reason to hate me; perhaps just a natural impulse towards mischief, to be the first to break bad news. "She wrote to me," he said; and if he saw that this dug deeper into my wound, again he gave no sign. "Can't say that Carey often writes to me. But this—I suppose she thought her only brother ought to know. There'll be all that tiresome business about a wedding; personally I can do without weddings, for me or anyone else. But my sister—or half-sister—it looks as if I'll have to go."

Henry Bowring. I could see him now, standing in the seething foam of the beach on that evening of the party . . . The food on my plate now tasted of nothing. I said, "When—when are they getting married?"

"Ah. Well, that doesn't seem to emerge. I don't know why. Doubtless something to do with Ma. I always got the feeling that she didn't want Carey to marry; that she wanted to keep her around. But Henry Bowring Junior is I believe a rich young man, and perhaps the Empress's finger has touched him with favour. Perhaps he's managed to persuade her that he's one of her fervent fans, and but for the age-difference, he'd marry her. However that may be, no date's mentioned."

Some small comfort in this.

"It was rather an odd letter," Jonathan was saying. "Carey, when she *does* write usually rattles on as if she were talking to you. Heaps of useless but quite funny information. But this was only a few lines, beginning, 'I think you ought to know'. Such an odd way for Carey to begin a letter; as if she were writing to a solicitor. The letter's somewhere about—d'you want to see it?" He was looking over his shoulder, as if trying to remember where it was. I didn't answer, and he took my silence for agree-

313

ment, and went over to the desk. He lifted the file of paper, and what appeared to be a paperback book fell to the floor. He picked it up hurriedly and put it back beneath the file.

"What's that?" I asked.

"Oh . . . a page proof. Some months old now. I read it for a friend." I didn't know why he sounded as if he wanted the question, like the book, out of the way.

"Labour of love," I said.

"Not exactly. No," he added; "not love." He opened a drawer. "Yes, here it is."

He put the blue airmail paper on the table at my side.

As he'd said, the letter was short. "Dear Jon, I think you ought to know that I'm engaged to a guy called Henry Bowring, Junior. He was at my twenty-first party; I don't know if you remember. Ma seems to be pleased. I expect it's the right thing. How's London? And yourself? Give my love to old friends, if I have any. Send me news, when you've time. Your loving and now promised sister, Carey."

I said at last, having taken the stab of her writing: "She doesn't sound over-the-moon."

"No; does she?" If he knew what was in my mind, he still showed no evidence of it. "But then she knows I'm not an over-the-moon type of person. D'you think she's going to ask me to give her away? I will if I have to, but can't think of much I'd like less. Nothing against my charming sister; but I'd feel an ass."

I pushed the letter away. I didn't want to think of that wedding, with its excitement and flowers and guests and champagne—and Carey at its centre, the wife of Henry Bowring, Junior. Yet the whole thing made a kind of sense. Carey wasn't a girl to stay unmarried; so far as I knew she hadn't got far in her profession: Henry Bowring, perhaps, was an easy way out. . . .

With an effort I finished my meal. Jonathan poured more wine into my glass, as if he thought I needed it,

314

which I did.

He said, "I must say I don't envy Mr Henry Bowing Junior—"

I looked up swiftly, but he went on, "Oh, not for being married to my sister; she's a nice enough girl; pretty too. But Ma hovers close, and always will. And Ma's can be quite a problem, but when they're Emma, if you see what I mean, that's more than a problem: that's a time-bomb."

"Apparently he's willing to take it on."

"Perhaps he doesn't know the whole of it. Or thinks he can get out from under. People who are very rich sometimes think they can. Buy themselves out, I mean. But you can't buy yourself out of Emma—absolutely not, I'd say."

"Perhaps Henry Bowring will take Carey far off—like the West Coast—"

"Ma," said Jonathan, "will arrive with a bang and a flash of light; you can bet your bottom dollar. Trouble for Henry—rather a good title, don't you think?"

I didn't say much more; and as soon as I could I left him. He made a few polite remarks about my going so early, but I think he knew well enough what made me go.

Once alone in the streets, I could see little but the blue airmail paper of Carey's letter, and the words spelled on it.

I knew them by heart, for they were so few, and so oddly formal. ". . . give my love to old friends, if I have any . . ." Was that an oblique gesture towards me? "My love". If I had Carey's love, I had everything in the world I wanted, but the phrase could mean nothing. My only true comfort came from the tone of the letter: a few blunt facts with no frills at all. I hadn't till now read the letter from a young woman announcing her engagement, but I felt that something more might be expected: some eulogy of the young man, talk of honeymoons, perhaps?

I went on walking through the dark London streets, nearing winter now. Walking eased my mind, which grew tired, shuttling back from hope (the formal words of the letter) to despair: "I think you ought to know that I'm engaged to a guy called . . ."

I shifted restlessly through various prospects of action. Write to Carey, pleading with her? Telephone her? Even borrow the money from my father, go to the States and confront her? For minutes at a time they all seemed possible; then the bludgeon of distrust would fall, and I would see them as impossible. Or perhaps I feared another rebuff from Carey which would be worse than the first.

I didn't see how it could be resolved; and the thing that happened hadn't even touched my mind.

At first, as was I suppose natural enough, I saw more of Barbara Myers. I wouldn't be the first or last to do with a second-best love; and such a marriage could succeed well enough.

No need to marry, of course; I wouldn't be Barbara's first lover, nor she mine. But I wanted to have some announcement to fling back at Carey, to give something of the wound I'd received. Not perhaps a very honourable reason for marriage; but that's how it was.

One evening we lingered together in the theatre after the performance had ended. The "closing notice" had gone up on the board, and the house had been more than half empty. Barbara was gathering props from the stage, which, now that the actors had left it, had the desolation of all places from which entertainment has departed.

"It was a nice set," she said, surveying my efforts to represent the ballroom of the last act.

"*Was* is the operative word."

"Yup—but it's a shame. It's a *good* play. You want to know what happens."

"Not enough people do, it appears."

"We were short on publicity. No big names—"

"Big names cost money; this management's working on a shoestring."

"Oh—money." She ruffled her short dark hair (no one could look less like Carey); "what about art?"

"Two different things," I said.

"Not always. Shakespeare made money... D'you know I've worked on *Othello* and forgotten the handkerchief: can you believe that?"

"I can believe anything in the theatre," I said. "Come on, let's pack this in and go and eat."

With the theatre behind us with its unoccupied seats and its large canopied darkness, we went out together.

We found a small Italian restaurant, and I ordered everything I could think of, together with a bottle of Chianti. Barbara looked at me with pleasurable surprise. "Going to town?"

"This is a night out," I said. (Keep Carey far to the back of your mind; you can't go on loving someone who's three thousand miles away and marrying someone else; there's no future in that; and at your age you want a future: who doesn't?)

"Fine," she said, "I'm all for nights out. Especially with you."

Pleasing to hear ... and why shouldn't I be in love with Barbara? She was pretty and intelligent, and we worked in the same world, had the same outlook on things, so far as I could tell. Though I was sure she'd had one love affair, she didn't sleep around; I could tell that, and there was no reason why this evening shouldn't end with us in bed together; and after that, marriage. Well, however long it took to get a marriage set up. (And then I could write to my father and tell him that I was going to be married; and be sure that this information would in the end reach Carey...) No reason at all why Barbara and I...

None, except that I couldn't forget that night on the Vineyard, and the quarrel in the bedroom; and the strained silent parting the next day. I couldn't forget waiting in Greenacre Park on East 51st Street, and walking the hot New York streets home . . .

I heard Barbara's voice: "You've gone away."

I looked up. "Sorry. Dreaming."

"Didn't seem to be a very happy dream."

"Are any dreams happy?"

"Now and then. I said I liked an evening out, especially with you. Some kind of answer needed to that, isn't there?"

I put my hand on hers. "Lots of answers," I said. "First, I like you a lot. And I want to be with you for a long time. A long, long time." I drew closer to her, and the little tongue of desire licked us both. I put my mouth against her cheek, close to her ear. I said quietly, "I'd like to be with you tonight—all night. All through the long night—you'd be nice to hold."

Her eyes were drowsy, as mine were: then the waiter came and put large plates of spaghetti Bolognese in front of us, and the spell was broken; and she woke up.

She began to eat her meal. "'Like you a lot'," she observed drily. "That's kind of short-changing, wouldn't you say?"

Perhaps this was going to be more difficult than I expected. "Understatement," I said.

"Ah. Understatement of what?"

"How I feel."

She went on eating from her plate of pasta. "I'd like to belive that," she observed, as if she spoke of some abstract theory.

"True," I said, for sitting here beside her, aware of her affection and the pleasing face with its wide mouth and the cropped dark hair, what I felt for her seemed strong enough.

She stopped eating and looked at me, elbow on the table, chin propped on her hand. This was one of those restaurants where lop-sided candles were supposed to make the atmosphere more romantic than it was. The light from our candle caught the gleam of her dark eyes, and they weren't drowsy any more; they surveyed me with amused judgement.

"No good denying," she said, "that I fell for you from the start. Does that sound immodest?"

I grinned. "It sounds fine. Undeserved, but fine. Tell me a man who doesn't like to hear it?"

She remained in the same position, her fork abandoned on her plate. "Well . . . perhaps one who has other—let's say—things on his mind."

I faced this with as blank an expression as I could. "People were always telling me, when I was young, that I was absent-minded."

"I wouldn't have said that. But I think you've got something you'd like to talk about, and it isn't to do with me."

I was silent, while the candle flame curtsied and swung. I looked at its light in the dark red of the wine, and saw again the Vineyard party and all that had happened then . . . Talk about it? Perhaps she was right and I wanted to; but I could not; I couldn't talk about Carey to anyone.

I wanted to get back to the mild easy affection we'd started with. "We've all got problems," I said. "They're mostly dull; it's not worth spoiling an evening with them. I told you—I've thought a lot about you. I want to be with you. I don't only mean tonight. I've thought—I've wondered—if you'd think of marrying me?"

The words had come out before I expected them. I had spoken impelled by a need to escape her questions which brought Carey to my mind.

Barbara sat back in her chair. "Well, now! A proposal! More than I expected. A whole lot more."

She became silent then, and it distressed me to see that tears had stopped her voice. She quickly brushed her hand across her eyes. "What a wonderful idea. Something settled; married to Rick Ashley—a whole splendid life opening out; the kind of life I want."

"Then—" I began.

"I've never wanted to marry anyone before; but you . . . that would have been something different. Ah, yes; indeed."

Her voice was still not quite in control. I said, "Would have been?"

She wiped her face again. "Yes; you see it would be such a fine thing—"

"Well then—" I didn't know whether I was relieved or hurt by this prevarication.

"But you see I don't think I could marry a man who had a suitcase, as it were, which he couldn't unpack. Which I wasn't allowed to see."

I tried to brush this away. "We're not seventeen. Who hasn't a snake in the cupboard, or whatever you like to call it?"

"I don't think I'd call it a snake."

"People who get married don't have to give a blow-by-blow account of their past. If they did the number of marriages would drop to nought per cent. What's past is over."

Her head was down; she was drawing on the table-cloth with one finger. "Don't think this is over."

"This?"

"Whatever's eating you. Because something is."

"Something eats everyone. I want to start again."

"A rebound?" she said. "I never think that's a good idea. I know it happens, but . . ."

She made an effort to eat more of her pasta, then pushed the plate away. I thought that I'd made a mess of this evening, but I didn't quite see how. Perhaps I had underestimated any woman's ability to perceive those things which one doesn't want her to know.

"I meant it," I said stubbornly; "I meant it when I asked you to marry me." It seemed I did, too; the more so since she had retreated into doubt.

She shook her head.

320

"I did," I said; "and there's no reason on earth why not."

Soon we left the restaurant. I held her hand, for I didn't want this to be the end of it. I said, "Come with me. Talk to me a bit longer. I *have* asked you to marry me: doesn't that give me some sort of privilege?"

She turned to me then, and I held her in my arms, close in the cold night street. I could hear the drifting laughter of men and girls as they passed by. I didn't care. I wanted to retrieve something from this, and I kissed her with force, as I'd kissed Carey—no, I must keep Carey from my mind. Especially if Barbara was going to read it.

She was shivering a little as she drew away from me. "All right," she said. "All right, I'll come back."

Perhaps the evening wasn't lost. I walked with my arm about her. I didn't like the way she'd had to control her tears when I'd talked of marriage; in our work together she'd always been resilient, optimistic, riding cheerfully over disaster.

My bedsitting room was in its usual state of muddle, with books and records and sheets of cartridge paper spilling about. I didn't apologise. I made her sit in the one comfortable chair and said, "I'm going to get you a drink. Then we can cheer up. It's rather a bad sherry, but it's all I've got."

She looked up at me, smiling, and I felt happier and more confident.

We drank the poor sherry. I crouched down beside her and she stroked my head, as if we'd made love, and this was the calm after it.

"You're going to stay here, aren't you?" I said. "You're not going away?"

She looked round the room, with a dream-like inquiry, as if she tried to sum it up: whether it would be a good place.

"No . . . I shan't go away yet."

It was a beginning, I thought, and I leaned forward to

kiss her.

And then the telephone rang.

At first I knew merely the irritation of interrupted physical encounter. Why did one's friends always choose the wrong time to telephone? I said "Hullo?" briefly and without enthusiasm.

"Rick? Is that you?"

I said, cast into a great depth of surprise: "*Emma.*"

"Yes, of course it's Emma; I want to know about Jonathan."

The whole thing was making less and less sense. I had almost forgotten Barbara in the room behind me. I said, stupid with surprise, "I thought you were still in New York."

"So you were wrong. I flew in this morning."

I said, seeing the sudden opening of strange country, "*Is Carey with you?*"

"Carey?" The name might have been of small importance. "Yes, she's here—"

My heart gave a sudden twisty jump. "Jonathan says she's engaged—"

"What? Oh ... yes. Yes—"

"Is he with you?"

"Who?"

"Her—her chap. Henry someone."

"Oh—no. No." The voice was impatient; whatever her feelings about Henry Bowring Junior, she didn't want to talk about him now. "I want to know where Jonathan is. Is he with you?"

I couldn't imagine why Emma should want to see Jonathan so urgently, nor why she should think he was with me. I said, "No," being reminded again, for I had almost forgotten her, of Barbara.

"I've spoken to one or two of his friends, and they said you'd been seen together." It sounded odd, as if we were conducting a clandestine love affair, which God knows

322

we weren't.

I said, "We meet now and then."

"And you know all about this book, I suppose?"

The conversation seemed to belong more and more to Wonderland. "Book?"

"He must have talked about it."

"Jonathan doesn't talk about anything much. We just meet and have a drink. He told me about Carey—"

Clear that Emma hadn't time to talk about Carey. "I think you'd better come round to see me—"

"I don't know where you are—"

"I'm in your father's house."

It had odd Biblical overtones. "My father? Is he there?"

"No. I came over alone."

"You said Carey was with you."

"Oh—yes, yes. You'd better come now. I've got to get to the bottom of this. Get a cab. Come now."

Before I could say more she had put down the telephone. I turned and faced Barbara. "I haven't any idea," I said, "what that was about."

Barbara had got to her feet. She was lighting a cigarette with a hand that shook a little. She said at last, "Maybe not. But I think I grasped one thing."

I faced her in silence, still confused by the sudden sound of Emma's voice.

"What Carey is," said Barbara, slinging her handbag strap over her shoulder. "She's the suitcase. The one you wouldn't open."

I said, "I'm sorry."

"Oh—no need for that. Always better to have things clear. Who is she?"

"Her name's Carey Gardner. She's Emma Pride's daughter."

Barbara gave a small whistle. "*That* must be quite an undertaking. From all I hear."

She stood looking about the room, as if she wouldn't

323

see it again, and had some need to impress it on her memory.

I put my hand on her arm, but she moved away. "No ... I like things to be clear-cut. I knew all the time, really. Stupid to push away one's instincts—they're nearly always right."

I said, "I'm sorry," again.

She gave me a glance, half-amused, half-sad. "I don't think one has to be sorry for being or not being in love. If Carey Gardner's Emma Pride's daughter, *and* engaged to someone else, seems to me you've got problems. But they're yours. I can only wish you luck. Good-bye, Rick. See you at work. The best thing, after all."

"The play's closing," I said.

"Oh—yes; everything closes. But—don't they say?— another door opens. I can find my own way down."

I let her go. I hadn't time to feel the discomfort, maybe the remorse which would come later.

I had only one thought: Carey was over here, the mere distance of London between us; and I went out into the street and found a cab.

Chapter Three

As I travelled north the perplexing conversation turned over in my mind. Why should Emma ring me of all people soon after arrival in England? And summon me late at night to come and see her?

Book? Jonathan?

All at once, as the winter streets passed by, a small picture fell into my mind. Jonathan's room; and his desk, with the anonymous file of typewritten paper. And the book which he had retrieved—hurriedly, it seemed—from the floor.

What had he said? A page proof he was reading for a friend . . . And I had said "Labour of love". What had he replied? "No; not love."

It didn't make much sense; but a small chill touched me.

Here was my father's house; the old house at the edge of Hampstead Heath, which I remembered from childhood. And Emma was here, presumably because when she was in England now she usually rented a house, or stayed in an hotel. Unreality hung about me as I went to the door. The crowded trees of the Heath whispered at my back, their branches stripped of leaves, wearing only the foliage of foggy air.

It was Emma who opened the door. I hadn't seen her since that sad and silent departure from the Vineyard. I stood, taking the small shock. For this Emma not only showed the lines of age and anger, as she had then, but something deeper, a mask of distress which wasn't only drink (though she swayed as she stood there) but the expression of one who has looked into a future which is unendurable.

I said, "Hullo, Emma." And added as she didn't move, "You asked me to come."

She turned quickly then, taking a pull at a cigarette. She wore a dark blue dress, gripped tightly by a belt. It seemed to me that she'd grown very thin. The words went up in my head "But you used to be so beautiful!" I didn't speak them. I walked into the house with apprehension because I still couldn't quite believe that I should see Carey. And what good would it do to see Carey? Who was engaged to Henry Bowring, Junior?

But at least he wasn't there.

I walked into the well-remembered sitting-room. It smelt of smoke and spirits; and of crisis.

From a corner of the room, Carey moved towards me.

And I thought, oh God; this is love, and I don't want it; it's no good, and I was getting free . . . But the sight of her, so familiar, so much part of my life and all my hopes brought a moment of such relief and joy, and pain too, that I could find nothing to say to her.

She greeted me as if perhaps she understood, and held out her hand. I took it as if it were some unexpected gift. "Good of you to come," she said; "we seem to be in some sort of trouble."

Emma flung herself on to the sofa. "I'll say we're in trouble." Her voice was slurred; the half-filled glass stood beside her. She picked up a book with a bright blue and yellow jacket. "Seen this?"

"I don't know what it is."

"Are you quite sure?"

I glanced at Carey who was standing alert, on guard; she looked both sad and apprehensive.

Emma held out the book to me.

Since it seemed to be the root of this crisis, whatever

326

that was, I took it with caution as if it might explode.

Which was perhaps wise, as the author of the book was given, in bold yellow letters, as "Jonathan Pride". The book was called *Skid-Star*, which seemed a pretty terrible title to me, but at least gave an idea of what this was all about.

Emma said, "Are you trying to tell me that you didn't know about it?"

"N-nothing at all," I said. "It's the first time I've seen it." But that memory of the book which fell to the floor made me hesitate, and stutter; and Emma pounced.

"I don't believe you."

I had more confidence now, stirred by the challenge which was untrue. "I didn't even know that Jonathan had written a book."

"He's done that all right," Carey murmured. "Without telling any of us."

"Using my name—" said Emma, lighting another cigarette. (I forebore to say that it was his name too; that—whatever he'd done—he had the right to call himself Jonathan Pride.) "And a cheap, vulgar bit of work it is; written in basic English, to say the least—ugly words, all over the place." Again it was no time to observe that Emma used these words herself when she was in the mood, and her children heard them. She glanced at me again. "I don't see *how* you couldn't have known. It's all there."

"What's all there?"

"That time—at the party. On the Vineyard. He's written all about it. Everyone'll know who he's writing about; everyone. And it's cruel. Cruel and horrible. No, damn it, I'm not going to cry. No, I'm not."

Carey moved across the room to her mother and put an arm on her shoulder. "It's not as bad as you think, Ma. There's one hell of a lot of novels. They get lost in the flood."

"This won't," said Emma, with bitterness. "He's been

too clever; he's made it sensational. He's written about me as if I were . . . oh, God, how *could* he? He's my son; how *could* he? God, I never want to see him again . . . Yes, I do; I want to tell him what I think of him; just once; I want to tell him . . ."

Carey was stroking her mother's neck. "I should cool it, Ma. It isn't worth all that."

"But he's my son. I loved him . . . Not as much as I loved you, perhaps, but I loved him. I can remember when he was small . . ."

"Don't cry," Carey said; and I could see that same compassion which she'd shown to her grandmother all those years ago when she'd wept for a daughter (Emma herself) who didn't speak to her on the telephone from America. And seeing it, my love grew deeper; and I had to keep reminding myself that this was no good; Carey was to be married, and what we had to concentrate on was Jonathan's book. Or rather, what it had done to Emma.

Emma said, returning to me, "How can he have done it without your knowing? When it's got all that about the party—when you were so rude to me, and I slapped your face—"

I tossed the book down. "All right," I said. "I'm sorry Jonathan's put all that into a book; but I didn't know anything about it; and, as for the party—he was there, wasn't he? He saw everything that happened. He didn't have to consult me about it. And if he had, I'd've told him to drop the whole thing."

She looked at me, her face marked with tears. "I don't see how he could have done it; my own son . . ."

But I could see. Perhaps once Jonathan had loved Emma, as a small boy; but that love, so neglected, so casually returned, had in the end become resentment, then hatred. For only hatred, surely, could have driven him to write what must be a cruel (if true) portrait of his mother. And not entirely true, I thought; to produce something sensational, as he apparently had done, he

328

must have exaggerated; suppressed the good in Emma, for it was there; and the pity for her, too.

"Get him, Carey," she said. "I must speak to him: I must face him; tell him what he's done . . ."

"Better not tonight, Ma," Carey said gently. "It wouldn't do any good. Besides, you tried to ring him and he wasn't there."

"He might be back."

"Truly, Ma; it'd be better not to see him tonight. You'll only have a row and that'll make you feel worse."

Emma held out her glass for more drink, and as Carey dawdled, said, "Hurry up; I need that; don't let's have any prissy stuff . . . It'll help me to sleep."

Reluctantly, I thought, Carely refilled the glass. "More than that," Emma said; "C'mon; give."

I watched each movement of Carey's, as if I had later to describe what I had seen. Though tired and anxious, she was to me more and more beautiful; and for moments at a time I could fool myself that things were all as they had been; that Carey, whom I loved beyond all else, belonged to me.

Emma made a grab for the telephone. "I don't care whether it's better to see him or not; I'm going to ring him again." Her hand was shaking so much she had to put the receiver down, then start again. Carey and I watched like warders. Please God, I thought, she gets no reply.

But after a few rings which echoed clearly in this familiar lighted room the ringing stopped, and I heard Emma say: "Jonathan?"

Impossible to hear the voice at the other end; Jonathan always spoke quietly.

"I want you here," Emma said; "now; right away . . . you know damn well why . . . don't *lie* to me; you *know*; about this book, this damn, filthy book you wrote; about *me* . . . of course it's about me; you've put in all the things that happened . . . Carey's twenty-first party; you put

329

that in . . . it's meant to be me; you can't say it isn't—and it was cruel, cruel. . ." The other voice took over. I watched Emma as she listened, grabbed at her glass and drank from it; went on listening. The voice—Jonathan's voice—seemed to be going on for a long time.

Then, without a further word, she put the telephone down and began to cry.

Carey went to her. "I told you not to ring him, Mama."

Emma wept. "He said . . . he said I'd never done anything for him. Never cared a damn about him. Left him whenever it suited me. It's not true. Not true. I was—am—an actress. What else could I do?"

"Nothing, Ma," said Carey.

"How *could* he speak to me like that? Oh, God, I must see him; make him take those words back; if he won't come here, I'll go to him . . ." She took another gulp of her drink; rose, swaying, to her feet. Carey gripped her arm.

"Please, Ma . . ."

"I was good to him; I gave him things . . . He had everything he could want . . . I must see him; hear him say it isn't true, that I treated him so badly . . ."

I took her other arm. The evening with Barbara seemed so long ago that it might have belonged to a different life. There was only Emma, distracted with drink and grief; Carey, white-faced and determined, and myself bound to help her.

Emma pulled herself with surprising strength from both of us, and staggered to the door. She stood there with her back to it, as if we were the ones who wanted to escape.

I looked at her, desperate, unlovely; yet paradoxically with some of the loveliness still there: the Emma who had swept across stages, bowed to applause; died beautifully as Juliet, as Desdemona; made people laugh as she delivered a line with perfect edge; made them weep, as she communicated by the smallest gesture, that the grief in her heart was too much to contain . . .

I glanced at Carey beside me. I thought she too remembered all the past; remembered what Emma had been, and that it was almost too much for her. I took her hand, and held it hard.

She didn't look at me, but she didn't take her hand away. She just said, "You can't go, Ma. Really, you can't go. If you have to see him, see him tomorrow."

"Tomorrow . . ." Emma said. "I don't know about tomorrow."

"Tonight isn't the time," I said.

Emma turned to Carey. "You wouldn't have done that, would you? You couldn't say that I've been cruel to you?"

The smile that drifted across Carey's face contained everything. "No, Mama."

"You've meant so much to me. Everything. I couldn't help being away . . . couldn't help . . ."

Emma began to cry again.

Carey said, "I've always loved you. Come along now. Rick's going to help me get you upstairs. You're going to bed."

Emma wiped her face. "Did you mean that?"

"Mean what?" Carey said.

"That you've loved me."

"Why, of course." Carey had her arm round Emma, myself on the other side.

Emma said, "I don't know . . . I'm not sure . . . if it can be true. If it can . . . You can't undo the past; you can't take back the things you've done . . . Why should it be like that?"

We moved towards the staircase. It was more difficult to move her than I'd supposed: I tried to take the greater weight, but Carey, her head down, showed a sinewy determined strength.

At last we got her to the top of the stairs. Here she leant against the wall and said, "Why wouldn't you let me see him? I wanted to say ... there were so many things I wanted to say."

"Not tonight, Mama," said Carey. I was surprised—though perhaps I should not have been—at her command, at the way Emma obeyed her. Pity touched me again, for this was Emma Pride; and she was an ageing woman, drunk and shocked, helped to bed by her daughter, and the son of a man she'd once loved. Her face was raddled and smeared; and I thought that no one would applaud her now.

Carey said, "I'll get her into bed. You wait for me downstairs."

On the sofa I sat and glanced through Jonathan's book. For something which had caused such distress, it looked very slight; and from what I could read hadn't much except the advantage of a skilled journalist's style. I doubted that Jonathan would—apart from this—make a novelist. But that wouldn't help Emma. The book had an American publisher, which maybe accounted for the fact that I had heard nothing of it. As yet.

I read a page here and there, then flung the book down, already sickened by it. I could hear little but the brush of traffic outside the room, travelling fast on the night road; and Carey's footsteps above me. Now and again her voice came, quiet, persuasive. I called "D'you want any help?" but she answered, "No; it's O.K." Emma, it seemed, was protesting no more.

I wandered to the window: across the road stretched the foggy dark of the Heath, crowded with winter trees and silence. I was impatient for Carey to return to me; yet I didn't see how this evening was going to end, for Carey was entirely concerned with Emma; and I with this useless weight of love which like an uninvited guest had no part here.

Quiet deepened. At last Carey came downstairs and flung herself beside me on the sofa.

"Is she all right?" I asked.

"She's asleep." I saw that Carey had a small bottle of tablets in her hand. "I let her have two of these, and then, when she was drowsing off, I put the rest in my pocket." She played with the small bottle, turning it this way and that, as if she judged its weight. "She forgets she's taken them and then takes more." In the quiet firelit room we sat together like those exhausted after rescue. Carey said, looking aside, "I don't know what's best to do. How to help her."

"Seems to me you help her all you can."

She shook her head. It was growing late, but she didn't seem to want me to go. I said, "How on earth did it happen? Emma and the book?"

Carey put her head back on the sofa. "Oh ... like everything happens with us. A good friend (how good, one can't say) told Ma about this book, and she read it— and then she missed her performance at the Lincoln Center and they cancelled her contract, and she went into one hell of a spin. I wasn't working—so off we were, at Kennedy, checking our baggage, and then we were here. This morning. Ma works fast."

Her hand lay beside me on the sofa and I covered it with my own. She gave a small smile of acknowledgement, as if she were too tired to do more.

"I don't know what to do about her," she repeated. "She's always picked herself up; come back; but now ..."

I was silent. I couldn't see the figure which we had helped up the stairs commanding an audience again; but this wasn't the time to fight as I'd fought in her room on the Vineyard; it wasn't the time to say that if Emma's career was sliding to disaster Carey couldn't do anything to stop it, nor could she deal single-handed with the results.

"The revenue boys are after her too," Carey said; "she owes an awful lot of money. You wouldn't think it, the way we live; but she does. Thousands of dollars. I don't know how we get out of that one."

"We?" I said.

"I seem to get caught up in it. Henry, of course, was prepared to pay—"

"You mean *Henry Bowring* was going to underwrite Emma's tax debts?"

"Seemed like it."

"And you were going to marry him because—"

She shook her head, and I knew a fall of heart.

She said, "I'm not as noble as that. No martyr, me. Henry's a nice guy; kind, clean about the house; quite funny at times."

"You said *was* prepared," I observed, tearing a small piece of paper between my fingers, not looking at her.

"Well, I couldn't let him. I don't think you can let people do things like that, do you?"

"Maybe not 'people'," I said. "But the man you're going to marry—"

She gave no answer to this; it was as if she hadn't heard. She still turned the little bottle in her hands. Her glance went to the staircase as if she were listening. "She's asleep now. So long as she doesn't wake—"

I said I didn't think anyone in Emma's condition would stir till morning.

"You don't know Ma. She never sleeps long. She never has. And she doesn't like waking up. She's afraid."

I too looked up towards the room where Emma was. Something of that fear seemed to penetrate the room where we sat together; the fear of a woman who saw the edge of an abyss close to her feet. I glanced at Carey beside me. The marks of fatigue on her face which detracted from her beauty only strengthened my love. I said, "I'm staying with you."

She turned her head drowsily. "It may be a long night."

"Never mind."

I feared she might tell me it was best I should go; but

334

she said only, "I'm glad you're here. You know all about it. About her."

True enough, I thought. I would like to have added, "Unlike, perhaps, Henry?" but I did not. I had to tread gently here. This late night companionship had a quality which I feared to break. For this space Carey belonged to me; and if I didn't look beyond it, I could tell myself that all was well.

The night was now very quiet. Only the occasional car pursued its lonely way on the road; lively voices sounded somewhere far off: a party breaking up, perhaps. For a little while Carey slept, her head turned towards me. Though I longed to kiss her, I did not. I looked for a time at her face in sleep, tired, vulnerable: the face of the young woman I so greatly loved. Though we sat close, I could not believe that we would be together for long; the plan of things seemed to be that Carey and I should drift together, and by some means Emma should part us. She would, I thought, part us again.

The fire burned low. Quietly I rose and made it up. Restless I pulled the window curtain and looked out. The road was dry, empty, with a carapace gleam under the lone street lamp. From a house not far off one light burned, and I wondered who also, and for what reason, was awake. Work? Grief? Love? I felt a bond of companionship with that other man or woman, still awake.

Carey stirred on the sofa. She blinked at me drowsily as if trying to take in the strange fact of my presence, then smiled. "I'm going to see if Ma's all right."

While she was upstairs I made coffee in the familiar kitchen; the place, though clean, smelt of disuse.

Carey came down, quietly, as if we were playing a game. She flung herself back on to the sofa. "She's still asleep. She didn't hear me; she didn't wake."

She took her coffee, drank it gratefully, and smiled at me. "I'm glad you're here," she said again.

I kissed her then, lightly, and she said, "Dear Rick. I

wouldn't have liked this alone."

"You know perfectly well I'd do anything in the world for you. And I'm sorry about last time. On the Vineyard. I said things—"

"Don't go back. It isn't any good. That was another time. We're here now."

I said, "I love you. I always have."

She gave a glance towards Emma's room. "But the problems are still the same—"

"All right. I don't care. I'll do anything . . ."

She kissed me. "It's easy to say that now—"

"I mean it."

"Perhaps you do."

"But you're going to marry someone else, all the same?"

The grey eyes, Emma's eyes, turned to me then. "I've sometimes wondered if I'll marry anyone."

"That's absurd—"

"Sh, don't talk so loud; you'll wake Ma."

"*Are* you going to marry him?"

"Don't ask questions, Rick darling. It's been a long day. And a long night."

Better not to pursue it. But now I had this small growing hope. It survived oddly in the night quiet, with the sensation of being on guard.

Carey slipped sideways on the sofa towards me and slept again. Gently, so as not to wake her, I put an arm about her. Then, lulled by comfort and silence, I slept too.

When I opened my eyes I could see the first dim light through the drawn curtains, a gleam here and there on polished surfaces. Something odd about this slow return of light, as if a stranger came into the room.

Carey still slept. Silence from upstairs. In spite of what Carey said, Emma had apparently slept through the night . . . The day when it came fully would be different; we would have Emma, and doubtless Jonathan; and the turbulence, as they expressed it in aircraft, would be back with us. But just for this moment I could look at Carey and love her, in silence, before the world came in.

I made more coffee and as I brought it to her, Carey woke. "Morning?" she asked.

"Just."

I put the tray down on a table before us. Her dress was crumpled, her hair uncombed; she wasn't yet free of her dream. Again I kissed her, and I thought she gave the kiss some return. "What an odd night," she said. "Sleeping with you, yet blameless."

"No fault of mine," I said.

She smiled, stood up and rubbed the shine of sleep from her face. "I'll go and see to Mama. She must have slept. I'll see what she wants—orange juice, maybe: she gets thirsty."

Quiet still held us. The grey that wasn't light, but was something other than the dark, filled the room like mist. I went into the kitchen as she climbed the stairs. The fridge was empty, but I found a can of orange juice and opened it. I was glad to have something to do. As I took down a glass I wondered how this day would go. The night, spent close to Carey, was over now: the day could separate us.

It was as I began to pour the orange juice into the glass that I heard her voice. It was so loud that my hand shivered and I spilt the juice.

"Rick! Come here!"

I fled up the stairs, and into Emma's room. At first it looked like any bedroom where the sleeper hasn't yet woken. Then I saw Carey's face; and that Emma was not asleep with her head on the pillow, but lying askew, head down, half out of the bed, as if she were plunging towards the floor.

I helped Carey lift her back. Emma's face was colourless, blue about the lips; her skin cold to touch. I put a hand to her wrist and felt for the pulse.

It was there; faint, unsteady, but there. I said, "She's

alive."

Carey said, "Just. But look—"

I saw, rolled on the floor, the empty bottle, companion to the one Carey had brought downstairs.

"She must have had another bottle," Carey said. "One I didn't know about. She's taken a lot, I think . . . Get an ambulance; quickly as you can. I'll stay with her—"

I was already downstairs, already dialling the easy and dangerous number. The day had overturned; these moments on the telephone seemed unreal. "Which service do you want? . . . "Ambulance," I said; then gave the address, and ran once more up the stairs.

Carey crouched by the bed. Emma lay now with her head back on the pillow. She looked as if she were already dead; but as I drew closer I could hear the rapid breathing. Too rapid, I thought.

Carey wasn't crying. She crouched there beside Emma, holding her hand, and with the other wiping the forehead which gleamed with sweat.

Carey was talking quietly, as if she feared to wake Emma; "I didn't know she had more. I didn't know. She must have hidden them . . ."

"You did all you could," I said. "You did everything."

"Not enough. Not enough."

I didn't answer that, but put one arm about her shoulders.

She said, "I did tell her I loved her, didn't I? I said it; last night, before she went to bed."

"Yes. Loud and clear."

"But I don't know if she believed me . . . It must have happened while I slept. Why did I sleep?"

"Because you were flat out."

"I tried to keep awake—" she began, but then we heard the sound. The sound that killed the air, killed thought.

I ran to the window and said, "They're here."

Carey got to her feet as if to meet some momentous encounter. I still held her.

She looked down at Emma, with a deep sadness, with a regret that held all the past. "I think it's too late."

Chapter Four

In winter Up-Island was almost deserted. The gaudy places of summer, the beaches, the dunes, the wild roses and the purple vetch were drained of colour as of life. The summer residents had closed their houses and returned to Boston or New York; Chicago or Montreal, or places east and west. Snow brought immobility to what had been a green blowing place; only the sea gathered strength. On most days the sea was a blanched green, and on the Atlantic shore drove in with the true energy of storm. But sometimes the waves were quiet, and the whole Island wrapped in a whispering fog; ice touched the swaying masts of the ships in harbour where the gulls alighted, as if for refuge.

But winter, I found, is a beginning, not a death.

The death was over. Newspapers, crowds, a chorus of contradictory voices, lay behind us now. The voices, the headlines had spoken loudly, all it seemed in tacit agreement that an actress who'd given them much fodder in her lifetime could only be of fervent interest to all who could read or listen, at her death.

They spelled it out; everything was there. The old stories of diaster: her failure in *The Newcomer*; the rumours of drinking, drugs, lovers ... photographs of Emma from youth (expecting all things) to middle age; to a short time before her death (skeleton thin, her beauty gone). Mercilessly, it seemed to me, these stamped upon the morning papers the story of that life at whose end

Carey and I had watched so quietly together. Afterwards, quiet was lost in confusion. The scene at the crematorium might have been a first night. We were all there (even Jonathan, even Carey's father); men and women of the theatre who had played (and suffered) with Emma; and the people—the great crowd of people who had come from varying motives (relish, regret, even—in some cases a kind of love) all pushing, their heads lifted to see the cortège pass by; to see the faces of the famous; to be able to go home and say "I was there".

"Death by misadventure" the Coroner had decided; perhaps with mercy. How many believed him? Drama is more acceptable than accident: "Of course it was suicide," people said; "of course she took an overdose . . ."

My father and Marguerite made the decision: they would take Carey and me first to New York (Carey had—as you might say—an appointment in New York) and then to the Vineyard house. Even in winter the Island had beauty and quiet, a healing quiet; and the house would be warm against the Atlantic cold.

So on this winter's afternoon, wrapped in a duffle coat, I walked to the edge of the garden, a mystery of bare branch and mist. Even so early the light was fading, and it was hardly possible to remember this place as it had been in summer, when the music of the party had sounded, and we had swum in that now icy sea.

My father and I had come yesterday from New York to open up the house; Marguerite was bringing Carey today, when Carey's business was over. Marguerite had said she and Carey would drive and come on the ferry to Vineyard Haven, via Woods Hole. No problem about a reservation; so few people came to the Island in winter.

I waited. I wanted, when she came, to see Carey alone. Grateful though I was to my father and Marguerite, I wanted to see her first without them . . .

I heard the sound of the car. Even then I couldn't run

341

to her; and in the end she found me.

She didn't ask why I stood here, alone, in the foggy Island dusk. Still in her winter coat, she stood beside me and took my hand. She kissed me and her lips were cold.

I said, "Is it done?"

She said, looking out to the fog of sea, "Yes; it's done now."

"Did it hurt him?"

"I guess so. You hurt someone, most of the time, don't you?"

I thought of that brief lost evening with Barbara. "It seems so. But you're sure?"

She turned to me then. "Oh, yes; quite, quite sure. As sure as one ever can be of anything."

I held her then, clumsily, because of our bulky winter clothes, and kissed her cold lips. "And we shall be married, you and I?"

"Yes."

I didn't say much more. I just held her there in the garden which had seen so much; within sight of the shore where Emma had come running to us, so long ago.

She said, her arms about me, as if she too remembered this, "I shan't ever forget her."

"You don't have to forget her."

"But I want to remember the good things. When she was happy. For she was happy sometimes, wasn't she?"

"Sure," I said. "There were good times."

"Other people will forget her. When they've done talking and saying the things that hurt—they'll forget. But I shan't."

"Jonathan?" I said.

"I don't want to think about him any more. It's done now. I was so angry at first, so blindingly angry . . . I told him so. But then I thought—maybe, in the end, it would have happened to her, anyway . . . I guess some time it would have happened. She couldn't take all she'd got. Now, I just don't want to see him. Perhaps one day, I will

342

again. But not for a long time."

A long time, I thought.

She said, "D'you know who I've thought of? Ben."

"Ben who?"

"You don't remember? Ben Hardy: the young actor who died; we found his photograph, you and I, here on the Vineyard. She loved him. She was going to have his child. Now . . ." She looked beyond my shoulder. "Puzzling, isn't it? All gone now. Lost."

I held her more tightly. The words echoed in my head: "Death after life doth greatly please."

The air darkened, the cold pierced more deeply; lights shone from the house, lonely, welcoming.

I kissed her once more, for this was the end of waiting. Then, arms about each other, we went in together.

The hall was not large. The company too was small 'by invitation only'. Outside hung the winter's dark, and the taste of the sea.

The hall was 'Down-Island', in Vineyard Haven. This was my father's plan. He sat with Marguerite further along the row of seats. The projection equipment stood in a small glass-fronted cabin at the back of the hall. Those who came into the hall came quietly, figures moving in the dusky and muted light. They spoke quietly too. With Carey beside me, I watched them. Even in this half-light it was possible to recognise colleagues from the theatre, well-known names. Amongst these were friends from the Vineyard: those who had come to Marguerite and my father's house, and played and danced; and swum from the shore below. They were, you might say, a company of friends.

An audience who sat, but still only talked quietly together in the waiting dark.

So great a contrast with that other occasion when all the people had come, in England, and the name of Emma Pride had gone easily from mouth to mouth, as if she

343

moved among them, elusive, and they craned their necks to see her.

This was better, I thought. With all her love of the theatre, Emma would have approved of this.

I turned to Carey beside me. "Are you all right!"

She nodded. I held her more closely, and she drew to me as if I were a refuge. She seemed very slight within my arm, limp but safe, like someone rescued.

My father climbed on to the small platform as the hour of seven struck. His face, I thought, still showed traces of grief; more signs of humanity too. His concern for Carey and me after the dark hours of Emma's death persisted even now.

He said, "This is a celebration, not a memorial. A celebration of a fine actress who like all the best, was unique. Whoever else we see, whoever else we applaud, we can't see another Emma. Her best work was on stage; that is lost to us. But we have the movies she made, and from them, my wife and I, together with Emma's daughter, have gleaned these few extracts. We offer them in love."

He moved back to his seat. All the lights dimmed, except the light from the projection room. Carey's face was calm, serious, looking up to the screen, waiting.

"It's all right," I said. "This is a good thing."

She gave a small nod.

The first pictures came on to the screen. Monochrome: the early movies. Other actors at first, and then Emma. A young Emma, laughing, speaking in that inimitable voice. I felt the shock go through us all, for it was impossible to believe that this Emma was not alive: that somewhere we could not find her again.

I glanced at Carey, for it was only for Carey that I was afraid. Only Carey, with me, had been in the bedroom that morning. But she kept control, her face (so like the youthful Emma's) still in the flickering light. If she wept, she gave no sign: a child in silence, deep in unfathomed thought. Given to the shadow of the woman who moved

344

on the screen, who had been her mother. Who was not, I discovered, an enemy any more, for I think there are no enemies among the dead.

Here was a still picture of Emma with a young man of fine looks—Ben Hardy; I remembered what Carey had told me. Emma and Ben were turned to each other in gentle easy affection, as if nothing but pleasure waited for them . . .

And now we saw an older Emma, perhaps thirty, even more beautiful, in spite of what appeared to be old-fashioned make-up. She played a love scene with a light tenderness; and again she reminded me of Carey . . .

And again in this Vineyard Haven hall, fear touched me.

I held her more closely; and I said to myself that it wasn't going to be like that; it wasn't going to be like that for her. She was Emma's daughter, but she was mine now, and her life wouldn't be the same. The young woman on the screen who had come to grief wouldn't be repeated. Whatever storms hit us, I would bring Carey through them, and the end would not be like this.

Different, I told myself; another kind of life.

Dear Reader,

You have been reading a Piatkus Paperback, one of a new range of novels which we hope will offer you what you want – an enjoyable, well-written story with realistic characters which leaves you feeling good at the end (though we don't promise that it will always be a happy one).

If you have enjoyed this book, please recommend it to your friends and look out for our distinctive pink, grey and cream covers in your local bookshop. If you don't see them, please ask the bookseller to order them for you.

Among other novels we are publishing at the moment are *The Kingdom of the Rose* by Margaret Bacon, the story of the changing role of women over a period of eighty years, *Sisters* by Debby Mayer, the story of an independent young woman who unexpectedly finds herself guardian to her eight-year-old half-sister and *An Honest Woman* by Anne Christie about the breakdown of a modern marriage.

We would love to hear from you with comments about our new series and if you would like to be put on our mailing list please send a large stamped addressed envelope to

Piatkus Paperbacks
5 Windmill Street
London W1P 1HF

Thank you for reading us.

Judy Piatkus